PRAISE FOR MICHAEL LIBLING

The Serial Killer's Son Takes a Wife is a terrifying novel that thrusts the reader into hairpin twists and turns right up to the last moment. Michael Libling is a gifted author, and his skillful prose, along with the story's unexpected developments, made it impossible for me to put this petrifying book down.

—SHEILA WILLIAMS, EDITOR OF *ASIMOV'S SCIENCE FICTION.*

The Serial Killer's Son Takes a Wife is sharp, funny, thrilling, and endlessly original. Michael Libling gives Riley Sager a run for his money!

—NICHOLAS KAUFMANN, BESTSELLING AUTHOR OF *THE HUNGRY EARTH* AND *THE STONE SERPENT*

By turns hilarious and terrifying... all rendered in Libling's razor-sharp prose and piercing observations of small-town life that build relentlessly to a Grand Guignol finale. It's the Coen Brothers meet Thomas Harris ... and I can't recommend it enough.

—LAWRENCE C. CONNOLLY, NIGHTMARE CINEMA AND PRIME STAGE MYSTERY THEATRE

Only a mind as demented as Michael Libling's could conjure a book like *The Serial Killer's Son Takes a Wife*. Only a writer as flat-out funny as Michael Libling could remind us that 99% of 'slaughter' is 'laughter.' And only a storyteller with the genius of Michael Libling could somehow, amidst gasps and giggles and plot twists galore, make us care.

—PAUL WITCOVER, AUTHOR OF *LINCOLNSTEIN* AND MANY OTHERS

Libling doesn't just go for the jugular, he goes for your entire throat, then reaches all the way down and grabs onto your heart. Full of feeling and freakish delights, this is a wild, unpredictable story that will amaze and startle readers by turns. What if Patrick Bateman from American Psycho had been a family man? What would his son be like? Libling answers that question in this terrifying and darkly humorous tale of hereditary horror.

—IAN ROGERS, AUTHOR OF *EVERY HOUSE IS HAUNTED*

Michael Libling is a brilliant writer. Anyone who's read his first novel, *Hollywood North*, knows this already. His second, *The Serial Killer's Son Takes a Wife*, is just as brilliant, giving us, as it does, the same breathtaking mix of riveting ideas and heartfelt humanity that makes all of Libling's work so memorable.

—BRUCE MCALLISTER, AUTHOR OF *DREAM BABY* AND *THE VILLAGE SANG TO THE SEA*

Michael Libling writes like that affable stranger on the next barstool buying you drinks as he charms you with his stories. Next thing you know, you've woken up in a bathtub full of ice with your kidney missing. Once you start reading this dangerous, slippery novel, watch yourself. You won't be able to stop, as much as you will sometimes want to.

—WILLIAM SHUNN, AUTHOR OF *THE ACCIDENTAL TERRORIST*

The Serial Killer's Son Takes a Wife is a remarkable novel ... a sequence of trapdoors which plunge the reader from serial killer mystery to visionary horror ... from its protagonist, the son of that serial killer, who fears family history will repeat ... to his enigmatic wife, Cori ... and on through the crumbling partitions of his past. Libling's debut novel, *Hollywood North*, along with his short stories and novellas over the previous decade, have occupied their own undiscovered country, bordered by continents of horror and mystery. This novel, in its electric shocks and transgressive force, fulfills all the promise of that earlier work. *The Serial Killer's Son Takes a Wife* raises and answers central questions of anxiety and existence. Libling, a major writer, takes chance after chance and surmounts them all.

—BARRY N. MALZBERG, AUTHOR OF *THE LONE WOLF*
CRIME SERIES, *BEND AT THE END OF THE*
ROAD, AND MANY OTHERS

Loads of fun and full of ice-cream-flavored digressions and cheeky warnings of bad things to come, *The Serial Killer's Son Takes a Wife* is a raucous, deceptively dark road trip that tantalizes and twists until it's too late to go back.

—TANYA GOUGH, AUTHOR OF *ROOT BOUND*,
FOUNDER OF STORYBILDER.COM

The title of Michael Libling's novel *The Serial Killer's Son Takes a Wife* confronts the reader with a reality few of us ponder: What must life be like for the family of a serial killer? Our avoidance understandable, the shame, too dark, the pain, too extreme. And the novel doesn't shy away from the gruesome and bloody details of the violence perpetrated by the killer. What is more shocking is that Michael Libling has written one of the funniest books I have ever read. The book does a wonderful job conveying the thoughts of a young man trying to live in a world where his father murdered over two dozen people. However, the humor is what gives this narrative ballast. I laughed out loud dozens of times, sometimes with tears in my eyes. The wit in the plot, the dialogue, the insights, the similes, and the metaphors is of a comic altitude few writers can reach. What do you call a book that digs into the mind of a serial killer's son with belly-aching laughs and rapier wit? Wonderful!

—JAMES LADD THOMAS, AUTHOR OF
LESTER LIES DOWN AND *ARDOR*

The Serial Killer's Son Takes a Wife by Michael Libling is an experiential and heart-stopping mystery soaked in the supernatural. Libling is a Canadian treasure, and his follow up to *Hollywood North* is at times surprising, and at times wrenching. I loved every page of this book ... it took me to an unexpected place and left me little time to catch my bearings before something else floored me with a left hook. The action and dialogue are fast-paced and kept the story moving briskly. This is deftly written, at times witty, and at times bloody terrifying. And that final revelation ... !

—TIMOTHY S. JOHNSTON, AUTHOR OF *THE SHADOW OF WAR*

Michael Libling has a genius for inserting a blade ... the healing surgeon, or the nurse of death?

—CLARK BLAISE, AUTHOR OF *THIS TIME, THAT PLACE*

THE SERIAL KILLER'S
SON TAKES A WIFE

.

THE SERIAL KILLER'S SON TAKES A WIFE

MICHAEL LIBLING

WFP
WORDFIRE PRESS

The Serial Killer's Son Takes a Wife
by Michael Libling

THE SERIAL KILLER'S SON TAKES A WIFE
Copyright © 2023 Michael Libling

EBook ISBN: 978-1-68057-456-2
Trade Paperback ISBN: 978-1-68057-457-9
Dust Jacket Hardcover ISBN: 978-1-68057-458-6
Library of Congress Control Number: 2023940919
Kevin J. Anderson, Art Director
Vellum layout by CJ Anaya
Published by
WordFire Press, LLC
PO Box 1840
Monument CO 80132
Kevin J. Anderson & Rebecca Moesta, Publishers
WordFire Press eBook Edition 2023
WordFire Press Trade Paperback Edition 2023
WordFire Press Hardcover Edition 2023

Printed in the USA
Join our WordFire Press Readers Group for
sneak previews, updates, new projects, and giveaways.
Sign up at wordfirepress.com

To my wise, kind, and courageous daughters,
Carrie, Lindsay, and Margie,
who knew what they were in for,
yet still read the pages that follow,
albeit with one eye shut
and the other half open.
No father could ask for more.
I'd call them "awesome,"
were I the sort of person
who used the word "awesome."
Love you girls!

*"Years later you realize there are some stories
you never write down. Some stories you only tell
and tell only to someone you don't know well,
maybe after the loss of a sibling or an auto accident,
in a quiet place over a cigarette or coffee."*

KURT OLSSON, SOME STORIES,
BURNING DOWN DISNEYLAND

*"Oh, Henry Dickens had a wife, a son so they claim,
Candy was his cover, his calling was to maim.
Children and their mommies, daddies all the same,
Peanut brittle was his weapon, Brittle Butcher his nickname."*

WILLOW STORROW, 4TH VERSE, THE
BRITTLE BUTCHER OF HILLSDALE

*"Insert up to three quotations at the beginning of your
manuscript. Quotations impress editors and readers by
demonstrating you are a serious author who is well versed
in the vast literary tradition. Selected quotations need not
be relevant to your book's content, only that they appear to
be so. Readers will have forgotten them by the end."*

ANNA CARMEN HOPE, BESTSELLERITIS!: HOW TO CATCH IT!

CONTENTS

I NEED YOU TO KNOW

You hold in your hands the only authorized and true account of what went down before, during, and after the Hillsdale incident. Accept no imitations. Any other purported version is the product of a fast-buck artist's feeble imagination, cobbled together from rumors, lies, and hogwash. Nobody has told this story or will tell this story the way I tell this story, because this is my story.

Anyhow, I've been told to say these pages are unsuitable for readers under eighteen or faint of heart. Explicit language, adult themes, and violence predominate. Bad things happen to bad people and worse things happen to good people. I tell it as I lived it. Reader discretion is advised, which is something else I was told to say. Do not claim at some later date I failed to warn you. I tell you this not as a threat, but out of concern for your safety and well-being. There are individuals currently at large who could react with hostility to complaints or criticism directed my way. Trust me here. Please.

—Robert "Bobby" Blessing, June 2023

PART ONE
FAMILY LIFE

BEWARE THE QUIET ONES AT THE BACK OF THE CLASS

Interveiw with Myself by Bobby Dickens
(Mrs. Cole's English class, Room 6)

Bobby: What is it like to be the son of a serial killer?
Myself: I don't know.
Bobby: Do people treat you diffrent?
Myself: If they find out.
Bobby: How do they find out?
Myself: I tell them some times.
Bobby: Why?
Myself: I don't know.
Bobby: What happens then?
Myself: Some think its a joke. Some go away. Some don't.
Bobby: What is the best part about being the son of a serial killer?
Myself: Scaring people I don't like.
Bobby: What is the worst part?
Myself: Missing my father.
Bobby: What do you want to be when you grow up?
Myself: I know what I don't want to be.

Teacher's Comments: *I find this disturbing. Threatening classmates is unacceptable. See me after class! Your spelling also needs improvement.*

LET ME GET THE CHILDHOOD CRAP OUT OF THE WAY FIRST

Put yourself in my shoes. I was twelve years old. My family was wrecked. I was seeing a shrink. And my mother up and changed my name. Didn't ask me. Didn't warn me. Just left the decree for me to find on my pillow —a goodnight kiss-off from her and the Great State of Double Whammy. All because Dad killed a couple of people. Okay, a bunch. But still.

I pulled up my pajama bottoms and stormed into the hall, shirtless, barefoot, batshit. *I'd show her.* I'd rip up that stupid paper and throw it in her face. *Damn right I would.*

But she wasn't in her bedroom or the living room or the kitchen. She was way ahead of me, as always, across the yard in the cottage in her studio at the rear, doing God-knows-what to God-knows-who for God-knows-why. The hours she spent holed up in there, year after year, week in, week out ... And since Dad had been removed from the picture, her hours had quadrupled. Just when I needed her most.

No shocker. More than once I'd heard her tell my father, "He was your idea. You know how I feel about children." My wicked stepmother was my own mother.

I paced the porch, the planks soft and cool underfoot, the air warm and serene, and my mother's court-sanctioned betrayal of me and my dad toxic in my fist.

I'd show her. *Damn right I would.*

I started, stopped, stewed, as the flash of Mom's camera strobed blue-white through the cracks of the shutters and into the night. *Or were those lasers blasting from her eyes?* I wouldn't put it past her. Wouldn't put anything past my mother.

The photography was for her business. Her website. There was truth in this. A half-assed truth. It was the whole-assed truth I worried about. I had witnessed enough by then to fear enough.

To hell with it. To hell with her.

Down the wooden steps I went.

Across the dewy lawn I charged.

By the hand-painted wooden sign I wavered.

BLESSING'S CHRISTMAS COTTAGE
ORNAMENTS, GIFTS & BRIC-À-BRAC
HEATHER BLYTHE-BLESSING, PROP.

My legs were banana peels.

My heart was a grenade.

Maybe changing my name was a good idea, after all. Considering.

I let the paper slip from my hand and onto the stoop.

I retreated the way I'd come. Back to my bedroom and the 24/7 shuffle-play of my brain.

I buried my face in my pillow, did what I often did, steered my dreams to another family, another life. Pretty much any other family, any other life.

Mom greeted me at breakfast, her smile off-the-rack, her empathy a level teaspoon. "Sleep well?" She tipped the box of Grape Nuts into my bowl, passed the milk for me to pour. "You'll get used to it, same as everything else. If anything, I should have made the change sooner. We need to move on."

I conceded nothing. Not to her face.

For twelve years I was Bobby Dickens and then, overnight, Bobby Blessing.

Blessing was a goddamn awful wussy way to go. Too churchy. Too sibilant. At odds with the badass I had worked so hard to be. Not that Dickens had been a piece of cake. Put a Dick anywhere near a kid's name and you're asking for trouble.

My mother was looking out for me. In her own way, I suppose. Couldn't have been easy: Dad busted and holding on Banrum's death row, while she trawled the fallout with me in tow.

Change of name changed nothing.

Wasn't a soul in town who didn't know what my old man had done. What he might've done too. If he hadn't already been tagged with every unsolved murder in America, he would be soon.

Wasn't a soul who hadn't looked at me and seen a chip off the old block. The shame I carried. The humiliation. The death wish. There is little upside to having a murderer for a dad. Unless you expect to write about it someday, cash in on the infamy, make yourself come out spanking clean.

Wasn't a soul who hadn't pointed a finger at my mom, bandied about how much she knew and when she knew it. It wasn't shame with her, it was defiance, a compulsion to rub her tenacity in their faces.

Thus we did not *move on* as Mom had said. We toughed it out in Hillsdale for three more god-awful years before she relented, decided she'd had her fill of the town. Her fill of me too, as it so happened. Because she also decided it would make my life easier if she was no longer a part of it.

She didn't pussyfoot. "People disappoint, Bobby. None more than family. The less family in your life, the stronger you will be. And you, more than most, need to be strong." She was relocating to Europe, which was as specific as she got. She would be dumping me somewhere near Boston.

She was bringing her pioneering approach to parenting to bear once more. She might as well have pinched my nostrils, stuffed a sock down my throat, run duct tape across my mouth.

I was fifteen. I wasn't ready to be on my own. A boarding school, no less. As if the Hell of Hillsdale had been my warm-up. "I don't mind being disappointed, Mom. Honest."

"Alas, sweetheart, I do."

"You think I'll disappoint you?"

She glanced at her watch. She had a flight to catch.

"What if I get hit by a truck or something? What if I need to talk to you?"

"For heaven's sake, darling, we barely talk now." She rummaged in her purse for a scrap envelope, scribbled a name and number on the back, and pressed it to my palm. "The lawyer, the one who'll be sending the money, he knows how to reach me. Do not abuse the privilege, Bobby. Genuine emergencies only. Episodes of teen angst do not qualify."

"But summer ... Christmas ... I'll see you then, at least, right?"

"The school has an excellent program for students who remain in residence during vacation periods. You'll be well cared for."

"But what about when they, you know, when Dad gets, well, you know?"

Word was, my father's bromance with Death had grown personal, their intimacy blushing, a mutual admiration society grounded in the arbitrary, extending to both victim and methodology. Adopting Death's model, Dad was more than open about his guilt, while more than vague on motive. The best the profilers could come up with was *eeny meeny miny moe*, as near to perfection as a killer, serial or run-of-the-mill, can hope for.

Dad was also bored to death with death row. The pleas for commutation and subsequent delays annoyed him to no end. Given the chance, knowing him, he would have taken an axe to the meddling do-gooders and abolitionist junkies who petitioned on his behalf. He was pushing to meet his Unmaker, and the powers that be were looking to oblige. While we'd been more Darth and Luke than Mufasa and Simba since his arrest, I'd been counting on Mom to be there for me when he finally got his wish. "I mean, what'll I do when it happens?"

"Oh, surely you will think of something, darling. Write a poem. Isn't that what teenagers do? Or spend more time with what's-her-name, that therapist of yours—that Cutcheon person. I must warn you, however, do not expect closure. In my experience, the concept is woefully overrated."

Mom could live with being single, single mom not so much. She was burying me alive. For my own good.

Her façade faltered as she moved to hug me, repressed affection on a longer lead. The offer was too late. I broke her grasp, ducked beneath her goodbye kiss. "Yes, well," she said, "if this is the way it must be. Not your doing, Bobby. In no way your doing, sweetheart." *Were those tears in her eyes, on her cheeks?* Europe beckoned. She was gone before I could verify one way or the other. Just as well. I had my own tears to contain.

I muddled through the gauntlet of high school, the preppy B&B she had surrendered me to in the wastelands of Worcester. I made no friends, did not try, rebuffed all who attempted otherwise, and held my own against the privileged pricks who mistook me for a whipping boy. I will spare you the boarding school drama. You've seen the movies; you've read the books. Take the brutality, eliminate the triumph, and call it *Bobby Blessing's Schooldays*.

Come time for college, I fluked my way into an institution that favored the aggressively average. I proved the point by dropping out spring break of senior year. Eight weeks later, May of 2012, I resurfaced in Syracuse and stumbled into a career jerking sodas and riffing hot fudge at Frosty Freddo's on Erie Boulevard.

Freddo showed me the ropes, ordained me with his wisdom: "There's no better environment in which to learn the ways of the world than the frozen dessert industry. Anybody who's ever been up to their armpits excavating a tub of hard-frozen Butter Praline will say the same."

I did not tell Freddo I knew better, that one education trumped ice cream: having a serial killer for a dad.

They say he murdered twenty-seven innocent people. Do not believe it. The real number is higher. I don't know how much higher, but probably a lot.

According to Dad, he didn't murder, either. He killed. There is a difference.

Murder is a crime of pleasure or vengeance or passion or impulse or happenstance or stupidity or negligence or insanity. Killing is a service.

You might think my father was a bad man. He was.

You might think you know the whole story. You don't.

You are not alone. I didn't know the whole story either.

3
BASIC MARKETING FOR ICE CREAM VENDORS

My father was Henry Taylor Dickens. You might have heard of him. The Dickens sticks in peoples' minds. It's a cute name for a killer. His nickname was cute too—the Brittle Butcher—though not as cute as it might have been. He could have been the Candyman, for instance, had it not been claimed in the early '70s by two unrelated scumbags who lived in Texas, one of whom poisoned his son on Halloween with a treat tricked out in potassium cyanide.

It was Rory Thomas, an old-school newspaper guy from Chicago, who came up with the Brittle Butcher. He's famous for coining nicknames for serial killers. Spree killers too. Just not rampage killers. Rampage killers never get nicknames. There's no romance in school, concert, and shopping mall shootings. I spare no sympathy for any. Each and every perp is deserving of obscurity for all eternity. I apply the same to my dad, though it is too late to rein in his celebrity. This book will not help, of course. I apologize for this. And for my hypocrisy.

Rory Thomas turns up on TV whenever the body count ups the nation's fear levels—you know, when you double-check the locks on your windows and doors, when you scope out the back seat of your car for crazies lying in wait, when you survey windows and rooftops for snipers adjusting their sights. Every network has their own Rory Thomas, but no talking head has a more envied track record in capturing the public's imagination. His speculation on *the who* and *the why* typically features three or four catchy options that roll off the tongue, while inspiring a nifty logo. After Dad's arrest, less canny media tested Twisted Dickens and David Slaughterfield, but literary allusions never go anywhere. Clever doesn't cut it. Alliteration does. Then too, peanut brittle has that indefinable feel-good working for it, a Rory Thomas trademark.

The first person Dad killed lived in Montpelier, Vermont. His name was Alain Cousins. It was 1988. Mom and Dad were on their honeymoon. They were driving to Quebec City and spent a night in Montpelier, where Dad squeezed in some alone time.

Cousins had a wife and two daughters. He installed garage doors for a living. My father pulped his skull with a 36-inch winding bar.

I don't know what a winding bar is. I can't say my father knew, either. He pulled the winding bar from the rear of Alain Cousins' van. It was never his practice to show up prepared. He was more into improv. He once killed a man with a vintage milk bottle. Another with a cuckoo clock. He broke his rule only once. The last time. The peanut brittle time.

Dad was a candy wholesaler. Right into the 2000s, he carried on the old-fashioned way, servicing his customers' stores in person. Most were a dying breed of mom-and-pop shops, small-town throwbacks to a more obliging era. Despite my mother's know-how and success, he'd opposed taking his business online. Thus, come December, the trunk of his Impala was packed with boxes of candy canes and peanut brittle. Had Dad reached for the candy canes, Rory Thomas might have gone with the Candy Cane Killer, which, if you ask me, would have been catchier than the Brittle Butcher. Such is fate. Either way, the killing would have retained the earmarks of improv. In this respect, the Improviser would have been the ideal nickname, had the ink not dried on Brittle Butcher before Dad's pattern came to light.

You might say I followed in my father's footsteps. Confections. Should killing people prove to be genetic too, I figure they'd call me something like the Waffle Cone Killer. Waffle cones can be dangerous, especially if dipped in chocolate and left to harden. You could drive the cone into somebody's throat or slush up their brain through an eye socket. You'd need to practice, of course. Strike the collarbone first and the cone could crumble.

I didn't plan on ice cream. My first choice was to be the next Rory Thomas. Coming up with nicknames for serial killers struck me as a fun way to make a buck. It was one of the reasons I spent three semesters in Journalism. Alas, my disillusionment grew with the curriculum. The only course offered on the nicknaming of serial killers was at the graduate level, a lousy partial credit at that.

I stuck with Frosty Freddo just shy of three years, until the January I took off for Penn State and what they call the Ice Cream Short Course. The smiley-face at the registration desk greeted me with a lemon-chiffon grin and a promise of "seven days of udder bliss." A month later, diploma in hand, I moved to Malta in Upstate New York and before May was done, my bank account was drained and Loony Scoops was up and running. You couldn't beat the location, Highway 9, south of Saratoga Springs, between Homewood Suites and P.J.'s BAR-B-QSA. *Oh, man, the ribs, the brisket, the music.*

Georgia Treasure is the flavor that put Loony Scoops and me on the map.

A Dixie-inspired mélange
of oven-roasted Spanish peanuts,
thick swirls of caramel fudge, a splash of peach,
a hint of mint, and decadently rich
triple-chocolate truffle ice cream.

Week after opening, I delivered a bucket to the *Albany Times Union*. Next I knew, Lenora-Jo Coffey, the paper's legendary food and wine critic, was on the phone and making my day, her voice matter-of-fact and paper thin, in jarring contrast to the Baby Jane headshot that accompanied her feature: "So help me God, Mr. Blessing, your Georgia Treasure is the most divine thing I have licked in all my life."

A day later, she was propped on a stool at the soda fountain, while I puttered about with tastings. She was so unlike the Lenora-Jo portrayed in the paper, I was about to ask for proof of identity when she said, "Don't tell me you don't know?"

"I guess I don't."

Nope, this couldn't be Lenora-Jo. She was closer to middle age than coffin age, librarian assertive with a book-smart haircut and probing blue eyes behind no-frills frames. No turban. No hula hoop earrings. No push-broom lashes. No eyebrows arched in infinite delight. She cut to the chase: "Lenora-Jo Coffey, she isn't real."

"Seriously?"

"It's common knowledge."

"Not to me."

"The paper made her up. Years ago. I'm the ninth."

"Like Betty Crocker ..."

"Anonymity is a food reviewer's greatest asset."

"I feel stupid," I said.

"My fault. I shouldn't have assumed."

"So if you're not Lenora-Jo, what do I call you, then?"

"Miss Coffey, of course," she winked, and raised her phone to eye level, urging me to face the camera as I faced away from the camera.

Best to interject here before upcoming events convey the wrong impression.

First off, I don't want you to think that, as author and main character, I'm setting myself up to be some sort of James Bond or kinkster hunk from Fifty Shades of Grey. *I have never been God's gift to anybody. Notwithstanding the melodrama that contaminates my life, I embrace the humdrum. As a Certified Public Accountant by the name of Allison once said to me in the dying seconds of a slow-going evening of speed-dating, "Do you work at making yourself forgettable or does it come naturally?"*

Governed by parentage, I sought to stay below the radar, even as the need to promote my business ramped up. I was store-brand vanilla with negligible aftertaste. I played up the ice cream, played down the maker. That's not to say I came without features. I was self-sufficient, cooked, cleaned, made my bed most mornings. I knew the difference between a Phillips screwdriver and a Torx, a haymaker and a hook. I kept fit, no small feat considering my everyday proximity to fats and sugars. My life's goal, however, was invisibility, which is why I ended up in ice cream.

The uniforms alone kept me out of the limelight. While Loony Scoops bypassed the sanitized dress whites, geeky bowties, and brimless garrison caps of days gone by, my theme of chocolate brown polo shirts, yellow-brown baseball caps, and pleated khakis still screamed castrato.

That said, and with respect to Lenora-Jo and the significant other soon to enter my life, I was a humble purveyor of frozen desserts—a career soda jerker—and, as history records, no man in my profession has ever had studmuffin and his name appear in the same sentence.

Dairy-driven romances have never captured anybody's imagination, outside of a 4-H clubhouse.

Done with the photos, Lenora-Jo retrieved a spiral-bound notepad from her leather case and bade the show go on.

I was in my element, I tell you, my genius on display as I swapped my signature concoctions in and out, scoops and sundaes, milkshakes, floats and smoothies, cakes and cannoli, diligently ascribing the supernatural to each, as Lenora-Jo dipped and divined, quizzed and jotted, her tongue swirling, her chef-de-cuisine squint inscrutable, and confirmation of her Food Network training. She gave me nothing. Nary an *ooo*, *ah*, or *yummo*. She could make or break Loony Scoops and we both knew it.

"And this last?" she said. "What was it you called it?" Her tongue was slow to relinquish the spoon.

I circled out from behind the counter, settled onto the stool beside her. "Coco Rico."

"Coco Rico?"

"Yeah."

"Well, Crème d'Orgasme would be far more à propos, don't you agree?" she said with a purr, and spun to rest her New Balance pinks on the edge of the stool, a toe-curl from my crotch. "Would you want to have dinner sometime?"

I acted as if this was normal. "What? Like a date?"

"Whatever works. Lunch. Coffee. Carousel in Congress Park. No pressure. Really. I just thought perhaps ..."

I was flattered, excited. An older woman wouldn't be looking for either a commitment or my life story. A two-night stand at Ice Cream U was the last I'd come to anything resembling a relationship. The years before and the months since had seen a series of guarded, go-nowhere flirtations, underscored by my accustomed normal: horny, lonely, starved for intimacy, horny, lonely. *You try carrying the baggage that was my father. See how far that gets you on the dating scene.* Even by this standard, Lenora-Jo the Ninth was a non-starter. She was a reporter. I knew reporters. Dozens. Hundreds. Thousands. Newspaper reporters. Television reporters. www.bullshit.com and .net and .org and .wtf reporters. As inviting as she was, I would not risk it. "I'm sorry," I said, loathing myself and my deep-seated paranoia. "I can't."

Her face fell, though she was quick to pick it up. "All good. Nothing ventured, nothing gained. My mistake. Sorry. I just thought ..."

"It's not you," I said. If we didn't part on good terms, there was no telling the damage she could do. "It's me."

"Whatever." She cut short a forced yawn and gauged the distance from her stool to the exit. I had embarrassed her.

"It's just, you see, I was taught not to mix business with pleasure."

"Funny, I've always believed business should be a pleasure."

With my brain flailing north and my mouth flagging south, I blurted the blurt of all blurts: "It's because you remind me of my mother." *Oh shit, oh shit, oh shit! Where the hell had that come from?*

She winced, shuddered as she tried to contain it, but the laughter rushed out of her, crescendo upon crescendo of disbelief slapping me in the face. This was a good one. *Best she'd ever heard.*

In fact, she did not remind me of my mother. While the surrogate Lenora-Jo Coffey had plenty working in her favor, she was no Heather Blythe-Blessing. *Who could be?* On the other hand, if there was a surefire line to let a woman down easy, this had to be it. *You remind me of my mother.* A cockblock for the ages. Inspired!

"Look, I'm fine," she said, gulping giggles as she packed up her belongings. "I'm a writer. Rejection comes with the job. I deal with little boys like you all the time. The loss is yours." She beelined it to the door.

I backtracked to save my ass. "It's not that I don't like you."

"Stop the whining. I'm a professional. I promise, I'll be writing the puff piece of puff pieces. You'll love it."

"Much appreciated," I said. "Really."

"I would have been fine with the truth, you know. It just never occurred to me that you were ... Well, I'm not the homophobic sort, if that's what you're worried about. But all your baloney, my God, what is wrong with you?"

I did not protest, did not attempt to refute her theory. It was perfect. I should have come up with it myself. The kicker was her question: *"What is wrong with you?"* I was grateful she didn't hang around for my answer.

Leonora-Jo was true to her word. From the moment her write-up appeared in the *Times Union*, Loony Scoops boomed. *"Most heavenly ice cream in the state and, dare I say, the country."* Folks came steadily and in droves. Halfway through my second year in business, Corinne Meredith Widdoes came too.

HOW TO FIND A GOOD DENTIST

Some days, a shot of espresso did the job. Other days, I sought relief in an affogato—three shots of espresso and a liberal scoop of *Cappuccino Di Cremona* gelato. This was one of those days.

Business was dead. I'd had three customers since lighting up the *Open*, takeouts for birthday cakes, each prepaid. Ice cream and winter don't mix at the best of times, but the cakes and hardpacks paid the offseason bills. Throw in a blizzard and a guy might as well stay in bed.

I sat by the window, nearing the bottom of my cup and a sluggish five o'clock, when the headlights swept through the parking lot. My expectations were zero. I was ready to close up, grab dinner from China Wang in Malta, and settle in at home with a movie. My guess, the driver would U-turn to BAR-B-QSA a hundred yards back. I drained the last of my affogato and stopped dead at the sight of the apparition in the window.

A drop in barometric pressure will do that to you, or to your brain, at least. Not that I believed in the supernatural or much else by then. And a phantom in a snowstorm had to be abnormal even for the paranormal. The wind was pushing forty. Ice pellets pelting. Drifts up to your nostrils. White on night, no sign of life, except for this ethereal waif, peering through the vapor, looking to get a rise out of someone or something. I wondered why she (or it) hadn't opted for better weather and a busier time, the opportunity to freak out more than my gang of one. But then she vanished as abruptly as she'd appeared, dispersed into the ether, down vest, cozy fleece, and ectoplasm. An instant later she traipsed through my door and taxied to an unhurried landing at my table. Angel of Death come to collect a soul past due.

She pocketed her gloves, tossed off her hood, brushed snow from her vest and bangs. And there I sat, the oblivious male lead in a déjà vu screenplay: the tenderfoot newly arrived at the ranch, waiting for Billy the foreman to show up in a pickup truck, except Billy turns out to be a spirited babe in a cowboy hat and the story writes itself.

"You're still open, I hope?" She unzipped her vest, loosened her scarf. "I'm not too late, am I?"

My diaphragm rebooted. I got to my feet. "Too late for ... uh...?"

She appraised me with a quizzical grin, her brown eyes probing, and raised her hands to indicate the surroundings. "This is an ice cream shop, isn't it?"

"Ice cream?" Her hair fell in soft waves to her shoulders, the shade a buttercream the overhead lighting somehow mined for platinum.

"I'm sorry. Am I missing something? Did I wake you up?"

Dazed is what I was, arms straight to tabletop, elbows locked, knuckles flat. I must have looked like I was set to detonate. "I'm sorry. Yeah, I guess you caught me napping, sort of. I wasn't expecting you."

"Me?"

"Anyone. The weather ..."

"So you are closed?" She flicked her scarf back to her neck.

"No, no. I'm open. Wide open." I pointed her to the counter and the backlit overhang that was the menu. "Take your time. Anything you want, on the house."

She eyed me with suspicion. "That's not necessary."

"To come out on a night like this ... for ice cream. Yeah, it is necessary."

"Well, okay then. Thank you," she said. I had the feeling she had more on her mind, but she let it pass. Seconds later she pointed: "I know I shouldn't, but this sounds wonderful."

Vermont Volcano Sundae!
Ribbons of pure Vermont maple syrup,
crunchy nuggets of pure Vermont maple sugar,
and the most awesomely vibrant vanilla in the galaxy.
Topped with Everest-inspired peaks of farm-fresh whipped cream, crisp
slivers of home-baked raspberry wafer,
and the fiery essence of South Seas cinnamon.

"Still, you've got to let me pay," she said. "I insist."

"Look, I'm just glad to have company. It's been a long day."

"We'll make a trade, then. I pay for the ice cream, you talk my head off. Deal?" She offered her hand and I was happy to reciprocate, though wisely kept it brief. She'd done next to nothing, said next to nothing, and yet I was drawn to her. She was a small planet with a gravitational attraction akin to Jupiter, fragments of unknown worlds in orbit about her. I didn't say this out loud, of course; I wasn't a dope, doped-up, or Pablo Neruda.

Forgoing poetic (and pathetic) allusion, I let my actions do the talking. Indeed, I gave that sundae everything I had, scooping, saucing, sculpting, and sprinkling to beat the band.

"You're an artist," she said, as she watched.

"It's too beautiful to eat," she said, as I set the glass tulip before her.

"Well, almost," she said, as she submerged her spoon.

"Oh, my," she said, as the first taste touched her lips. "Oh, my."

She was around my age, twenty-five, twenty-six, though self-possessed in ways I couldn't come close to. You could see it in her eyes: the amusement, the knowing, as if any surprise would fail to surprise. She came across as the storied girl-next-door, ambitious and eager and quick to leave home, only to return years later with worlds in her pockets.

I made myself another espresso, a double, and took a seat at the counter, two deferential stools between us. Lenora-Jo Coffey's sneaker on my crotch had been a lesson well learned.

Her. Me. And the wavy orange and blue stripes that animated the walls and ceiling of Loony Scoops. Our tête-à-tête had all the makings of those super-vivid dreams that send your hopes soaring, opening your life to wondrous possibility, before the crushing reality that arrives on awakening.

"First time here?" I asked, as syrupy suave as a shot of Buckley's Original.

"Once before. Labor Day weekend."

"Did we talk?"

"You were busy. The place was packed. Not like now."

"Yeah, always best to hold off on ice cream until there's a snowstorm."

"I'll keep it in mind." She burrowed deeper into the sundae, her spoon emerging with a taste of pretty much everything. "And you, Rob, been here long?"

"You know my name?"

"It's embroidered on your shirt."

"My middle name is Idiot," I said.

"I'm Cori, by the way," she said, and extended her hand a second time. I held it a fraction longer than before, waited for her thumb to signal time-up.

I told her how I got into ice cream and ended up in Saratoga. She told me how she was new to the area, had gone to McGill University, up in Montreal. "I was so anxious to get back to the States, I took the first job offer to come along. I thought I'd be miserable here, but I'm not. Saratoga. Lake George. Even Queensbury. I love the area." She looked me in the eye. "I really do."

Smitten had never been part of my vocabulary. It ranked alongside *fiancée* and *marvelous* as words no man should ever speak aloud. But as I chatted with her, *smitten* is where I sensed I was heading. She was spooning up the last of her sundae when I got to the question I'd been avoiding. "You're not a writer, are you?"

"Like books?"

"Like a reporter."

She paused to parse my question, and again looked at me like I might be off my nut. "Why would you think that? Do I give off vibes or something?"

"Just wondering, that's all."

She shook her head as if she might have finally had enough of me. She took a ten-dollar bill from her purse.

"I told you," I said, "it's on the house."

"Okay, if that's how you want it." She took back her money and slid her business card across the flecked Formica, through a dollop of marshmallow topping, and onto my palm. "We'll do a trade-off, then."

CORINNE MEREDITH WIDDOES, DDS
ORAL CORRAL DENTAL
WEST HIGH STREET, BALLSTON SPA, NY

"I could use a good dentist," I said, in the great dairy-romantic tradition.

She laughed. "You're an interesting guy, Rob."

"You think so?"

"I do."

"Because interesting is the last thing I try to be."

"Clearly, you need to try harder."

"Yeah, well, I'm glad you liked the *Volcano*. Hope you'll come by for more sometime"

"Only if you'll let me pay."

"I promise," I said. "If it'll help, I'll charge you double next time."

She was the girl every band in history has sung about—a pop-song crush in melody, verse, and yearning. And for reasons yet unknown, she had transcended the lyrics to touch down in my life. I watched for her daily, but soon saw her passion for ice cream was dictated by the weather. She showed up solely on the stormiest days, when business was dead and I was alone. According to the love guru who resided at the sub-basement level of my brain, this was a good thing. At this rate, I'd soon be writing my own songs.

Six visits down, Cori's tally was formidable:

One *Vermont Volcano Sundae*.

One *Pistachio Parfait*.

One double scoop of *Georgia Treasure* on a cake cone.

One double scoop of *Salted Caramel* in a handcrafted waffle bowl.

One *Amorous Amaretto* frozen cannoli.

Lastly, three-quarters through one *Kiwi Mango* milkshake, she poked her straw aside, pondered me a moment, and said. "I'd give anything to see what you look like when you're not wearing brown or an apron or that baseball cap."

"What? You've got a problem with my sense of fashion?"

"To put it mildly ..."

"We'd have to meet somewhere outside of here, then."

"Are you asking me out?" she said.

"Like a date? Yeah. Guess I am."

"About time." She pecked me on the cheek and cut a hasty exit.

5

DATING TIPS FOR SONS
OF SERIAL KILLERS

I decided to tell Cori about my father on our first official date. With others—three, anyhow—I had waited until the third date, which is where the budding relationships ceased to bud. That's why I waited. But not with Cori. The more I got to know her, the more I dreaded the void she'd leave when she left. The sooner I scared her off, the better off I'd be. Cori too.

I didn't work Mondays in winter and she started only after lunch. A breakfast date was just about our speed. She had suggested Coffee Traders in Saratoga. "Ever had a Death Wish?" she'd asked.

I began to formulate a bullshit denial when it dawned on me she was talking about the coffee brand. "It's what we serve at Loony Scoops," I said.

She was holding fort at a table in the back, mug in hand, as I ambled through the door.

"Wow," she said, admiring my getup—Asics, Levi's, navy sweatshirt, black ski jacket. "A whole new you."

"Revelatory, huh?"

"Earthshaking."

We hugged. She kissed me lightly on the lips. I kissed her less lightly. And my heart sank in anticipation of the blowback to come. Death Row Dad was breathing down my neck. *Spit it out, boy. Spit it out.*

The morning rush was over, the queue short. I explored the

chalkboard menus by the cash up front, ordered a large Death Wish along with a bacon grilled cheese for me and an egg and avocado wrap for Cori. She offered to pay, as expected. "I'm taking you out," I said, flashing a wad of fresh one-dollar bills. "Your donations to Loony Scoops should cover it."

Coffee Traders is compact, homey, and three times as long as it is wide. First impression is funky on the side of grunge, with a hipster vibe that starts with the staff and ends with the shelves of vintage candy at the rear. There are a dozen tables throughout and a scattering on the street for when the weather cooperates.

We concentrated on our sandwiches, segueing into uneasy small-talk that hiccupped through the predictable—the weather, the menu, the baristas, the baristas' tats, the baristas' piercings, the baristas' hair. Neither of us had counted on awkward, but awkward it was. Calling it a date had formalized whatever had been developing between us. The newness sucked. We needed to find our old selves again, to the extent we had old selves. Cori addressed the obvious: "I wanted to come here because of the intimacy. But it's having the opposite effect on us. Like we're on a blind date."

"Blame me," I said.

"What's going on?"

"Ah, nothing," I lied. "Work stuff. I'm sorry." *Spit it out, boy. Spit it out.*

"Anything I can help with? Should I be coming more often, eating more sundaes?"

I laughed. "Nah. Just give me a couple of minutes. I'll be okay. I'm sorry. Really sorry."

She followed up her wrap with a caramel macchiato and a muffin chaser. "Food is fuel," she said. "I try to get a run in every morning. Four, five miles, at least."

"So that explains it," I said, without a clue as to what *it* was, and worried my *it* came across as smarmy.

We had never strayed far beyond the superficial. Rehashing the same-old/same-old was starting to wear. We both knew it too. The ins and outs of ice cream. The ins and outs of dentistry. Books. Movies. TV. Apps. Android versus Apple. Abridged and redacted anecdotes of our respective childhoods. We were sidestepping the elephant in the coffee shop—our true selves.

We'd talk, go silent, and begin anew. I had my reasons for keeping the conversation generic, but what were hers? Unless putting up barriers was all we had in common.

I wasn't ready to give up on her or me, but I was entering the homestretch when Cori called it. "This can't continue. Not like this."

"I know," I said. "There's something I need to tell you."

"And me, I need to tell you something too."

I let her go first, thinking she might let me off the hook, part ways with me for her own good reasons, rather than the one good reason I was about to provide.

"That night I showed up at your place for the first time, it wasn't by chance. The thing you need to know, the thing I haven't told you, I liked you even before I met you."

I hadn't seen this coming.

"You see, there'd been this story about you, and there was this picture—you were putting a cherry on a sundae ..."

"The *Times Union* thing? That was two years ago."

"Almost. Yes. I was still in Montreal. I was googling the area and, well, you popped up. And I can't tell you why, because I don't know why, but there was something about it. About you."

"C'mon, a soda jerk putting a cherry on a sundae? Oh, yeah, every woman's fantasy—Brad Pitt with a scoop."

"No, honest. I swear. Now I won't say it was love at first sight or anything so dumb, but I couldn't get you out of my head. Like it was fate or whatever." She was blushing. I was blushing. Every soul in Coffee Traders should have been blushing. "And now, truth is, you're in my head more than ever. I like you. I like your messy brown hair and the blue of your eyes and the way you listen to people, like you're listening to me now."

Oh, Jesus! I combed my fingers through my hair. *Ah, jeez.*

"There's something special and good about you, like I've known you all my life. I know, I can see, I'm scaring you off, coming on too strong, too fast. But I can't keep it in any longer. I am never this forward, not with anyone. Not ever. I just need to know if you feel the same, if whatever we're doing is worth pursuing. Because right now, the last hour, it doesn't feel good in any way."

"Like we've hit a wall," I said.

"Exactly."

Now as breathlessly goo-goo-eyed as this scene appeared to the Coffee Traders' faithful, and as warm, loving, and heartfelt as the moment was to Cori, I found myself at the mercy of the adolescent me.

My hormones were in free fall, my heart along for the ride. Beneath the table, my right leg was shredding to the Metallica blasting in my braincase. I was twenty-six years old going on sixteen. I wanted to jump into bed with her. I wanted to have children with her. I wanted to spend the rest of my life with her. Hell, I wanted her inside and out, banality be damned. I needed to put an end to this misery, swap it out for a more familiar misery. "My father is a serial killer."

"Pardon?" She tilted her head, squinted, as if I might be speaking in tongues. "What?"

I groped for a nicer way to put it. "My father. He killed people. Lots of people."

"What are you saying?" Simultaneous translation would have been helpful. "He's like a serial killer?"

"Not *like*. He is."

I watched, waited. Next, if true to the pattern established by my previous unrequited true loves, Cori would say, "Are you trying to be funny?" or words to this effect. And with combined disgust, pity, indignation, and terror, she would denounce my cruelty, my tastelessness—"Joke or not!"—and on a swell of bitter tears, off she'd scoot, forever traumatized by the sick fuck she'd been so foolish to have fallen for.

She brushed muffin crumbs from her sleeve. "You're serious?"

I was at a loss. I'd never been obliged to take the big reveal further. Why was she still sitting there?

"Who did he kill?" she asked.

"Anybody. Everybody."

"Why?"

"He never said."

"Never?"

"Nope."

"C'mon, he never told you?"

"Far as I know, he's never told anyone."

She raised her mug, savored the warmth. Behind us, a barista tidied up the candy shelves. He was dressed in black. His hair was green. The holes in his earlobes were the size of quarters. His arms were a gallery of tats, the Millennium Falcon and Sonic the Hedgehog the highlights.

"I'm sorry, Cori. Sooner or later, you'd find out. Better to come from me."

She propped her elbows on the table, rested her chin upon a

latticework of fingers. She stared me down, direct and matter-of-fact. "Are you one too?"

"What?" I'd heard her, all right. She was not the first to ask.

"A serial killer, Rob. Are you one too?"

I tried to read her.

She folded her arms across her red-knit sweater, rocked back on the legs of her chair. "It's not a trick question."

What did she expect me to do, confess I did not know for certain? Killing one or two people might not be a disease, but killing upward of twenty-seven likely was. No stopping, once you start. Like those hapless OCDers who tie and untie their shoelaces a kazillion times a day. Could killing be passed on father to son, same as high cholesterol, male pattern baldness, or a career in confections? And it wasn't like I'd never had the urge. *Like who hasn't?* Everybody wants to kill somebody sometime. "No," I said, with less certainty than I would have liked. "I am not one too."

"Wow," she said. "Just plain wow. Do you think so poorly of me? Do you think I would have asked such a ludicrous question if for one second I believed you were?"

"I'm stupid."

"And I'm stupid for making you feel stupid."

"Talking about him isn't easy. Scares people off."

"Is that what you wanted, to scare me off?"

I shook my head.

"So you were testing me?"

"Look, for better or worse, my father is a huge part of who I am. I hate it. But I live with it. And anyone who's going to share my life, whether it's five minutes or fifty years, has to live with it too."

"Share your life? Now who's rushing things?"

"You know what I'm saying. It doesn't scare you?"

"Of course. But you don't."

"You haven't heard it all."

"And if I do?"

"That's up to you."

"You think you're the first boyfriend I've had with skeletons in his closet?"

"Yeah, Cori, but my skeletons are skeletons."

"Agreed. Your baggage is a bit heavier than most boyfriends'—"

"Really? You're not going to run?"

"Let's just see if I'm still here by the time you're done talking. So you had better make it good. I want to know everything."

I told her as much as I dared, though not all that I knew. I kept it simple. Henry Taylor Dickens. His kills. His arrest. The incriminating peanut brittle. The nickname. His confession. My conversion from Bobby Dickens to Bobby Blessing. My exodus from Hillsdale. My mom's exodus from me. Boarding school. Dad's ever-delayed execution. And how I had built my life not upon the succor of friends and family, but by avoiding it.

"Early on, my mom sent me to this psychologist, Doctor Cutcheon. She said there was only one thing I needed to understand: Happiness is a myth. The best anyone can hope to be in life is less unhappy. If I could accept this, the rest would fall into place."

"That's a terrible thing to tell a child."

"Worked for me."

"If you say so."

Cori sat quietly for a long while, plotting her escape, no doubt. It was only fair I give her the out. "No need to stick around. No hard feelings. In your shoes, I would have been gone an hour ago."

"Really, you fit into a women's size seven?" she said. I laughed, though she wasn't kidding. She was feeling sorry for me. Had it been anyone else, I'd have been pissed. Wasn't my nature to solicit pity. Sympathy gave me the hives. "You know, I'm thinking, you just might be the loneliest person I have ever met. How have you survived? How do you carry all this inside of you? How are you even you?"

"Dr. Cutcheon."

"I'm not so sure."

"Kids are pawns. She made clear it wasn't my fault. And there was nothing wrong whether I loved my dad or hated him. But the toughest part, you know what it was? It wasn't coming to terms with what he'd done. I knew what he'd done. It was how the papers and TV made him look, how everyone lapped it up, as if he was less than human. I know it sounds nuts, Cori, but my dad was a good guy. Until he wasn't. I'm not saying people didn't have cause to fear him, it's just ... I dunno."

"So which is it? Do you love him or hate him?"

"You tell me. What would it be if he was your father?"

"He's still alive?"

"Prison. Florida."

"Do you visit him?"

"What?"

"Do you visit him?"

"I haven't seen him since the day he was caught. Not in person, anyhow. I mean, every now and then I'll come across something. A news thing. Those true crime shows. A podcast. I try to stay away from them. They're all bullshit. I wrote him once or twice at the beginning and he wrote back, but we had nothing to say. All of a sudden we were strangers. Later, with my mother taking off and all, I needed to take care of me."

"Surely you must want to see him before he dies. Once more, at least?"

"His execution has been set and changed so many times, I've stopped keeping track. It's been so long, when I think of my father, it's in the past tense. Sometimes, he's not even real to me. I'm not sure his physical death will make a difference. Truth is, I haven't thought of him in terms of The Living for years."

I'd taken her breath away. She blotted tears from her cheeks, mascara running. I apologized, though in the dark as to what I was apologizing for. She'd asked for it. This was uncharted territory, don't forget. Never had the discussion gone beyond "my dad, the serial killer." I had told Cori stuff I'd never told anyone, myself included.

She squeezed my hand as I walked her to her car. She was parked in front of Northshire Bookstore, which I guess prompted her to say, "You should write a book."

"Yeah. Right. I'll become a role model, show how children of serial killers can grow up to be normal, healthy human beings, leading fulfilling and productive lives."

"You never know," she said. "There are plenty of screwy kids out there these days, some screwier than you."

"Screwier than me? C'mon?"

"You have no idea," she said, and twirled to face me. She threw the flats of her hands onto my chest, backed me up against her BMW. A red 650i.

"You mystify me," I said.

"Aha! So my plan's working ..."

"Yeah, from the day I met you, I've seen you as more of a Prius type."

She sort of smiled, fixed her eyes on mine, guided my hand to her mouth, kissed me on the fleshy round of my thumb, and took a not unpleasant nibble. "I've got two hours before my first patient. All that sadness you keep inside, I know exactly what you need."

"A miracle cure?"

"An established therapy."

"Your place or mine?" I said.

"Smooth."

"I've got more, if you want. I've memorized the entire *Playa's Handbook of Cheesy Things to Say on a First Date*, cover to cover."

"Too cute," she said, patted the top of my head, and pushed me into the car.

6

QUESTIONS EVERY BRIDE SHOULD ASK

I'll end the suspense before this enters romcom territory: I married her.

I'd been accepted sorry-ass past and all by a woman who, in a rational world, would have been more rational. Woody Harrelson's dad had been a hitman. Keanu Reeves's dad dealt heroin. And Charlize Theron, her mom shot her alcoholic father right in front of her. They'd done okay, and I could too.

Cori had her own take: "Any man so forthcoming about something so horrific on a first date has to be a keeper." I did not question her reasoning. I did not stop to ask what could be in it for her.

As it turned out, dead or almost dead dads were something we had in common. And the good news kept coming: Her mom was dead too. I could not have asked for more. Taking me home to meet the girlfriend's parents had long been a worry.

"So tell me, young man, what line of work might your father be in?"

"Serial killing, sir."

"How interesting! And your mother?"

"She's a comic book."

We were sitting on her bed when Cori got around to the details of her parents and their ends. "There were no signs of violence. No suicide note. I think they might have been going at it in the backseat, if that makes any sense. I mean they weren't kids." Her voice quavered. "My babysitter found them. The car was in the garage. Windows were shut. Engine running. They'd been out Christmas shopping. I still have Dolores Bea, the Cabbage Patch doll they bought that night."

"Gosh, Cor."

"It was inevitable, I suppose. They were both recovering alcoholics. They met at AA."

"I can't believe you never told me."

"You have your own issues."

"Yeah, but still ..."

"My aunt, she took me in, you know, after ... without her ... I was lucky, really. Eden Prairie was a good place to grow up. Aunt Maureen, she saved my life. I owe her everything. She's why I went into dentistry. I wanted to be everything she was." Cori searched her closet, exhumed Dolores Bea. The doll resided upright in the box she'd come in, her eyes wide and watchful, as she came to grips with the shock of meeting her big sister's husband-to-be.

I had never been much good with people who opened up to me. Never knew what to do or say, how to position my head, purse my lips, or where to place my hands. I had my own junk to contend with and the sob stories of others came off anemic by comparison. Cori changed this, to the extent she could.

The closer we grew, the more in tune I became with the intimacy guidelines, hanging in for as long as she needed, never too quick to break away. Where I came up short was on the consolation side. I struggled to distinguish genuine compassion from the Hallmark variety, and I'd self-censor in lieu of dribbling the mush aloud. My forte was empathetic silence. I worried I was failing her; Cori claimed my concern made her love me more. "It's how you hold me, Rob." My drug was the nearness of her. A marathon stay at the Betty Ford could not have weaned me from the scent of her *Violet Blonde*.

Our wedding was small. Loony Scoopers on my side—part-timers Dawn, Jenna, Amber, Justin, Oliver; co-glaciers Patsy, Louise; consultant and co-packer Darryl. Oral Corral Dental associates on her side, only two I knew well enough to name—Laurie the dental assistant and the head guy, Dr. Fred Beckman, the *Dr.* imperative.

No family attended. Aunt Maureen from Minnesota, Cori's surrogate mom, had died the year before we met. (Yeah, I was three for three.)

BAR-B-QSA catered.

Cori wanted to know if I had told my father about her.

"Why would I?"

"I just thought ..." She was hurt.

"Please, Cor, when it comes to my father, don't. Just don't."

My mother was a no-show too. Here, Cori was upset for me. "You did ask her, didn't you? You said you did."

"I did. I swear."

As for the wedding gift Mom sent, I kept silent; I'd yet to figure out what to make of it, never mind what to do. I toed the storyline, how she was off in Europe, how she'd lived there for years without visiting home, how we didn't talk much.

"Where in Europe?" Cori asked, sensing her groom was being less than truthful. I had no answer. All these years later, communication between Mom and me continued to be filtered through her New York lawyer. Money too.

"She never was the same, you know, after my dad ..." I'd created a backstory for Mystery Mom, a collection of alibis and excuses for all occasions. My sick sad life was Cori's aphrodisiac of choice. Why dilute it? Besides, my father was millstone enough for any bride. No point throwing Heather Blythe-Blessing into the mix. Murder is one thing, sex and murder a whole new horror.

7

CAPITALIZING ON THE
UNSUNG PERKS OF INFAMY

*Life is one long knot in the gut
interrupted only by extended bouts of anxiety
and fleeting moments of unwarranted euphoria.*

—Robert Blessing

... There you have in writing my lifelong credo. And a damn fine and levelheaded credo it was, until Cori came along and the euphoria felt neither fleeting nor unwarranted. Maybe Cutcheon was wrong. Maybe happiness was not a myth. Or maybe married life had turned me into a sap and, before long, I'd pay the price.

We were coming up on our first anniversary when the unraveling commenced. A Tuesday morning. I was at work. The phone rang. The first of what would be three sketchy calls.

I canted to the left, a gallon jar of maraschino cherries under my arm, as I fumbled for the receiver. The caller introduced himself as a math teacher from Ballston Spa High School, a status calculated to grant him instant standing and respect.

He lived down the road in Wilton, and he had a bone to pick: "My wife nearly choked to death last night because of you."

I eased the jar onto the table, racked my brain for an alibi, my instinct more fight than flight. *Where was I last night? Who was I with? What was on TV?*

"That ice cream of yours, with the chewing gum ..."

"Gumball Choo Choo?"

"Well, son, one of your gumballs caught Charlie right at the back of the throat, come up through her straw like a shot."

I played the straight man. "She was drinking it? A milkshake?"

"If I'd been out, God knows, I'd be planning Charlotte's funeral."

Now to my way of thinking, a flavor that goes by the name of *Gumball Choo Choo* might lead one to count on a gumball or two, and one might want to proceed with caution if inclined to make an asshat milkshake of it. *And where the hell did she come up with a straw wide enough to accommodate a gumball?*

All the same, the remorse gushed out of me by rote: "Look, I'm real, real sorry, sir. Please, next time you're in the neighborhood, let me make it up to you and your wife."

The guy did not laugh, he guffawed. His spittle engorged both ends of the line. "Well, son, I can be there lickety-split. I'm in my car as we speak. In your parking lot."

I sent him home to wifey with four complimentary tubs, a t-shirt, a fistful of plastic spoons, and a brotherly slap on the back.

Customers had shaken me down plenty over the years. It was the cost of doing business. Buy them off, shut them up, keep the bottom feeders satisfied, Stupid Charlotte and MathMan the latest in a long line.

It had worked like a charm too, or so I thought, until a few days later when the Saratoga County Department of Health put me on notice. There'd been a complaint. No details, only that *"action was pending pursuant to review of said food service establishment premises."*

Stupid Greedy Lying Charlotte and her mutant milkshake. Makes you wonder about people. You bend over backward. You give them every reason to love and forgive you. *Four tubs and a t-shirt, don't forget.* And still they come at you. Tells you all you need to know about the milk of human kindness, room temp or deep frozen.

I had nothing to hide. Not when it came to ice cream.

June of 2019, Cori and I celebrated our anniversary and the best damn year of our respective lives. I had spared her the news about the Saratoga County Department of Health, projecting an admirable stoicism as I waited for the other shoe to drop.

I hadn't expected the shoe to belong to Lenora-Jo Coffey, the *Times Union* food and wine critic. She caught me on my cell. Caller number two.

"Nice to hear from you," I said.

"Is it?"

"I hope so."

"I assume you're aware, in addition to my regular column, I am now the paper's featured blogger on food-related issues. *Coffey's Cream*?"

"Sure," I lied. "It's great."

"Yes, well, the purpose of my call is to fact-check a story." She read me the headline: "'Is ice cream a weapon of choice for the son of the Brittle Butcher?'"

"What's that supposed to mean?" I said, hackles rising.

"You tell me."

"There's nothing to tell."

"I am doing you a courtesy, a chance to tell your side, Mr. Blessing. Or are you more at ease with Mr. Dick?"

"I don't know what you're talking about."

"So you claim not to be the son of Henry Taylor Dick?"

"Not quite."

"According to my sources—"

"For Christ's sake, it's Dickens. D-I-C-K-E-N-S. Not Dick."

"Calm down. It was a slip of the tongue. I would not have let it go to press as such."

"Either way, I am not my father."

"You know what they say, though, Mr. Blessing, the apple doesn't fall far from the tree."

"Why are you doing this?"

"My blog had over seven thousand unique visitors last month alone. Do you know how good that is? People are interested in what I have to say. An exclusive like this will go viral, put me on the national stage."

"An exclusive what? There is no story."

"Don't let it be said I didn't give you every opportunity to rebut."

"Look, if we got off on the wrong foot, I'm sorry—"

"Oh, you will be."

"The piece you wrote for me was great. I thanked you. I sent flowers, ice cream. You even got my name right."

"You lied to me."

"I what?"

"You told me you were gay."

"I never said any such thing."

"You led me on."

"I led you nowhere."

"I was willing to give myself to you."

"What, you're so irresistible, no guy has turned you down before?"

"Never a single one. Never a straight one."

"There's a first for everything."

"You humiliated me."

"I don't see how."

"You married my dentist."

"What? Cori? Is this a joke?"

"You should have fucked me when you had the chance. Now I'm going to fuck you."

Coffey had talent, I give her that. She was candid about the rumors and innuendo that drove her exposé. She stated at the outset the accusations against me were tenuous. *Alleged* appeared no fewer than eighteen times as she detailed my guilt. The unnamed couple from Wilton. The heads-up from the Health Department. Plus incidents I barely remembered and others I could swear had never happened.

Yeah, Coffey had it all and then some, including how generously I treated disgruntled customers. Nonetheless, by the end of her diatribe, even I was ready to steer clear of Loony Scoops. Whatever I had or hadn't done, the case was open and shut.

> **Could it be the county's pending legal actions against Robert "Bobby" Blessing are not as frivolous as they may appear initially? It must be noted that the founder and proprietor of the popular Loony Scoops ice cream establishment on Highway 9 in Saratoga is alleged to be the son of the notorious Henry Taylor Dick, who is alleged to have murdered twenty-seven innocent Americans in cold blood between 1988 and 2002.**

No sooner did Coffey's blog go live than *alleged* Loony Scoops customers came alive, going wide with gaggy thingamabobs and what-nots they had fished from my ice cream. I was hung, drawn, and quartered on Twitter, as outraged tweets and retweets of my misdeeds flew in from ice cream fanciers nearby and far-flung. Saratoga, Halfmoon, Clifton Park, Schuylerville, and Glens Falls. Canberra, Taiwan, London, Edmonton, and Whatthefuck. If the item existed in the material world, Loony Scoops ice cream contained it in the frozen world.

Coffey's Cream hit the viral jackpot. Likes. Shares. Shares of shares. Retweets. Retweets of retweets. Every damn warrior on the web took the story to their freeze-dried hearts. The trolls spared no flavor, except *Mango Basil*, which was a bust to begin with. Harder to take were the trolls who made it personal.

█████████████████████ – Jun 21
Die moron. Lock yourself in you're freezer and die die die dei die die
#DeadlyIceCream #FoodCrimes @CoffeysCream @LoonyScoops

█████████████████████ – Jun 21
I hope he chokes on his own vanilla. #LoonyScoops @CoffeysCream

████████████ – Jun 21
Am I the only one who wants to see this Blessing clown drown in a vat of his own toxic sludge? #LoonyScoops @CoffeysCream @LenoraJoCoffey #icecreamkiller

█████████ – Jun 22
Kill him same way he killed the poor folk who ate his ice creme.
#LoonyScoops @LenoraJoCoffey @CoffeysCream #Killicecreamkiller

███████████████████ – Jun 22
Wanna bet a snowflake judge lets #RobertBlessing walk. Don't let the #icecreamkiller get away with murder. #Killicecreamkiller #stophimnow

███████████████████ – Jun 23
Protect your children. #RobertBlessing is a #pedalphile. Lock him up.
#icecreamkiller @CoffeysCream #pedalphiles #HenryTaylorDickson

██████████████ – Jun 24
His name is Dickens, not Dick. I went to school with Bobby Dickens or whatever he calls himself now. The whole family was messed up.
@LenoraJoCoffey @CoffeysCream #serialkillers

████████████████ – Jun 24
Rot in hell you ████ scumdumpster piece of ████ ██ █████. Were coming for you. #RobertBlessing #icecreamkiller #BrittleButcher

█████████ – Jun 26
Desth to motgerfukkers!!!!!!!! #BrittleButcher #icecreamkiller @SaratogaNY

Dick would be amended to Dickson and, later, Dickson to Dickens. If Coffey offered a mea culpa, I missed it.

Loony Scoops and I were done. All my work added up to zip. It was *Home Sweet Hellsdale* all over again. Helpless. Hopeless.

There was no hiding the facts from Cori, now. She strove to be the voice of moderation. "You've been through worse," she assured me, muted reference to Death Row Dad. "You'll get through this too."

"I should close up while I'm ahead."

"I've got a good job. I make good money. Take advantage of it. Move on to something else. Start fresh. Write that book."

"What I need is a lawyer."

"Are you crazy? A lawyer will only keep the story alive. You don't want that. I certainly don't."

"Jesus, Cor, I'm not allowed to defend myself?"

"As if anything you say on social media or anywhere will make a difference? Really? People believe only what they already believe. You, of all people, know this."

"And what about my father? How'd Coffey find out? Who tipped her off?"

"I wasn't the first girl you told, Rob. You had to have known it would get out sooner or later."

"You saying I wanted this to happen?"

"Did you?"

The drop-off in business was immediate. Only the uninformed, the unwired, and a coterie of loyal fringe-dwellers stuck by me. Some sought to cheer me up with what they imagined to be the silver lining. "Hey! No more waiting in long lines for ice cream. Woohoo!"

Even Frosty Freddo, my old mentor back in Syracuse, came out of the woodwork, dropped me a note.

> Ever heard of the Palmieri Cheese Company? Back in the day, they were the largest supplier of mozzarella to pizzerias in the Northeast. Then one day news breaks that pipes from the factory's toilets are leaking into the cheese vats and had been for years. And what happened? I'll tell you what happened. Palmieri is now the largest supplier of mozzarella in the whole United States of America and who knows if they ever fixed the plumbing. Do you get what I'm saying? As long as it tastes good, nobody cares what shit is in it, even if it's shit.

While I appreciated Freddo's email, I was too discouraged to pay it much heed. Depression had sent me a formal invitation and was waiting on my RSVP. But then, late on the afternoon of the second day, the fan stopped spinning and the shit stopped flying.

You know those old movies where some screw-up screws up worse than usual, and the cops and debt collectors and local hoods start tightening the screws, and just when you figure the poor sap is screwed-beyond-screwed, his friends and neighbors and loved ones, his unaccountably hot wife, they show up en masse to bail him out, and everybody cries and laughs and applauds?

Well, that's what happened to me. Sort of.

It didn't go down all at once, and it wasn't as tearjerky as *It's A Wonderful Life*, for instance, but it was enough for Cori to say, "I told you so."

Five days in, the online outrage was isolated to an undercard of overmatched Johnny-come-latelies. Loony Scoops was back on track and gathering steam.

My takeaway baffled Cori. "I'm more of a nobody than I thought," I said. "Figured I was worth a week of outrage at the very least."

"Why did I marry you, again?" she asked.

There was no one factor as to why it blew over so quickly. There were a bunch.

One: Fatigue, for sure. A combination of mile-long Twitter threads and short attention spans.

Two: The relative insignificance of Loony Scoops. I was no Baskin-Robbins, no Ben & Jerry's. My extinction would be light on bragging rights.

Three: The fearless anti-trolls and their hashtags, #ResistanceLoonyScoops and #SaveOurScoops. (I suspected Cori led the charge here, though she denied all.)

> ▓▓▓▓ – Jun 22
> Dear @LenoraJoCoffey: Shame on you for indulging in reprehensible muckraking. Casting unwarranted aspersions on a legitimate small business owner is beyond the pale. I hope he sues you.
> #ResistanceLoonyScoops #SaveOurScoops

> ▓▓▓▓ – Jun 25
> LoonyScoops is the best ice cream ever. Give the kid a break. He's getting a raw deal. @VisitSaratogaNY #SaveOurScoops

Four: My counterintuitive marketing.

I'd kept a running tally of the junk reported to have turned up in my ice cream. I joked to Cori how I should include a handout with every purchase. "To make life easier for customers who might want to jump on the bandwagon."

She didn't laugh. "It's not a half-bad idea. Fight stupid with stupid. What do you have to lose?"

I beefed up the list a tad, printed it up on the morning of the third day. People laughed, gobbled it up, and shared it. The list went viral, outdoing even Coffey's hatchet job.

LOOK WHAT I FOUND IN MY LOONY SCOOPS, TODAY!	
Check (√) and enjoy!	
Only ice cream	Some ugly mystery thing
Egg shells	Screws/nails, pristine
Budweiser cap	Screw/nails, rusty
Pearl earring	Broken chopstick
A Harry Potter earring	Seashell
Human or animal tooth	Guitar or banjo pick
Insect, dead	Matches
Insect, alive	Coins
Band-Aids, with scab	Chess, checkers, Monopoly
Intact or scab-free	or other game piece
Acrylic fingernails	Beads
Buttons	Fishing lure
Xmas ornament(s)	Hair accessories
Staple, paper clip, or	An orthodontic device, child or
other fastener	adult
Animal hair	*G.I. Joe* accessories
Human hair	*Barbie* accessories
Glass, wood, or metal	Earbuds
Hubcap	The Iron Throne
Clark Kent's tie or	Star Wars, Simpsons, or similar
eyeglasses	figurine(s)
Judge Crater and/or	The Sasquatch and/or
Jimmy Hoffa	The Abominable Snowman
Rodent fetus (mouse,	Wholesome, all natural
hamster, etc.)	ingredients
Legos	Other: _____

Five: The good in people.

I'd stopped looking for the quality from an early age. The return had never justified my effort. Perhaps the trick to finding good was not to seek it, but to accept it. Faith is a wonderful thing. Lets you see everything without seeing anything.

Yup, across the board, the Saratoga County faithful and business community stood firm in my defense. Folks turned up at Loony Scoops in droves to blast the naysayers who had vilified their ice cream of choice. Even the math teacher and his lovely wife, gumball-choking Stupid Charlotte herself, pledged their allegiance. "Cross our hearts and hope to die, Mr. Blessing, our lips have been sealed. Swear to God in Heaven, we never gave the time of day to that snoopy reporter or anyone. It's a crime what they've done to you. Lower than low."

Curiosity seekers slithered in too, mingling with the locals. I could spot them, of course. *Smell them.* But as long as they were firming up my bottom line, I tolerated the finger-pointing and whispers and photo ops. Just sucked it all up. Didn't so much as blink when asked to autograph their books and the horseshit pages devoted to my dad. You would not believe the shitload of so-called encyclopedias of serial killers out there.

The Pictorial Encyclopedia of Serial Killers & Murderers
The Encyclopedia of Serial Killers
The Encyclopedia of Modern Murder
Bad Girls Did It!: An Encyclopedia of Female Murderers
The A to Z Encyclopedia of Serial Killers
The Wikipedia Encyclopedia of Serial Killers
Human Monsters: An Illustrated Encyclopedia of the World's Most Vicious Murderers
Serial Killers Encyclopedia

Yup, I signed them all. Britannica and World Book might be on life support these days, but not these babies. The books are a category unto themselves, a publishing staple up there with miracle diets and thrillers with *The Girl* in the title. During Dad's trial, pen and paper were regularly shoved in my face, but this was a first for my so-called adult life, and in the wake of Coffey's attempted assassination, I'd turned sufficiently mercenary (i.e., practical) to go with the soul-crushing flow. *Make hay while the sun shines.*

I trusted none of it. I trusted no one. My sixth sense was pessimism.

My seventh was cynicism. Bad stuff finds me. Always has. Started in the womb. My mother pressed her hands to her belly and there I was.

Sure enough, as if on schedule, John J. Tavasi, MD, MPH, Commissioner, Saratoga County Department of Health, announced publicly that *"an expedited investigation into recent revelations concerning alleged irregularities and infractions of said dairy establishment has been launched."*

Enthusiasm for my plight waned. The vocal became less vocal. The Wilton Loony Scoopers, the Little League ball team I had sponsored since the day I opened, rubbed salt in the wound, dropping me in favor of the Valvoline in Halfmoon. So much for the free cones I'd shelled out after every win. In retrospect, I wished they'd been bigger losers.

Coffey's handiwork and the ensuing ups and downs had spelled trouble for Cori too. We were having dinner, some pesto and pasta thing she'd culled from a waiting-room issue of *Bon Appétit*, when she got around to telling me. She'd kept it to herself for days.

Her boss, Dr. Beckman, had serious concerns. "He's worried about 'the bad press,' as he put it. He wants me to take some time off 'until the distasteful little matter goes away.'"

"I thought he had more brains ..."

"No you didn't. You know he's an ass." She mimicked his squirrelly tenor: "'We are concerned your familial notoriety will prove a detriment to patients. As dentists, my dear, we strike sufficient fear. Why exacerbate the problem? Your husband's notoriety could well render difficulties for us as well, no need to mention.'"

"You kidding me?"

"Don't worry. All's fine. He backed off. But you might be a little angry with me."

"Why would I—"

"For what I did."

"Which was?"

"Promise not to freak."

"What did you do, Cori?"

"Promise you won't freak."

"Tell me."

"Promise."

"I promise."

"Well, I guess, I sort of mentioned how my husband wouldn't take particularly kindly to the news."

"And?"

"And that it's not a good idea to get on his bad side, if you know what I mean—family history and all."

Violence by association is the great unsung perk of infamy. I'd put it to good use too, plenty of times. "The asshole fell for it?"

"You should have seen his face," she said, encapsulating in six one-syllable words the adventure that was married life with Cori, an ongoing reveal of facets unseen and unforeseen. I admit, when I first laid eyes on her, my hypothalamus processed only the basics on the sexism meter —*beautiful, sexy, hot*. Clearly, I can be as insensitive and shallow as any other guy abandoned by evolution. But before you stop reading and cancel me for life, you also need to know my love for her was because of the person she permitted me to see. Funny, kind, and independent. Mercurial, mordant, and whip-smart. She did not suffer fools gladly, though suffer them she did, until you crossed her subjective line and God spare your pissant soul. All this to say, a veiled suggestion of extreme violence was a nifty, if twisted, addition to Cori's substantial repertoire. "The unspoken threat is fun," she said. "It's like dentistry, but with a soupçon of death."

"Fear changes everything," I said. "When I was a kid, I had this don't-mess-with-me look."

"You? Like a badass thing?" She sat back in her chair. "Show me."

"It's been so long." I wished I hadn't let the crazy thing slip. "You'll laugh."

"Maybe I can use it on Beckman."

"Sounds like you did fine on your own."

"C'mon, Rob. You don't bring up something like that and keep it to yourself."

"You won't like it."

"Let me be the judge."

"It's dumb."

"C'mon."

"No, I'm serious, you won't like it. It's not anything you need to see."

"You don't scare me, Robbie." She was teasing, I know. But I also heard the challenge. *You can't scare me, Ice Cream Boy.*

I rose from my seat, kicked the chair aside. I adjusted my stance to the stationary swagger. I assumed the demeanor, smiled the smile that wasn't a smile. Cracked my wrists, knuckles, thumbs. Curled fingers into fists. Let my focus drift to where she wasn't, to where she'd be when I was done with her. To *what* she'd be. Breathed deep, then not at all.

There was nothing to it, really. Jekyll morphing into Hyde.

Her giggle tailed off. "You don't scare me," she said again, less confident now, unsure as to whether I was horsing around or prepping a dive from the high board into an empty pool.

"But I could," I said, with an intensity I intended and regretted. Two quick steps and I was in her face, staring her in the face, without seeing her face.

She held my eyes a fraction of a blink, her face as white as my knuckles. "Stop it," she shot back. "Don't you ever ... What the hell was that? What the hell was that?"

I stood down, returned from the place I'd been, reminded myself to breathe. "You wanted to see it."

"It wasn't you."

"I thought you'd laugh."

"You weren't funny."

"I'm sorry." I reached for her hand, but she'd have none of me. Her entire purpose in life was to bus the dishes from the table. My guilt soared. "I'm sorry. Honest. I don't know where it came from."

"Yes, you do. Don't lie to me. You damn well do."

I gathered up the forks and knives, spewed apology upon apology. She froze at the sound of the clatter. Glanced at my hands, my face. "What the hell is wrong with you?" Shook her head. Fled the room.

I didn't get it. Took a moment.

The knives in my hand. *Jesus.*

She had seen only the knives in my hand.

If you had your doubts about me before, chances are you've got more of them now. Strike two! I know how bad the above makes me look. But I am not that guy. I have never been that guy. Except when I needed to be that guy. And I never was or needed to be that guy with Cori. She asked and I showed her. I warned her she wouldn't like it and, sure enough, she didn't. That's all there was to it. At worst, miscommunication. Think about it. It's my book, right? I'm writing it, right? Would I have told you any of this if I actually was that guy? At the very least, allow me the opportunity to explain, same way Cori allows me to in the next chapter. Stay with me till then. It's all I ask.

I was at her heels, nearing the top of the stairs, when my cell rang. Why I stopped to answer, I'll never know. The third caller.

"Am I speaking to Mr. Robert Blessing?" Caller ID came up empty. "God bless, it is an honor to speak with you, sir."

"Look, I don't have time—"

"Should the hour be inconvenient, sir, I apologize. However, I am hoping you will indulge me a moment or two. It is in reference to your father's last words, sir, as alluded to in the very excellent *Death Row Digest* podcast—"

"Are you reading from a script?"

"Yes, well, several sources suggest your father will not actually deliver his last words ..."

"Who are you? How'd you get this number?"

"... Rather, Mr. Dickens says he will leave them to you, his one and only child. I was wondering if you—"

I did not throw the phone, I punched the damn thing dead. I'd change the number the next day.

I know I shouldn't have. I did not want to. I opened iTunes, found the podcast, and fast-forwarded.

A corrections officer speaks, his voice distorted:

"So I ask him one day. I says, 'Tell me, Henry, planning on any last words? I mean, it'll be real helpful to your victims' families, you know, give 'em some peace of mind.' All those folks, not knowing why he did what he did. Imagine living with that. Senseless deaths and such. I was just saying, you know, suggesting he make amends. Never figured to get a rise out of him. But Henry, he looks me dead in the eye, man to man, and says, 'When I'm dead, ask my son. He'll have them for you.'"

I swear, I hadn't a clue what my father was talking about. Not then.

8
SURVIVAL SKILLS FOR
TROUBLED YOUTH

Dad's fans were fawning freaks and creeps and they came in every size, shape, scent, and flavor. "Paparazzi," Mom called them, "albeit without the charm and social skills." She kept her distance. I did too. But as time wore on and my isolation grew, I became more open to them.

Theory is, small towns take care of their own. Just don't deviate from community norms, like coming out LGBTQ or having a working serial killer in the family.

Mom and I had lived in Hillsdale all our lives, yet the town turned on us so fast you would have thought our hands were bloody too. It wasn't what anybody did, more what they didn't. Like look at us. Speak to us. Include us. Unless they were looking to punish us. We were plenty popular then.

When I wasn't being shunned, I was baited, a pint-sized stand-in for the Brittle Butcher. Pariah for some. Quarry for others. Threat to all.

It wasn't fair. Dad hadn't killed a single soul in Hillsdale proper. The closest he'd come was a good two hours away. Kyle Keegle. Easton, Pennsylvania. Number twenty-four. Keegle was the collector of vintage milk bottles I mentioned earlier. He displayed them in the windows of the café he owned. The bottle Dad used to kill Keegle had an etching of Hopalong Cassidy on it. Hopalong Cassidy had been a movie cowboy who liked to drink milk. Dad bashed in Keegle's head and tore up his throat with the busted bottle.

My father's fans were my saving grace, the closest to what I might call friends. Infamy by association can be a rush. Fat Donald. Ellie Forehead. Sammy Gummy-gums. Five-Chin Joan. While I never did learn their actual names, they were the only people at ease with me or, more correctly, the idea of me. Mostly, they didn't hate me.

The autograph seekers who'd come by Loony Scoops were the first I'd dealt with since leaving Hillsdale. Caller number three was in the same boat. I didn't resent them. Didn't welcome them, either. But I was curious. What had earned my father their morbid loyalty after all these years? Did every killer's kid put up with this crap?

"Who called earlier?" Cori asked, as I finally made it up to our bedroom.

I hung back by the doorway, options open. "Wrong number."

She eyed me with skepticism, dog-eared the page of her paperback —*The 7 Habits of Highly Effective People.* She read a lot of books like this. Don't know why. She was the most highly effective person I knew, excluding my mother. "You're still keeping things from me," she said.

"You're better off not knowing."

"If you can't trust me ..."

"You don't want to know what I know."

"Please, don't take this the wrong way, but I think you need to see someone."

"I'm seeing you. Nice view too."

"Don't be cute. You know what I'm saying. A therapist. Someone."

"I suspect Dr. Cutcheon is retired by now."

"Thank God."

I dropped onto the bed beside her. "What is it you think I'm hiding?"

"I never want to feel threatened by you again. Do you understand?"

"But I wasn't. I was just showing—"

"Because if you do, if you ever dare ... you have no idea what I'm capable of."

"You don't have to worry."

"So what was that at dinner then? It was like you'd shut the lights and a different person switched them on."

"It was nothing."

"Not from where I stood. It was funny, silly even, but then ... I don't know."

"I've told you, I got into a lot of fights as a kid. That's why Mom sent me to Cutcheon. She worried I'd get hurt or, I guess, do the hurting. She didn't want me living my life like that."

Cori took my hand, wove her fingers through mine. "You've never made her sound quite so motherly before."

I played it down. "Yeah, well, she had her moments." Left unmentioned was my boyhood affinity for violence. *Peas in a pod* was how my mother put it, aligning me with Dad. "She did her best, except when she didn't. Anyhow, the crazy look was Cutcheon's idea."

"Why am I not surprised?"

"Say what you want, Cor, but without her, I doubt I'd be here now. She gave me some pretty good tools." I did not elaborate, explain how Cutcheon encouraged me to embrace what she dubbed my "pseudo-psychopathic persona," to revel in the defense of my father even should his actions be worthy of no defense whatsoever. My glory lay in my commitment. "She didn't want me looking for fights, just that I be ready to fight. That's how the look came about. People expected me to be this violent little bastard, but that didn't mean I had to be. Cutcheon's idea was to raise expectations to the extreme, to raise the red flag that I wasn't only violent, but one crazy, rabid, insane motherfucker."

"You looked the part tonight, I tell you."

"These assholes, they'd come along, figuring that punching me out would make their reps. I'd stand there, let them mouth off. I wouldn't so much as peep. I'd just give them a sneak peek at the damage I might do—an advance screening of the badass that raged within. You want to talk about rage? Hell, Cor, it was in every fiber of my being. And I'd show them too. The worst kind of violence. Unpredictable and unrelenting. A bone-shattering kind of violence. None of it needed to be real, only that it could be. Movie psychos had nothing on me. I wore menace the way other kids wore Yankees caps."

"And this look, it worked?"

"Most of the time, yeah."

"And when it didn't?"

"It was about self-discipline. As long as I made the effort to keep my emotions in check, I earned Cutcheon's gold star." I did not tell Cori that, more often than not, I preferred to take a beating than to set my alter ego free. My fear was that the make-believe scary fuck would turn out to be the permanent me. Because there were plenty of times my discipline faltered and the make-believe scary fuck was me.

Some equate passivity with weakness, but passivity has been my greatest strength. By the time the good doctor was done with me, I accepted pain and confusion as willingly as I might have allowed the Lord Jesus Christ himself into my life had Mom sent me to a preacher instead of a psychologist. I summed it up in terms Cori would appreciate: "Dr. Cutcheon helped rebuild my self-esteem."

"With a badass look? I'm not so sure, Rob. It's hardly Psych 101. Sounds closer to the Bible. All she taught you was to turn the other cheek. With an edge perhaps, but ..."

"What you saw tonight was nothing." By the time Mom left me in Worcester, I stacked right up there with any whack-job who ever sliced and slashed. I had the deranged posture down pat, every pore hell-bent and hairy. Glassy eyes, fevered twitch, spastic fists, stutter clotted with drool. "A piece of work, I was, all right. You should've seen, Cor, I could turn jerks into chicken shit with no more than a fistful of allusion."

"Not to mention your wife."

I shrugged. I was fresh out of sorry.

"Think I can't see through you?" She rolled to her side, looked me in the eye. "You're so full of shit. You were just as happy when that stupid look didn't work, weren't you? Am I right? Scaring people was fun, but I'll bet you liked beating them up even more. I mean, the way you talk about it, the words you chose ... scary fuck ... spastic fists ... hair ripped from scalp. You didn't pull that out of thin air. That comes from memory."

"I'm not like that anymore."

"You were one tough little bastard, weren't you?" She fluffed her pillows against the headboard. "Question is, when will you stop being this tough little bastard—this Bobby Dickens kid?"

"Is that how you see me?"

"To be honest, not until tonight." Forgiveness was imminent. Her sleepshirt fell open; she did not cover up.

"Funny thing was, you know, through it all, everybody looking at me cross-eyed, expecting I'd be some kind of monster ... All I ever expected was to die."

"You remind me of my father. He'd get this look sometimes."

"Your father? You remember? Weren't you a baby when your parents died?"

"Was I?" She played with her hair a moment, fingers twirling butter into gold. Her hand strayed idly to my chest, then lower, and the conversation dangled.

I played it cool, perhaps a bit too proud of my newfound candor, smug in the knowledge I'd atoned for my misstep, when she grabbed my t-shirt by the collar and bunched it tightly, her fist at my throat. I did not resist. She had cause to strangle me. Instead, she straddled me. With the ruthless finesse of a *SmackDown* diva, she yanked the shirt from my back and over my head, taking my nose and ears with it.

"The strange thing is," she said, her negligible weight shifting to my crotch, "what you just told me, I find comforting. It's good to know you can protect me."

"I could. I would."

"As long as it isn't you I need protecting from. You should know, I can be a tough little bastard too."

"You weren't so tough tonight."

She slapped a hand to my mouth and squeezed till inner cheek met inner cheek. "What about now?" she said, and raked five fingernails across and down my chest. I could have turned the tables. Easy. But jeez, this version of my wife worked for me too. And the view of her from my back, well, it was always something to behold. Believe me, for a depresso once destined to a life of one-night stands, I counted my blessings, no pun intended.

She assessed the art she'd carved into my flesh, pondered the need for a touch-up or two. Best I could tell from the angle, my chin glued to chest, it was the letter *C* rendered in five parallel and slightly bloody furrows.

"You've explained *how* you frightened me," she said, absently retracing her penmanship with a finger, "but you haven't told me why."

"You said I didn't scare you."

"So?"

"I don't like to be underestimated," I said.

9

OPTIMISM FOR BEGINNERS

Cori read the letter from the Saratoga County Department of Health and handed it back. "We'll look back on this one day and laugh," she said, knowing we wouldn't be doing either. I'd been exonerated, the complaints against me "unfounded and spurious." Commissioner Tavasi had signed it, along with a handwritten postscript: *My kids love Loony Scoops!*

I whited out the Tavasi children's endorsement and forwarded the letter to Lenora-Jo Coffey. I also uploaded scans to the platforms that had gone after me, but the scummers were too busy trashing other lives to notice. No retractions. No apologies. No likes. No retweets.

Three months after the call from Stupid Charlotte's husband, it was as if the whole thing never happened. Freddo had been right. *As long as it tastes good, nobody cares what shit is in it, even if it's shit.* By August my sales surpassed the year before.

The regulars who had bailed on me were replaced by new regulars. And, of course, the know-nothing tourists kept coming. The bogus claims would come up now and then, and an occasional fan would drop by to shake my hand or stare or have me sign an *encyclopedia*, but the mudslinging had run its course. So had I. I'd refined the art of going through the motions.

"Sell it," Cori said, one late summer morning as I headed out to work. "You can't go on like this. Find something else."

"If I could, I would."

"You're biding your time, on standby for the next bad thing. Stop. Just stop." She turned my head with both hands and planted her lips on my mouth. "Make sure you're home early. If that hurricane blows through the way they say it will …"

"Don't worry."

"I just want you to be happy. It's not like I can't afford to carry us." Beckman had upped her salary, commensurate with her skills, popularity with patients, and reputed mad dog of a partner. The fact she'd inherited major bucks from her aunt to go along with the long-invested payout from her parents' life insurance policies didn't hurt either.

"No way you'll carry me unless I'm in a casket."

"Jesus, Rob! Sometimes, your sense of optimism …"

10
THE REVERSE STOCKHOLM SYNDROME IN PRACTICE

I was icing "Happy 50th Anniversary Alma & Lowell" onto a canvas of dark chocolate fudge when the kid stormed into Loony Scoops, hopped-up tics and hammy bluster. "Hands where I can see 'em, asshole. Up! Up! Move it! Move it!"

The streets were empty. Hurricane Jerry had been teasing since noon. Now, as Cori had warned, playtime was over. Wind scatter-bombed the rain in torrents. Hurricanes are not usually accompanied by lightning, but this night Heaven and Earth defied meteorological logic.

He stood grinning, gun leveled at my chest. "The fuckin' cash, man. Open the fuckin' cash."

I'd told Cori how I'd faced my childhood battles with the expectation I would die. This was only partly true. Everyone expects to die. I expected to be murdered. I'd been sure about it since I was eleven. Not once, however, did I figure on a weenie-ass frat boy schooled on Grand Theft Auto.

"You think I won't bust a cap up your ass?" he said. "You think I won't?"

"Oh, I'm pretty sure you will." His eyes were black, except for the whites which were pink. I made an appeal for the ice cream cake in progress on the table before me. "I need to put this in the freezer. Their daughter is coming by tomorrow to—"

"The fuckin' cash, man. Open the fuckin' cash." A raggedy red soul patch bobbed in sync with his lower lip, raising fears he'd eaten Elmo and forgotten to wash up.

It's not that I wasn't afraid. My heart was hopping, skipping, and jumping, while my brain was shopping for insoles at Fleet Feet. And though the gun he waved in my face was real, the rest of him reeked of wannabe.

The Skidmore hoodie, crisp, green, and Tide bright. The Knicks cap, brim flat. The GAP camo shorts. Maybe his mom had dressed him. I felt embarrassed for the dick. Who wears shorts to an armed robbery?

"You pledging? I mean, if that's the case—"

"Fuck you! The cash, man. The cash." He threw his arm straight out to emphasize the gun at the end of it. He lunged, pulled up short, lunged again, a spray of spittle on a cartoon cackle. I flinched to keep him happy, reassure him I recognized he was one scary dude.

That's the trouble with amateurs: no discipline, no focus on the prize, as if the mission is to put on some idiotic song and dance for a captive audience. Armed robbery as burlesque. All threats aside, he wouldn't mean to pull the trigger, it'd be the gun's fault. His plea would be manslaughter. Good people would vouch for him. His mom. His pastor. His sixth-grade English teacher. His soccer coach. His dermatologist. A crappy end for me, for sure. At least I'd have the satisfaction, albeit fleeting, of being proved right. About my murder, I mean.

Outside, a car horn sounded, more burp than beep. My murderer-elect turned his head and waved his gun to silence his buddies. A Subaru. An Outback. *Jesus!* Then again, considering the water pooling on the streets, good traction in a getaway vehicle couldn't hurt, despite the lack of street cred. The suicidal smart-ass in me couldn't resist: "Borrow the car from Grandma?"

"I'm fuckin' gonna kill you, Butcherboy."

Butcherboy? Had I missed something? Was Butcherboy the latest catch-all alongside Bro, Dawg, Amigo, and Dude? I sensed he'd gone off-script, his threat increasingly credible. My don't-mess-with-me look was worth a shot.

I adjusted my stance, the stationary swagger. I assumed the demeanor, smiled the smile that wasn't a smile. And could take it no further. The thing was so damn dopey. Letting Cori in on the details had ruined it. I felt stupid, self-conscious. Worse, the punk hadn't noticed. He had this habit of looking toward me, but not quite at me. My biggest regret in this moment was never having discussed with Cori the name to put on my headstone: Dickens, Blessing, or Dickens-Blessing. Or maybe just plain Dick, because I more than qualified.

"You're really pushing it, fuckface."

"Your gun, that's a Glock, right?" I hadn't a clue. I was looking to defuse the situation.

"How the fuck do I know?"

In the first few months of Loony Scoops, there was this Mr. Greenberg who'd show up on Tuesday afternoons and order a banana split with three scoops of vanilla. No chocolate. No strawberry. Only vanilla. Never varied. He said he preferred to keep life simple since retiring from the force; he'd been a hostage negotiator in Newark for twenty-two years. Were I ever to find myself facing death by violence, he advised, I should express interest in my would-be executioner, admire their expertise, praise their savvy choice of weapon, and empathize with the hard luck and unfair system that led them to such desperate measures. Done right, I'd pull off a reverse Stockholm and save my ass. If the guy could see me as a potential best bud rather than a victim, he'd be less inclined to blow my brains out.

"I know what you're going through," I said. "I've been there." I set my piping bag on the table and wiped the fudge from my knuckles onto my apron. I smiled, prepared to introduce myself, shake his hand, offer to buy him a coffee.

"You think I'm some kind of retard?"

It was then I recalled why Mr. Greenberg no longer visited on Tuesdays. He had refused to co-sign a loan on a Honda CR-Z for his daughter. He was pushing for a more practical Honda Civic. She stabbed him in the heart so many times, the resulting mince would have made a good burger.

The punk-in-training raised three fingers. "You got two seconds, man." The Outback revved in the lot. His pals were getting antsy. "Two seconds, man."

"I got nothing to give you, I swear. If I did, I would." I could have opened the cash drawer to prove my point, but the outcome would be the same.

He gripped the gun with both hands and shifted his aim to my head. "Wum," he said, though I think he meant to say *one*.

11
HOSTAGE NEGOTIATION
FOR DUMMIES

Being in the wrong place at the wrong time is the crappiest of all ways to die. Of course, it's never really about one time and one place. It's about the getting there.

Had Alma and Lowell not met some fifty years before, their daughter Barb would not have ordered an anniversary cake at the last minute, I would have locked up early, and some luckless bastard behind the cash at Doug's Liquor would be staring the Sophomore Slayer in the face instead of me.

Had my father not done what he did, I might have become an astrophysicist instead of a soda jerk.

Had Mom not hauled us out of Hillsdale, I might still be living at the house on Appleton, working Dad's candy business or Mom's Christmas Cottage crap.

Or maybe I'd be into my second decade of pushing up daisies in Parchment Hill Cemetery.

Whatever, the punk hadn't listened to much I'd had to say. Perhaps I could get through to him with the kindly advisor schtick. "If you're going to rob an ice cream parlor, use your head. Look at it out there. It's coming down in buckets. The sky's falling. Nobody's eating ice cream today. There's nothing in the till. Come back when it clears. Tomorrow. Next week."

"Don't diss me, man. Nobody disses me, man." Why he felt the need to say everything twice I do not know. I also had the feeling he'd never used *diss* before.

"I'm not dissing you," I said, never having used the word before, either.

He sandwiched the gun between two palms and, once more, extended his arms, turning his wrists until the gun was parallel to floor and ceiling. Shooting me sideways would be way cooler than straight on.

He calmed, his grin fixed. "It's not the money I come for, anyway."

Thunder bellowed with a ferocity better reserved for the end of the world. Lightning illuminated the fissures. The lights of Loony Scoops winked and blinked.

"I come for you, Butcherboy."

"Ah, Jesus."

"I hear you're some scary piece of work, huh? Like you iced a bunch of clowns or something? Like some Cannibal Lecture or something?"

Butcherboy. *Brittle Butcher.* Ah, jeez, just what I needed. "That's not me," I said.

"Yeah. Right. And this here's a water pistol. It's my turn now, amigo. I'm the one they're gonna talk about. Because the only news bigger than Cannibal Lecture is the guy who offed Cannibal Lecture."

"You're confusing me with my father," I said. "Also, it's Hannibal Lecter."

He shut one eye, puckered up like he might blow me a kiss, grunted a multisyllabic "Fuck," shut the open eye, and fired.

12

WHEN GOOD CALLIGRAPHY GOES BAD

His final *fuck* fucked him. Amateurs and their yakkety-yak-yak. Too many movies. Too many long-winded super villains. When my father killed, he didn't mess with the dramatics; he killed. A slaughterhouse on two legs, he was. You don't have to approve of his crimes to respect his work ethic.

In the breathless millisecond between the wannabe's extended *fuck* and his flick of the trigger, I gave the anniversary cake a heave. Alma & Lowell took the bullet point-blank. The cookie sheet on which the cake had rested grazed my shoulder as the bullet carried it to the wall. And the cake carried forward to make an impromptu sundae of the dumbass's dumbass face.

I hurdled the soda fountain behind us and scrambled to the corner where the drawers met the floor. I made myself small and hoped to hell he'd run. His point-blank miss should've been all the incentive he needed to clear the hell out. Likewise, saving my own life should have been all the incentive I needed to have barricaded myself in the freezer or, at least, gone for the kayo.

He vaulted onto the countertop, napkin dispensers, jimmy jars, and straws flying as he bounded down to where I huddled. He squatted above me, lowered the gun to my ear. I braced for the last sound I'd ever hear, and got the tinkling of a bell. Someone had entered the shop. I hoped for cops, got a best bud instead: "C'mon, Dobsie. Somebody's coming. A car. C'mon, man. Jesus, Dobsie! What the fuck happened to your face?"

Dobsie dragged a sleeve across his face, his gun hand steady. His head was slathered in chocolate fudge and cappuccino cream, his eyes asquint in 14 percent butterfat. The Toxic Avenger and Incredible Melting Man slimed into one. "Not going anywhere," he shouted over the thunder. "Not until I waste this fucker."

"Jesus, dude, you crazy? Take the cash and screw. C'mon!"

"You used my name, Emory. I got no choice. He'll squeal."

"Listen to him," I said, a last-ditch effort. "You don't want to do this. It'll ruin your life."

"Not as much as yours, Butcherboy. You're gonna make my rep."

"I'm not who you think I am."

"Whatever." He gave a farewell salute with the gun in the same instant the lights flickered. I thought perhaps he'd just killed me, my brain dissolving to black. But then the thunder rolled over us, cannonading with a force the building shuddered to withstand. Lightning struck again, successive bolts of white and blue and green. Another clap of thunder. And Loony Scoops turned a merciful, miraculous pitch dark.

I did not waste God's free pass. I jerked the prick's hairy legs out from under him and swung his sorry ass off the counter before his misfire hit the ceiling. And with a move I hoped to see someday on *Dancing with the Stars*, I slammed the sweet spot of his Paleolithic skull into the cold ceramic floor. Like riding a bike. One never forgets.

He wasn't quite out, wasn't quite with it. He was under me now, scrambling on hands and knees, fingers skittering across my shoes like ten blind mice. He was frantic, desperate to locate his frigging gun. I dropped down, locked my arms around his neck, and wrenched him to his feet.

Ah, the primal pleasure, as I drove his back into the chrome of the counter, my knee up into his nuts. And with the heel of one hand rammed flat beneath his chin and the other fast upon his belt, I launched him sprawling into the sludge of the ice cream cake he had so callously forced me to trash. A waste of fine calligraphy. *The guy who killed Cannibal Lecture, my ass!*

I couldn't see him, couldn't hear him. I leaped onto the counter, squinted into the seamless murk. It was a rush, I tell you, lording it there, fists at my hips, chest defiant. Hadn't felt this much power in years. I was hungry for more. Then the bell above the door tinkled, again. "Rob?" came the voice. "Rob?"

Lightning ripped another slice of night.

No mistaking the silhouette in the doorway.

No mistaking her ever.
No mistaking the clamor as the asshole thrashed to reach her.
"Cori!" I shouted.
I'd kill him. I'd kill him.

13

A NOTABLE OMISSION IN THE SKIDMORE COLLEGE SYLLABUS

The backup generators whirred to life. The freezers hummed, LEDs glowing green. The emergency spotlights hesitated, then stunned bright white, Maglite beams crisscrossing the combat zone.

The Sophomore Slayer lay motionless at Cori's feet. Blood streamed from his nose and mouth, swirled with the ice cream. Cappuccino strawberry. Cori's umbrella sprouted from the loser's thigh.

"I came to see where you were. I was worried. You hadn't called. I thought he was you." I wrapped my arms around her. "He grabbed me. I reacted. I do that. I knew he wasn't you. After, I mean."

"You did good," I said. I gave her the short version of how he'd come to rob me.

"Is he dead?" she asked, a shiver of apprehension.

I knelt beside him, monitored the uneasy to and fro of his chest. "He'll survive."

"Should we call an ambulance, the police?"

"Wouldn't be good for him. And a whole can of worms for us. Look at him. We roughed him up good. They'll question who the real victim is. Try talking your way out of that."

"He tried to rob you."

"No," I said, "he came to kill me."

She looked at the body on the floor and back to me.

"He's thinks I'm the Brittle Butcher."

"You? Your dad? I don't understand."

"He seemed to think killing me would make him some kind of hero."

"My God, Rob."

"Yeah." I pulled her umbrella from Dobsie's leg. The wound was deep. She'd packed a wallop. I wiped the bloodied end of the umbrella on his hoodie.

Cori extended her hands. "If you don't mind," she said. I wiped the blood and ice cream from her driving gloves and she reciprocated by lifting a corner of my apron to clean my chin.

A cell rang. Kelly Clarkson. *My Life Would Suck Without You.* Could the punk-ass have been any more uncool? His eyes rattled open. He raised a finger, but his hand failed to follow. I scanned the lot; his buddies had turned tail. I dug the phone from his pocket.

"Dobsie? Dobsie?"

"Hey, Em—Emory," I said.

"Dobsie?"

"All good, man," I said. "All good. Meet me outside. Hurry."

"You sound funny."

"Yeah, well."

"You kill him? Did you?"

"All good, man. All good. No worries. No worries. Hurry. Hurry." I clicked off.

I knelt by Dobsie's head. "Do your homework next time. Know who you're dealing with. Avoid individuals with behavioral issues. And keep it simple. Don't make it personal. If you're going to rob, rob. If it's to kill, kill. Get in, get out."

I could see the agitation coursing through him, building like a bag of Orville Redenbacher's in the microwave. Maybe he thought I was getting set to slit his throat. He let rip a panicked cry, threw himself to the side, and made another move on Cori. I now got to see what the blackout had concealed.

Cori evaded his grasp with the agility of a cat on a rat, hard-landed her heel on his right hand, and high-stepped onto his left. Wired she was, as she stomped, stoked by the girly *yip yip yip* from his throat and the chilling *pop pop pop* of his knuckles. She was going in for the kill, a back-kick to the jaw, but pulled up at the surrender in his face. She alighted daintily en pointe. A snug tug on each of her gloves marked the decisiveness of her victory. *Kung Fu Dentist—in theaters now! 97 percent fresh on rottentomatoes.com!*

"Jeez, Cor."

Her smile was in the realm of sheepish as she examined the heels of her ankle-high hiking boots. "I've taken a few self-defense classes over the years."

"And you were afraid of me—my stupid badass look? It's me who should be afraid of you."

"Perhaps." She was nonchalant, a twinkle in her eye.

Together, we dragged Dobsie outside, negotiated his disobliging frame through the rising waters, over the parking stanchions, and propped him up against the window, beneath the jubilation of the poster that hyped *Saratoga's Only 5-Scoop Cone*. Cori retreated inside, left him to me.

I squatted between his splayed legs, balled the front of his hoodie into an unforgiving fist and parked my knuckles in the hollow of his throat. I jerked him near, wanting him to hear every word. The elements raged without let-up. The savagery buoyed me.

"Listen," I said. He gazed slack-jawed through droopy lids. "I am the victim here, not you. You brought this on yourself. You're hurt bad. You need to get to a hospital. Understand? A hospital. Where the doctors and nurses, and likely the cops, will want to know how you got banged up. You've got two choices: shut the fuck up or make something up. Because if you or your amigos breathe about me or my wife and what went down here tonight, the next place you'll rest your empty head will be the deep end of a body bag. And that goes not just for you, Dobsie, but your buddies, your pal Emory, your mommy, your daddy, and every human shit who has helped to make you the sorry-assed fuck you are today. I know who you are, I know where you live." I slit his throat with my finger. "I am not who you think I am, Dobsie. But I promise you, I can be."

I let the wall break his fall. I was sore, soaked, and tired.

My curbside sermon complete, I returned inside to find Cori sprinkling Skor bar crunchies onto a *Toffee Tornado* sundae. "There you go," she said, as she set it on the counter.

"For me?"

"Who else?"

"It's perfect. You're some fast learner, lady."

"It's fun once you get the hang of it."

She scooped assorted sorbets into a cup for herself.

I dimmed the emergency lights, angled them low, sufficient for us to see out, but not outsiders to see in. We sat well back from the windows, our legs dangling from the countertop, two crazy kids taking in a show.

"What did you say to him?"

"Not much. The spoken word version of my badass look, I suppose."

The Outback coasted into view, passed in front, circled back.

"What if they come in?" Cori whispered.

"Sounds like you're hoping they will."

Dobsie's accomplices took it slow, before summoning the courage to retrieve him. They gathered him up quickly, pranksters from Sigma Delta Douche swiping the rival fraternity's mascot. They stuffed their fallen leader into the rear of the Outback. The doors blew shut as the Subaru hydroplaned into the fringes of Hurricane Jerry.

"Can I have a taste?" Cori asked, and I fed her a spoonful.

"I do make a good sundae, if I do say so myself."

"You looking for a job?"

"You never know."

Cori helped me mop up.

I picked up the gun, wrapped it up in a towel, set it aside.

"What if he had shot you?" she said, her arm at my waist.

"Yeah, well, he didn't."

Lastly, I got around to the redo of Alma and Lowell's anniversary cake. Cori watched as I worked, joining in toward the end to demonstrate her skills with frosted ribbons and rosettes. "My Aunt Maureen owned a bakery," she explained.

"I thought you said she was a dentist, why you went into dentistry."

"She was my inspiration. Not because she was a dentist, because she gave so many people so many cavities. Besides, fondant and dental fillings aren't all that far removed."

"If that's the case, then you and I were made for each other. We just might have a goldmine here, Cor."

"Right. You rot the teeth ..."

"... and you fix them."

"I'll be sure to leave a box of my business cards by the door." She dabbed a fingertip of chocolate fudge onto my nose, brushed up close, and licked it off. Making love atop a soda fountain was a first for both of us.

We were ready to go, when she asked to see the gun again. I unwrapped the towel. "I want it," she said.

I double-checked the safety. "No, you don't."

"Yes, I do."

"Not a good idea, Cor. The serial numbers are filed down and—"

"I want it," she said.

"Trust me, you don't."

"If they come back. If they find out where we live ... Give it to me."

"Do you even know how to use it?"

"They came to kill you, Rob."

"Yes, but if you've never—"

"It's a Bersa," she said. "A Thunder .380, matte finish, double action, eight-plus-one capacity. Super compact with a checkered polymer grip. Made in Argentina." She slipped a slender finger through the trigger guard and deposited Dobsie's gun in her bag.

"What are you, a secret agent? CIA? Wonder Woman?"

"How did you ever guess?" she said.

And there's the thing about that night. We were troubled, but in no way shaken. Not how you'd reckon innocents of sound mind to behave in the aftermath of violence. *The kid had tried to kill me. My wife had almost killed the kid.* It was not a first for me. I'd been well schooled, had lived the larger part of my life in the barrens of dispassion. But who or what had messed up Cori?

14
LIFE-CHANGING DECISIONS FOR THE IMPULSIVE

She nuzzled in the crook of my arm, sharing my pillow. The power outage extended from Schenectady to Warrensburg. A candle burned on the night table, the scent apples and cinnamon. Shadows ebbed and flowed across the ceiling. "I don't want you working there anymore," she said.

"Tonight was a one-off."

"It's been a year of one-offs."

"Nothing's happened. Nothing will."

"You lie like a rug. You forget how well I know you—what goes on in that brain of yours."

"Nothing is going to happen."

"How many more crazies are out there? What if it's the son or daughter of someone your father killed next time? A husband? A wife? Somebody looking for revenge?"

"You've seen too many movies. I am not my father. People know the difference."

"Tell that to Dobsie."

"C'mon, Cor. He was nobody."

"A nobody who could have killed you. And what about those creeps who show up with those disgusting books? Coffee table books about murder! Seriously? And you sign them like it's normal. You think I haven't noticed?"

"They're my father's fans."

"Do you want to be killed? Are you hoping to be?"

"I told you, I just expect to be."

Her sigh trod the boundaries of mourning.

"I've been thinking," I said, feeling my way, though I'd rehearsed the conversation in my head a thousand times. "If you're open to it, there is something I'd like to try. It was your idea, really."

I told her I wanted to write a book about my father, my mother, and what it meant to be trapped between the two. I'd been keeping notes for years. *My Personal Journal of the Damned.*

And then I told her *where* I wanted to write the story. This was where my mother's wedding gift came into play. I'd kept it from Cori long enough.

I will not lie. I hoped she'd nip the whole dumb idea in the bud.

As for the book I was going to write, this isn't it.

PART TWO

WHAT WE MEAN WHEN WE TALK ABOUT HOME

15
HENRY TAYLOR DICKENS SLEPT HERE

The five-hour drive from Saratoga began as an exercise in labored enthusiasm. Doubt lobbied the crawlspace of my brain, while aggressive and passive duked it out for supremacy. We'd uprooted our lives on whim and wishful thinking.

"Breathe," Cori said. "You look like you're about to give birth."

"Probably triplets."

"Lose the doubt. You're doing the right thing."

"How can you be so sure?"

"I wouldn't be here with you if it wasn't."

Cori had been on board from the get-go. The change of scenery. The joy in shoving her letter of resignation up Dr. Beckman's prissy ass. The challenge of starting her own practice. The new house. The book I was going to write.

Frosty Freddo came through too. Eager to expand, he'd come up from Syracuse to take Loony Scoops off my hands. The money would be enough to keep us going for a year at least, never mind the bucks Cori had in hand or what her new Hillsdale practice would be bringing in.

Now here we were, a Monday morning in October, the air mild, the sun pumped, and the leaves undecided between green and gone. If returning home was a fun idea, the notion I could write a book was a rib-tickler.

Cori's belief in me was grounded in a parallel reality. Other than the posters of sundaes, shakes, and flavor-of-the-week plastered about Loony Scoops, she'd never known me to be much of a writer. Truth was, I'd never had any great desire to write, even with my three semesters in Journalism. Like I said, nicknaming serial killers sounded cool. Mostly

77

though, I had wanted to know what made reporters tick, if there was any thrill in badgering next of kin.

Now, as the miles piled up, so did the scenarios for what might lie ahead. Horror stories overshadowed romcoms ten to one. Whatever Cori's anxieties, if any, she expressed them in silence, a pat of my hand, a buoyant smile, a squeeze of my thigh.

At the billboard welcoming us to Hillsdale, I reminisced to Cori how local business types had once petitioned the Chamber of Commerce to add a postscript:

HOMETOWN OF HENRY TAYLOR DICKENS
"THE BRITTLE BUTCHER"

"Serial killers are good for tourism," I said. "Once they're caught, anyhow."

"Or dead," she said.

"Sorry you agreed to this, yet?"

"Only sorry you feel the need to ask. We're in this together, Rob. I wish you'd remember."

Landmark by landmark, I gave her the short-form tour.

Gables' Fresh-picked—a roadside stand and acres of orchard: "Best apple turnovers ever."

Bibber & Sons Ford dealership: "Mr. Bibber was mayor. He had no sons, only daughters."

The Great Wall Restaurant: "Used to be a Greek diner."

As we reached the top of the hill, I pulled to the curb and idled the Pilot in the shadow of St. Luke's Church. Downtown Hillsdale simpered below, clean, compact, and born-again smug.

"Like a movie set," Cori whispered in awe. "It's pretty."

"One way of putting it." Where she saw charm, I saw the hateful little burg of my childhood, where small minds and smaller hearts pressed the agenda, the veneer of the place so brittle with conceit, its continued existence defied the laws of physics. If Hillsdale was a movie set, the movie was *Drag Me to Hell*.

Across the street was Country Furniture Outlet. "It used to be a bowling alley," I said. I could have told her more, should have told her more. But how much dumb shit could I cram into her head before she tapped out and split? And this, I'm telling you, was some dumb shit.

A Saturday morning in August of 2005. I'm fifteen and seething, as I walk the town for a final time. A cavalcade of one, no stops scheduled. But there in the lot adjacent to Jimmy's Spares 'n Strikes is a tractor trailer, cargo doors wide open, and nobody in sight. An invitation. Spur of the moment, swear to God.

Up and in I go, and the box cutters call to me by name. "Bobby. Bobby." I grab one for each hand. Assess the cargo. And boom-kablooie blows the top of my head. I am bananas. I am postal. And I am in for the kill, hacking high, slashing low, a Muay Thai assassin crashing a Ninja jamboree. Front kick. Side kick. Axe kick. Roundhouse. First stack. Second stack. Third. Fourth. Until the cartons collapse one into the next, mutilated bellies disgorging calcified guts.

Bowling balls is what they were. Twenty, thirty, a ton. Mottled pinks, fluorescent blues, seasick greens, and lustrous ebonies. Thundering onto and across the deck of the trailer. While I'm hopping, skipping, dodging, as my off-the-cuff tsunami gathers momentum, on course for the hill, the downtown, and the unsuspecting pinheads overdue for payback.

I do not stick around to watch. I run before the damage is done. And forgo the opportunity to be forever remembered as fondly as my mom and dad.

Sirens sound as the news makes the rounds. Tongues are wagging.

Who would do such a damn fool thing?

Hillsdale citizenry step to the fore. Witnesses galore.

Two Asian kids were seen hanging around the bowling alley.

Nope, the kids who did it were black.

Uh-uh, Latino.

Nope, a grizzly on a Harley.

Wrong again. A trio wearing red berets, gangbangers from NEW YORK CITY.

The only homegrown suspect is Kenny the Wino, who was dead three months by then.

But the thing that throws me, it's not the bowling balls folks are up in arms about. What the hell! It's the truck. It's the truck that rolled down the hill. It's the truck that bowled down the people. What the hell!

Mom and me, we leave Hillsdale that afternoon as planned. Mom is moving to Europe, me to wherever-the-fuck. "Did you do it, Bobby?"

"No."

"Are you sure?"

"Yes."

"I'd understand if you did."

"I didn't."
"You can tell Dr. Cutcheon. She said you could call her anytime."
"I didn't do it."
"But if you did ..."
"I sure wouldn't tell you."

I shifted into drive, resumed my personalized tour. The Dollar General where the Tivoli stood until the fire. The gazebo on the village green, where summer concerts are held. The streets, many named after First Ladies.

"Progressive," Cori said. "I feel at home already."

Cars still parked diagonally to the curb, headlamps winking and grilles grinning, flirting with passersby. Traffic was light. Locals had never done much driving *in* town, saving the wear and tear for out of town.

"Is it like you remember, Bobby?"

"Pretty much."

"Is that a good thing?"

"Your guess is as good as mine."

I revved the Pilot, turned off Main, up Robards, past Franklin Park, and onto Appleton. The house at 18 left us speechless. The rambling old Victorian was where I grew up. It was my mother's wedding gift to me and Cori.

16

HISTORICAL HIGHLIGHTS OF HILLSDALE: 18 APPLETON*

---

* Built in 1905 in a Free Classical Style by renowned architect Norris Daimler II—as referenced in *Historic Hillsdale: A Walking Tour* (2006 pamphlet).

The house was not as large as I remembered, yet it was everything I remembered. The wraparound porch, so broad it served as a platter for the birthday cake that was the house itself. The wooden swing at the far end. The white wicker loveseat and its plush vinyl cushions, ideal for building forts. The bare windows on the lower level, lace skirting the tops and cheering the corners, a custom my mother borrowed from the Dutch and adopted in the weeks following her parents' deaths. Bare windows meant a person was open and above board, even when they were far from open and below board.

Variations on the topic were a favorite of Mom's, which was odd, considering she had so much to hide. "People who have things to hide are never as vigilant as those who feed on deception. You'll come to learn," she'd said, "the only way to protect yourself is to have nothing to hide."

"Then why did you change my name?" I had asked.

"It's your raincheck, sweetheart, a temporary reprieve from the inevitable. It gives you leeway to set the rules, to choose how you want the rest of your story to go."

What would my mother say now that I was about to cash the raincheck? How would she feel about me writing a book, airing our family's bloodied linen in public, leaving nothing for the next Lenora-Jo Coffey who comes along?

"The house, it's amazing." Cori jolted me back to the present, nuzzled close, her arm looped through mine. "So much more than I anticipated. Who was the architect—Mary Shelley?"

Dread rapped a rim shot off my chest, improvised a jazz solo on my eardrums. While Cori was satisfied to soak up the grandeur of the old place, I reverted to the dumbstruck ninny who had watched as the cops drew their guns and hustled his father to the ground. *Do something. Do something. Save him. Save him.* Good memories were washed away in the deluge of bad. My eyes darted from window to window, a face behind every pane. That goddamn house was staring back, demanding answers as to why the hell I'd come back.

From across the yard came a twang and a bang. The screen door of my mother's former Christmas shop swung back on itself as April Bright hobbled from her beauty spa. She chugged toward us across the lawn, hands waving a mile a minute.

"I didn't recognize you, right off," she gushed. "You've grown so tall, Robert. Couldn't recall for the life of me whether you said yesterday or today. And you must be the bride. Oh my, but you are a sweetie. Surely, you will put every lady in this town to shame—just like your mama did, Bobby. Oh my, but so elegant that woman is! An honorable soul, if I do say. It was only last week we chatted." Hobbit and Southern belle rolled into one, this was April Bright. And now I'd just learned she had one up on me: a relationship with my mother.

Once Mom was set on leaving Hillsdale, she had tried to sell the house, but my father hadn't been what you'd call a poster boy for local real estate. Outsiders called it Hellsdale.

Sure, visitors would come by to gawk and gossip, chat in disquieting tones of how this was the home of the homicidal maniac Henry Taylor Dickens, a.k.a. the Brittle Butcher. Choosing to own the property wasn't quite so cut and dried. The stench of rotting corpses wafting up from the foundation was not a big selling feature, the facts having no bearing on the heebie-jeebies.

My mother was set to board up the old place when April Bright came to the rescue. "My brother, Tusk, he's served time for crime. I know what it's like to be shunned, Mrs. Dickens. I also know you and your boy had nothing to do with the evil deeds done. So if you're looking for someone to mind your home, I've a proposition."

Mom had known April from Stan's Photo and Hobby over on

Lavinia Scott Road, where she'd buy her cameras and stuff to shoot the knick-knacks for her Christmas catalog and, later, her website. According to Mom, April's honesty regarding her wayward brother validated the woman's basic decency. (Pretty much how Cori summed up my telling her about Dad on our first date.)

"I must confess, Mrs. Dickens, I am not acting wholly out the goodness of my heart. It is not the house I covet, though it is a splendid home. It is your shop I wish to discuss."

So went the story, anyhow.

Blessing's Christmas Cottage stood sixty feet from the main house. Mom had run her business from it since college. The mail-order and web sales had given her financial independence, the inheritance from her parents the bonus. This was the story too. There were a lot of stories.

April was a trained beautician. She wanted the cottage for her salon. I asked Mom how anyone so goofy-looking could make anybody beautiful. Soon after, Mom handed me a biography of Toulouse-Lautrec.

In exchange for taking care of the main house and property, April was given the cottage rent-free. She promised that on the day my mother returned, the house would be as spick and span as the day she left. "Cross my heart and hope to die, Missus."

Mom arranged with her New York lawyer pal to send April a monthly check for upkeep. It was evident April had kept her part of the bargain. On the surface, the house appeared unchanged. Except for the porch. Now dark green.

It had always been red.

Every spring my father would paint it. I would help.

Ours was the only house in town with a red porch. The siding was white, the shutters and gables blue. During the Hillsdale centennial celebrations, Dad won a red, white, and blue ribbon for having the most patriotic home in town. Patriotism had nothing to do with it. Dad worried he would track home blood. (He knew a lot about blood, how it could have a mind of its own. He called it *red vengeance*. I know a lot about blood too. And red vengeance.)

April topped out at a thumb over five feet, pushing sixty at least, with a rabid energy your average cokehead would have envied. She was more homey than homely, with an ingratiating perkiness she used to steamroll all obstacles in her path, real and imagined. She had once been the sort of woman the majority of men bring home to mother, which is what her husband must have done before skipping out on her. April's was a sorry tale of betrayed love my mother would mention only as a casual aside, a hushed nugget nestled within a less soapy conversation.

Before I could stop her, April hoisted my duffel bag from the rear of the Pilot and slung it over her shoulder. The bag bobbed against the walkway as she limped ahead.

"Now don't you two worry a whit." She huffed and puffed as she unlocked the door. "It's not the Blessings people recall with fear, it's the Dickens. And the only Dickens anyone worries about is locked away; may your father be at peace, Bobby, no matter what demons possess his tortured soul. So don't you youngsters fret. People have short memories for even the wickedest of happenstances, and Hillsdalers the shortest of all."

Once inside, we hoped April would leave us be. We thanked her, promised to come by her salon soon, catch up on old times, and thanked her again. And again. She didn't get the hint. Even after we'd dragged every box, bag, and suitcase from the Pilot she jabbered on, insisting she had to show us the house.

Topics flew from her mouth as bees from a burning hive. The intricacies of the beauty business. The sad story of her sister, Faith, who might still be alive had she had any. Her brother, Tusk, a tormented soul, though sweet of spirit. How to keep celery green and crispy. How wonderful this house used to be at Christmastime, the decorations and all, and how she prayed I'd revive the tradition.

After the kitchen, dining room, living room, den (off the landing), seven bedrooms, and three bathrooms, we were coming up on the attic leg of the grand tour when Cori braced herself against the doorjamb of the master bedroom. She'd go no further. "Surely, you have clients waiting in your salon."

"Good Lord, yes!" April cried.

We opened the bedroom window to let in some fresh air and watched as she trekked across the yard.

"What happened to her leg?" Cori asked.

"I don't know. Arthritis?"

"Is she wearing a prosthesis?"

"Not that I remember."

"How do you think she'll react when you tell her she has to move out of the cottage?"

"I'm not looking forward to it."

"Yoo-hoo!" April called up to us. "Did I mention, Bobby, your young bride is the prettiest little thing? Anytime you fancy the services of the county's finest beautician, my dear, you come on by. The miracles I can work, it will be my privilege."

Cori beamed appreciation, her accompanying groan for my ears only.

"One more thing," April shouted. "Don't y'all pay any heed should mindless folk bring up the old bugaboo about ghosts and strange doings hereabouts. Never once have I been given pause, supernatural or unnatural."

A disgruntled client, hair in curlers and hands aflutter, corralled April outside the cottage.

"She really say this house is haunted?"

"You believe in ghosts, Cor?"

"Not usually."

"Me, neither."

"Something about her though ... hate to say it ... so cloying. You sure we can trust her?"

"My mother did. So probably not."

"And, God, her perm. If she thinks she's going to touch my hair ... I know the type: Her specialty is making thirty-year-old women look sixty. Someone should sue her for malpractice."

"At least we can't fault her for the way she kept this place."

"Oh, yeah?" Cori knelt at the fringe of the Persian carpet and turned away in disgust, hands up. "I'm not touching it."

I plucked the condom from between the tassels. "April has been a busy girl. Who'd have thought?" The condom was dry and cracked. "You don't see many black ones. Sexy, no?"

"Gross."

"If this is the worst we find ... c'mon, Cor, you can't deny the house—"

"It's easy to see why your mother didn't let it go."

"Yeah. She got rid of me, instead."

"That's not funny, Rob."

"It's true."

"Jeez, Rob, cut her some slack, already. Finding out your husband of thirteen years is a serial killer doesn't happen every day. There's no handbook to consult. No *Cosmo* quiz."

"It wasn't fun for anybody."

Cori bear-hugged me from behind. "But this will be," she said, taking me with her as she toppled backward onto the bed. "Shall we give them a show?"

"What?"

"The ghosts." She ran a finger the length of my fly, unzipped, and stopped. "Wait. On second thought, let's change the sheets first."

I can't say when we dozed off. I'd been dreaming of Cori, so her scream didn't connect right off. But her fingernails did. My heart leaped from my chest and the rest of me followed bolt upright.

Dusk filled the room, lending scant illumination to the creature that loomed at the end of our bed. Whatever the hell this thing was, it had fangs.

17

SEE COLORFUL LOCALS IN THEIR NATURAL HABITATS

The guy's name was Tusk. No mystery why. Made you wonder if his parents weren't Dobermans. He was April with a canine bent. "So you're who come back," he said.

I grabbed for my underwear and jeans.

He was talking to me, though his focus was Cori. She eyed him warily, sheets clenched to her chin. Angry. Violated.

"How'd you get in?"

"Door was open. Anyhow, I got a key."

Cori sat up. "You have a what?"

"Who the heck you think kept this place up, huh, Blondie? You think April done it on her own? You got me to thank, little lady."

He was taller than his sister (who wasn't?), though not by much. Squat, compact, except for the gangly limbs, he was a hodgepodge of spare parts, more likely slapped together in a Hollywood backlot than the product of a human womb. He was something you might stare at out the corner of your eye, and turn away shamefaced if caught in the act. His head would have fit nicely at the end of a novelty keychain. Yet, he elicited no pity. Hairline to neckline, he frothed belligerence.

"I banged your door, eh, ten, twenty times easy. Some old guy's waiting out there. Mighty pissed too. Says you owe him money."

I followed Tusk outside.

Joe Di Iorio was pushing seventy, with the finger-snapping air of a stale-dated Sinatra. He wore a yellow windbreaker zipped to the neck, the knot of a tie bulging above the collar. His baseball cap was white, with a green and black logo of a steering wheel and *Steer-U-Rite* smack center. He was dean of a driving school which, according to Cori, made him the most reliable candidate to drive her BMW from Saratoga to Hillsdale. He'd been a patient of hers and she'd hand-picked him for the task. His price was half of what he would've charged anyone who wasn't Cori.

Joe did nothing to conceal his disappointment or the single long-stemmed rose in hand. I checked over the car and counted out the balance owed. Joe held his ground, reluctant to part with the keys. "I need to see Dr. Corinne."

"Bet you do," Tusk muttered.

"Sorry, she's sleeping," I said.

"My arrangement was with her."

"You can give me the keys, no problem."

"No disrespect, sonny, but it was me she asked to transport the vehicle. I'm not about to trust a luxury, high-powered automobile to just anyone."

"I'm her husband. It's okay." Joe was the latest among Cori's forlorn minions. Hell, I'd suffered the pangs myself. Only difference, I was the forlorn minion she married.

"Keys," I said. "Now."

"Fine," he grumbled. "But only because I know about you." He slapped the keys onto my palm, poised to defend against my imminent attack. I turned, walked away.

"Hey!" He tendered the rose, softened. "Any chance you'll give this to her?" I sighed, snatched it. "And the bus. Next one's at eight. Either of you fellows up to giving a good Samaritan a lift to the depot?"

Tusk jumped in: "Budgie's, diner up on Main, there's your depot. Four blocks that way, two that. Five minutes. Can't miss it."

Joe chewed his lip. "What if I got an abscess?" He pressed a hand to his cheek. "Yeah, I got an abscess."

"She's sleeping." I swear, I thought the guy might cry.

"Well, you tell her from me then, her car smelled sweet like her. You tell her Joe Di Iorio said that. Joe Di Iorio. She's got my number." He looked to the BMW with longing, to the house with greater longing, and moped up Appleton in the opposite direction Tusk had directed. I had no desire to correct him. Neither did Tusk.

Tusk lowered the tailgate of the pickup parked at curbside. A spanking new Ford Super D F-450 Platinum—eighty thousand bucks if a dime. "Nice," I whistled, straddling the line between tough and friendly, as if winning the handyman's respect would make a profound difference in my life.

He spit a toothpick onto the road. "Grab an end, would ya? I brung you the ladder. And them tools." I kept my hands in my pockets. He raised his voice, pointed to the bed of the truck. "C'mon, grab an end."

I can be a sucker for authority even when there isn't any authority to be a sucker for. I hauled the ladder from the truck, expecting Tusk to hold up his end. He didn't even try. I stumbled backward onto the grass, kissing the rungs as they thumped off my nose en route to knees.

Tusk was blunt. "You goof on your roof and you ain't gonna be on your roof long."

I weighed my odds as I regained my feet. One punch to his marshmallow middle would do the job. "Why in the hell would I be on my roof?"

"Your Christmas crap. April says you come back to do the Christmas crap. Like in the ol' days, with your Mom."

"I never told April—"

He dropped the toolbox, clearly aiming for my toes. "I don't by nature borrow out tools, especial to types who don't know which end is up. But April's got in her head you're all right, so who am I to say?"

How was it his sister spoke so well, whereas he was a cautionary lesson on the perils of in-breeding?

"Good luck," he said with zero sincerity, and climbed into his truck. "Just can't figger you. Like who comes all this way to dress up the ol' homestead for Christmas? Nuttier than a nutbar."

"Nutbar. Yup, that's me."

"Nutbars are dangerous. Nutbars get folk killed."

"Up to here in cornpone wisdom, aren't you?"

"You think I don't know? The Christmas crap? I know it's not why you come back."

"And how's that?"

"Because you'd be an idiot if it was. And April's been on my ass ten years to stick that junk up. Now she's got in her head you're her bitch. So why then, huh? Why you come back?"

No way I'd tell him it was to write a book. Talk about your sissy shit.

"You shamed of somethin'? You doin' somethin' you shouldn't be doin'?" Moonlight ricocheted from the truck's side mirror to his tusks. The effect made them longer, sharper, tuskier. "I know what your daddy done."

"Fuck off," I said, my patience spent, in contrast to my infinite patience with annoying Loony Scoops customers. "I'm here to write. Satisfied?"

"You a blogger?"

I inhaled, faced him again on the exhale. "A book."

He slammed the dash. "No shit!"

"No shit."

"Well, if you need help some, gimme a call, you hear?"

"Yeah. Right. You're at the top of my list. Absolutely."

"No shit! A book." The asshole was impressed.

He started the engine. "Hey! Almost forgot." He waved me closer, a staple gun in his hand. I went to take it, noticing too late his eyes had gone wonky, a slot machine spinning blanks. Jeez! The guy was stroking out. I ripped the door wide and he crashed on top of me, peppering staples into my face as we fell.

"Accident. Accident." Tusk staggered to his feet, threw up his hands to plead his innocence. "I got this here 'firmity. Body does stuff I don't ask it to do. Gotta up my meds."

I could have sworn I was tuned to *Animal Planet*, how he bounded back to the pickup and swung up into the cab. "Good luck there with your book-writin'," he sputtered, before flooring the F-450 and tearing up Appleton.

———

It wasn't easy explaining to Cori how five heavy duty staples came to be embedded in my face, mainly because she had to yank the staples out before I could. She dabbed my wounds with hydrogen peroxide. "It's assault," she said.

I popped a couple of Advil. "Just another day in Hellsdale. You'll get used to it, hon."

"There's something not right about that man."

"Ya think?"

"I know."

"On the other hand, Cor, it could be his way of welcoming me to town. 'Howdy, stranger! Mind if I shoot some staples in your face?'" Cori's laugh was halfhearted. Mine was half of halfhearted. It hurt too much.

I gave her the key to her car along with Joe's rose. She rolled her eyes. "He's upped his game. Usually it's a carnation. And the other key?"

I didn't know what she meant.

"The house key. From Fang."

"Tusk? Ah, jeez ..."

"I don't want him in this house, Rob. I don't want him anywhere near me."

"That gut of his. You could take him easy, Cor. The way you handled that Dobsie kid ..."

"How long was he standing in our room? Did you see his face? His eyes? I was naked and he was still undressing me."

18

THE TREASURES TO BE
FOUND IN THE CELLARS
OF OLDER HOMES

According to a 2017 story in the *Times Union*, New York State Senator and gubernatorial hopeful Larry Gamelin was so enamored of my writing, he vowed to replace his team of speechwriters "with the genius who composes the blurbs for Loony Scoops."

Genius. Right. That was me—*William Milkshakespeare*.

When I got down to writing for real, not a damn thing happened. Not a word. Not a frigging title. For three days, I stared that goddamn computer in its stony gray face, until I came to the realization my parents' lives and Vermont Volcano sundaes were as much alike as swamp and sky.

Cori had been on my back about cleaning out the cellar. *"Death by fire may appeal to you, darling, but not to me."* Getting rid of the junk now struck me as a terrific idea, even if I'd never felt at ease down there. Cellars are nothing but pre-fab graves. Why bide your time in one before your time? I didn't exit cellars, I fled them.

A barricade of boxes, crates, and trunks loomed before me, wall to wall and floor to ceiling, a good twenty feet deep. There had always been a load of stuff piled against the back wall; now I wondered if, before our getaway, my mother hadn't hired an engineer to calculate the most efficient means to store our family's lifetimes. I was a tomb raider picking through the remains of the dead and the dead-in-transit.

A few days earlier, Cori had seen on some news site that my dad's execution had been scheduled yet again. "Don't fall for it," I'd said. "Give it a couple of weeks, and they'll announce yet another date."

"But what if it's for real this time?"

"I don't play that game anymore."

"You should see him, Rob."

Oddly, the first item of any note I came across in the cellar was Dad's alligator sample case, his name embossed in gold, his business cards inside.

HENRY T. DICKENS
WHOLESALE SWEETS, CONFECTIONS & SUPPLIES

I moved on to the baseball bat. A Louisville Slugger. Thurman Munson autograph model. The cops had examined it for blood residues. They never could accept Dad's improvised modus operandi.

I hung onto the bat as I ventured deeper. Cellars, you know? Gotta be prepared.

A box of my old stuff. Baseball mitt. Trading cards, Star Wars and WWF. Magic Cards. A Game Boy. And in a tiny plastic box, the black toenail I'd saved, a souvenir from the toe I'd stubbed on the night Dad killed Bonner Doyle and Debra Curdovic. Victims twenty-five and twenty-six according to the Feds.

A box of comics. Including *Astride-OM*, the Fotoromans stuff from Europe. My mother had foisted them on me shortly before our leaving.

Suitcases. Clothes. Some belonging to my mother's parents, my elusive grandparents, who had died on the very same day of what my mother claimed, in her questionable sorrow, were unrelated causes. It was at their funeral my father met my mother. "It was the day my life began," Dad would say. He meant it too. He never spoke of any past before that day. No parents. No hometown. No schooling. Not even the cops could shake his story. Every trail came up cold, every lead false. Henry Taylor Dickens was born at thirty-nine.

Cori interrupted my reverie, called down from the top of the stairs. "Rob, can you come up? There's someone here to see you."

To the right of the furnace was Dad's workout bench and rack of weights. He had worked that shit like he was out to kill, which in fact he was. He was never a big guy, but he was damn near the strongest. But it was the stuff behind the furnace that required a closer look.

Five kitchen chairs circled a big-ass spool of electrical wire. The chrome of the chairs was dull, the vinyl cracked. The seats regurgitated stuffing. Atop the spool, Styrofoam cups filled with ashes and butts— tobacco, weed, and hybrids. And melted condoms. Black condoms. Like the one we'd found on our bedroom floor.

At the center of the spool, propped back-to-back against each other, were three photos.

My mother. Frame warped, glass cracked. She posed in a black dress beside a Christmas tree. Lips and nails burgundy, smile expansive, cleavage plunging. She preened the way celebrities do in *People*, goddessy casual.

My father. In black and white within the faded Kodacolor. Charcoal suit. White shirt. Black tie. Shoes polished. Hair slicked back. The fifteen-year age difference between he and mom more pronounced than I remembered. He winked at the camera, his shoulder turned, as he strung candy canes about the middle of the Christmas tree—same tree as in the photo of my mother. Their first or second Christmas together, '88 or '89. Before me, anyhow.

The third photo. Little me. On a tricycle. A fireman's hat on my head. No smile on my face. No Christmas tree, either.

"Rob," Cori called again. "You coming up?"

Behind the chairs, running from the corner and out along the wall, a good thirty cases of empties. Coors and Bud and IPAs, stacked four and five high. Wine too. Cheap stuff. Boone's Farm Strawberry.

Welcome, ladies and gentlemen, to another stirring episode of The Secret Life of April Bright and Brother Tusk. What else was I to make of it?

I gathered up the cups, tossed the lot into an empty carton, and spotted a checkered rag draped over a yellow pail.

It wasn't a rag, it was my father's shirt. His Paul Bunyan shirt. The shirt he'd wear for chores, his sleeves rolled to biceps.

I shivered at the touch, though the shirt was dusty, stained, and stiff. It was also stuck to the bottom of the pail, as if dunked in paint and left to dry. Brown paint. Dark brown. It had to be paint. *Nothing else it could be, right Bobby?*

I should have torn the place apart straight away. But Cori, she needed me upstairs. Priorities. I exited the cellar. One purposeful step at a time. I did not flee.

A man sat hunched at the kitchen table, knuckles resting on a spiral notepad. He wore a gray jacket, blue tie, black trousers, and blue Skechers. "Oh," Cori said, as she poured his coffee, "here's my husband now, Detective."

19

VISITORS ARE INVITED TO SIT AND CHAT WITH FRIENDLY LOCALS

Detective Sam Hotts had arrived fresh from a 1940s casting call for expendable sidekicks. Or from Albany, anyhow.

He was broad in the shoulders and soft in the middle, coasting to retirement on the cushiest cases to hit the blotter. He emptied a packet of Stevia into his coffee. Speaking was an effort, syllables spliced with stifled yawns. "Your wife tells me you know this man, that so?" He slid the photo across the table.

The face was familiar. "Who is he?"

"Rob …" Cori prompted, irked by my cluelessness.

"Are you sure?" Hotts tapped the photo. I gave it another look, shook my head. "Your wife tells me you saw him a week or two ago."

"Joe?" I said, recognition dawning. "Joe Di Iorio. Yeah. Sure. Of course. The smile threw me. What's this about?"

"That's where I'm hoping you can help me, Mr. Blessing. It would appear Mr. Di Iorio has gone missing."

"Wow." I told the detective what I knew, how he delivered Cori's car and I paid him.

"Check or cash?"

"Cash. Two-fifty."

"Convenient."

"What do you mean by that?"

"And then?"

"He left."

"That was it? You didn't see or hear from him again?"

"He was going to catch a bus. The eight o'clock, I think."

"What about his behavior? Was he agitated? Happy? What you might call unusual in any way?"

"I'd only seen him once before, back in Malta, the night he came to get Cori's Bimmer. To be honest, I can't say what *unusual* might be for him." The cellar, my father's shirt, the bucket. I was off my game. Hell, I'd just used the word *Bimmer*, spoke it aloud like some douche. What would I do next, blurt a confession? Better to say less than more. No need to bring up Joe's distress at Cori's brush-off. Hotts would peg me for the jealous husband and cuff me straightaway.

"And the bus? Where's that exactly?" Hotts asked

"Budgie's Diner on Main."

"What about Tusk?" Cori leaned against the kitchen cabinet, half-standing, half-sitting. "Have you spoken to him?"

"Tusk?" Sam Hotts asked.

"Yeah, Tusk," I said. "He was there with me. You should talk to him."

"So it wasn't only you and Mr. Di Iorio, but this third party too?"

"It was Tusk who told Joe how to get to Budgie's."

"The diner on Main where the bus stops."

Cori peered from behind the rim of her coffee mug. "You definitely want to speak to him, Detective."

"And why's that, Mrs. Blessing?"

Cori shot him a dirty look. "Correct me if I'm wrong, Detective, but isn't it customary to cover all the bases?"

Hotts turned fidgety, smacked his lips. "Well, now that you bring it up, Mrs. Blessing, I do have something of a rather indelicate nature to ask, with regards to your relationship with Mr. Di Iorio. If you prefer your husband not be present ..."

"Oh, this ought to be good," she said.

Hotts looked to me, before shifting his gaze to his thumb and hangnail. He cleared his throat. "Mr. Di Iorio's wife believes her husband was having an affair. She says he was coming here, not to transport the vehicle, but to run off with you, Mrs. Blessing."

It took some doing for Cori to gain control of her laughter.

"Mrs. Di Iorio claims that since you became his dentist, he stopped taking care of his teeth, so he could see more of you."

"Oh, jeez," I said. "Unbelievable."

"Do you honestly expect me to dignify any of this with a reply, Detective Hotts?" Cori said.

"Only conveying the facts. No one's accusing."

"I assure you, Detective, if and when I choose to cheat on my husband, it will be a step up, not down."

"Gee, thanks," I said.

"Well, ma'am, with all due respect, you do drive an Audi, correct?"

"Bimmer," I said.

"A 650i," Cori added.

"It's a scientific fact, women who drive BMWs are more prone to cheat on their spouses."

Cori scoffed. "I think we're done here, Detective."

"As you wish." Hotts flipped open his notepad. It had been a prop till then. "How do I get in touch with this ... uh ... uh ... Mr. Tusk, is it?"

"April," Cori said. "His sister works just across the lawn. The so-called beauty spa ..." And for my benefit: "Soon to be my dental clinic."

Hotts drained the last of his coffee. "You sure you don't have anything more for me, Mr. Blessing? Ma'am?"

"Goodbye, Detective." Cori carried the detective's mug to the dishwasher.

Hotts dealt his business card onto the table. "Well, if you do ..."

I wondered if Tusk would tell Hotts what I had not. Joe Di Iorio had headed off the wrong way that night, and neither of us bothered to set him right.

20

ROLLERBLADING AND MUSIC
ARE POPULAR PASTIMES
AMONG LOCAL YOUTH

Cori poked her head up through the trap of the attic. "Not writing today? Seriously, Rob?"

"Taking a break. Thought it might be fun to put up my mother's old Christmas decorations."

"Maybe you should finish cleaning out the cellar first."

It was Halloween, the weather more summery than fall. "Yeah, but this stuff, once it turns cold ..."

"But *this stuff* isn't why we came here."

"Neither is the cellar."

"I agree. So write. Just write."

"My brain works better in the afternoon."

"Don't suppose you'll show me what you've got so far?"

My memoir continued to progress slowly. I'd formatted the page numbers and typed *CHAPTER ONE*. "I've been writing."

"I didn't say you hadn't been."

"I'd just rather keep it to myself for now."

"Well, if you're looking to do something constructive, give April Bright notice. It's not fair to her or me. I want my clinic up and running by spring."

"That's why I'm doing this, Cor. I figure once April sees the lights up, it'll soften the blow."

"Talking to you lately is like reasoning with a four-year-old." A few minutes later, her car peeled out of the driveway. She didn't say where she was going.

It took most of the morning to scavenge the crates and boxes and haul them down. Few were labeled. They'd been stored in haste during Christmas of 2001 when my father's luck ran out.

The reindeer and sleigh, the three-quarter-scale crèche (farm animals, Baby Jesus and family, the Wise Men), Frosty the Snowman with the corncob pipe that blew smoke rings. I'd forgotten how much of this stuff my mother had. Not that her annual display was ever about Christmas. It was about promotion. Nothing went up unless she had the item for sale.

Cori caught me on the porch around noon. I helped her carry in the groceries. "Are you really going ahead with this, Rob?" Her mouth was set, her dimples taut. Boxes, wires, and odd contraptions were strewn across the porch, like a plane crash postmortem on a hangar floor. "You came here to write, not play Santa. We're here a month and you're giving up. This isn't you. C'mon, Rob ..."

"I told you, afternoons work better for me. A person can't start writing just because he feels like it. Or his wife tells him to."

"You never had a problem before."

"Ice cream is different."

She muttered something I was better off not hearing and huffed into the house, only to reappear an instant later. "I picked this up a while back, just in case." She wielded a thick hardcover book as if it were a meat cleaver. Yellow Post-Its rippled from between pages. "Writer's block is common." She read from the book: "'Writer's block is as natural a part of the creative process as dotting an I and crossing a T.'"

"I'm not sure it's my problem, Cor. In order to have writer's block, I'd have to be a writer. I've got soda jerk's block."

Exasperation drowned her giggle. She was on a mission to save me. She shoved the book into my gut. "Read it."

"Will I be quizzed?"

"In ways you can't imagine."

"You really want me to do this, don't you?"

"I wouldn't have followed you here if I didn't. But the way you've been acting ..."

"It's the town," I said. "It gets under my skin and ..."

"That's an excuse and you know it. You're better than this." I gave the book a generous once-over. *Bestselleritis!: How to Catch It!* By Anna Carmen Hope.

"It has five stars on Amazon. At least give it a chance. Because right now, Rob, you're wasting not only your time, but mine. You've turned into, I dunno, a slacker. I want my husband back."

"I promise. As soon as I'm done with the decorations."

"And I promise I will hold you to it. Do you want a sandwich?" she asked, conciliatory. "Tuna?"

"Love one, yeah," I said, and she went inside.

I expected inspiration would strike, sooner or later, but I didn't see it coming from a woman who made up her own diseases. *Bestselleritis?* C'mon, eh?

I noted the title page and Cori's inscription:

> *To Rob, my love, with love*
> *May you find freedom in your words*
> *and peace within your prose*
> *Forever yours, Cori*

Jesus, I thought, *I should hire her to write the book.* As if to confirm the notion, Anna Carmen Hope passed judgment from the back cover. I could almost see the stick up her ass as it poked through a nostril. I winced, and in the same instant caught sight of two kids blading up Appleton. A girl and boy.

First glance, the scene was the hook from an Ariana Grande video. Second glance, Halsey.

The girl whipped along with grace and ease, guitar slung high across her back. The boy floundered six strides behind, a Dungeon Master who needed to lay off the Lays. Best guess, they were sixteen, seventeen, a fail-safe storyline of young love and opposites attract. I thumbed the book open to a Post-it as they glided by, but a clash of chords recaptured my attention. The duo had changed their minds and direction.

They hovered at the foot of the driveway. Her guitar now slung across her hips, fingers on frets, right hand lazing on the strings. Two backpacks rested on the walk between the boy's rollerblades. He pulled off his helmet, set free a bristly stand of muskrat hair. The girl wore no helmet, tossed her curly auburn all the same. I flashed a neighborly smile, thin, no show of teeth, and right away the girl called up to me. "A serial killer used to live in there."

I hoped I hadn't heard her right.

"They say he killed a hundred people." She fell short of foaming at the mouth, though not by much, and I knew the closest this kid had come to violent death was movies, TV, and Xbox. She looked to her friend for backup. "A hundred, right, Justin?"

Justin was occupied, fighting to prevent his skates from escaping with his legs.

I choked down whatever it was I wanted to say. Anna Carmen Hope was smirking now, I swear, anxious to see how I'd handle these kids so damn intent on getting a rise from me.

"Like you had to have heard of him?" the girl said. She twirled a full 360, red wheels spinning, guitar riffing. "The Brittle Butcher?"

Every cell in my screwed-up head shouted at me to end it here, go inside.

"Like because he killed people with peanut brittle."

Common sense did not prevail. I strode up to the pair, extended my hand in boyish good cheer. "Hi, I'm Bobby Blessing," I said. *These were kids. Just kids, after all.* I'd meet them on their terms. As for my reversion to Bobby, it's who I'd always be in this town. Rob and Robert were for other people and places, Cori among them.

The girl blocked my hand with her guitar. "Bobby? That's a little boy's name." Her laugh was Cori's note for note, down to the blissful undertow.

"Ha!" Justin sniggered, lips sealed to minimize the chrome strung across his teeth. "Bobby Blessing sounds like a prayer."

"Sounds about right," I said.

"You're new here, huh?" Guitar Girl said. "Nobody's lived here like forever."

"Yeah, well, somebody lives here now," I said.

"I wrote a song about him."

"You what?"

"It's called 'The Brittle Butcher of Hillsdale.'"

Justin piped in. "It's really good too. Play it for him, Willa."

"No," she said, a coy appeal for additional coaxing.

"Yeah, play it," I said. My dad was nothing to sing about, but this was too freaky to pass up.

"Yeah, Willa. C'mon." And then to me: "She's really good. She's won all sorts of singing contests. I keep telling her to go on *America's Got Talent*. Bet she'd win too, no sweat."

"You really want to hear it?" she said.

"A free performance from a future superstar? Definitely."

"Well, I guess, maybe the chorus ..." She strummed a chord, adjusted the tuning. Her voice was shaky sweet:

> *"Be afraid, be afraid, be so very afraid,*
> *Hillsdale has a killer, the worst God ever made.*

A monster who prowls with candy and hate,
For the boys and girls who happily play,
For the boys and girls he'll happily slay.
Be afraid, be afraid, be so very a—"

She stopped, distracted. "She your wife?"

I looked behind. Cori stood at the open door, sandwich on a plate. For no good reason, I felt like an ass. I stepped back, mindful of the distance between the kids and me. "Good song," I said.

"I'm still working on it," she said.

"And you're a really good singer too. But I gotta go—a ton of chores waiting."

"Aren't you scared, living in there?" she said.

"Should I be?"

"I'll bet your wife's scared. I'd be."

Justin gave her a nudge. "C'mon, Willa. We should go." He followed up with a veiled warning, made sure I heard: "Our moms will be wondering where we are."

Willa swung her guitar to her back. "What about ghosts? They say your house is full of them—all those kids he murdered."

"He didn't murder kids," I said.

"Yes, he did."

Justin shrugged the backpacks onto opposing shoulders, and almost hit the ground as he reset his helmet. But Willa held firm. "Hey! What's that you're reading?"

"I'm done with it." I showed her the book. "You want it?"

"Wow!" She eased *Bestselleritis!* from my hands. "Look, Justin."

"Cool. Let's go." He let the blue backpack slide to his elbow and Willa zipped Anna Carmen Hope inside.

"Are you a writer?" Willa asked. "I've got loads of ideas. Oh my God, have you read *The Fault in Our Stars*? Oh, and *Cinder*? If singing doesn't work out, I'm going to write books. It's not much different from songwriting, except more words."

Justin tugged at her arm. "It's getting late."

"Well, see ya, I guess." She waved, and gravity pulled her up the walk.

I called after them. "Good luck with your singing, Willa."

"It's Willow," she corrected. "Like the tree, Bobby." Justin yelled at her, but whatever his gripe, she wasn't fazed.

She skated from view, arms and legs pumping without effort. As Justin flailed in her wake, he flipped me the bird.

"Friends of yours?" Cori asked.

"They wanted me to know a serial killer used to live here."

"Oh, I've heard that too," Cori said. "Perhaps you should write a book about it."

To my relief she didn't ask what had become of *Bestselleritis!* I'd been a thoughtless asshole. And thoughtlessness had consequences. More than I could have imagined.

21

THE PLACE TO BE FOR AN OLD-FASHIONED CHRISTMAS

First week of December, the Ghosts of Christmas Past annexed the neighborhood. "It's magical," Cori said. She was awed by the lights and contraptions. I was awed by the fact no fuses blew. The crowds were another matter. I knew they'd come, yet felt unprepared. I might as well have stripped naked and cartwheeled up Main announcing the return of the killer's kid.

"Stupidest thing I've ever done," I said to Cori.

"You're young," she said. "Give it time, you'll top it."

Neighbors, April's customers, ice-skaters bound for Franklin Park, seniors, kids, and church groups, all had their favorites. I was proudest of the nativity scene, the animals with their bobbing heads and swishy tails, Baby Jesus and the Virgin Mary with their luminescent halos, and the Wise Men harmonizing on ninety seconds of *Silent Night* every twenty minutes. "My God, you'd swear Pentatonix is singing," April swooned.

Some visitors made mention of the giant candy canes, gumdrops, and cookies wired to the soffit and how this had been the home of "that candy guy who killed people," but few made the connection to me and those who did were anything but hostile. I realized then, or at least deceived myself into thinking, the past is most important only to those for whom it was once the present. To all others, it is hearsay, as relevant as the history books on their grandma's bookshelves. For me, the line was drawn between those who had once feared my father and those ignorant of what the fear was like.

Second night, a young woman with two kids in tow, and a third on the way, marched up and asked if I remembered her. "Bonnie McHale?" she said.

"Bonnie. Of course. Wow."

She took a deep breath to steel herself and let rip with emotions she'd bottled up inside for years. "I was one of the kids who didn't treat you right, you know, after your father ... I've always felt bad. But now, being a mother, seeing things ... You didn't deserve it, Bobby. I just wanted you to know how sorry I am, how wrong I was. I'm glad you're back. I am so happy for you, I really am." By the end, she was choked up and teary-eyed, and I was near the same. I thanked her, forgave her, and we shared a hug that held until she noticed her kids had wandered off.

The owner of Basil's Blooms, the flower shop on Main, came by too. His mustache rode his lip like a caterpillar hanging ten. He drew me close with a two-handed shake, introduced himself as Basil Bloomfield, and spoke with almost as much passion as Bonnie McHale. "Please, on behalf of the Hillsdale Business Owners Association, allow me to thank you for your community-minded spirit and the light you bring to our fair town. I say this, son, both figuratively and literally, fully aware of your tragic lineage. I'm new here, myself. A mere four years. But welcome, son, welcome to you and your splendid wife."

Yeah, it was nice, though not all popcorn balls and shortbread. Four nights in, a young guy with a stringy goatee and a doting twig of a woman affixed to his hip emerged from the crowd and asked, "You're Henry Taylor Dickens's kid, aren't you?" I didn't answer, which was all the answer he needed. "Awesome meeting you, man." He pulled an autograph book and Sharpie from a canvas rucksack.

"Yeah, awesome," his girlfriend echoed, her thighs wrestling with what I perceived to be an urgent pee.

"I don't do autographs," I said. There was something off with these two. More off, that is, than the usual run of Dad's fans.

"You signed one for my bud."

"Not me."

"Yes, you did. You did. At your ice cream place up in Saratoga. You signed his book same page as your daddy's mugshot."

"Yeah, well, I don't do that anymore."

"Mind if I give you some advice?" Goatee stepped up, clamped a hand to my shoulder. "Your lights are nice, Bobby, but they don't belong on this house. Too many eyes, if you catch what I'm saying."

I maneuvered out from under his hand. "I don't have time for this, okay?"

"Hey, don't be like that. We're on your side, man. With you every step, man."

His girlfriend piped in. "Do you think they'll fry him this time?"

"What?"

"Your daddy," she said. "Death-day? Come March? The sixth?"

"Sixteenth, Caitlin," Goatee corrected.

"I'm pretty sure it's the sixth," Caitlin insisted.

"Uh-uh. Sixteenth."

"What's the dif? March, it's all the same."

Goatee stabbed the autograph book with his Sharpie. "Sure you won't reconsider?"

I shoved my hands into my pockets and slunk off. When I looked back, they were gone. But they'd left me troubled. Not about the date I didn't want in my head, but the fact they were so young. Any fan I'd ever known was nearer my dad's age than mine. Never as young as these two.

It has crossed my mind from time to time that when the Human Genome Project is analyzed in full, the difference between autograph collectors and serial killers will be revealed to be a single genetic marker.

The good news was, Goatee and Caitlin excepted, my seasonal extravaganza did not appear to have spurred a pilgrimage of Brittle Butcher fandom. Few regular folks cared a whit whose house they were gawking at, as long as the lights were pretty. The only talk of it being haunted came from a kid and his mom I happened to overhear.

Kid: "Haunted houses don't have Christmas decorations, do they?"

Mom: "No, they don't, dear. They certainly don't."

And that suited me just fine.

Screw my fears and doubts. Christmas lights belonged on 18 Appleton as much as any house in Hillsdale. I had every right to be here, not that I was obliged to broadcast the news, of course. Apart from the pair of autograph hounds, my father was old news.

The crowds also pointed up how alone Cori and I had been. Neighbors were eager to welcome us. The Messners from down the block, Al and Marie, came on like best friends, raving how our display had invigorated not just Appleton Street, but the whole damn town.

"You gotta see, man," Al had said. "People are putting up lights around here like they haven't in years."

Marie had confessed to Cori they'd been worried about us, the new neighbors. "You never know what you're going to get. Ten years ago, two houses down, well, trailer trash would have been a step up. But looking at you two, we couldn't have asked for more."

Cori let the *trailer trash* slip by without comment, which took some doing. She knew we needed friends.

The four of us made plans for dinner and a movie.

Yeah, things were looking up. "I told you putting up this stuff would change everything for the better," I reminded Cori.

"You never did," she said, which was the truth. "But that doesn't mean it hasn't."

When I was a kid, *The Daily Chronicle* would do a story on our Christmas decorations most every December. They'd take our picture too. Mom and Dad and me, full of good cheer and the spirit of Saint Nick or Jesus or Klar's Department Store on Main. After Dad's arrest, the last of these photos was picked up by the wire services and splashed across the country, except Mom and me were cropped out. If you looked closely at Dad's left shoulder, you could see Mom's hand resting there— the tips of her Rita Hayworth fingernails, anyway. Rita Hayworth was a movie star. Dad always said Mom looked just like her. Only prettier.

It was like old times when the photographer from what was now *The Weekly Chronicle* showed up. I feigned shyness. I did not want a repeat of Saratoga and Lenora-Jo. I handed off the photo chores to Cori, but she begged off too, a clear comedown for the photographer. "The house should be the star," she said.

The compromise was to have him shoot her from behind, her arm around the tallest of the Wise Men, the house looming bright before her. "Did you give the Wise Man a woody?" I asked.

"Only the photographer," she replied.

The photo made the front page. Cori was especially happy the article spelled her name correctly, Dr. Corinne M. Widdoes, and made note that her new dental clinic would be accepting patients of all ages by spring. She loved the *all ages* part. My name did not appear. And not a peep about the Brittle Butcher.

Hillsdale had changed. I could live my life here. Yes, I could.

Cori shook me awake. "Somebody's outside." It was 2:00 AM. She was at the bedroom window. A sliver of moonlight illuminated her face.

A 4x4 idled at curbside.

Three men were in our yard.

One carried an axe.
One carried a sledgehammer.
One revved a chainsaw.

22

ACTIVITIES GALORE FOR ADULTS
AND YOUNGSTERS OF ALL AGES

Now you might think, as I relate the events that follow, our lives were a daily succession of unpleasant encounters and comic book horrors. This is not the case. In time, as you will see, *Bestselleritis!* would be returned to me and I would come to take Anna Carmen Hope's advice to heart, especially page 93:

No reader, save the vanishing elite and pseudo-erudite besotted with dreary classics and the impenetrable sludge deemed contemporary literature, craves the mundane. Unless the information is integral to the plot, avoid protracted descriptions of the everyday. The reader assumes Jack goes to the toilet and flushes, that Jill inserts her arms, one at a time, into the right and left sleeves of her coat, and that Sally shuts the door after she has transited the threshold.

So, while I might not dwell on the trivial, you can rest assured that, in between the messy stuff, our lives were wholly ordinary.

Each day at sun-up, Cori would jog her four, five, or six miles, with me plodding along on the occasions she'd cow me into action. (In many ways I was no better than that Justin kid on Willow's tail.)

We'd go to Wok In The Park in Kenner for Chinese, Vietnamese, and Thai. We'd order pizza from KK's Italian Oven on Main, half everything for me and half all-veggie for her. When curry called, we'd make the trek to Taj in Cameron Springs. Breakfast at Budgie's was a weekend ritual. No comparison to Mom & Pop's back in Ballston Spa, though decent enough.

Saturdays, we'd do the farmers' market, Target in East Butterfield, or the big mall off 88. Cori and Victoria's Secret were like sisters. The staff at Anthropologie, lululemon, and Burberry knew her by name, Haute Heels and Aldo by size.

We went for hikes up at the State Park and bought ice skates for the rink at nearby Franklin Park. I'd played a little hockey as a kid and Cori had done some figure skating.

We'd go to movies. We splurged on a 55-inch Samsung with sound bar and subwoofer. We signed up for Netflix, Hulu, HBO, and Prime. We got hooked on *Top Chef*, *Schitt's Creek*, *Watchman*, and *Succession*.

We got better acquainted with Al and Marie Messner, both home and away. Went to the Hillsdale Players' production of *Little Shop of Horrors* at the high school auditorium. Had dinner with them almost as often as we did on our own, Wok In The Park a favorite of theirs too. Al loved General Tso's as much as I did, while Marie sided with Cori on the snow peas, broccoli, and that tofu insanity.

Marie was your firecracker type, a dark-haired pixie with a playful PhD swank. Best of all, she laughed at any dumb joke I made. It was a great laugh too, welling up from the heart of her. Al was more on the pensive side, the kind of guy you couldn't help but warm to, even if he did correct anyone who called him Albert or Allan. "It's plain Al. Do I need to show you my birth certificate?" Cori hit it off with them too. Marie had a degree in biosciences, so she and Cori had plenty to talk about. And Al and me, well, we both liked Knob Creek bourbon, Macs over PCs, and killing time on YouTube.

Sure, there was the evening it got uncomfortable, when Al asked if we were aware a murderer had owned our house. He thought he was being funny, but Marie was quick to hush him up. Al accepted our somber nods and let it lie.

While I was busy doing my thing, lying to Cori about my writing, procrastinating with the Times Spelling Bee, or finessing the Christmas lights, Cori did hers.

She redecorated the rooms, one by one, a little touch here, a little there, before observing, "I might be wrong, Rob, but I'd swear the bedrooms have been slept in, like April or Tusk might have been running a B & B on the side." She'd found another black condom in some sheets, a joint in a night table drawer, and a potato peeler and a tube of lipstick under different beds. "Maybelline. Berry Blackmail."

She moved ahead with her plans for the clinic, secure in her faith I would soon evict April Bright. Cori went so far as to fly in an interior designer from Cincinnati who specialized in dental offices. They visited the beauty salon on the pretext of becoming customers. April was beside herself with excitement, failing to note the floor and window measurements they took. "Imagine! Two beautiful city girls choosing April Bright's Beauty Salon and Spa!" As usual, she rhapsodized over Cori, babbling to clients about her hair, her skin, her figure, her fashion sense, her living-right-next-door, and how her mother-in-law had been quite the looker in her heyday too. "She's a dentist too, would you believe? A woman dentist? You'd think she'd be a movie star. Oh, don't be so modest, my dear, you most certainly could."

The problem with the ordinary, it's transitory.

The chainsaw went from revving to whining.

Cori kept watch at the window as I scrambled to find my clothes. Sleeping in the nude has its pluses, but come an emergency, the seconds you lose making yourself decent can be the difference between life and death. "Take Dobsie's gun," she shouted after me, as I tripped into my jeans and hit the stairs.

"They're kids," I shouted back, and opted for the Louisville Slugger I'd stashed in the umbrella stand.

I burst onto the porch, and a howling broke above the buzz of the chainsaw. Agonized. Relentless.

Two of the kids had taken off, tires screeching, taillights streaking up Appleton.

The third kid, the jackass with the chainsaw, convulsed at Frosty's feet, thrashing and grinding. His fist was frozen to the throttle. Blood sprayed from where his left arm had been. His thigh was gone as well, a freshly butchered brisket marinating in the grass. And next to the brisket was the Virgin Mary's severed head.

Cori held her post at our bedroom window, phone in hand. She waved. I waved.

I kicked the kid's right hand, dodged the blade, kicked again, and the chainsaw sputtered dead.

The kid's cries grew weaker.

Sirens wailed.

23

THE FORCE THAT'S WITH YOU
(MOTTO OF THE HILLSDALE POLICE DEPARTMENT)

We hung back on the porch as the paramedics went about their business. Cori filled me in on how the Virgin Mary's head had come to rest near Frosty, some thirty feet from the nativity scene where her decapitation had occurred.

"Something scared them. Like someone was coming at them from the side of the house. They ran, but the kid with the saw, I'm telling you, Rob, it was bizarre. The head came flying at him out of nowhere, knocked him right off his feet. Except the saw kept going. And then his arm ..." She was a far cry from the warrior who'd kayoed Dobsie. Inflicting damage can be a rush, witnessing the same unnerving. Better to be the perp every time.

"And you're sure you didn't see anybody else?"

"I was watching the boys. But you'd have to be pretty strong to throw the Virgin Mary's head so far, right?"

"I guess. It's solid wood. They don't make Virgin Marys like they used to."

"It's not funny," she said, and stopped to watch the paramedics wheel the kid into the ambulance.

"No sheet over his head," I said. "That's good, I guess."

The cops waited for the ambulance to pull away before approaching.

"Uniforms," I groaned. "The fun never ends."

"They're not all out to get you, Rob."

"The one on the left is, guaranteed."

"You know him?"

"Wade Griffiths. My best friend. Until he wasn't. He's taller. Bigger. But the fucker hasn't changed. That fucking red hair. Just my luck."

"He's cute," Cori said. "A baby face."

"Trust me, Cor, I'm cuter."

Wade Fucking Griffiths. Here's all you need to know in 112 words:

"Because your father's guilty, people assume you and I are guilty too."

"But we didn't do anything to anybody, Mom. And Daddy never did anything to them."

"Someone has to pay the price for what Daddy did. We're all they have."

"It's not fair."

"It's human nature. People are frightened. If this had happened to Wade and his family, we'd be shunning them same way they're shunning us."

"Not me. I would have stuck by him, no matter what."

"But most people aren't like you, Bobby. Even then, none of us really know how we'll handle any tragedy until we're facing it."

"Wade and me, we were friends forever."

"Forever isn't over."

"Hey, Wade," I said.

"Heard you were back, Bobby. Detective down from Albany, Sam Something, mentioned he had a sit-down with you. Saw that write-up on your lights in *The Weekly* too. You are his wife I'm guessing, ma'am? The dentist?"

Cori kept to the shadows, beyond the dirty yellow glow of the porch light. "Hi," she said.

"Yeah, your mom always put on a great Christmas show, Bobby. Loved coming by your place back then. The hot cocoa and cookies." Wade smacked his lips. "Meant to drop by sooner, but you know how it is."

"No," I said. "How is it?"

"Busy like you wouldn't believe. The local force, we're down to four full-timers now. We're small, but deadly." He winked, clicked his tongue. "But never mind that. Jeez, you and me, how many years is it? Plenty of water under the bridge, eh? None of us getting any younger."

"Yup," I said. I wanted to grab Wade Griffiths by the throat. I wanted to wring him by the neck. I wanted to smash his face until he didn't have a face. I wanted to beat him down so hard they'd peel the fucker off the pavement. "Yup."

The older cop cut in. "Scur Goldwater, Acting Chief." His face was creased and cracked, eroded by a lifetime of regretting whatever it is a small-town cop might regret. "I don't suppose you remember me, son."

"I thought it might be you, sir," I said.

Wade snickered, felt his duty was to fill in the blanks for Cori: "The Chief was working the desk the night they brought Bobby's father in. You know, the Brittle Butcher?" Clearly, he'd been hoping I'd been dumb enough to have kept this tiny detail of my past a secret from her.

Scur coughed into his armpit and neither he nor I bothered to correct the asshole on his version of events. "Yes, well, if you don't mind, Officer Griffiths, might be best to save your reminiscing for later." Scur addressed Cori. "It's mighty chilly out here, miss, and the lighting's not the best. Might we go inside? I know it's a crazy hour, we'll try to keep it short."

———

I flicked on the kitchen lights and it was like the cops saw Cori for the first time. Blue jeans. T-shirt. Bedhead. Bare feet. They whipped off their hats so fast you'd think they were geeks gearing up for a tête-à-tête with the homecoming queen.

We gathered at the kitchen table. The cops pulled out their notebooks. Cori put on the coffee.

Wade jabbered as we waited for Cori to join us. His shifty eyes kept shifting to Cori's backside, and it took some doing not to jump him. And then it took a whole lot more doing. "If it wouldn't have been for your dad, Bobby, I might never have pursued law enforcement as a career. A piece of work he was, huh? Anyhow, I hear it's gonna be a go this time. The execution, eh? March something. Long overdue, you ask me."

Acting Chief Goldwater scratched an ear, examined his fingertip for wax.

I pushed back from the table, eyes burning into Wade's skull. From across the kitchen, Cori shook her head *no*. I kept my response low-key: "Go fuck yourself, Griffiths."

Wade could not believe his ears. Apoplectic is what he was. His eyes narrowed, which took some doing, since his eyes were slitty to begin with.

"Go fuck yourself," I said again. I'd been dreaming of this moment for years.

His nostrils flared. His nose whistled. "I can take you in for that." He was red in the face, dry in the mouth. "I can cuff you right here, right now, and take you down to the station. Disrespecting a police officer. Threatening a police officer. Assaulting a police officer. Obstructing justice ..."

I leaned across the table and into his face. "Go. Fuck. Your. Self."

Wade leapt to his feet, chair toppling behind him. He had the gloat of a gunslinger, fingers loose at his holster.

"Cream and sugar, officers?" Cori asked brightly, tray held before her. "Cookies or biscotti, anyone?"

"Well, thank you kindly, miss." Goldwater relieved her of the tray, cast a disapproving eye toward Wade. "Chill, Griff. Chill."

"You always had an axe to grind." Wade's face was a circus, a contortionist's sideshow as he labored to reclaim his nonexistent cool. He righted his chair, dragged it up to the table, stirred his coffee with the wrong end of the spoon. "I can't for the life of me understand why in God's great name you'd want to come back. What did you think was going to happen, Bobby? A welcome home party? Balloons?"

"A parade would've been nice," I said.

Cori took her seat opposite Scur, me to her right, Wade to her left. And the idiot failed yet again to keep his stupid trap shut. "That photo in the paper, ma'am, didn't do you justice. They should've shot your front." Cori liberated an almond from a rectangle of biscotti.

"I take it they don't offer cops sensitivity training around here," I said, as Cori gripped my knee.

"You done?" Scur said to Wade. "Are you done, Officer Griffiths?"

Wade flashed a brave smile, sat back.

"So, now?" Scur said, and the interview began.

Cori described the scene as she saw it, before handing it off to me. I left out nothing, surprised protocol didn't call for separate interviews. But that was Hillsdale for you.

"And you're sure whoever frightened off the kids wasn't your husband, Mrs. Blessing?"

"Rob was in the house. He had to get his shoes, and the bat, of course ... He knocked the umbrella stand over when he grabbed it. He swore, and shouted up to tell me he was sorry he'd broken it. It was a lovely antique piece too. White ceramic. Whatever happened with the boys was over before Rob stepped outside."

"You had the bat in your hand when we pulled up, Mr. Blessing. What exactly did you do with it?"

"Nothing. Never had the chance."

"What were you planning to do with it?"

"I dunno. Scare them off. Defend myself, if needed."

"Ha!" Wade slapped the table. "'If needed,' my ass! You were always a hothead, Dickens. You never needed an excuse to throw a punch."

"You're wrong," I said. "I never had a temper until the pricks in this town—pricks like you, Griffiths—started piling on. What did you expect me to do? Let you treat me like shit? We were friends, Wade. Best friends. And you turned on me like it was nothing."

"Your father murdered twenty-seven people in cold blood. You call that nothing?"

"More coffee, anyone?" Cori asked, carafe at the ready.

The blowhard yammered on. "And get your facts straight, Dickens. It wasn't me who turned on you; you turned on me. You went into lockdown. Nobody could talk to you. "

"Your version."

"Yeah? And those fucked up faces you'd make. Your crazy eyes. Everybody saw, you'd gone mental, man."

"The look took practice, trust me."

"You didn't scare me, though, did you, Bobby? Remember when I bloodied your nose?" Wade's smile was smug as he gauged Cori's reaction to his boyhood heroics.

"Yeah, you were quite the tough guy," I said. "You jumped me from the bushes. You shoved a broomstick through the spokes of my bike. And then you kicked me while I was down."

Wade dismissed me with a flip of his hand. "What did I tell you, Chief? Nuts then, nuts now."

"Let's try to be civil here, shall we?" Scur clenched his teeth, breathed in, breathed out, a hiss fore and aft. "As I was saying, Mr. Blessing, about the baseball bat? Is it possible, are you sure you didn't take the bat to the kid's head and he tripped onto the chainsaw? Could you have threatened him with it perhaps? Even a mild tap, no one would fault you. You'd only be guilty of defending your own property."

"They were kids, sir. They were letting off steam. Scare them? Yes. Hurt them? Uh-uh."

Wade coughed, crossed and uncrossed his legs.

Scur kept it together. "From what I understand, your holiday decorations are vintage, correct? Worth a pretty penny, I'd wager. Who wouldn't be upset? Communities like ours, these days, vandalism is a scourge. Some young punk rubs you the wrong way and you can't help but go ballistic ..." Scur put it to Cori point-blank. "Did your husband take the bat to the kid, Mrs. Blessing?"

"I know what I saw." Cori held her ground. "The boys ran. Mary's head caught the kid in the back. The SUV took off. And next thing I saw was my husband standing in the yard. I expect the boys were too spooked to have noticed him."

Scur swirled his tongue around the inside of his cheek. "Well, I guess, we'll hear the kid's version when he comes to, God willing. It seems pretty open and shut, except—"

Wade seized the opening. "Except since you come back, Bobby, we got one guy who's missing and a kid who's half-dead. And both of them just happened—just happened!—to cross paths with you. Get real. Think we were born yesterday?"

"Officer Griffiths makes a point, Mr. Blessing. Now, me, I don't rule out coincidence. You and the missus seem like nice people. But it might be best if you keep a low profile the next while, if you know what I mean. It's a tight-knit community. You don't want folk talking."

"Wouldn't be the first time," I said. "Guilty until proven innocent. It's the Hillsdale way."

Wade cast an evil eye, stumped for a snappy comeback. Cori and Scur adjourned to the hallway. Surly footsteps followed, Wade and me, snide by snide.

Scur and Cori paused to admire my mother's grandfather clock. Mahogany with maple inlays. Brass dial. "You ever want to sell this," Scur said, "you let me know." He scribbled a note, carried on to the vestibule. They chatted as Wade and I sulked up the hall. Scur was showing Cori his teeth and gums. "You'll be first in line. I promise," she said. "Should be open early spring."

Scur thanked Cori, as he corralled fragments of the shattered umbrella stand with his foot and shuttled them to the wall. The bat propped in the corner merited no more than a glance. "I'll leave word for the morning crew to come by and see if we can't find some trace of this mysterious vigilante of yours, Mrs. Blessing."

"Call me Cori, please."

"Much as I hate to say, this being the festive season, might I suggest you put a cap on the lights and such? Kids these days, God love 'em. Frankly, we don't have the manpower to patrol like we used to."

"Maybe you'll luck out, Bobby." Wade's contempt verged on parody. "Maybe the kid will bleed out before ratting you out."

"Well, now," Cori said, clasping her hands, before extending her right to Wade. "I've heard so much about you. So nice to finally meet."

"You too, ma'am, miss."

"And what I said to Chief Goldwater applies to you too. I hope you'll consider me, should you need a dentist."

"Here's hoping I do," Wade said, more pearly yellows in a single smile than I had ever seen.

Cori pshawed, eyes downcast, and all at once her feet shot out from under her and a blameworthy shard of white ceramic sailed across the floor. Backward she yelped, arms flung wide, and you should have seen her Hail Mary, as she grabbed the doorframe to break her fall, as her right leg kicked up and out, and her right foot carried through to bust a bullseye on Wade's nutsack. The sucker retched forward, and the hard top of Cori's head crashed into his nose on the rebound.

Wade faded to the floor.

"Oh, my God," she cried. "I am sorry, so sorry. Are you hurt? Are you hurt?" She dropped to her knees, lifted his bloodied head onto her lap, and called for me to fetch a towel and ice. I held my place, mesmerized by his nostrils. Open hydrants, they were. A Holstein huffing snow. Only after Cori's sixth or seventh appeal did I collect what she'd asked for.

Scur could have been watching TV poker for the emotion he mustered. "No worries, miss. Accident, plain and simple. If not for your acrobatics, you'd be concussed along with him." The veteran cop had made a career of seeing only what he wanted to see, and he didn't want to see this as anything other than what it had to be. "Can't tell you how often I've told him to wear his cup. And headbutts, well, you got to be prepared."

"I hope nothing's broken," Cori said.

"The boy's a bleeder, miss."

Scur helped Wade to his feet. Cori apologized again. Wade glugged forgiveness, towel and ice at his face.

They were out the door and across the porch when Scur stopped and turned. "Best to sweep up the rest of that umbrella stand before you take another header, miss."

24

WHERE GOOD NEIGHBORS
MAKE GREAT NEIGHBORS

"That was the most beautiful three seconds of my life," I told her, once we managed to stop laughing.

"I don't know what you're talking about," she said.

"It was ballet. A three-second ballet."

"I slipped on a piece of ceramic. I could have killed myself."

"Tell me, Cor, is there anything you can't do?"

"Why? Do you have a request?"

We never made it to the bedroom.

Sleep should have come easy. Should've.

Chances are, you went to school with kids who could name all fifty states and the capitals of each, Jefferson City, Missouri, the badge of honor. Me, I could recite all twenty-seven of my father's victims, where they lived and how they died. Had I the lowdown on the unattributed unknown, I would have been able to rhyme them off, as well.

While Dr. Cutcheon deemed my preoccupation accomplished, she also declared it unproductive. "The weight is your father's to bear, Bobby, not yours." Fat chance.

Reciting the list was how I fell asleep most nights from the age of twelve. I weaned myself from the practice once I hooked up with Cori. Although her dismantling of Wade had salvaged the night, I found myself running down the dead once more, top to bottom and back again.

Henry Taylor Dickens Victims and Weapons List
(Unaudited)

1. **Alain Cousins**, Montpelier VT—winding bar
2. **Thomas Brunt**, Manchester MA—beach umbrella
3. **Parker Saludos**, New Haven CT—fishing rod, twine, and bait
4. **Olexandr Kalashnik**, Schenectady NY—ski pole
5. **Andrew Barlow**, Wells ME—barbecue fork
6. **Amjad Zulfikar**, Patterson NJ—bumper winch, galvanized aircraft cable
7. **Royce Hum Whitaker**, Concord NH—scalding water, shower head, hairdryer
8. **Shelley Elise Fairchild**, La Prairie IL—cuckoo clock
9. **Hugh Goodleaf**, Patterson NJ—garden hoe, garden hose
10. **Peter Bougadis**, Hoboken NJ—oven door, grill, commercial freezer
11. **Cozen Lem**, Erie PA—brick
12. **Keith Champagne**, Alexandria Bay NY—camera bag strap, refrigerator, duct tape
13. **Francis Bernstein**, West Lebanon NH—1/4-circle display cabinet, oak base
14. **Gary Roth**, Sunrise FL—brass lamp
15. **Amy Rodrigues**, Pompano Beach FL—mobility scooter
16. **Andrew Powers McVeeny**, Akron OH—hammer, nails
17. **Denny Lebel**, Cape Porpoise ME—lobster bait spike
18. **Walter Bowman**, Kingfield ME—chunk of ice, basketball net
19. **Joe Austin**, Oneida NY—belt and buckle
20. **Kim Seung Jo**, Iron MI—knife and/or cleaver
21. **Matt Cope**, Danville CT—Drano, Liquid-Plumr, twine
22. **Denver Allen**, Lester IL—baseball bat, baseball, cleats
23. **Ratan Bachan**, Saginaw MI—photocopier, pencil
24. **Kyle Keegle**, Easton PA—vintage milk bottle
25. **Bonner Doyle**, Hershey PA—knife
26. **Debra Curdovic**, Hershey PA—knife
27. **Abel Willing**, Woodstock VT—axe, tire iron, drill, Xmas tree baler, peanut brittle

Light of dawn, I made my way outside to search for clues, to learn what frightened off the teens. I scoured the grounds, the perimeter expanding with each pass. What would Sherlock Holmes unearth that I could not?

The hoarfrost gave up nothing and I soon conceded my powers of observation were limited to blood and the blatantly obvious. It wasn't solely Mary's head the bastards had severed, but Melchior the Magus's too, the remains of their halos crunching underfoot.

"Hey, Rob. Good morning, man." Al Messner loitered on the sidewalk. An air-puffed hairball named Françoise zipped about Al's ankles, winding her leash as she spun. A Bichon Frisé. A breed no self-respecting man should be caught walking. "Wow! What in God's name happened here?"

"Kids. Last night. One of them fell on a chainsaw."

"You serious?" Al freed himself from the leash and joined me at Frosty's side. "Holy cow! Would you look at that!" Blood spattered the plastic snowman's underbelly.

Françoise squatted, peed.

"Yup, it was quite the show," I said.

Françoise jumped onto my leg and started humping. I shook her off.

"You and Cori must be sick about it."

"No kidding. Cops came. It was pretty disturbing."

"Jesus. I heard the sirens, but never thought ..."

"We're exhausted. Some night, I tell you."

Françoise sniffed about Frosty, her object of affection since my rebuff.

"Was the kid hurt?" Al asked. "Bad, I mean?"

"Lost an arm and part of a leg, from what I saw."

"Karma, eh?"

"Huh?"

"And what they did to your Christmas stuff! Kids today, spoiled rotten. No values. No ethics. And morals? Not even in the dictionary. Goes right back to the parents."

Françoise flipped to her back, rolled in the grass. Al jerked the leash, but Françoise wasn't much into cooperation. "Bitch needs a hearing test. C'mon, girl! Come." He reeled the dog toward him, squatted to see what the fuss was about, and promptly gagged. "Oh, God. I'm gonna be sick," he said, and was.

The paramedics had overlooked a finger. A pinky. Easy to miss in the dark.

I scooped up the finger with a garden trowel and stored it on ice inside a plastic sandwich bag. I phoned the station.

"Hillsdale Police Department. Liz Wyman, speaking. How may I help you?"

Neither Chief Goldwater nor Officer Griffiths would be coming on duty till later in the day. I told her who I was, recapped the night before, and what Françoise had found. "Should I bring it to the hospital?" I said.

"No rush. David succumbed to his injuries early this morning, poor thing."

25

WHERE A HELPING HAND IS
ALWAYS CLOSE AT HAND

Tusk came by about ten to help dismantle the displays. "Am I the only sane one in this family?" Cori had said when I'd mentioned I'd enlisted him.

"He claims he's upped his meds."

"Don't come crying to me when he takes a hammer to your head."

"I have no choice, Cor. There's too much to take down myself. Better to get it done sooner than later."

My wife and the handyman had not come face to face since his unscheduled cameo in our bedroom. With an uncharacteristic formality that bemused Cori as much as it did me, I introduced her to Tusk and vice versa.

Tusk threw out his hand with boyish zeal. "Missus," he said, his voice cracking.

She observed the progress of his hand as one might note a mammoth cockroach scavenging the baseboard. She composed herself with an unspoken mantra, cinched the belt of her robe, and proceeded to load the dishwasher. "Hi. Sorry. Hands full," she said, her focus on the flatware basket.

Just as well. His fangs spumed the glandular equivalent of cappuccino onto his puff-pastry lips. And to think I figured the guy asexual, despite Cori's previous assertion. *"I was naked and he was still undressing me."* In any book I'd read or movie I'd seen, characters like Tusk were either comic relief, basking in the afterglow of the hero's love-life, or a slavering miscreant, eliciting pity, repugnance, and deserved annihilation, usually culminating in a fall from a bell tower.

Speaking of miscreants in high places, we were up on the roof dismantling Santa's sleigh when I got around to Sam Hotts. I worried our treatment of the missing Joe Di Iorio would come back to haunt us.

"That detective guy from up Albany way? Yeah. Sure. Nice fella. Big fan of mine."

"What's that supposed to mean?"

"My book. Ol' Sam loved it." Tusk unscrewed the red bulb that was Rudolf's nose.

"A fan? You loaned him a book? Like you actually read?" I hoped I didn't sound as condescending as I probably did.

"I read sometimes. But not the thick ones. How about that book of yours? How's that goin', Bobby-boy? Goodly or badly?"

"Badly."

"Maybe this ain't the place you should be doin' your writin'? You might get it goin' more goodly up where you come from. A comfy chair. You gotta have a comfy chair." Boarding Tusk's train of thought was a never-ending exercise in patience and comprehension.

"I'm here till the book is done," I said.

"Or you die tryin', huh?"

"Um ..." I braced for the hammer to my head, as Cori had predicted. "Die trying?"

"You're here till the book gets done. You said so. So if it never gets done, you die here."

"Ah, right, I get you."

"Whatever you're gonna do, ya gotta finish, yeah? Fireman. Repo man. Jailbird. Parolee. Roustabout. I done 'em all till I was done doing 'em all." His dialect was a moving target. He skipped from Cajun to Canadian to Brooklyn to Troll to Harvard Class of '39.

"How long did you serve?" I asked, fuzzy on the political correctness.

"Nope. Never did."

"But you said, your sister said ..."

"Oh, you mean the slammer? I thought you meant bartendin'." He brayed with hilarity, way too jolly for anyone on a rooftop on the cusp of winter. "Eight years, all told." His spittle froze in flight to my face.

"Wow. Rough."

"Yes, siree. Eight years, three crimes, one big-ass gazoonie. That's me."

Wrongly or rightly, I concluded this to be perfect segue to the booze and smoking lounge I'd stumbled across behind the furnace. "Is it you or April who's been partying in my cellar?"

I lifted Rudolf's forelegs as we prepared to lower the smallest of the nine to the ground. Tusk looped the rope around the reindeer's middle, as our attention turned to the yard below and Cori trotting toward April's salon.

She was in her jogging gear. Headband and ponytail. Red jacket and black pants, red stripe along each leg. Her sneakers, the ones with the purple trim. It was a late start for her, though understandable considering the night before. After my snooping about the yard, she'd surprised me with pancakes, scrambled eggs, and grilled tomatoes. I did not mention Françoise's discovery. After Tusk turned up, she'd gone back to bed.

She skipped onto the porch of the cottage, now salon, and only then did I see the kraft envelope at her elbow. Tusk whistled. "Pray she don't come out lookin' like my sis. Be the last hard-on you ever get, Bobby-boy."

I shrugged off the comment, shifted back to the cellar.

Tusk was quick to deny his guilt. "Wasn't me." Rudolf landed without incident.

"Cigarettes. Beer. Wine. No big deal. We're cool here, man. I was cleaning up and got curious, that's all. There were these photos too, of my mom and dad. And this bucket of paint—with my father's shirt."

"Wasn't me."

"April, then? Also, any chance you guys were renting out rooms in the house?" He steadied the ladder as I swung from the roof onto the rungs. Coiled extension cords and strings of lights hung from my shoulders. Lamb to the slaughter, I was. One shove would do the job.

"Wasn't nobody," he said.

"Had to be somebody."

"Not if it's nobody."

I upped the speed of my descent. "Eight years, huh? What were you in for?"

He gripped the top of the ladder, peered down. "People," he said. "I hurt them."

26

IT HAPPENS IN HILLSDALE!

We were hauling the last of the decorations up to the attic, when Tusk took a break on the landing outside the den. "Your writin' cave?" he said, noting the desk and computers.

"More like my prison," I said, the words ill-considered, but he let it ride.

"Maybe you'll show me that book of yours."

"Nothing to show."

"When there is."

"Don't hold your breath, man."

Job done, we rammed Tusk's ladder into his truck. "Couldn't have done this without you," I said. The decorations that had taken weeks to go up had come down in less than a day. "You saved my butt."

"Maybe you'll let me do it again."

I returned his staple gun with misgivings. The gesture should have triggered an apology for his meltdown weeks earlier, but the guy was too thick to pick up on it. At least he refused to take any money for helping me out. "April brought it on you, anyway, her danged nagging over that Christmas crap."

I'd no sooner hoisted his toolbox onto the tailgate than he shoved the book into my hands. "Look and see," he said. *The Stainless Steel Ride* by Raymond T. Culley.

"Yeah, I hear it's pretty good." I'd seen a review in *Entertainment Weekly*. Cori subscribed.

"It's mine," he said.

I didn't mean to patronize, but the fact he owned a book was startling. Hardcover, yet. "Like books, do you?"

"Mostly just mine. But the movie, now, that's a whole other cauldron of kettled fish."

"Yeah, they always screw up the movie versions. You ever see Stephen King's *Dark Tower*?"

"A bunch of lawyers, agents, and shit—them Hollywood fucks ain't gonna hoodwink me. 'Come back with figgers that make sense and I'll sign,' I says to Ginny. 'But don't bring me no doodly.'"

"Ginny?" I was missing something. "Not sure I follow."

"Ginny Childs, my agent?"

"Oh. Your agent. Sure. You bet."

"You been hearing me? My book. I'm talkin' about makin' my book a moving picture."

"Yeah. Your book. 'Moving picture.'"

"How many times I gotta tell you?" He wrested *The Stainless Steel Ride* from my hands and folded the dust jacket to isolate the photo on the flap. "See. My book."

Struck dumb, I was, in the biblical sense. I gawped, transfixed by the face scowling back at me. I ran my finger across the surface, probed for a telltale edge, evidence the jacket had been doctored. The black-and-white photo of author Raymond T. Culley was Tusk, a sneer more arrogant than belligerent, but unmistakably Tusk. "Holy fuck," I said, absent the exclamation.

"R.T. Culley. That's me. My alternative ego. The *T* don't really stand for nothin'. It's for folks who know me, for the Tusk."

I gawped some more. And gawping wasn't anything I'd done much of.

"In prison, real nice writer lady, Miss Anna, come down from Atlanta couple times a month to set with the boys who had an inclination for such doings. Says I'm a natural."

"But you don't even speak the language," I said, failing to self-censor. "And this ... this ..." I skimmed the pages, indicated words, sentences, paragraphs, punctu-fucking-ation. "I mean, the *EW* review was glowing. Best novel on prison life ever written or something. Funny. Frightening. Chester Himes on steroids. Shit like that. But? But? This is a prank, right? You're pulling my leg?"

"It's the God-sworn trute," he countered, offended I'd suggest otherwise.

"There. That's exactly what I mean. No offense, Tusk, but you can't speak for shit."

"Listen up, Bobby-boy, all you hear is my talkin' skin. And up on the roof and thereabouts, what you seen is my workin' skin. But they ain't nothing like my writin' skin. It's like them foreign folk—them Frenchies, like that See-line Dee-yon—how she can sing our American songs and sound just like us. Not like no Frenchie, none. It's how I write. Comes out my head and down to the paper, and I'm singin' like a Frenchie, Bobby-boy. And I got money to buy me a shiny new truck and April a curling iron and any other doodad she cottons to. Miss Anna said I was a flambant."

"There! You did it again. It's savant. Savant."

"Yep, that's me. Savant."

"Jesus, why waste your time with this handyman shit? Your book's a bestseller. They gotta want you to write another?"

"Can't write no more till I've lived some more. And livin' is what I've been doin' last spell or so. Gatherin' notes, makin' observations, learning about the folks I want to write about." He winked, right eye, left eye, both eyes. "Maybe I'm gonna write about you next."

"Un-fucking-believable."

"Unless you get round to writin' about yourself first."

"I'm nowhere, man. Nowhere. How do you fill the pages? How do you do it?"

He raised a hand to his ear and snapped his fingers. "I picture what I want to write in my head and whatever I see flows out my brain, down my arm, into my fingers, out my pen. All there is to it."

"You write with a pen?"

"Computer, typing machines, all that pounding bruises up the fingers, plugs up the pipes." He tapped my forehead. "Typing constipates the brain."

"I dunno, without a computer ... I use a pen, my hand cramps up."

"Then do it Miss Anna's way, the talkin' way. Didn't work for me, 'cause like you say, I talk like a mental defector, so I keep my mouth shut when I write. But a whip-smart college gradient like you, I betcha—" He stopped cold. Perhaps his brain had discovered whose body it was trapped in. I didn't bother to fill the dead air, spellbound as I was by the saliva bubble taking shape between his lips. His eyes crossed as he too observed its progress, his writing seminar resuming only after the bubble popped.

"Yeah, so, where was I? Oh, yeah ... So you start talkin' out loud, like I'm doin' now. You talk about what you see and what you hear inside your head. Then you write down the words you talked out loud and keep goin' till you're done. Nothin' to it."

"This Miss Anna, she a heavyset woman, big glasses, dark hair—a shock of white out front?"

"Skunk-head we call her. She works wonders for us boys in the clink."

"Maybe I should rob a bank."

"There's an idea, Bobby-boy, but I dunno ..." Tusk stroked his chin, weighed my suggestion. "It's rough on the inside. And that missus of yours, you don't leave no woman like her on her own."

"Nope, guess you don't." Pointless to mention I'd been joking.

He handed back the book, but kept a grip. "Anyhow, it's twenty bucks. I'm giving you the friends 'n family cost."

Now it was my turn to wonder if he might be joking. He wasn't.

I dug into my pocket for a twenty and saw Cori emerge onto the small porch of the cottage. She held the screen door ajar as April stretched to hug her from the step above. They chatted, tittered. The whole thing had the look of a conspiracy.

Cori hopped off the porch. She handed off the envelope as she passed me by, her smile on loan from the smart-ass cat who ate the canary. "The deed is done," she said. "She's out first of March."

"That easy?"

"So easy, in fact, you could have done it." I watched her go, from canter to lope to you can't catch me.

April padded onto the porch, clutched the railing as if she might snap it. She was watching Cori too. What's that they say ... *if looks could kill?*

27

IDEALLY SITUATED FOR YOUR WEEKEND GETAWAYS
(OR THE JOURNAL IN MY HEAD)

WEDNESDAY

A week before Christmas, Cori announces she's flying to New York for the coming weekend. She'll be meeting up with an old friend. "Patty Daniels. I've mentioned her. From Montreal? McGill?"

"I don't think so."

"You're a man. You hear only every second word, anyway."

Cori seldom talked about old friends. I think it was to spare my feelings. I did not have old friends, Wade a case in point. But Cori, she could be the reigning queen of Facebook, Twitter, and Instagram had she been interested. Nope. Not a single account. "Think about it," she once said. "Those best served by social media are the antisocial."

I'm bummed she doesn't want me tagging along. We haven't been apart since the day we were married.

"I haven't seen Patty in ages. Trust me, you'd be bored to death."

"Not if she's anything like you."

"Are you leering? What are you, like seventy?"

"I was being charming."

"By whose definition?"

"Not yours, I guess."

"Anyway, Patty and me, we're planning on finishing up our Christmas shopping. And, if you don't mind, I'd like to surprise you this time around."

I back off. I've been idling in an abstract reality, my obsession with the Christmas spectacular at 18 Appleton disconnected from the holiday it was alleged to trumpet. I've also been looking over my shoulder, hoping to get the jump on whatever would be coming at us next. Now I need to think about ribbons, bows, and a gift Cori will never see coming.

THURSDAY

I offer to drive her to the small airport in Kenner and pick her up on the return. "Better to park and fly," she says. "This time of year, the weather, you never know."

"Where will you be staying?"

"Oh, some hotel Patty booked." Her flippancy with the details, it could have been my mom talking: *"Oh, somewhere in Europe, sweetheart."*

FRIDAY

She tries to slip out without waking me. Except I've been up all night.

I stow her suitcase in the trunk of the BMW. I'd thought she'd opt for a carry-on; it's only a weekend, how much clothes does she need? "You are coming back, right?" I say.

"You're joking, I hope."

"Maybe."

"Well, then, I guess you'll just have to wait till Sunday night to find out."

We hug. We kiss. She starts to leave, then comes back for another of each.

She waves from the car and is on her way.

I haven't felt at loose ends like this since I was nine, when the stray collie I'd harbored for the summer was claimed by its owner and dragged into a van.

The sun has yet to rise. I can go back to bed or give the writing another shot. I have lived alone most of my adult life. I am expert in the science of solitude. Or used to be before Cori.

I toast up a couple of waffles and put on enough coffee to see me through till lunch. Next I know, I am face down on folded arms at the kitchen table, hyperventilating my way out of a fifty-fathom nap without any recollection of slipping under.

The coffee maker beeps.

Daylight seeps through the slats of the window.

I yawn, stretch my neck, turn my head. Blink. Squint. *Holy, Christ!* I don't know who or what, but it's standing in the hallway, checking me out from the in-between, where light submits to shadow.

The wind whooshes out my mouth, my nose, my ears, my eyes. I can hear it, goddamn it. And a queasiness surges into my gullet and into my tailbone.

He's poker thin and as gray as smoke, with a jack-o'-lantern grin of rusted teeth and wasted gums, his lips a washer-fluid blue. He's what you expect to find puked onto the New Jersey coast in a mess of hospital waste, except his shirt is vanilla white and his pants a crisp blueberry gray, cinched to the ribcage. He's Death on a starvation diet and he's pleased as frigging punch to see me. *Jesus!* He twitches his nose. The fucker twitches his huge hairy nose, flutters veined lids, his eyeballs set to pop like bubble wrap. He's got a rubber-band on his left wrist and he's snapping it with his right. The guy's got urges.

I'm on the knife block in a flash, grappling for the longest, sharpest, deadliest. I whip about to face the scuzz, and there is no one to see.

Not a whisper.

Not a creak.

I could call the cops, but conclude my death at the hands of an unknown assailant the more palatable option.

I lug myself to where he was, sidle into the hall, knife out front. The fear rushes out of me. Shame rushes in. Cori gone two hours, and my brain has jumped the shark. The evidence does not lie. My intruder might as well have been the goddamn grandfather clock. *Does Dr. Cutcheon have a hotline?*

I search the upstairs, if only to save face with myself. At Cori's bedside, I supplement the carving knife with Dobsie's gun. And off we go, Paranoia and me, hunting room by room, closet by closet, knowing full well my quarry is an illusion, leakage from a ruptured dream.

At the cellar door, I click off the safety, descend into the stillness.

A suitcase juts from the jumble. Hard shell, olive green, and dislodged from where it had been. Or maybe it hasn't moved at all. I can count on one hand the times I've been down. I nudge it back into place. Symmetry is comforting.

The party zone behind the furnace yields a different story. The photos of Mom, Dad, and me are gone. The chairs have been stacked one atop the other and moved against the wall. It might have been Cori, but my bet is Tusk. I only wish he would have carted out the empties too. He should have warned me he'd be dropping in. It was all Cori needed, Tusk skulking uninvited.

My father's shirt is gone. The bucket too.

I give the place a final once-over, pause to inspect a carton with my name on the side, the handwriting my mother's. Keepsakes. Papers and drawings. Seems I drew a lot of dragons and fighter jets. There's school stuff too. Like the infamous *Interview with Myself* that got me suspended for a week and prompted Mom to send me to Dr. Cutcheon. My teacher had seen it as a threat. The principal agreed. (That's my Chapter 1, should you care to read it again.)

I write. Or think about trying to write.

I surf the Net. News sites. *Rolling Stone.* See what's new on iTunes. I google Cori.

How's it possible I've never googled her?

McGill Faculty of Dentistry. *Zip!*

American Dental Association. *Zip!*

City of Eden Prairie, Minnesota. *Zip!*

Corinne Meredith Widdoes generates two matches: oralcorraldental.com and scoremydentist.com, where she rates ****½ out of *****. Rave reviews too:

"Gentle touch."

"Painless."

"Professional."

"Can't wait for my next check-up."

"Eye candy is good for the teeth."

One negative:

"I would not send my husband to her in a million years."

I try variations. Cori Widdoes. Corinne Widdoes. Meredith Widdoes. I search again. LinkedIn, Facebook, though I know she avoids them all. I mess with her name. Cori Widows. Corinne Widows. Corky Windows. (Yeah, I'm a little punch drunk.)

Nothing.

Weird.

Have I married my father? Does my wife's life story begin on the day she joined the staff of Oral Corral Dental in Ballston Spa? What do I really know about her beyond what she has told me?

I call Tusk, tell him I need his house key. He asks why. I lie. "Because we've got friends coming from out of town."

"You got your nerve," he says. "What you done to my sister."

"You can drop it in the mail slot or I can come get it. Whichever's easier."

"She's gripin', like it's my doin'. I says to her it's a good thing. She can get herself a fancy new saloon. Or open up that horny-pathy hospital she's always blabbin' about."

"Homeopathy?"

"Homey-pathy, horny-pathy, who gives a shit? It's not like I don't got the bucks. Got me an eye on that strip mall over by Scott Road. Movie deal's mostly done too, huh? Agent's talkin' about some indie nobody to direct. Me, I'm holdin' out for Score-seas or Eastwood."

"Look, you can't keep letting yourself in whenever you feel like it. Cori, I mean, you can understand, it's not right. It stops now, okay?"

"What you done to my sister, after all the help I give you on your book."

"Just bring me the damn key."

I call Hillsdale's only locksmith, leave a message. "I need a lock changed. Sooner the better."

I text Cori:

WHAT ARE YOU
DOING AT THE
MOMENT?
WRUDATM XOXO

She does not text back.

I pick up *The Stainless Steel Ride*. Haven't touched it since Tusk sold it to me. A gold seal on the cover trumpets *National Book Award Finalist*.

The dedication is as cryptic as the author:

For Anna, the Ducks, and the Ding Wing

I turn to the photo of Raymond T. Culley. I don't get it.
I read the opening sentence:

All eulogies are fiction.

I'll never get it.

I crave a roast turkey sandwich on caraway rye. Dijon. Dills. Honey barbecue chips. A Cherry Coke. There's that new deli on Main. *New York Style.* The fresh air will clear my head.

Half a block ahead, Wade Griffiths stands by a white Mercury Marquis, his foot on the bumper. He's writing a ticket. He has a bandage on his nose.

I check to see if Cori has texted. *What's going on with her?*

Common sense tells me to cross the street. But allowing Wade any victory, however inconsequential, is more than I can concede. Worse, I slow my pace as I approach. Wade doesn't disappoint. "I hear the bitch ... er ... wife's out of town," he says. His eyes dart in rotation, from me to the license plate to the ticket in progress. "You and the babe going through a rough patch, are you? She beat you up same way she did me?"

This will not end well. For me, anyhow. I brace to take him on as my focus drifts beyond his right shoulder to the opposite side of Main. Someone is waving to me from behind a glass door. Wade's trash talk recedes to filler.

I cannot look away. The grandfather clock has followed me. He's changed to a suit that'd do a corpse proud, a triangle of hanky in breast pocket. He's got a pencil-thin mustache and oily black hair that's slicked front to back. The white of his scalp bleeds through in stripes. I know him. The shop is the giveaway. Basil's Blooms. The florist. And the figure is Basil Blooms himself. Or Bloomfield, anyhow. He'd come by for the Christmas lights. He'd made a big deal of welcoming me to town. Today he salutes me, and with a theatrical flourish, urges me to move along. *Exit stage right.* I nod my gratitude. He nods forbearance. A truck rumbles past. Clouds chase the sun. Basil vanishes within the motley reflections.

Wade yells after me. "Where you going? Hey, I'm talking to you. I'm talking to you, Dickens. Get your fucking ass back here."

SATURDAY

April Bright shambles out of Budgie's as Al Messner and I shamble in for an early breakfast.

Last I saw April was when Cori gave notice to vacate the cottage. Most days, I avoid her. She can't go two seconds without filling me in on her latest call with my mother. *"Only last evening she was asking after you and your precious wife. Rest assured, I told her you and your little lady were managing just fine. Oh, but I am sure she knew. Just making chit-chat, she was. You know your mother. What a hoot!"*

When I was working on the Christmas display, she turned up daily, patient zero in an outbreak of nitpicking. *"Don't forget Frosty's pipe. The Wise Men will sing, won't they? I loved them best. The halos! Oh, the halos!"*

On the night we threw the switch, April was first on the scene, toting her so-called Gifts of the Magi. Her world-famous sugar cookies for me: *"Practically two full cups of sprinkles per batch."* And a gift card for Cori: *"Three spa or beauty treatments of your choice up to a $105 value."* Noting the 90-day expiry date, Cori had murmured a discreet, "Thank God."

This day, I hold Budgie's door for April, greet her with a politician's hello, sincere, affable. She growls through a clumsy sidestep and exits onto Main.

"Miserable little hobbit," Al snipes, as we watch April drag herself past the restaurant window.

"She's pissed at me and Cor. We asked her to move out." I give him the details over smoked ham, mushroom omelet, home fries, and Texas toast.

"Well, you can't blame her entirely," Al says. "On the other hand, she must realize she's had it pretty good all these years. Rent free, c'mon! And Cori offered to give her free dental care to boot? Marie and I should be so lucky."

"Part of the deal," I said.

"It is your property, after all. You have every right to use it how you see fit. Any lawyer would agree."

"That's why Cor had a lawyer draw up the papers to vacate." I scrape the last of the blueberry preserves from the ramekin onto a wedge of toast. It's in the jams and jellies that Budgie's edges out the competition. "Funny thing is, April was fine with it at the time."

"She needs to suck it up. Free dental care, c'mon! What Marie and I wouldn't give for that. Nope, no excuse for her behavior, Rob. Let's hope that nut-job brother of hers doesn't take a hammer upside your head. Would you believe that cretin actually wrote a book?"

"Jesus, Al!" How many more well-wishers would warn me about Tusk, his hammer, and my head?

"You own a gun?"

"No."

"I'm not telling you what to do, Rob, but if you were smart ... Vote for the Dems, sure, but you got to think like you're GOP. That kid dying on your lawn, something's in the air. Best be prepared. But, oh man! Free dental care. Now that's really something. Wow."

I call the locksmith, again, leave another message.

I should let it lie. I owe April nothing. It isn't like I haven't severed most ties to my idyllic childhood. I'd long stopped caring what others thought of me. It is a war I cannot win. Except in April's case. I am hoping for a truce. For old times' sake.

April glares through cloudy lenses as I enter the salon. "I got nothing to say to you," she says, and waltzes an industrial-strength hair dryer across the checkered linoleum. She brakes behind the only customer in the shop. She lowers the chrome dome over a silver-blue head of pink curlers and kicks the engine into hyper-drive.

She drops a magazine onto the woman's lap. A Kendall Jenner cover.

"I'm sorry," I say. "I should have said something sooner. But you know how it is. Cori explained to you."

"A poor woman works tooth and nail to earn a respectable living, and you yuppies come along all la-di-dah and throw me onto the street."

"Cori needs a place to work. It's not personal, April."

"Not personal? Not personal?" She purges the roof of her mouth with her tongue. "Your wife and mother are one and the same. Selfish. Two-faced."

I channel Job—the patient guy from the Bible: "C'mon, my mom's been more than fair with you. So has Cori. We're trying to do the right thing here. Tusk tells me you want to open a homeopathy hospital. Getting out of here will be good for you. New business. Fresh start."

"On my terms, not yours. You think I don't know what your mother does? What she's been up to. How she makes her money. Too good for the rest of us? Don't make me laugh. No cottage, no deal. I'll show you. I'll show everybody."

The demon hairdresser of Appleton Street lifts her bum leg a quarter turn and shuffles to the cabinet adjacent to the sink. She rifles a drawer and bustles back in an Oscar-caliber portrayal of anguish. She cuffs my wrist, swats a postcard onto my palm. "Quite a woman, your mother. Murders her folks and uses their memories to peddle perversion."

"That's a lie and you know it. It was an accident." I parrot the half-truth as though it were the whole.

"The audacity. To claim her livelihood in Christmas knick-knacks. To defile the Lord's birthday. Ha, how do you like them melons, Bobby?"

I give the postcard short shrift. I have seen my mother in her working gear only once before: the night the cops came for my father. "But it's me you're dealing with now. I am not my mother," I say, a departure from *I am not my father*.

April shushes me, draws the line between us with a hangman's finger. She snatches back the card and launches a show-and-tell so venomous, I cease to breathe for fear of airborne toxins. "This isn't a swimsuit. Your mother isn't dressed for trick-or-treating. My goodness, are you stupid or dumb? Open your eyes. Look. See. This is what your mother is."

I give up. No role more thankless than peacemaker. Gloves off: "Fuck you, April. Fuck you and your bullshit. You've had it good. Way too good. You think I don't know about you and your little scam—the Airbnb or whatever you were running out of my house. Hell, be grateful I don't sic a lawyer on you."

I've touched a nerve, all right. She hobbles up to me on her one good leg. "You can't prove a fucking thing."

"I guessed right then."

I go for the door. April dips beneath my arm, beats me to the lever. Her gimpy leg pivots left, right, and back again as she unloads the postcard at my face. And, hell, I see the curveball coming with the subtlety of a Richter 8.6 in the San Fernando. Her teeth. Her bridgework. Her lips, puffed and puckered, a grotesquerie of mutated duckbill. She mashes her mouth onto mine, a slushy smack that's leech as much as lip. She tastes like spearmint, if spearmint were kimchi.

"What the—Christ!" I lift her from me, spit the memory while it's fresh, and plunk her ass down on the nearest table, shampoos and conditioners tumbling, rolling. I push up against her legs, grip her shoulders, press down to contain her.

She has the persnickety air of accomplishment about her, as if she'd storyboarded the sequence in advance. Her oily grin jacks her cheeks up past her eyebrows. She licks her lips. "I've always wondered what Evil tastes like."

"Any more shit out of you, and I promise you'll also know what Hell tastes like. I had a great teacher. I'm guessing you remember him. I'm guessing you remember what he did."

"You're threatening me."

"Not at all. You see, like my dad, I don't make threats. Cori gave you notice. Make sure you're out." I snatch back the postcard. "Or else."

"I'll tell Tusk."

"What was his role—bellhop?"

"I'll tell the police you me-tooed me."

"Go ahead."

"I'll tell your mother."

"Oh, no. What's she gonna do, spank me?"

I dial K.K. Pizza. I order an everything with extra mushrooms.

"We're not allowed to deliver to 18 Appleton."

"What?"

"Boss's orders."

"But you always deliver. We're the best damn customers you ever had."

"Sorry." The kid hangs up.

I redial. "Let me speak to the boss."

"Manny? You wanna talk to 18 Appleton?"

Manny hurls himself onto the line. "No deliveries. No pizza. No nothing."

"What? We're your best cust—"

"I could fuck up your pizza. Bleach. Mr. Clean. Dog shit. But I am a man and not an animal like your father."

Not again.

"My name is Manfred Keegle. Mean anything to you?"

Oh, crap. Another Bobby Blessing moment. I never see the piano falling until I'm under it.

"Kyle Keegle was my father. Your father murdered him. In cold blood. I was nine years old. Still want your fucking pizza, eighteen-fucking-Appleton?"

"I didn't realize." *Number twenty-four. Easton, Pennsylvania.*

"Do you know who found his body? Me. Your father beat his brains in with a milk bottle. Ripped open his throat. A fucking milk bottle."

"Hopalong Cassidy," I say, but, unlike his dad, he's not into collectibles. I could ask why he moved to a town where the man who killed his father once lived. Then again, I'd been dense enough to do the same.

"I was nine years old, you goddamn cocksucking shitbag."

I do not say what I am thinking: *And I was eleven. Can't you see, we're both victims?*

I open a can of ravioli, no-name brand. I eat it cold. I hope to get lucky, be dead of *E. coli* by morning.

I fall asleep at eleven, wake at midnight. April Bright and Manny Keegle are taking potshots at my brain. I chase them out by counting down the Brittle Butcher's victims. By nineteen (Joe Austin, Oneida, New York, belt and buckle), it's Cori I'm thinking of, where she is and what she's doing.

I am a White Stripes' song. *I Just Don't Know What To Do With Myself.*

I text Cori: U AWAKE

I resume my count in reverse. Eighteen. Walter Bowman, Kingfield, Maine. Rendered unconscious with a chunk of ice, stripped naked, and hung till dead from the rim of a basketball net in his neighbor's driveway.

SUNDAY

The Violet Blonde gift set at Nordstrom's is a no-brainer. Next up, Victoria's Secret. There's this lacy baby-doll thing Cori would look great in, but I've never bought lingerie and I'm iffy on the measurements. I see a guy in the same fix as me. He's giving an approximation with his hands. I will not be this guy. I point to what the breathy salesgirl calls a "devilishly amorous kimono." I select mauve in small, and move on to lululemon.

I go through the racks, unable to recall all that Cori owns or what she needs. The salesgirl suggests a gift card and escorts me to the cash. It's a cop-out, but it's late in the day and Cori will be home before I know it.

"How are your ghosts?" the cashier asks me. Her smile is familiar, mischief in her pale green eyes. It's Willa ... Willow, the rollerblade/guitar girl. She's not so tall without her skates. Or without shorty whatshisname beside her. Justin. Jumpy Justin.

"You work here?" I say.

Her smile defaults to caustic. "Duh?"

I laugh it off, mutter some baloney about a lack of sleep.

She punches up the total. I pull my wallet from my jacket pocket and out sails the postcard of her majesty, my mother. *Thanks, April. Fuck!*

Willow collects the card from the counter. "Oh. My. God." She knows what she's looking at. "Sexy scary."

A second cashier takes a peek and chirps, "Ick! Kinky sick! Where'd it come from, Willa?" Willow nods to me. They labor to suppress their giggles.

"It's not what you think," I say, which is pretty much what a creepy old dude would say.

"Right." Willow returns the postcard.

I keep my head down, pay with VISA.

"I hope your wife enjoys it, Bobby," Willow says. "She's very pretty."

"She's not my wife."

"Oh, your mother then?" she laughs. As if.

"Yeah. My mother," I laugh. As if.

The girls allow me a brief head start before doubling over in shared hysterics.

I'm out the door and in the driveway before Cori kills the ignition. A thin mist camouflages the drizzle.

"Miss me much?" she says.

"Oh? You were away?"

"Very funny."

"Would've been nice if you'd answered my texts."

"It was a girls-only weekend," she says, as if this explains it. She makes an umbrella of a *Runner's World* magazine and scurries for the shelter of the porch.

I haul her suitcase from the trunk. "Where's the rest? Thought you went shopping."

"Your gifts are taken care of."

It's only when we step inside I notice her hair. "You don't like it?" she says.

She's gone from butter blonde to sorta-red/sorta-blonde.

"I needed a change. It's closer to my natural color. What about the cut?" It's short and businesslike.

"You can run for Congress."

"Makeovers keep a marriage fresh. They allow you to cheat on me without cheating on me."

"Happy to oblige," I tell her.

She cups her hand firmly, and too briefly, at my crotch. "Unfortunately, for you, I have other things to take care of first."

I carry the suitcase up to our bedroom. She asks about my weekend, how the writing went. I bullshit how the solitude was a godsend. (I might not have progressed as a writer, but my lying skills are razor sharp.) "Another twenty pages."

"The book helped then?" she says. I fumble for a plausible answer. "The one I bought for you—*Bestselleritis!*"

"Lots of good stuff in there, Cor. And Tusk, he's been helping too."

"I will never understand how that man wrote a book. What's it called, *The Steel Ride*? I saw people on the plane with it."

"*Stainless Steel.* You should read it. It's good."

Since the move to Hillsdale, I have become proficient at failing to live up to her expectations. Although she has not complained, I sense there is a limit to how much more she might take. She will inevitably come to see I am her excess baggage. She can do better.

Speaking of baggage, I lift her suitcase onto our bed, while she goes to freshen up. She shouts to me from the bathroom. "Don't open it. You'll ruin the surprise."

There are no luggage tags. I want to ask why, but worry how I'll sound. Suspicious. Accusatory. I'm circling each, that's for sure.

Again, she calls through the door: "I'm desperate for a run. You up for it?"

"Now?"

"Tomorrow morning. It'll do you good. Might jog your brain."

I lie in bed, attempt to think like a real writer. *A Bestselleritis! kind of writer!* I reconstruct each thought, dredge up words I didn't know I knew.

Outside, a guileless thaw succumbs and a frigid, northerly wind descends upon Hillsdale. Ice writhes upon the roof. The rafters creak empathic torment. A full moon bleeds cadaveric shadows, racing as rats before glacial floodwaters across the floors, the walls, the bed.

Ugh. That's not me, not my voice. Not any human's voice.

Cori sleeps unawares, lovely, lacy, and seraphic, while I wait for the sky to fall.

Even if I could write, I wouldn't write like this. God, no!

18 Appleton is the house I grew up in, the house I have returned to with a stranger I call my wife, the house with the sprawling green porch my prudent father painted red. Across the lawn, the cottage. A cobbled path to roadside, where a heather-painted wooden sign once swung.

BLESSINGS CHRISTMAS COTTAGE
ORNAMENTS, GIFTS & BRIC-À-BRAC
HEATHER BLYTHE-BLESSING, PROP.

Long ago, on stormy nights, when phantom terrors surfed the winter winds, I would listen to the rasping of the sign upon its hinges, and imagine this to be the Spirit of Christmas, reassurance amid the tumult.

Listening to my brain makes me want to throw up. Some of me doesn't feel like the rest of me.

Cori awakens with a start, a cry trespassing on her dreams. The cry is mine.

"What's the matter, Rob? You sick?"

"No."

"You frightened me. What were you saying?"

"I don't know."

"Were you sleeping?"

"I'm not sure."

"It sounded like you said, 'Get the fuck out of my house.' Who were you talking to?"

"I don't know."

"Then what are you doing?"

"Lying here, thinking how hard it is to write vivid description when it's not about ice cream."

"Count sheep. Please. It's quieter."

I go down to the den, wake my computer, and it's there on my desk, adjacent to the router. As if it had never left. As if I had conjured it. *Bestselleritis!: How to Catch It!*

Can't be. Is Cori aware I'd given it to Willow? Did she buy me a replacement in New York? I flip to the flyleaf. She's written the same inscription as before. Word for word.

> *To Rob, my love, with love*
> *May you find freedom in your words*
> *and peace within your prose*
> *Forever yours, Cori*

No sense pretending. It's the same damn book, of course. Cori's Post-Its in place. And it's been well read, the pages thumbed, the jacket smeared with sauce. A fingerprint on Anna Carmen Hope's cheek. Ketchup or jelly. Streaky. Sticky. The culprit had tried to wipe it clean.

The book falls open to a *Twilight* bookmark and page 93.

I give it a read. It's not half-bad. Could even be helpful. But the next two pages are stuck together. More ketchup. And I tell myself this has got to be Willow's idea of a joke. Something like: *"Hey, Justin! Let's spook out the old creep. We'll give him his ghosts, all right."*

Could be the girl knows Tusk. Could be he let her in. Or delivered it on her behalf.

Sick sense of humor. I give Willow credit. She has succeeded. I am creeped out.

Ketchup. For sure.

I toss the book into a drawer. Head back up to bed.

The weekend sucked. Monday will be better. Cori is home. Come morning, we'll go for a jog, leave yesterday behind.

Everything will be okay.

PART THREE

WHAT WE MEAN WHEN WE TALK ABOUT THE HOLIDAYS

28
SUSPECT

"Too damn hard on the knees," I called to Cori, as we skirted the no-vacancy side of Parchment Hill Cemetery and loped through the open gates into the landscaped heart of Lazy Green.

The cold didn't nip, it ripped, and the sky hung so damn low I half-expected it to break away in slabs of gray. A white Christmas was promised, three days to go, but for now the pavement underfoot was bare and brutal. Downhill was uphill. Uphill was Everest.

My lungs were running on empty, my legs no better than dopey, when we came upon the cop cars: A Hillsdale black-and-white, State Police black-and-yellows, and backups from neighboring towns. Dodge Chargers. A Ford Expedition. Ambulances too. More flashing lights than a UFO flyby.

Were I anyone but the sorry product of my nominal upbringing, this would have been the moment I woke up, Cori spooning warm behind me. But as you know by now, where I am is rarely where I want to be.

The main attraction was a whitewashed Colonial from the early 80s, when Lazy Green was dubbed The New Development. Fifty years on, the cachet still applied. Hillsdale never did garner much momentum when it came to change.

The blood wasn't obvious. Unless you've got it in your blood. I can spot red on red, a pinprick from a hundred stories.

Upper floor. Second window on left. The shades hung bent and broken, eyelids paralyzed mid-wink. Like the house itself had stroked out from the trauma.

There were ten clean dabs where the fingers touched down, when survival remained a possibility. Broader, darker streaks below, the heels of the hands when the final blows came. And hapless dots and dashes down to the sill. Acceptance. Resignation. Lights out.

Fear ranged the backfield. Paranoia took the hand-off.

A cop came tripping out of the house, braced himself against the railing, and puked onto a chokeberry bush. Once. Twice. He glanced up, flustered by the crowd, and parlayed the vomit trifecta. He was State Police. Griffiths and Goldwater were nowhere to be seen.

Dread burrowed in. What made me think I could come back to this town? I'd have been better off to have dug my own grave and jumped in. I was clueless as to *the who*, but damn well knew *the how* and *the what* would lead back to me.

I'm a natural born suspect. Like I've said, bad stuff finds me.

"Don't stop." I trod pavement as Cori waded into the mourning zone. "Keep moving," I said, as we cruised among the dazed and devastated.

They gathered in clusters, sleep-deprived mothers and fathers, daughters and sons. Fuzzy slippers and bathrobes, jackets thrown over pajamas and nighties, shoulders hunched against the chill. Had these people half a brain among them, they would've ducked inside for warmer wear or, smarter yet, stayed clear away. But I knew from experience, few are willing to miss the moment that makes the story. Ghouls and fools, my mother called them.

Two cops extended the police line, yellow tape strung between hydrant, trees, fence, and lamppost. A pickup coasted up the street. A city worker pitched orange traffic cones along the curb to keep bystanders at bay.

There was crying too. Sobbing. Weeping. Hankies glued to frostbitten fists, sorrow rife on bad-news breath. *Inhale at your own risk.* It was all too restrained, as if the horror could be stashed away for later enjoyment, teardrops and tokes. Even the cops had fallen prey to Lazy Green propriety, reduced to Sunday-service whispers. That was the neighborhood for you. Hillsdale's finest.

Cori and I pieced the crime together as best we could, a grisly scenario assembled from snatches of conversation, speculation confirmed by hearsay.

A family of four. Morrow. Or Toro. Or Sorrow, maybe. The entire family, anyhow. Slaughtered. Mom, dad, boy, girl. Upstairs. Downstairs. Carnage. Everywhere.

"There's nothing more to see," I said, but Cori would not be moved. Not now. Not when the ritual upstaging had begun. No tragedy is complete without it. Sure, I know, the intent is to honor the victims. Still, it has always struck me as stealing thunder from the dead.

A thirty-something mom with a second-wife strut, underdressed in black velour bathrobe and open-toed slippers, led the procession. She broke from the crowd, bore down on the house, a spray of red carnations ablaze in hand.

From his perch on the porch, Trooper Upchuck observed the woman's approach. His Dasani bottle on the railing, his dry-heaves in abeyance, the cop was jonesing for redemption. You could see his brain go full-on Cumberbatch as the woman ducked beneath the police tape and arranged her offering at the base of the white picket fence. *Like how'd she come up with flowers on such short notice?* Prime suspect. Case closed.

A heartbeat behind, a kid pranced, Hello Kitty pajamas billowing from beneath navy pea jacket. She ditched her teddy alongside the flowers and, next you know, Lazy Greeners were rushing helter-skelter, crisscrossing yards and streets, frantic to cobble together their own manifestations of grief.

"We'll stop by the florist later," Cori said. I nodded in sober agreement. My cynicism never did hold sway with her. She said it was my third-least endearing trait, after pigheadedness and a secrecy that bordered on the pathological.

The cop cars backed out. The ambulances backed in. "C'mon, Cor." But my dear sweet wife's attention had swung to the makeshift memorial.

Some teenage chubster was taking his star turn, headlong into a rip-roaring breakdown.

His mom moved to comfort him. His dad struggled to contain him. The kid wrenched free, threw off his coat and his parents, and hit the ground howling, laying further waste to this bitch-slap of a morning.

Hell. I knew him.

His eyes were red and puffy, his mouth contorted to this side of wonky, but hell, *I knew the boy.*

I tugged at Cori's sleeve. "Now. Please. Let's go."

Justin. Oh, goddamn hell. Jumpy Justin.

I searched the crowd for long, curly, and auburn. A girl with a guitar. Desperate now to seek her out, to counter thoughts I did not want to think.

And there they were, Justin and his folks, shuffling toward us, the boy resisting, as if bungeed to the scene of the crime. *This was no place for him. Why weren't they taking the poor kid home?* "Why aren't they taking the poor kid home?"

"What?" Cori said.

And there they were, settling in to the right of us, Justin's shrieking de-escalating to blubbering, his tears a blotch upon his father's parka. "Why, Daddy? Why her? Poor Willa. Who'd do this, Daddy, who?"

I looked to distance myself, find an out. The crowd hemmed me in.

That's when Justin lifted his head.

That's when his face filled with the fear of me.

29
FANTASIES

I squeezed Cori's arm. "Can't stay," I said, and took off before she could protest. They were wheeling the first of the four bodies from the house. There wasn't much to it. A kid.

I cut through the crowd and onto the street, dodged the flower girls, teddy bear wranglers, and prayer circles.

I ran past the memorial. It'd be a mountain in no time.

I did not look back, knowing I would remain in Justin's sights long after I was out of his sight. I could hear the cock of the hammer, the click of the trigger he so badly wanted to pull.

Cori caught up a couple of blocks on. "I'm sorry," she said. "I should have realized."

I could not speak. I picked up the pace, rounded the corner onto Skelton, and careened through the gates of Lazy Green, going as fast as I could to get as far away as I could. For once, Cori struggled to keep up with me.

"I've got a bad feeling," I said. *Duh.*

"It'd be cause for concern if you didn't," she said.

I plopped onto the living room sofa and Cori into the overstuffed leather armchair my father had favored for reading. She was in my head, as usual. "You think it's going to come back to you, don't you? I saw that boy looking at you, how you tried to avoid him."

I asked if she remembered the teens who'd bladed by around Halloween. Cori kicked off her sneakers. "They told you a serial killer used to live here," she said. She propped her feet on the coffee table, crossed them at the ankles.

"Well, the girl—"

"She played the guitar for you—that insane song about your dad."

"Her name was Willow. That house up on the Green. It's her, Cor. Her family."

"My God, Rob, I feel ill."

"Me too."

"But this has nothing to do with you."

"It's going to. The cops will add it up."

"Add what up?"

"The old man you got to drive the car from Saratoga ..."

"Mr. Di Iorio. Joe."

"He's still missing. And the kid with the chainsaw. You know he died, right?"

"And you're connected to all of them. Is that what you're saying?"

"Who I am, who my father is ... Anybody else, it'd be a series of bad coincidences."

"But that's all it is."

"It's bigger, Cor. I can feel it. Ever since we came here ... I'm being watched. I'm being set up."

"By who? The ghosts?" She was humoring me, using the voice wives use when they suspect their husbands are having a breakdown.

"Whatever it is," I said, "it's closing in. When you were away, there was stuff I didn't tell you."

"I knew something had happened, how you were acting."

"April went ape-shit on me."

"Really? Why?"

"Jeez, why do you think?"

"But she was fine with it."

"Not so much. I tried to smooth things over with her, but she—"

"She told me she'd wanted to relocate for ages, that she'd outgrown the space. Her brother even had some spot picked out for her."

"Everybody's fine until they have the chance to think, till others throw in their two cents. I'm telling you, she was crazy. It was like she wanted to kill us. And my mother too."

"Your mother?" Cori took her feet off the table, not quite sure how to assemble the pieces I was putting to her.

"Remember how we thought she might have been renting out rooms in here?"

"Like a bed and breakfast ..."

"Not sure about the breakfast, but she pretty much confessed to the bed part."

"So our coming here cut into one business and now, with the cottage, the other."

"Yup. And then Willow ..."

"The rollerblade girl."

"I saw her Sunday. Up at the mall. I finally got around to Christmas shopping and, well, she was the cashier."

"Please don't tell me you came on to her, Rob?"

"Of course not. But there was something."

"I'm listening."

"I should've told you."

I went to the vestibule and retrieved the postcard from my jacket pocket. I handed it to Cori, head down, as if presenting a note from teacher. "This is why the cops will be coming for me."

"Porn? Rather soft core, wouldn't you say?"

"When I went to pay, it slipped out of my pocket and into Willow's hands. This other girl, working with her, saw it too. It wouldn't matter much, except now ... with the murders ... I mean, if Justin makes me into some sort of creep and the police start piecing shit together ..."

"But why, may I ask, were you walking around with porn in your pocket?"

"It's not porn, Cor. It's my mother."

She stared at the card, then at me, then the card, configuring the shape and size of her incredulity. "This is Heather? I knew you hadn't told me everything about her, but I never imagined ..."

"April was kind enough to give it to me."

"I'll bet she was." As much as she tried, Cori couldn't help smiling. "Sure she's not just dressed for Halloween? I mean, this is classic cheesecake. I've seen ten-year-old girls dress up like hookers. Wait! You're not telling me your mom was a hook—"

"She's a dominatrix."

"Holy shit. You have got to be kidding."

"I wish I were."

"A woman's gotta do what a woman's gotta do, I suppose."

"The Christmas shit wasn't her main source of income. Mom was always taking photos in the back of the cottage. Everyone assumed it was for her website. But it was mostly for stuff like this."

"Selfies."

"Yeah. You could call them that. April was the only one who knew, aside from Mom's clients or the models who'd come by—what she'd call salesmen and business associates. April worked at the camera shop where Mom bought her supplies. She must have seen what Mom was up to. My guess, Mom paid her off to keep her quiet. Sex workers don't go over well in small towns, even if there's no sex involved. And Mom was already hated, don't forget. Good looking. Smart. Money. She knew it too, had this air about her, like she was above it all. Even as a kid I could see it. The way she spoke to people."

"So April blackmailed her, and the cottage was the payoff?"

"Not sure my mother would have given in to blackmail. I suspect it was more of a thank-you for shutting up when it mattered. We were leaving town. I doubt Mom cared what anyone knew or thought at that point. When she made the house our wedding gift, I'm guessing she figured April had been thanked enough."

"That night the police came, the nice one ..."

"Goldwater."

"... When they were leaving, he asked me how you were doing. He said, between your mother and your father, you never caught a break."

"He would know. Wade didn't get it quite right. Scur wasn't working the desk the night my father was arrested. He was the cop who brought my father in."

She reexamined the postcard, daughter-in-law assessing the competition posed by mother-in-law. "So then, besides the photos, she did her dominatrix thing here too—in the cottage?"

"Not a lot, I don't think. Nobody from around here, from what I understand. She was pretty discreet. Referrals. Mostly doctors. Mostly from Europe."

"They'd come all this way?"

"In her sophomore year at college, she spent a couple of semesters in Rome and Amsterdam. I don't know how it happened exactly, but she started modeling for medical textbooks—anatomy books or whatever. There was this one, *Eve Erectus* ... and she started getting recognized in public. Medical students had a real thing for her."

"I'll bet."

"It was around then the dominatrix gig came up. Some girlfriend got her into it. It paid way better than the Christmas stuff she'd been selling. And it wasn't like she was required to have sex. It was more like play-acting. And then one of her clients, this Dutch guy, had this idea. He was a publisher of Fotoromans. They're like comic books, but with photographs instead of illustrations. Anyhow, he said she was the first professional dominatrix he'd ever met who wasn't ugly, overweight, or smelled of herring. He created a Fotoromans series around her—*Astride-OM*. She tortured men and saved the universe at least once an issue."

"So that's what those kinky comics in the cellar are. Funny, isn't it, how Martians and megalomaniacs share a weakness for well-endowed Earth women clad in leather?"

"Since she was in Europe for only three or four months a year back then, they needed extra shots for the comics. That's where her photography came in. Later, when *Astride-OM* switched to illustrations, the photos were needed to help guide the artists. She was huge too. She rivaled *Asterix* and *Tintin* for a time. In England, they called her *Astrid, Omnipotent Mistress of the Universe*."

"Your mom, she must have been every adolescent boy's masturbatory fantasy."

"Don't go there, Cor. Uh-uh."

"How is it you know all this? The Internet?"

"Just because my mom's a domme doesn't make me a glutton for punishment. I know all this shit because she told me."

"Oh, but this keeps getting better and better."

"It's how she broke the news about leaving me and moving to Europe. 'A more sexually enlightened continent,' as she put it. The *Astride-OM* collection came from her. She figured it would help explain her situation better. Gave me the lot before we left town. I guess she wanted me to have the same reading opportunities as kids in Europe."

"Twisted bitch."

"There's a copy of *Eve Erectus* in the cellar too, if you're interested."

She crossed to the sofa, snuggled tight beside me.

"They're going to be coming for me, Cor."

She cupped my head in her hands and kissed my forehead. "Oh, my dear sweet darling, you are so utterly, wholly, totally fucked. Except for your secret weapon."

"What's that?" I said.

"Me," she answered.

30
BAD

DECEMBER 2021

After twenty-six official kills and twenty or so unofficial, Henry Taylor Dickens should have known better than to go after some yahoo in Vermont in December.

Abel Willing worked in a tree nursery outside of Woodstock. Christmas tree buyers swarmed the lot, competing for trees the way Black Friday shoppers wrestled for Beats. Dad did his homework, so he knew Abel was an early riser, first on the job and easy to isolate. While he could have killed Abel on Saturday as planned, Dad proved himself sensitive to the needs of others, in this case, the tree-buying families. Rather than put a damper on anyone's weekend, he postponed Abel's execution from Saturday to Monday.

The crime scene extended across an acre. Although heavy snow, first responders, and sloppy cops contaminated much of it, the investigators' theories were for the most part on the money. Later, Dad corroborated or corrected the sequence of events. He was nice that way.

Dad struck from behind with an axe as the tree farmer was climbing down from his Dodge Ram. Except the axe head flew off on the backswing, leaving only the handle to connect with Willing's neck. Dad was in deep doo-doo from the get-go. Willing was a barroom brawler of local repute. He outclassed my father in height, weight, and reach. Where Dad had him beat was on the speed and the fact Willing had been stunned by the initial blow. They tussled some, Dad dodging and evading with neither doing much scoring, until Willing delivered with a steely left that sent Dad sprawling into the bed of the pickup. Would have been game over too, if not for the tire iron. As Willing moved in for the kill, Dad walloped the sucker's skull into the bleachers.

Dad rolled Willing onto a sled and dragged him to the processing yard, where he hoisted him onto the tree baler. The man was still alive, cried out something, but Dad forgot what.

Abel Willing's coworkers discovered his body beneath a pyramid of balsam and pine. He was bundled in netting, and prepped for market with a slit throat and a one-inch hole in the crown of his battered skull. A one-half-inch by four-inch rectangle of peanut brittle had been inserted into the hole. This same piece of peanut brittle had been used to cut Mr. Willing's throat.

Had it not been snowing, my father would have arrived home by early Monday afternoon. But the roads were a disaster, and the plows and salt trucks were having a rough time keeping up. He pulled in after dark. My mother was in her studio. Blue light flitted like lightning bugs through the drawn blinds and shutters.

With Mom occupied, Dad smuggled her Christmas gifts into the house. The delay in the killing of Abel Willing had allowed a couple days for shopping.

I was watching *Fear Factor* when he called to me from the side door. His face was bruised and scratched. His hands were swollen and cut up. I'd seen similar before. Hazards of the candy racket, I'd been told, boxes tumbling from shelves and whatnot.

I hid the shopping bags as instructed, while Dad returned to unload the car. He had a gift for me too, he teased. I never found out what. The Impala and its contents were impounded for evidence.

I waited on the porch as he puttered about the trunk. Flurries whirled on random gusts, my view pixelated, as if censored by Mother Nature.

Neither of us paid much attention when Jürgen Hirsch and his rented Ford Taurus pulled onto the asphalt strip adjacent to the cottage. Men often visited Mom at odd hours. Most of her *importers* and *exporters* were European and kept "continental hours," as Mom put it. It was baloney of course, but living in a backwater, you come to accept the harebrained customs of the world beyond your own, particularly hoity-toity Europe.

Jürgen Hirsch was like many of Mom's business associates. He was a cardiologist from Hamburg, Germany who had come for a session with *Astride-OM*, my Fotoromans mom.

In his rush to keep the appointment, Jürgen had blown through three STOP signs and hit two parked cars on Main. Astride's clients were well schooled on the importance of punctuality.

The cops might have cruised right past our house had it not been winter. My mother's Christmas display was Hillsdale's Disneyland. When it lit up, the town lit up. There was no missing the Taurus or the figure of Jürgen Hirsch sprinting into the cottage.

The cops followed Hirsch inside. They came out with my mother.

Her hair was as red as shame, unruly against bare back and shoulders. She wore clothes I'd never seen on anyone. No moms, for certain. She was dressed in leather or vinyl or both. *What does a kid know about textiles?* Hell, I didn't have words for half the stuff she had on. Took me years and multiple visits to fredericks.com and annsummers.com to match the names to the trappings. A black bustier, laces crisscrossing the bodice, and revealing more to me than any son should ever have revealed about his mom. Gloves up to her elbows. A cat-o'-nine-tails dangling from her hip. A G-string. Boots as high as her thighs. And those heels, holy moly! *How the hell could she stand, let alone walk?*

I wondered if the town, like my school, had a dress code and Mom was under arrest for breaking it. Perhaps Hillsdale didn't permit swimsuits in winter. Mom's swimsuit, anyhow.

I looked to my father, expecting he'd run to her, throw a blanket over her, berate the cops, demand answers. But he gawked like a stranger. A serial killer caught in the headlights. He did nothing to help her. Nothing to help himself. Trunk wide open. Evidence in plain sight.

Officer Goldwater would say it was instinct that led him to take a second look at Dad, though the APB from Woodstock surely contributed. Peanut brittle was fresh in Scur's mind and it was a busted box of the sugary confection the man by the Impala held. A gold box with red stripes. With more of the same inside the trunk. And—*holy crap!*—carpet stains that could be blood. And a tire jack with a hairy patch of what could be scalp.

Goldwater spun my dad up against the car, kicked his legs out wide, and drew his gun. His partner, Officer Timothy Ramsey, bolted from the cruiser, shotgun leveled. Dad offered no resistance, yet they belly-flopped him to the ground and whipped the cuffs onto his wrists.

Jürgen Hirsch slunk from the cottage and drove off in his rented Taurus. The cops didn't care. Perps beat pervs every time.

My mother stood shivering in the falling snow, bathed in the ballpark bright of her holiday extravaganza. Her lips so red. Her teeth so white. Her smile slight, knowing, and inexplicable. On the ground, my father strained to keep his face out of the snow, his smile as bewildering as Mom's. I waited for her signal, the moment we would rush to Dad's defense and beat the cops away. The signal never came. Whatever my parents' emotions, they ran counter to the storm kicking up in me. No panic. No fear. No anger. Nothing to worry about, son. *Accept.*

Mom paid no heed to Officer Ramsey's warning to keep her distance. She knelt in the snow at Dad's side.

"I'm sorry, Heather," he said.

"Don't be," she said. "Or I'll have to be sorry too. I can only imagine what you think, seeing me like this." She slipped off a glove and stroked my father's cheek, straightened his damp hair.

"I love you," he said.

"You always have," she whispered, and kissed him on the cheek.

She returned the glove to her hand, one finger at a time, smoothed out the wrinkles, and rose to her formidable heels. "You be good to him," she instructed the cops. "No matter what he's done."

That's when the van pulled up in front of our house and the Hillsdale Community Church Youth Choir trooped into our yard. They'd come to regale the crowds with their caroling and pass the hat for donations. Past Christmas displays helped loosen purse-strings. "Perhaps I'd best excuse myself," my mother said, as the boys, the girls, and their choirmaster goggled to a standstill.

Goldwater tipped his cap, cleared his throat with a respectful, "Ma'am."

As they maneuvered my father into the back seat of the cruiser, his eyes met mine, conveying what I liked to believe he wanted me to know: He did not hold Mom or me to blame. And, after this, I should never be afraid of anything again.

Every son wants to see their father in a positive light. Somehow, even knowing what I knew, what I had witnessed, I was that son.

Next morning, I awoke in panic. I could not remember what my father looked like. I could not find him in my head.

Much later, Dr. Cutcheon would ask how I felt when I saw them take my father away. I said, "Bad." In truth, I felt relief.

SEPTEMBER 2005

"You were young, Bobby. You didn't understand much about that night then, but I imagine you have a better grasp now."

I maintained my glum focus on the gravel shoulder of the highway. I gave my mother as much as she gave me. Nothing.

We crossed into Massachusetts, Mom clocking 120 in a 65 zone. "The speed limits in America are archaic," she said. As I saw it, she couldn't wait to dump me in Worcester.

"Daddy getting arrested and then seeing me—the clothes I was wearing ... you must have thought ..."

I turned up the volume on the radio. I rolled down the window.

She switched off the radio, powered up my window, and activated the child safety lock to prevent me from opening it again. "I'll be gone in a few hours and I don't know when we'll see each other again. I want to be sure you are clear on everything."

"If you're wondering if I still think it was a bathing suit, don't worry. I read the comics. I know who Astride-OM is."

Dad had figured in surprisingly few of our very few mother-son chats over the previous three years. Any issues I had were passed on to Dr. Cutcheon, and never once had Mom made reference to what she'd been up to that night. The closest she'd come was when she handed off her *Astride-OMs*. There was no mistaking this glorious nightmare of a super-hero was my mother. I lacked only an understanding of Astride-OM's role in the real world. Cutcheon might have helped, had I allowed her in. With respect to Mom, ignorance was safer than answers. But now she was kicking the cat out of the bag.

I put it to her. "Did Dad know what you were doing?"

"A better question would be if I knew what your dad was doing."

"Did you?"

She nudged the speedometer up to 140. "Did you?"

"You're a whore, right?" I meant to hurt.

She laughed. "Strictly in the business sense."

"People say men pay you for sex."

"Of course they do. It's how small minds work. A small-town girl does well ..." She smirked. "Painfully well, in my case. But I swear on my life, Bobby, I have never once taken money for sex. Do you know what a dominatrix is?"

"I don't care."

"You understand that *Astride-OM,* like all comics, is a fantasy, correct? A dominatrix is a woman who takes the fantasy and makes it real. That was what I did. It's what I do."

This was too much information. I changed the topic to one I could stomach.

"But your Christmas junk?"

"A nickel and dime business. It's never been worth the effort, then or now. I was in school when I began, don't forget. Bondage and discipline allowed me to supplement my income. Christmas knick-knacks and fetishes aren't as different as you might suppose. They serve identical markets. You'd be amazed how many of the items share the same molds and dies. Add a pleasant face, a pair of wings, *et voilà!* It comes down to painting and packaging. One man's dildo is another man's angel at the top of the tree."

"Dildo?" I asked. She took her hands from the wheel and applauded, as though it were a question every mom hoped to hear from a son. Inflatables. Strap-ons. Wall-mounts. Double-enders. Vibrators. Butt plugs. The art of pegging. Hell, she yammered on until I interrupted her encyclopedic dissertation with a curt, "Are we there yet?"

"As for my being a whore, it's simply not true. My performance has little to do with sex, sweetheart. It's therapy. Like marriage counseling. The less mainstream the fetish, the less a husband will be inclined to tell the wife. As a dominatrix, I have helped more people, more effectively, than any so-called professional therapist ever could. I provide the outlet so everyone stays happy. I am not a bad person."

"Is Daddy? Is he a bad person?" I should have asked what a fetish was. I thought it was a type of hat.

"We're much the same, he and I. We both made careers of less-than-mainstream vocations. Why? Do you think Daddy is a bad person?"

Guilt fed my silence. Mom loved to pick at scabs. If only she'd applied a Band-Aid on occasion.

"You understand my leaving has nothing to do with you, right? I'm more at ease in Europe. They don't judge me there. Indeed, they love me for who I am."

"I love you for who you are too," I said.

"That's not true. You love me for who you want me to be. And I am genuinely sorry, Bobby, but I will never be that person."

"Did you kill your mother and father?"

She repositioned her hands from the bottom of the steering wheel to the top. "Who told you that?"

"Same people who say you're a whore."

"It was an accident."

"What kind of accident?"

"I forgot to latch the door of my studio. They caught me in the middle of a ... Well, I was busy with a client."

"What were you doing?"

"What Astride-OM does."

"And that's it? They just died?"

"Something like that."

31
PLUSH

I was at the door and set to go for it. I'd be home before she woke up. She'd never know I'd been gone. And should it not work out, no one to blame but me. But then the hall light shot on and there she stood. "What are you doing?"

"Going for a walk," I said.

"At three in the morning?"

"I can't sleep."

"Where are you going, Rob?"

"Nowhere."

"Then why are you dressed in black? Why the flashlight and balaclava? You look like a burglar."

"I have to see for myself."

"Tell me you're not. You're not going up to that house. Tell me you're not that stupid."

"I need to know how, Cor."

"What difference will it make? They're dead, Rob."

"If it was a copycat killing ..."

"You can't go anywhere near there. That's all you need. All we need. But me, I can do it."

"Now who's crazy?"

"There's a better way. Without the risk. Just listen to me."

"You sure about this, Cor?"

"Trust me, I've done far worse."

"Yeah, but … well, you keep your phone on, just in case."

"Yes, sir," she said, chest out, spine aligned, salute crisp. "Shall we synchronize our watches too?"

"Just call, okay?—the second you're done." I handed her the bunny and she zipped the plush toy into her fanny pack.

"Stop worrying."

"I still think we should do it together."

"This is what I do. I'm good at it."

She pulled on her fingerless gloves, brushed my lips with her own, and trotted into the sun breaking on the horizon. Her ponytail bobbed above her headband, her speed increasing with her stride. The bunny waved from her fanny pack.

My biggest worry was that Wade Griffiths would be the cop on duty. I'd told her about my run-in with him a few days earlier. "He's got it in for us."

She laughed it off. "He's nothing but hot air."

"He's dangerous, Cor."

"So am I."

"Don't underestimate him."

I caught the news on the radio at 8:00 AM. The identities of the dead had been released.

The Storrow family. Longtime Lazy Green residents. Hillsdale was in mourning.

Mother, Kelly, thirty-eight, yoga instructor with a home studio. Maiden name Colborne. Hillsdale High Prom Queen, Class of '98.

Father, Matt, forty, a volunteer fireman, builder of luxury homes, originally from Los Angeles, one-time second-base prospect in the Orioles organization. He'd recently filed Chapter 11.

Willow, seventeen, high school senior, active in track and field, gymnastics, and swimming. Aspiring singer/songwriter. Worked weekends at the mall.

Ryan, twelve, up-and-comer on the BMX circuit.

The authorities were tight-lipped about the particulars, though one officer was quoted off the record: "Ever been to that abattoir up by Everton?"

The implication was obvious. *Tell me, again, how deep in debt was*

Matt Storrow? Yeah, another white male who couldn't hack it. Murder-suicide, evident to all. Except me, the cops, and Jumpy Justin.

I paced the floors, counted down the minutes. I should never have let Cori go on her own.

But the look on Justin's face, hell, I should have dropped to my knees and confessed on the spot.

The block was cordoned off to all but local traffic. Cori jogged on through. Unlike the day before, she didn't see anyone until she reached the house. A lone cop stepped from a cruiser and raised a hand as she approached. Trooper Upchuck, the cop who couldn't keep his breakfast down. His eyes were red, droopy lids fighting sleep. "Sorry, miss, but unless you can show me proof you live in the immediate vicinity, I'll have to request you depart the area."

"I just want to pay my respects." Cori gestured toward the memorial mound that fronted the house. She choked up. "For Willow." She freed the bunny from her fanny pack.

The policeman yawned, stretched stiff neck and shoulders. "Shift's almost up. Been a long a night. Friend of the family, are you?"

"We go back."

"A bunch of folk came by yesterday—from that Lulu and Lemons store at the mall. See that big wreath ..."

"Must have been awful in there," Cori said, a sad and wistful nod toward the house.

"Not anything anyone should ever have to see."

"How do you do it, Officer? I mean, deal with something so appalling?"

"It's my job, miss. You need a strong stomach, thick skin."

"How did it happen? A knife? A gun?"

"I'm sorry, miss, I'm not at liberty to divulge the information at this time."

"No, please. I'm the one who's sorry." She touched his arm. "I should never have asked. I just wondered, you know, because of Willow, if she suffered. I haven't been able to think of anything else. She was the sweetest girl."

"They all suffered, Miss. You get stuck up and down your torso with a ski pole or bashed up with a brass lamp ... Not that you heard it from me, please, Miss."

"I don't know how you do it, Officer."

"I try."

Cori knelt before the memorial, whispered a silent prayer, and deposited the bunny into the opens paws of a larger bunny.

"Thank you, Officer," she said. "You're what this community is all about."

"Oh, I'm just on loan. From upstate, you know, where the abattoir is?"

"It's been an honor."

"You too, miss, paying your respects, so early in the day. It's nice for the deceased, you know, people so caring and all."

I kept vigil at the window, worried the cops would turn up before Cori. My best guess was Justin's folks were taking their own sweet time, weighing the pros and cons of turning me in before turning me in.

By nine, an unconfirmed report said murder-suicide had been put on the back burner. Police were investigating credible leads and "a person of interest." No kidding.

My cell rang at 9:30. "Mission accomplished," Cori said. "Piece of cake."

"And?"

"Lamp. Ski pole."

"Shit," I said. "Oh, shit."

32

COPYCATS

Olexandr Kalashnik of Schenectady, New York was Dad's number four. He gutted Kalashnik with a ski pole, before skewering his brain. Or vice versa. It was one of his messier killings, and what prompted him to paint our porches red.

Gary Roth of Sunrise, Florida was number fourteen. Dad crushed his skull with a brass floor lamp. Crushing skulls was as close as Dad came to a pattern.

"It doesn't sound like anything a husband or father would do." Cori sought to rationalize the dead Storrows. "Men who kill their families aren't typically creative. They use knives, fists, guns, poison ..."

"Like I said, Cor, a copycat. With the execution looming, some asshole might be aiming to carry on the legacy."

"We should go to the police."

"And tell them what, their prime suspect has a theory?"

"If we explained ..."

"How many people did you run into this morning? Dog-walkers? Joggers? People are keeping to themselves. They're frightened. It's Christmas. The cops need to pin this on someone fast. Even if it's the wrong guy, they'll have put people at ease for the holidays."

"But what if he strikes again?"

"It's not if, Cor, it's when."

33
LAWYERED

The cops came for me late morning.

They parked their cars and trucks scattershot in the road and up the butts of my Pilot and Cori's BMW. They poured onto the scene, flak jackets and baseball caps, assault rifles and submachine guns, crouching low as they flanked the house. Every crime fighting resource in the tri-county had been mustered to take me, dead or alive.

Sometimes paranoia isn't paranoia. Sometimes it's self-preservation.

Wade was among those hunkered down behind the cars, rifles trained. God bless the dick and his Kool-Aid grin.

Two plainclothes cops crept onto the porch, sumo bulky in bulletproof vests. Pistols drawn, their backs buffed the siding as they edged up and in for the kill. Acting Chief Goldwater dragged up the rear, no vest and nowhere near as cautious as the others, a breaching shotgun slung casually at his side. As plans go, theirs didn't strike me as overly sophisticated:

Step 1. Blow away the door.

Step 2. Blow away anything that moves.

Upstairs, Cori showered. The assault would be done long before she was. The headline writers would be all over it:

WIFE SHOWERS AS BULLETS SHOWER HUBBY

My sudden and violent death would come as a shock to her. I hoped so, anyhow.

The doorbell worked fine, but the lead detective chose to tap the door. A dainty knuckle. No chance I would have heard it had I not seen the infantry roll up.

"Be right there," I called, and counted to three, resigned to my imminent aeration in a hail of gunfire. I opened the door slowly as wide as it would go. I raised my hands to my head without waiting to be told. Scur and his shotgun skated to the side and the detectives and their 9mm semi-automatics filled the breach. They were confused. *Who was this shoeless, unshaven, unarmed freak in Levi's and a Hollister hoodie?*

"Something funny?" the detective asked.

"Pardon me?" I said.

"You're smiling."

"I am?"

"You are."

The second detective, a woman, agreed. "Yeah, you are."

I didn't like how they'd positioned themselves. Wade had a clear shot at me. (Were my skin any color but white, odds are my story would have ended here.)

"Are you Robert 'Bobby' Blessing?" the male detective asked.

"He is," Scur said. He sidled to center, removing me from Wade's crosshairs.

I flashed to the image of my father in the snow, my mother kneeling, their smiles thin and out of place. "Sorry," I said, all lightness and politeness. "I smile when I'm nervous. Runs in the family."

"Oh?" the female detective said, snark propelled by smug. "Anything else run in the family?"

Scur spoke over the detective. "We need to ask you a few questions, Bobby. Be okay if we come in?"

I surveyed the street, the cops in my driveway. "Looks like you've got more than questions in mind. What's going on?" I sounded more fake than I'd rehearsed. I wasn't so dumb to let on I'd been expecting them, that was for sure. The rate at which the cops were dropping in on me of late, I should have opened a social club, charged annual dues. Was there any crime I wasn't suspected of? How and when had I assumed my father's rep?

"You can lower your hands now," Scur said, and signaled the uniformed cops behind him to stand down. "We're good here, gentlemen."

The cops bitched as they cleared the yard and street, tramped back to their vehicles. They'd been psyched for a showdown, not a stand-down.

I shouldn't have let them in, not without asking to see a warrant. Worry was, any objection would be confirmation of my guilt.

I led them to the living room.

As usual, I avoided my father's armchair in favor of the loveseat. Scur took the sofa, while the detectives conferred by the archway before taking their places: the male detective on the sofa alongside Scur, the woman behind Dad's armchair. She was buzzed, prepared for any eventuality. She had yet to return her gun to her holster.

Silence followed. Awkward. Like my third grade teacher holding our class hostage until the guilty party owned up to the boobs and dong scribbles on the blackboard. Five seconds felt like five minutes. Were they thinking I'd crack, blurt some cockamamie confession?

Detective Bill Walsh was black with a bouncer's build and a State Farm salesman's certitude. There was a natural warmth about the guy that was likely his best weapon. Hochstein, no first name offered, was slim, toned, and rigid in her verticality, a head taller than Walsh. Her face was round and smooth, with nary a crease or wrinkle. She'd never laughed too much, too long, or too hard.

Walsh cleared his throat as if the cue was prearranged, and Hochstein holstered her gun.

"Who else is here?" Walsh noted the staircase across the hall and the sound of running water from above.

"My wife," I said.

"She be done soon?"

"She likes her showers. Any chance you can tell me what this is about?"

"You were in the ice cream business, I hear," Walsh said.

"Up in Saratoga."

"You don't say!" Walsh sank into the couch, crossed his legs. "I got family up the road in Clifton Park. Might've been to your place. What's it called again?"

"Loony Scoops."

"Near the barbecue joint. Yeah, yeah. You had some crazy flavors, man. This chocolate one, with peanut butter and marshmallows ..."

"Fluff-Oh!-Nutsy."

"And the gumballs. My kid loved the gumball one."

"Gumball Choo Choo."

"Really good. You come up with those flavors on your own?"

"I took a course."

"There are schools for ice cream? Well, I'll be!"

Scur sat on the edge of the couch, hands in lap, legs on vibrate. He was biting his tongue, holding back on whatever it was he was keeping inside. Walsh, on the other hand, could've been attending a franchise fair. "You need a lot of ingredients, I take it. Where do you get your ideas? Cookbooks?"

"Something like that."

"And what about the off-season? I hear a lot of folk in the ice cream business go to Florida in the winter. Convenient, I'm guessing, for visiting your father."

"I was open year-round. I've never been to Florida."

"Interesting business, ice cream. Do you think it'd be something I might want to get into some day? The area's woefully short on good ice cream, wouldn't you say, Evelyn?"

Hochstein folded her arms atop the back of the armchair. "I'm a vanilla person."

"You're missing out, Evelyn. I'm telling you, this guy came up with flavors you wouldn't believe. Like what was that one I had? Marshmallow-peanut...?"

"Fluff-Oh!-Nutsy."

Hochstein's attention had drifted. She vacated her post, dropped to all fours by the coffee table. "Is this a Louis XIV?"

As interrogations go, this was the pits. The Reid technique was the go-to for most police departments and I had a good idea how it worked. A better idea than Walsh and Hochstein, anyhow. Start with the friendly chit-chat. Get the suspect talking. Establish a baseline. Gauge his reactions, the tics and twitches. Acquire a sense of guilt or innocence. And then lay it on thick. There were nine steps and they'd yet to nail the first. Hillsdale and vicinity needed more murders. These guys were rusty. It was cause for hope and worry.

"Look, if you need to ask me something, ask. I know the game."

"How's that?" Hochstein said. "You in the habit of being questioned by police?"

"Lately. Yeah."

"Why's that, Mr. Blessing?"

"The way it goes sometimes."

Walsh chuckled under his breath. "'The way it goes sometimes.'" He consulted his notepad, traded blank stares with Hochstein. "Could you tell us your whereabouts this Sunday evening past into Monday morning?"

"Why?"

Scur cut in. "You have the right to a lawyer. You know the drill, Bobby."

Hochstein hit the roof. "If you don't mind, Chief!" She double-jerked her head toward the hallway. "If I might have a word with you."

The two chatted beyond earshot. The front door opened and closed, and Hochstein returned without the Chief. She was done schmoozing. "Mr. Blessing, we are conducting a homicide investigation. Evidence has come to our attention that implicates you as a material witness."

Walsh translated: "You're suspected of murder, Bob."

"I'm what?"

"You're adorable. Simply adorable." Hochstein slapped the back of the armchair, no doubt wishing it was my face. "Is this how you want to play it?"

"I was home from late Sunday afternoon till early Monday morning."

"Anyone who can verify this?"

"I can," came the voice from the stairway. And there was Cori, drifting down from the second landing, Walsh and Hochstein enraptured by the spectacle of her descent. They weren't alone. She was wearing what I'd never seen her wear before. A button-up blouse in white, a tailored black jacket with matching pants, and leather flats. Pink lipstick. Mascara. And not a hair out of place. "What's going on?" she asked, though it was clear she knew.

The detectives flashed their credentials, as she made her way into the living room and took her place beside me on the loveseat.

"Mrs. Blessing, I presume," Walsh said.

"I also happen to be his lawyer," she said, unbuttoning her jacket.

My *what-the-fuck!* reaction escaped the detectives' notice, their attention rapt on Cori. Walsh flipped through his notes. "The information I have is you're a dentist, Mrs. Blessing?"

"McGill, Class of 2015."

"So—"

"And Fordham Law School, Class of 2017."

"Wow, quite the go-getter," Hochstein noted. "Impressive."

"Do you have a warrant, Detectives?" Cori asked.

"Just here to ask a few questions," Walsh explained. "There's been some murders, you may have heard, and, well, Mr. Blessing is a person of interest."

"You mean he's a suspect."

Walsh nodded grimly.

"And what exactly leads you to believe this?"

"Circumstances, ma'am."

"Yes, of course. Nothing keeps the justice system humming quite like circumstantial evidence and coerced confessions."

"We're not looking for problems here, ma'am," Hochstein said. "We're merely looking for your husband to shed light on certain recent altercations which he is alleged to have been party to and which may or may not impact the case."

I called them on the bullshit. "Is that why you showed up with an army?"

"You can ask my husband whatever you care to, on the understanding he has freely granted your request to be interviewed and the fact he has nothing to hide. But it is also my husband's prerogative to choose whether or not he wishes to answer your questions. You will be polite, respectful, and conduct yourselves in a professional manner, as forthright in your intentions as we shall be in ours. There shall be no badgering or subterfuge. You will ask and Mr. Blessing will answer, according to my counsel. Are we in agreement, Detectives?"

Hochstein clucked, "What next, hon, Atticus Finch's closing remarks to the jury?"

"If that's what it takes." Cori twinkled, cookie-cutter sweet. "We're on the same page then, Detectives?"

"Appears so," Walsh said.

"One more thing, and I apologize for asking, but if you wouldn't mind removing your shoes?" Cori said. "The carpet is an antique Kerman, 19th-century Persia."

The detectives glanced at one another, looked to see what might be special about the faded florals underfoot, reds and blacks and blues. "Who told you it's a Kerman?" Hochstein asked. "I can do a knot count, if you'd like."

"Please, just the shoes for now," Cori said, and the detectives ceded grudging compliance.

Cori took my hand as the scene played out, guided my fingers to her jacket pocket, tracing the form and shape of the Bersa Thunder. *Jesus! First she tells them she's a lawyer and now this?* I had paid little heed to the gun's provenance, the role it might have played, pre-Dobsie or with Dobsie. All at once, I felt more screwed than I already was. I nestled closer, conjoined twins fused at the hip.

Walsh withdrew a folded sheet from an inside pocket, passed it to me. "Know her?"

The camera loved Willow, even a poor photocopy from a high school yearbook. *Most likely to succeed* and *future superstar* struck melancholic chords among the dozen lines that survived the crop.

"I know who she is, but can't say I knew her. I met her exactly twice."

"You didn't have an altercation with her on or around October thirty-one of this year?"

"It was friendly. She stopped to talk. She was with a friend."

"We have a witness who says you made inappropriate remarks, that you were a little too friendly."

"What's that supposed to mean?"

"You tell us, Mr. Blessing."

"Next question, Detective," Cori said.

"You gave her a gift, didn't you? I'd call that friendly, considering you'd just met the girl."

Cori squeezed my hand.

I swallowed. "It was a book."

"What book?"

"A how-to thing. On writing. She was interested in it and I let her have it. That was it."

Cori gave me a sidelong glance, dug her nails into my palm.

"And what about this Sunday past at the mall? Are you going to sit here and claim Willow Storrow had an interest in pornography too?"

Cori was on it. "Badgering, Detective. Once more and we're done."

"With all due respect, this isn't a courtroom, hon," Hochstein groused. "Let us do our job."

It was one *hon* too many for Cori. "I'd be only too happy to, if you exhibited the slightest comprehension as to what your job entails, hon."

Walsh disregarded the sideshow. "Let me rephrase, Mr. Blessing. Did you give pornographic material to Willow Storrow on Sunday last at the mall?"

"It was an accident."

"How's that?"

"It fell out of my wallet. And it wasn't porn, it only looked like it."

"Looks like porn, but isn't porn." Hochstein pulled an earlobe, addressed the carpet. "Looks like a Kerman, but isn't a Kerman."

"It was a picture of my mother. An old one. She was wearing a Halloween costume."

"Can you produce this photo?"

"Asked and answered, Detective," Cori said.

"You were at the scene of the crime on Monday morning, correct?"

"So were a lot of people. Including my lawyer."

Hochstein picked up the thread. "The thing is, you and your wife were the only people from outside the immediate neighborhood to show up at that hour. In fact, you had to cover some distance to get there. This was before the news was out. I stress the *before*. What could possibly bring you all the way from here to Lazy Green so early on a Monday morning? Your father is a convicted murderer, is he not?"

"That's it. You're fishing, Detectives. My husband is as valid a suspect as either of you. There's a murderer on the loose. The sooner you find him, the safer all of us will be." Cori stood, but failed to draw the cops to their feet. The barrel of the Bersa poked from her pocket. No way they wouldn't see.

"So you're saying bad things just seem to happen when you're around. Is that it, Mr. Blessing?"

"We're done here," Cori said again.

Hochstein stayed her course. "Let's see, now. In the three months since returning to your childhood home, the residence in which your father masterminded his murders, we've got a missing driving school instructor from Saratoga, New York—a gentleman with whom you had business dealings. Two, we've got an eighteen-year-old boy who just happened to get butchered on your front lawn. Three, we've got the first non-domestic mass homicide in Hillsdale history, a family of four, whose daughter you spent a good deal of time and effort getting chummy with. And four, are you really going to sit here and tell us it's all some crazy coincidence?"

Walsh sighed wearily as he tied his shoelaces. "If there's anything you wish to tell us, Bob, I encourage you to do so now. It'll go easier on you later."

"It's not like we don't understand where you're coming from," Hochstein said. "We know it's not your fault. It's how you're wired. Genes. DNA. But you should also realize, it's only a matter of time. Once Forensics finishes up, we'll have our case, guaranteed."

"Get out of here," I said.

"Your call, Bob." Hochstein stepped into her shoes, tucked the untied laces under the tongue.

Cori held the front door open. Outside, a single police car idled, Goldwater at the wheel.

Hochstein couldn't let it go. "Your lack of cooperation is duly noted. Lawyer up all you'd like, but you're not out of the woods yet. I'll bet my badge you're mixed up in this, one way or the other."

"Pardon me, Detective, are you threatening my client?"

"Take off the blinders, Mrs. Blessing. Your husband carries on an illicit relationship with an underage girl who turns up dead and you— you continue on your merry way. You tell me what's wrong with this picture? Take a good hard look at who you're protecting here, *Hillary*."

Hand at the small of her back, Walsh steered Hochstein onto the porch. "Yeah, well, anyhow, might be best if Bobby didn't leave town for the next little while."

"You have a court order to that effect?" Cori asked.

"I'm just saying, Mrs. Blessing. It's for his own—hey, is that a gun in your pocket?" Suddenly, it was high noon, and Wild Bill Walsh was waiting for Cori to make her move.

Cori didn't bat an eye. "A hairbrush," she said, hand stock-still in pocket. "Would you like me to show it to you?"

Walsh stared for a moment, shook his head and relaxed. "Sorry. We're all a little touchy, these days, what's happened and such."

"Apology accepted, Detective."

"Yes, well, like I was saying, best to stick around. For your own good, Bob."

"Good news is," Hochstein added, "I hear there'll be a vacancy on death row, real soon."

Cori slammed the door on the cops and confronted me straight off, fury shrouded in a whisper. "You gave that girl the book? You gave that girl the book I bought for you? What were you thinking?"

"Me? What the hell were you thinking? A gun? What were you going to do, shoot them?"

"Unlike you, I was using my head. I wasn't sure if they had a search warrant. It was safer in my pocket than in the night table."

"And telling them you're a lawyer...?"

"How do you know I'm not?"

"You went to Fordham, Cor?"

"Law is like most professions. You need only two percent of what they teach you to be competent. The incompetent succeed on far less."

"Jesus, are you even a dentist?"

For a second, I thought she might slug me. "I am whatever I need to be," she said.

34

BANG

"What are you, a polymath or something?"

"I prefer to think of myself as a quick learner. If you must know, the dentist was a friend. She taught me how to drill and fill in less than two weeks. Freezing and pulling teeth took a little longer. I've become quite proficient. I get by quite nicely."

"It's like I don't know you anymore."

"I'm your wife."

"Why'd you marry me, to learn how to make a sundae?"

"I love you."

"And I'm supposed to believe that, no questions asked?"

"You're also a good lay."

"Thanks, you're not bad yourself."

"What about you? Do you love me, Rob?"

"You know I do."

"Then what else matters?"

"That has got to be the corniest line to ever come out of your mouth. How about the truth, Cor? All this time, I think you're one person and now I find you're someone entirely different."

"Entirely different? Honestly? Is that how you define me, by my career?"

"Careers."

"My work is an aspect of my life, not my whole life."

"You're like my father. He had no past before he met my mother."

"I have a past."

"Right. Parents who died from carbon monoxide poisoning. A dead aunt from Eden Prairie, Minnesota. No living family to speak of ..."

"I have family. I have you."

"It's too neat and tidy, Cor. Until a few moments ago, I believed you'd gone to school in Montreal. How much of anything you've said is true?"

"Why does it matter to you so much?"

"If I can't believe what you've told me, how can I believe anything you will?"

"Ask me anything."

"And you'll tell me the truth?"

"As much as I can."

"Not good enough."

"Really, Rob? You've told me everything I need to know about you? You have no secrets?"

"That's right."

"You used to be a better liar."

"Guess I've passed the crown to you."

"Yeah? Then where is it? Shall we play find the crown?" She softened, a smile behind the veil. Unbuttoned her blouse from the top down. Slipped her jacket to crooked elbows.

"No way," I said.

"Yes, way," she said.

"This is serious, Cor. We can't keep sweeping stuff under the carpet."

"But we can keep doing stuff on the carpet." She touched my cheek, and as I pulled her to me, as I wondered why any of this would sexually arouse us, the gun fell from her pocket, discharged on impact with the floor, and blew out the half-moon of stained glass that had distinguished the front door since 1954.

35

QUICKIE

We didn't stop. We couldn't take the bullet back, regardless of who might have taken the hit on the other side of the door. Nevertheless, mindful in our horniness that the Sonny and Cher of county law enforcement might barge back in, we made it a quickie that began on the runner in the hallway and ended on the staircase, a step below the first landing. The urgency established a personal benchmark in our relationship. Never had we crammed greater variety and desire into so few minutes.

Look, I sense your disappointment. Should you find this and earlier sex scenes lacking in graphic content, I defer to Anna Carmen Hope and Bestselleritis!, page 319, sidebar: "Gentlemen authors! Be implicit, not explicit. The panoply of Western literature is littered with dreadful examples of male writers attempting to depict sexual relations among heterosexual couples. Best to abstain than to share their shame.

Keep sex scenes short and vague on detail. 1) Begin the scene; 2) skip the middle; 3) exit the scene. Only women possess the required sensitivity and experience to portray realistically what a woman thinks and feels during lovemaking. Anything less is pornography, a sexist sphere in which men have excelled historically to their everlasting discredit."

"You should have had the safety on," I said to Cori.

"Where's the fun in carrying a gun if you can't shoot it?"

She assumed the devil-may-care stance of a comic book crime fighter. She was daring me to argue her point, and all I could do was question what possessed her.

Was she bipolar? *Tripolar?* Was she done pretending to be someone other than who she was? Or was she, like me, a lifelong and unrepentant liar?

"You were messing with me, right, about not being a real dentist?" I said.

"Would you feel better if I called myself a practicing dentist?"

She had all the answers, all the questions. There was no winning. Should I have been afraid of her? Probably, had I been anywhere near normal.

I belted up, buttoned up, and approached the front door as I would an open casket. I peered out to find we had lucked out.

Not that I kicked up my heels or launched into the *Hallelujah Chorus.* There was an envelope in the mailbox. No stamp. No address. Only a handwritten *Bobby B.*

Inside, a clipping from the *Bargain Bugler.* The twelve-pager had been a local freebie since before I was born. The paper's bread and butter was garage sale notices, auction listings, and grocery buys of the week.

The closest it came to news was a gossip column, Edith Dengler's *All Eyes! All Ears!*—and I had made the grade:

> **Canard or culpability?** Does the **Appleton** fall far from the tree? In light of the dastardly doings of late, authorities may wish to pose the query to the newest resident of **Hillsdale's** most infamous street. Anyone for **peanut brittle?**

A scribbled note was attached.

Good news is nobody
reads this rag save old
biddies. Bad news is the
word is out. Watch your
back, Bobby.
                    SG

At least one cop was on my side.

36
KEYS

I boarded up the window after Cori left for groceries. I'd almost called Tusk, guessing he'd have a more aesthetic solution, but used my brain for once. Next day was Christmas Eve and the Messners were coming by for dinner. Marie had pledged "the juiciest turkey you've ever tasted," while Cori promised to cook up "a storm of sides." No doubt she'd cozied up to an executive chef at some point too. I did not grill her on it. A truce had been called, a tacit agreement to leave unfinished business unfinished.

The dessert had been assigned to me. I made quick work of the spumoni, the recipe on loan from Valerie Bertinelli and the Food Network, and headed up to my office. I dug *Bestselleritis!* from the back of a drawer and got down to the business of destroying evidence.

I shredded the dust jacket.

I tore out the soiled pages and shredded them too.

I knew it was wrong, but what would you have me do? Who'd believe the book had just shown up on my desk? My prints were all over it. And if the ketchup turned out to be Willow's ketchup ...

The obvious solution was to burn the book. I would've too, had reading Anna Carmen Hope not also inspired me. I didn't want to dump the tainted copy until I could replace it with a clean one, and Amazon was sold out. Hell, was anybody not an author, these days?

Wrongdoing on pause, I got down to business.

I formatted a title page as instructed and pounded out some options.

MY DAD, THE SERIAL KILLER

THE TRUE STORY OF THE BRITTLE BUTCHER

SON OF THE BRITTLE BUTCHER TELLS ALL

KILLSDALE!

DAD, THE BRITTLE BUTCHER, AND ME

DEATH IN 27 FLAVORS

COPING STRATEGIES
FOR CHILDREN OF SERIAL KILLERS

WHY OUR PORCH WAS RED

DAD, THE DEAD, AND ME

AT HOME IN HELL

WHAT HAPPENED IN HELLSDALE

HELLSDALE!

LIVING DOWN THE DEAD

I achieved another milestone too. I wrote a paragraph I didn't delete immediately.

My name is Bobby Blessing and my father killed people. His name was Henry Taylor Dickens. His nickname was the Brittle Butcher. I didn't know the people he killed, except for two. I met them briefly. Still, I guess this makes me guilty too, which is why I am telling my story.

I was on a roll, a second paragraph set to flow, when the voices intervened. They were flat, hushed, here and gone, like a flame igniting propane.

"Get down here. You outta your head?"

"Gimme a sec, man. Let me soak it up."

"Cor? That you?" I called, knowing it wasn't, and panicked footfalls tore a strip off the staircase. I grabbed a letter opener and bolted onto the landing.

The letter opener had belonged to my father. The blade was silver, the handle a miniature coffin in faux-ivory and engraved with gold.

Reuk Brothers Funeral Home
11 Custis Avenue, Hillsdale
Phone Carter 3323

The Reuks had once occupied the building that became Dad's candy warehouse. The place was dark and cool, ideal for storing chocolate and corpses. The Reuks had relocated to a residential neighborhood nearer their customer base. The wisdom of the move was validated when they were called to collect my maternal grandparents. My mother had noted Mr. Reuk's sensitivity: *"We had to make two trips for the bodies, but charged only for one since the dearly departed lived but a stone's throw."* In Dutch, *reuk* means *smell*. Dad found this hilarious.

"Stop, or I'll shoot," I said. It was a letter opener. What else could I say?

I was no John Steinbeck expert, but I had read enough to recognize refugees from his pages, and these two fit the bill—a rat-faced George and a heavy Lennie, frozen in comic tableau at the bottom of the staircase and in flight for the cellar. Odd thing was, neither was unhappy to see me. Odder still, I had no fear. I was increasingly numb and dumb, accepting of a fractured reality in which my waking life was a running gag in a worst-case scenario.

"Who the fuck are you?" Fans of my dad, I guessed. The pair wouldn't be the first to make it inside, only the first since my return.

Heavy Lennie released the knob, shrugged toward the vestibule. "We're with him."

"Yeah, him." His ratty sidekick gnashed a cheddar smile and looked to me as if this was great news all around.

I kept them covered as I descended, a near peaceful aggression effervescing between gut and brain. I hit the ground floor and, wouldn't you know, their *him* was Tusk. "Friends of yours?" I said, as he let himself in.

"Bobby-boy?" His eyes adjusted to the light. "You're not dead?"

"What?"

"Them? Oh, yeah. Yup. They're with me."

"What the fuck's going on? What are you doing here?"

"Easy, now. Easy. April hadn't seen ya for a coupla days, said she heard a gunshot. Figgered your missus had put a bullet in you. Or the cops, they'd come and done you in."

"And these two?"

"Um, perry-medics? Ya know, in case you needed savin'."

Heavy Lennie snatched Rat-face George by the collar and scooted down the hall. "Best we get back to the ambulance, yes sir. Best we ... uh ..."

Tusk trundled the pair out the door. "Hurry it up, now. You boys get your meat wagon back to the hospital. Bye-bye. Thanks for comin'. Drive safe-wise." He turned to follow, one foot out the door. "You take care now, Bobby."

"Not so fast."

"What? What do you want from me? More writin' tips?"

"The key, Tusk."

"You kill them poor folk?"

"Give me the key."

"I know killers, Bobby-boy. But I look at you and gotta wonder. An enema is what you are."

"A what?" Best I could figure, he was aiming for *enigma*.

He snorted phlegm, chased it with a snigger. "Every inch of you shouts loner-psycho-whack-a-doodle, yet you couldn't take out itty-bitty April."

"The key."

He fumbled with his belt, unhooked a ring of maybe thirty keys. He singled out one, as if the only possible choice, and tossed it at me.

I stepped around him, looked outside. George and Lennie were sipping juice boxes and munching Lays by Tusk's pickup. "Looks like the ambulance left without them."

"Funny that, huh?"

"Knee-slapper." I tried the key in the lock before easing the door shut.

"Your window, that it? Is that what you want? I can put her back to like how she was. Well, maybe not so pretty, but—"

"You going to tell me who they are and what you're doing here?"

"I telled ya."

"You told me nothing."

"You goin' paranoidal on me, Bobby-boy, like you done with April?"

"Those guys, they part of your scam—the Airbnb thing you had going?"

"They're nobody."

"What'd they want in my cellar?"

"You'd have to ask them."

I took him by the arm. "Let's check it out."

"Jesus H. Cripes!" He shook me off, drove a fist into the doorframe. I eyed the baseball bat in the corner. "You wanna know? You wanna know?" He pushed by and stomped down the hall, slapped the grandfather clock as he passed. I trailed him into the cellar, weighed the outcome of a letter opener versus staple gun matchup.

And here I was again, in the cargo bay of my personal Titanic. While I'd skimmed the outer limits, my curiosity for what lay deeper intensified with every visit. So did my anxiety. The cellar was forever new to me, and never in a good way. Stuff I recalled as over here was over there. Junk unseen on previous visits sat in plain sight.

Tusk roared across the floor, a bull ripped on premium matador. "There." He pulled up at the furnace, cross-punched the water tank. His beetle-black eyes took in the cases of empties, the overturned spool, the fresh cache of cups and butts and ash. "So me and boys wanna shoot the shit every now and then, you got a problem with that? So we play some cards, drink a little, smoke a little, what ya gettin' all hot and buggered for, huh? Where's the harm in that? No harm to no one."

"How about because I live here and I don't want strangers coming and going, all hours of the day and night? How about that? How about you find yourself another hangout?"

"Fer Crissakes, Bobby-boy! I'm no stranger."

"Maybe so, but you come damn close."

"Fer Crissakes, have we disruptified you and the missus even ever? Nope. Did we rattle you or the missus so much as once? Did we wake you from your zees? Nope. This, it's our meetin' place, our waterin' hole—"

"And it's my livin' place, my sleepin' place, my eatin' place, my goddamn home, and I'm shutting you down."

"You can't do that."

"Watch me."

"Nah, what ya need is to come set with me and the boys. Chew the fat, crack open a few, share your daddy stories. It's the least you owe me, all I done for you. C'mon, Bobby-boy."

"You've had a good run, Tusk. You and your sister. I'm asking you nicely. Clean up this shit and clear it out. Whatever scam you're running is over."

"Fuck me."

"Not in this lifetime."

"You're makin' a big mistake, Bobby-boy. I got connections. A bajillion. New York fucks. Hollywood fucks. You get your book writ, no telling what I can do for you. In this racket, it's who you know, not what you write."

"Clean it up. Get it out."

"Nope. No way. Not on my own. Tell you what. After Christmas, I'll—."

"Today. Now."

"You're not being realistical."

"What about your paramedic buddies? They're outside waiting for you. Bring 'em in. Bring anybody. Whatever it takes, just get it done. Then get your fat ass out of here—every damn one of you. For good. Got it? You stay out of my house and out of my life."

"After all I done for you ... you're barking up the wrong hydrant, pal. You're lucky I'm on my meds, because ... well ... if I wasn't on my meds, you'd know I wasn't on my meds ... and you'd be wishing I was on my meds ... and I wouldn't give two shits who your daddy is."

"One hour. All I'm giving you."

"Or what, tough guy?"

"You might find I'm more of my father's son than you give me credit for. How's that?"

"Whoa-ho!" He doubled over, all belly, all mirth. "There's the boy! That's more like it."

I marched up out of there, best damn exit of my life. And not a staple in my face to speak of.

I returned to the den, determined to pick up where I'd left off, as George and Lennie tramped back inside, each calling for Tusk, Tusk calling for them.

I reread my opening paragraph. Not my best work in retrospect. Not up there with my ice cream classics. But not terrible, either. A little tinkering and I'd nail the sucker. But there was no tinkering or nailing to be had, only a steady ruckus as the trio hauled the cases from cellar to curbside. Distracting as hell, it was.

I thought it might be easier to brainstorm more titles. I scrolled up and a glimpse was all it took. I had an uninvited coauthor now, some sick fuck who'd deleted my titles and replaced them with one of their own.

CORI'S KILLER

Unless it wasn't a title.
Unless it was a signature.

37
REDEMPTION

As usual, Cori's cell threw me to voice mail. "Call me. Now."

I went outside to wait for her. Snow was falling.

Down by the curb, Tusk and his pals sorted through the last of the bottles, nickel and diming as they loaded the pickup, as slapdash as they'd fill a dumpster.

Tusk shouted something at me about lemons and lemonade, stepped up into the cab of his truck, and the millionaire freak gonzo author came through crystal clear: "Gonna fetch us a pretty penny down at the bottle exchange, thanks to you. You shoulda claimed your cut, Killer."

"Redemption is ours!" Heavy Lennie cried, and Rat-face George joined him in a celebratory do-si-do, before the pair hopped in beside their esteemed leader.

Tusk gunned the 450 up Appleton and I was left in a state of what-to-do-next amid the broken glass and rejected bottles.

I was cornered by circumstances. Nowhere I could go, no one to turn to. The police, hell, I wouldn't have a prayer. If Cori didn't turn up soon, I'd have to track her down on my own.

I headed back inside to get my jacket and car keys, and before I'd turned around, Cori came through the door.

"Jesus, where you been?" Agitation undermined my relief.

"I told you I'd be a while. I had errands."

"I guess I thought ..."

"What? You thought what?"

"Nothing. It's the time of year. The Ghosts of Christmas Past. Whatever."

"It's going to be a good Christmas, Rob, I promise. You'll see." Cori could promise pretty much anything. She didn't know what I knew. My wife could protect herself from *the known*. But from here on out, it was up to me to protect her from *the unknown*.

We were not alone, never had been. Best I could hope was that shutting down Tusk's social club would put an end to it. Optimistic, I know. This was Hillsdale, after all, the house at 18 Appleton. The Brittle Butcher had slept here. Could be *CORI'S KILLER* had too.

I expected to be murdered. I did not expect my wife to go down with me, whatever her agenda.

38
TURKEYS

Marie, Al, and their brined-in-bourbon turkey failed to show. Cori phoned, but they didn't pick up. Bastards.

"Maybe they forgot," Cori said.

"Don't kid yourself."

"What if something happened to them? Like Willow and her family."

"Nothing happened. Except seeing the cops here and making the connection to my dad. C'mon, Cor, do I need to spell it out? The whole town knows by now."

"We should check on them."

"I'm not going anywhere near their place. That's all I need. If somebody sees ..."

"Why do you always think the worst?"

"You're joking, right?"

"It could be a misunderstanding. They could've mixed up the dates. Maybe they think it's tomorrow night."

Snow had been falling since noon. Fat, fluffy flakes, ashen fallout from a nuked Heaven. We followed the tire tracks in the unplowed road, parading slowly in single file, before veering into the deep of the Messners' walkway.

The house was dark, save for a bald orange glow deep within. The aroma of roast turkey carried to our frozen noses.

"Ring the doorbell," Cori said, jogging on the spot to stay warm.

"This is stupid. Let's just go."

"Listen. Music. *The Little Drummer Boy* ..."

The doorbell was the antique mechanical kind that rang at the twist of a brass key. A wind-up toy, minus the toy. I gave it a good turn.

"Knock," Cori said, face framed by the gray fur of her hood.

I knocked.

The music stopped.

The porch lit up. The interior remained dark.

Al observed us warily through the beveled glass.

"Are you guys all right?" Cori called. Her voice carried an excess of concern. "Did you forget our dinner plans?"

Al stammered an excuse riddled with *ums* and *urghs*. Hieroglyphics or bronchospasms. Although we couldn't see Marie, we heard her. She was feeding him lines.

"We're sick," he said with abrupt clarity. "Bad colds. Terrible." He coughed for emphasis.

"Surprised he didn't say they had to wash their hair," I said to Cori.

Cori continued to give them the benefit of the doubt. "You should have called to let us know. I made all the fixings. And a mince pie. And Rob's spumoni ..."

Al groaned like he'd taken an arrow in the back. "Look, I'm sorry, I can't do this. You need to know, we've got guns." The porch went dark. "Three."

Cori railed, dumbfounded.

"I told you. C'mon. Let's go."

"No." She kicked the door. "Let them come out and tell us to our faces. They owe us that." She pounded on the glass, hollered. "Talk to me, Marie. Marie, I want to talk to you. Al! Cowards. Come out here." She put her shoulder to the door, pushed, pulled. Twisted the ringer till her thumb cramped up. "Goddamn cowards. You won't get away with this. You won't, goddamn you."

I peeled her fingers from the ringer. "C'mon, Cor. They have guns."

"I have a gun too!" she wailed at the door.

"Cool it. It won't take much for them to do something stupid. When people are scared ..." My wisdom went unheeded. Cori straight-armed me in the chest and stomped off the porch. She was all about the vengeance now, scheming, plotting. I knew the feeling, did I ever.

She raged up Appleton, a force to be reckoned with as she blazed a fresh trail. I kept my distance, hands in pockets, in no hurry to catch up. I'd seen her angry, but never this riled. It'd be a stretch before she calmed down. The heat she was giving off, the snow should have been melting for miles around.

Despite Cori's earlier promise, it was shaping up to be the gloomiest Christmas I'd spent since my last in this town.

We dined on the fixings. Maple syrup yams. Triple-mashed potatoes with garlic and chives. Green beans and mushroom casserole. Pan-fried oysters and Creole mayonnaise. In place of the Messners' turkey, I nuked a couple of knockwurst for myself and a Beyond Burger for Cori. We polished off two bottles, a Pinot Noir and a Riesling, living dangerously, no heed to pairings. By the time I rescued the mince pies from the oven and scooped on the spumoni, we were downright giggly.

"It's kind of fun, isn't?" she said.

"Huh?"

"Having people frightened of you."

"It can be."

"Did you hear Al's voice? It was like he thought you'd slash their throats first chance."

"As appealing as it may be, I'll leave the job to someone else."

"Well, if you're looking for volunteers …"

"Jesus, Cor." God, I loved my wife.

39

UNWRAPPED

Christmas morning, we awoke to the doorbell and a broadside of April Bright's backside as she speed-hobbled through the snow to her salon. She'd left a fruitcake on our doorstep. It was wrapped in foil, festooned with ribbons, and accompanied by a hastily heartfelt tag:

> *merry xmas happy newyear*
>
> *fondly April Bright*

"Fondly?" I said. "What the hell?"

Cori scooped coffee into the filter basket. "Contrition?"

"Retribution."

"Like if you pull the ribbons, it'll blow up?"

"More subtle."

"Drano? Cyanide?"

"Nah, April's more the crushed glass sort." I buried the cake at the bottom of the compost bin.

"You really think she would?"

"Wouldn't put anything past anyone in this town."

We did not have a Christmas tree. Dad's killing of the tree farmer, Abel Willing, had put a terminal damper on the tradition. Cori was fine with it, at ease with my cornucopia of unrepressed quirks. (She'd have to deal with the repressed ones at a later date.) Besides, a carpet of pine needles held little appeal for either of us.

We tag-teamed on a tray of coffee, croissants, scones, butter, and strawberry preserves, and moved into the living room. Our gifts were spread across the coffee table. We'd set a limit of four each, though I counted only three for me.

I started with the Violet Blonde gift set from Nordstrom's. Cori sniffed the contents. "Love it," she said, without editorializing on my lack of originality.

She countered with two books, neither by Anna Carmen Hope. *Ice Cream: A Global History* by Laura Weiss. *Mothers, Sons & Lovers: How a Man's Relationship with His Mother Affects the Rest of His Life* by Michael Gurian. I said "Cool!" to the former and "Jesus Christ, Cori!" to the latter.

"How brave of you," she said of my second gift.

Cori threw off her terry robe and slipped into the clingy silk. "Thank you," she said, spoofing every model who'd ever modeled. Sour lips. Butterfly lashes. Flash of boob.

"The salesgirl called it a 'devilishly amorous kimono.'"

"Ah, so that's how I'm feeling," she said, and bent to kiss me.

Next up was a razor, a Philips OneBlade. "It'll make it easier to keep your beard trimmed."

"I don't have a beard," I said.

"Then what's that hairy stuff all over your face?"

"Two weeks of stubble."

"Trim it," she said, "and we can start calling it a beard."

I'd been having second thoughts about the lululemon gift card. Murder tends to be a downer on so-called joyous occasions, and the card was a doleful bleat from The Great Beyond. Life is a countdown to Death, culminating in a series of lasts the near-dead never grasp until their last gasp. The last sandwich you'll eat. The last movie you'll see. The last song you'll hear. The last orgasm you'll have. For all I knew, this was Willow Storrow's last gift card. Would Cori see skinny pants and tank tops or the brutalized remains of the girl who sold it to me?

"So, this is how that poor girl saw your mother's postcard," she said.

"Yup."

The latest edition of *Real Writer* magazine was Cori's next gift. Her accompanying note (six exclamation marks) informed me a gift subscription had been purchased in my name.

My fourth to her was a plaque with *Dr. Corinne Widdoes DDS* routed into the wood. "I guess this makes you a real dentist," I said, "same way the magazine makes me a real writer."

"Though I suspect, my love, the number of teeth I've filled significantly surpasses the number of words you've written."

"You don't know that."

"I never see you write."

"It's not performance art."

"Very funny."

"I write when you're asleep. Or out."

"If you say so." She skipped to the final gift. "It's not on the table."

"I was wondering."

"It's not anything you're expecting."

"We'll see about that."

She gathered the wrappings from the floor. "You know last weekend, when I was in New York?"

"Yeah?"

"I wasn't in New York."

40
GUILT

"I was in Florida."

"Ah, Jesus."

"I went to Banrum. The prison."

"I know what it is, damn it."

"They're going to execute him, this time. They really are. You know this."

"I don't know anything. Nobody does."

"I arranged for us to see him. I have visitation certificates."

"For fuck's sake, kill me now."

"One for each of us."

"No way."

"New Year's Day. We need to be there New Year's Day."

"No way in hell, Cor."

"They usually take at least a month to get. And it's the prisoner who needs to ask, but they made an exception for us. The warden gave us special dispensation."

"Who'd you pretend to be this time, the Governor?"

"Does it matter?"

"Not to you, apparently."

"You need to see him, Rob."

"You're wrong. I don't."

"Best if we drive. We can take our time, spend a night in Savannah or Charleston."

"You're on your own. There's no way."

"If you won't do this for yourself, you need to do it for me."

"Gimme a break. What movie did you steal that line from?"

"I will not live with you and the guilt you'll carry if you don't take this opportunity to see him."

"You don't know the whole story."

"Good. You'll have lots of time to tell me on the way down."

"He doesn't mean anything to me. I've told you. He hasn't for years. What's it to you, anyhow?"

"Because you'll regret it for the rest of your life if you don't."

"That's my choice."

"No. Not if I'm going to spend the rest of my life with you."

41

SLALOM

I'm good at silence, as long as I'm the one imposing it. In this instance, it was hard to say who held the upper hand, Cori and her disgust for me or me and my outrage for what she'd done.

We lived together apart for the next few days, Cori moving forward with her travel plans while I skied marital slalom around her and her mission.

I spent hours in the den, made sure she saw me plugging away at the laptop before I'd shut the door, free to let my motivation slide. Blank pages stayed blank. My second paragraph crapped out at *The*.

My saving grace was *Bestselleritis!* I started over from the beginning and stuck with it till done. I came across another stained page, neatly excised it from the binding, and shredded it to substandard confetti. Again, I knew I was destroying evidence that might have exonerated me. I also knew, no matter how forthright I might be, the book and the blood would nail me to Jumpy Justin's cross as surely as if I'd murdered the Storrows on Facebook Live.

We broke the silence only at mealtime. *You want eggs for breakfast? The coffee grinder needs a cleaning. I'm making tuna, care for a sandwich? Any Perrier left? I feel like Chinese tonight, you?*

Yeah, Chinese. The stir-fry that brokered the silence.

We would have preferred Wok In The Park up in Kenner, but Hillsdale fell outside their delivery zone and the weather wasn't much for driving. We settled for The Great Wall on 88. It was never any good, which sounded ideal. Bad mood, worse food.

The promised thirty-minute delivery was three times that. Perfect for a starving twosome at war.

The delivery guy was ready with his alibi. "Whew! The roads, it's the crapocalypse out there."

He ran down the items on the bill and I handed him the cash. "Hey, cheer up, man," he said. "Ya got yer food. It's all copasetic." He pointed a finger, emptied an imaginary clip into my chest, his tongue and cheeks beatboxing bloodshed. He was no older than twenty, hip-hop baggy from the ankles up, backward baseball cap on shaven head. Only when he turned to go did I see the front of the cap.

He was either a graduate of the *Steer-U-Rite* driving school up in Saratoga or he'd gotten his paws on Joe Di Iorio's cap. "Your hat," I said, "where'd you get it?"

"Huh?"

I tapped the side of my head. "Where'd you get your hat?"

"I dunno. Some guy left it at the restaurant. Sweet, huh?"

"What guy?"

"Some guy. Jeez, man."

"Young? Old? Short? Tall? What color hair? Was he alone? Was he acting strange?"

"Fucked if I know. It was lying around. Boss said I could have it. What's your beef, man? Is it yours?"

"When?"

"When what?"

"The hat. When did you get the hat?"

"Three weeks ago. A month. Look, I gotta—"

"You sure of that?"

"Of what?"

"That it was only three weeks ago."

"Chill, man, chill. It's a stupid hat. Look, I got deliveries ..." He pushed back with a full-body shrug and heaved himself up the snowy walk to a wheezing Ford Focus.

I'd wondered all along if Joe Di Iorio's disappearance hadn't been his own doing. Another frustrated old coot skipping out on wife and life. After Cori had crushed his dreams, perhaps he'd gone with his fallback. There'd be no reason for him to be over on 88, otherwise. But to leave a clue as obvious as his dumbass ugly hat, not even a deluded old fart like Di Iorio would be that careless. Unless he was pulling a Hansel and Gretel, leaving a trail of clothing instead of breadcrumbs. Could be he wanted to be found.

The Focus grappled for traction, fishtailed up the street.

THE SERIAL KILLER'S SON TAKES A WIFE

Cori was setting the table as I came into the kitchen. I unpacked the bags, unsealed the containers.

"Damn," I said, "they forgot the General Tso's."

Cori raked a clump of rice onto her plate. "When haven't they forgotten something?"

When we were done, I put on a pot of water for green tea.

We cracked open our fortune cookies. Cori's read: *One close to you shall reveal a heretofore hidden truth.*

My fortune was blank. My lucky number was 11.

We were in our bed, the blinds raised, the room bleached with moonlight, and the gulf between us so cold and vast, not even make-up sex could span it. Cori's thoughts, I couldn't say, though I'm sure I figured in them. She was in mine, all right, featured corpse in a stainless steel showroom.

The Storrows. Pulped and punctured. Faceless, save for Willow.

Joe Di Iorio. Jilted. Rosé tears from hollowed-out eyes. Mouth a sodden crater.

A nameless sixth and seventh and eighth and ninth, row upon row of the hideously departed.

And Cori, lithe and lifeless, serrated splendor from bloodied ear to bloodied ear.

"I'll do it," I said. "I don't like it, but I'll go."

She touched my thigh, sought my hand. "You're sure?"

"We need to get away," I said, *get away* open to interpretation.

PART FOUR
WHAT WE MEAN WHEN WE TALK ABOUT FATHERS

42
BANRUM

We spent an overnight in a no-name motel off a nowhere ramp off the I-95 in North Carolina, checking in late and checking out early. Other than that, we drove straight through, alternated shifts at the wheel, and arrived in Gator Jump on New Year's Eve with time to spare.

Cori had left little to chance. She never did. Research had told her most visitors to Banrum favored the Days Inn and Red Roof, convening in the lobby to share their pain, zombies in training, emotions reserved for the awkward reunions to come.

Cori opted for the pricier Marriott.

Did not sleep. Could not shut down my brain.

Wanted to be dead.

Wished for weed, though I'd given it up ten years before.

Wanted to be dead.

Sat by the window, looking out.

Wanted to be dead.

At breakfast, I went light, poked blueberries from a buffet muffin, washed them down with orange juice and black coffee.

"I'm sorry I've done this to you," Cori said.

"No, you're not."

Her smile was angelic, at peace with the truth. "No, guess not."

"Not yet, anyhow."

"No matter how it goes," she said with conviction.

We were here. I would see him. It would be done. A blip on my timeline, whether he died in March, as Cori was convinced, or lived to die another day, his odyssey cruel, unusual, and fitting. It would be a New Year's Day to remember, nothing more. Sure, my dad might try to make amends, but so what? Too little too late. Forgive and forget. Fuck and off.

Wanted to be dead.

Cori drove. She'd deconstructed my turmoil, rightly concerned that with me at the wheel, I'd take us off the first bridge we came upon. She was resolute and single-minded, blissfully devoid of apprehension. End-times were near and my wife was rapture-ready. I functioned on dread alone, adhering to a script I had no hand in writing. Minimal reaction, therefore, when Cori stopped by Alamo to rent a black Chevy Suburban.

"What's the matter with my car?" I said. The Pilot had gotten us this far.

"I need to look the part."

"What part?"

"Trust me, okay?"

Palm trees flanked the road in geometric windbreaks from Gator Jump to Banrum. Friendly fronds urged us onward, past artfully deceptive boulevards and sprawling fields of green. The landscape evoked country club, luxury resort, gated community, and Ivy League campus—anything but state pen.

Banrum Correctional Institution was a product of the Cinder Block School of Urban Architecture. Function, form, and payback. A modern-day eye-for-an-eye executed with dispirited blindness. Acres of gray upon gray upon gray. Right angles and straight lines, witless and windowless, nondescript to the point of dystopian parody. These were bunkers, not buildings.

"Lovely, isn't it?" Cori said.

"Peachy."

"There's only one thing to keep in mind. From here on in, you're to call me Agent Ambrose. Agent Shannon Ambrose."

"What the—? Jesus, Cor, not again!"

She stashed her wedding ring in the glove compartment. "Agent Ambrose. Don't forget."

"You're a cop now? Tell me you're kidding, please."

"Agent Ambrose doesn't kid," she said. She wanted me to laugh. I didn't.

"You said we had visitation certificates."

"Your father would have had to agree to them. I had no guarantees he would. Even then, we wouldn't have had privacy. This way, we get to see him alone without anyone listening in."

"This is a bad idea."

I could have bailed. I should have bailed. But I'd come this far.

As instructed, I had dressed conservatively. Charcoal pants from my funeral suit, a blue button-down shirt, and custom-tailored misgivings. Agent Ambrose was prim in black top and gray business suit, skirt to knees, and flats rather than heels. She'd tied back her hair and wore little makeup. Night before, she'd swabbed the polish from her nails. But Cori would always be Cori, whoever else she was in the moment.

Whatever fraud my wife had perpetrated to make this visit possible, I had no expectations it would keep. They would find her out, then zero in on me, the killer's kid who had skipped town under suspicion of murder. At least I'd make it convenient for them: they could bunk me with my dad.

We'd started through the second checkpoint when a corrections officer asked us to stand aside and wait. Thumbs in belt, Agent Ambrose played her Bad Ass Motherfucker (BAMF) card: "This is ridiculous. Do you people not know who I am? I don't have time for this."

"Sorry, ma'am, it's come down from the warden."

She huffed with officious annoyance and set her toe to tapping.

You can't step two feet up the anus of Banrum without wanting out. Passing through unsettles. Passing time traumatizes. Imagine claustrophobia on crystal meth. Or the interior of a submarine, if a sub comprised a hundred acres. You can taste the place, a stew of diesel, chlorine, and rump. You can hear it too, a one-note drone through corridors stark and hollow. Sound blunders forward, footsteps and voices like cannonballs on hammered steel, fair warning of Doomsday and its ETA. Thus we heard the warden before we saw him.

My image of wardens had been honed by Bogart marathons on TCM. They were heavyset guys with Vaseline hair and Marquis de Sade morals. Tusk would have made the grade had he been bigger, brawnier, and owned a bank-manager tweed. That's all to say the suit heading toward us defied the stereotype. He was tall and fit, with curly blonde hair, rimless glasses, and a probable middle name one syllable removed from Asswipe.

"All's well," Cori whispered as he drew near.

I was set to slap my hands to the back of my head, when he greeted Cori with a prom-date hug, and she responded with infuriating delight. "Assistant Warden Mangold, how nice to see you again."

His mouth broke wide, a touchdown grin. "Curtis, please. Call me Curtis."

"Shannon," Cori returned, harnessing her inner Agent Ambrose. "Is everything all right, Curtis? We are on schedule, are we not?"

"All ready for you. Roy—Warden Bucara—he wanted to make sure I extended his regrets and, of course, wish you a very happy New Year."

"Back at you." Agent Ambrose was just one of the guys. "You can't fault a man for taking his family to Hawaii for the holidays."

"And you, I assume, are Mr. Dickens." The Assistant Warden took my measure without the offer of a handshake. "Decent of you to assist. Extremely rare for offspring of inmates to cooperate in such sessions."

"We're lucky to have him," Agent Ambrose noted.

"Glad to help," I said, though I didn't sound it.

"Mr. Dickens's presence is especially important now," Agent Ambrose said. "Circumstances necessitate my interrogation to go beyond our initial concern regarding national security."

What!?

"I must say," Mangold said, "the national security issue struck the warden and me as terribly odd. Can't imagine how Henry Dickens could be tied up in anything of that nature. Certainly not from behind these walls."

"I'd love to tell you, Curtis. But you know as well as I, things are not always as they seem, particularly with regard to felons of Mr. Dickens's intelligence and character."

"Don't get me wrong. My intent was not to pry."

"The recent murders in Hillsdale, of course, are another matter."

"That town up north? Yes. Saw something on Fox. Tragic."

"As it so happens, the man I'm here to interrogate is from the same town."

"Henry Dickens? I had no idea. You think he's involved somehow?"

"More of a Hannibal Lecter level operation. Pick his brain. See if he might provide any insights."

"I don't know, Shannon, he's a strange duck. Least threatening soul on death row. You wouldn't peg him for a killer. Then again, age mellows the worst of them. No matter, he'll be meeting his Maker soon enough."

"Fortunately, not before I'm done with him," Agent Ambrose said, which was apparently the wittiest thing Mangold had ever heard a woman say. And maybe, for a woman in law enforcement, he was right. His hairy-chested laughter dwindled to residual chuckles as he led us up the corridor.

I followed behind as Shannon and the Assistant Warden chatted.

Here I was, moments from seeing my father for the first time since I was eleven, and all I felt was jealousy. This self-important douche was hitting on my wife and there was damn well nothing I could do.

The deeper the jagoff took us into Banrum's innards, the more otherworldly the prison became, the odds diminishing we'd make it out alive. We branched off the main corridor and onto a narrow artery, down and about through offshoots and spokes, coming to a stop before a heavy red door at the dead end of a padded capillary.

Mangold punched a code into a keypad. A buzzer buzzed and he motioned me inside.

The door shut behind me. *Jesus Christ.* Mangold and Agent Ambrose remained on the other side.

They continued to chat each other up as I watched in soundproof frustration

Mangold's back was to me, while Cori's eyes were on me throughout. Her smile did not leave her face. That charmed and charming smile of hers. The smile every guy believes she's smiling just for him. It was tough to take, I tell you. Mangold had way too much to say and my lip-reading skills were shaky.

Finally, he reopened the door. "I hope you obtain the information you came for, Shannon."

"I'll do my best, Curtis."

He blabbed some jargon into his walkie-talkie and nodded somberly at the unintelligible reply. "Shouldn't be long now. So later then, Shannon? I'll hear from you? You can't beat P.F. Chang's for Chinese."

"Gimme a few days," she said. "Once my report is done ..."

"Yes. Yes. Of course." He shadow-boxed a jab-jab-cross. "Right. Will do." And Shannon rewarded him with her damned irritating delighted laugh.

I waited till Romeo made good his exit. "'Shannon'?" I said. "'Gimme a few days'? 'Curtis'? Tell me, Agent Ambrose, you out of your mind?"

"Stop obsessing over the means. It's the end that matters."

"What end?"

"Patience, Mr. Dickens."

The room they'd assigned had the ambience of a morgue, minus the cold storage. At the center, a small aluminum table was bolted to the floor. Three aluminum stacking chairs rounded out the décor.

Cori proceeded to housekeep, dragged two chairs to opposite sides of the table. She motioned for me to join her with the third. I brushed her off, took my seat against the Xanax-yellow wall, and set my heels flat upon the floor. This was her idea. The backhanded way she'd gone about it, this was on her too, Agent Shannon Ambrose and Assistant Warden Curtis Mangold the least of my issues. The decision to go along, of course, was mine, and I was out to punish her for it.

With lines thus drawn, and within this isolated colon within the ulcerated bowels of Banrum, we awaited the infamous Henry Taylor Dickens.

Wanted to be dead. Oh, God, did I ever.

43

THE OLD MAN IN THE
BAGGY BLUE JUMPSUIT

Slow, deep breaths. Word repetition. Alternate nostril breathing. Progressive muscle relaxation. I employed every calming technique I'd ever googled. "Think of the good times," Cori urged. And all I could see were the mutilated corpses of Bonner Doyle and Debra Curdovic, victims twenty-five and twenty-six, underscored by the aftermath and my father's efforts to candy-coat my return to ignorance and innocence. *Good times, oh yeah!*

The lock whirred from without. The buzzer buzzed. Two guards and an old man in a baggy blue jumpsuit shuffled in. Shackles scraped the floor. Shackles jangled from his wrists. The ghost of Jacob Marley come to call on Scrooge.

And there he was and there he wasn't, firestorm and firebreak, my father, unmistakable from eighteen years earlier, yet unlike the father I had known. The blue eyes were his, now sunken within charred sockets, but everything else about him had me scrambling through the back pages of an alarmingly suspect memory.

I sat on my hands, suppressed the tremors.

I'd expected the cooperative suspect I'd last seen in the back of Scur Goldwater's cruiser. Muscle-bound. Calculating. Melancholic. Dad was forty when I was born. Over fifty when imprisoned. He was now pushing seventy. Time and Banrum had taken their cuts.

His once curly brown hair was white and as lifeless as roadkill. His body was lean and stooped, his face skeletal from the nose up, lumpy mash from the nose down. Henry Taylor Dickens had been erased and resurrected, reimagined and redrawn. *Henry Taylor Dickens as reconceived by Neil Gaiman.* He'd been counted dead and gone so often, his life force was marginal at best. He was someone I used to know. He was no one I knew now.

I was disappointed. I had wanted to feel more than pity.

Eyes down, he looked neither right nor left. The guards secured him at the table. They reconfigured his leg irons and locked him to the eye bolt on the floor. They would have restrained his hands too, had Agent Ambrose not intervened. "We'll be fine," she told them.

"You never know with his sort, ma'am."

"I'll take full responsibility," she said. They glanced my way with tacit disapproval and exited without questioning Agent Ambrose's authority.

Cori waited till we were alone. "Henry," she said, with what I can only describe as affection.

He turned to see who had spoken, stopped at me. "Bobby?"

"Yeah."

His voice was halting, deathbed thin. "You look like your mother."

"Yup," I said, and instantly regretted I'd given him anything. He could not have cared less. He'd moved on to Cori.

An approximation of a smile stole across his face. "Shannon?" he said, her name exhaled, rather than spoken. And there was Cori, transformed once more. She leaned across the table toward him, tranquil and tender, a touch of their hands evolving into an ardent hug. Tentative at first, my father responded with creaky pats and taps.

I set aside my shock and awe for future reference.

"You remember ..." she said.

"Everything about you ... I couldn't not."

Cori's eyes were puddles, her anguish remote from the Cori I knew. How had he earned her tears? The man caused tears, for Christ's sake, he didn't earn them.

"What the fuck is this?" I said. "What the fuck is going on?" I'm not saying they were making out. Nothing like that. This was a father-daughter sort of love-in. Nice. But unsettling. Like I'd married my sister.

Questions skittered through my brain. "You know my wife? All this time, you two, you've known each other?"

"Wife?" Dad said. "Shannon is your wife?" Cori replied with a gentle nod, and he was so damn thrilled, he might have jumped out of his seat and kicked up his heels were he not chained to the floor. "Too wonderful! You married him, Shannon. You married Bobby."

I could have left the room unnoticed, how they carried on.

"And you made it all this way to see me. And with Bobby too."

Cori wiped tears from her cheeks. "I told you I would someday, Henry."

"I know, but—" My father paused, then asked the question already on my mind: "You didn't marry him to get to me, did you?"

She'd faked everything else, love would be a walk in the park, orgasm a no-brainer.

"I could have come alone, Henry. I just thought it would be good for the two of you, you know, to see each other."

"But how? How?" The chains at his feet snaked across the floor.

"The proper letterheads. An ID. A badge. Some selective computer hacking. The basics, really." She grasped his hand with mock formality. "Agent Shannon Ambrose of the FBI. I'm here to ask for your cooperation in an investigation, Mr. Dickens."

His smile came easy. "Quite the chameleon ..."

"I have my ways."

"But if they're watching, listening ..." My father's eyes darted about the room.

"Don't worry, Henry. The Director and I made clear this interrogation is strictly on a need-to-know basis. No ears. No eyes. National security is at stake. Evidence has come to light that the Brittle Butcher may be a heretofore unsuspected precious asset in the war on terrorism."

My father slapped the table. His laughter boomed. "Homegrown or global?"

"Your call, Henry."

"No telling what folk will buy if it's a pretty girl selling."

"So," I said, again, "is one of you going to tell me what the fuck is going on?"

"Come. Sit with us, Rob."

I shook my head, arms folded. I was a kid again, the old man sitting there. I slammed my chair up against the wall and held my place. "If you think we're going to kiss and make up ... forget it. Just forget it."

Cori took another deep breath, and said, "Your father killed my parents. I'm here to thank him."

44

GOD, JESUS, AND DAD

I tabulated the twenty-seven victims in rapid sequence and threw the claim back at her. "He never killed anybody named Widdoes."

"I was Shannon Ambrose, then."

"No Ambroses, either."

"Between sixteen and seventeen," Dad said quietly. "If you go by the Feds' list, the ones they've attributed to me."

I reeled off the specifics without thinking. "Andrew Powers McVeeny. Akron, Ohio. Ball-peen hammer to the head. Nail through the heart ... Denis Lebel. Cape Porpoise, Maine. Lobster bait spike through the heart, lungs, and belly."

Cori wasn't sure whether to laugh or cry. "You know them all? Like ... like that?"

"Except for the ones I don't. Your parents, for example."

"It was carbon monoxide poisoning. Henry made it look like an accident. He did it for me."

"Tell me if I'm missing something, please. They were your parents, for God's sake."

"They were abusive."

"Ever hear of social workers?"

"In Simonette, Michigan? Hah!"

"The police?"

"You think it's that easy? I was eight years old. They'd adopted me. What did I know? I was a replacement for a daughter they'd lost—a dear sainted daughter I could never be. Or so they repeatedly reminded me. And while they never said what happened to her, it was easy for me to guess. Do you want to know what they did to me? How many years they did it for?"

"What about school? Teachers? You could have told—"

"I had no one. My world was the backyard. If it hadn't been for the moms and dads on TV, I'd have believed my life was normal. I had no one. Until your father heard my prayers."

"Come again?"

"Your father, he heard my prayers."

"And you call me messed up, Cor?"

"Makes us a perfect couple, wouldn't you say?"

"You should have told me at the start. Why pretend to be someone you're not?"

"I intended to. In the beginning. I wanted you to know your father wasn't a bad man. But the more I got to know you, your animosity for him, the less I felt I could. What was I supposed to say? 'Hey, Rob, I forgot to mention, your dad killed my parents.'"

"So you did marry me to get to him, then. Holy fucking shit."

"Henry and I, we wrote letters. Lots of letters. For years. He asked me to find you. To check in on you. To let him know you were all right, what you were up to. I didn't expect to fall in love with you."

"You love me. Sure."

"It's the one thing I won't fake."

"But you could."

"I wouldn't. Not with you."

Had she memorized the sappiest dialogue from every romantasy she'd ever read? "And I should believe this? Despite everything?" I'd had my fill of her.

Dad provided a footnote. "Shannon was thirteen when I received her first letter. Always a different name. But I knew who she was. All she had to do was mention Simonette. The others, none ever thanked me."

"Remember that night, Rob, you showed me your don't-mess-with-me look and I ran up to our bedroom?"

"That's got nothing to do—"

"In that moment, you were my father, the look he'd get just before he'd ... Henry answered my prayers."

"Hold on. Let me get this straight. You hired him to kill your parents?"

"No. Listen to me. I prayed to him."

"What's that even mean? You're saying he's God? Jesus? Nobody answers anybody's prayers. This guy killed people and you got lucky,

Cor. He killed *your* people, people who maybe—and who knows if it's not more of your bullshit?—just maybe happened to deserve it. Blind luck is what it was."

"You're wrong. Your father answered prayers. Every prayer he could. They all deserved it. Everyone he killed did."

"Are you kidding me?" I stared my father down. "What kind of crap have you been feeding her?"

"It's the truth," Cori said. "Tell him, Henry. Please. He needs to know."

"Know what? That you both belong in straitjackets?" I jumped up, as close to bouncing off the walls as I could get. "There's gotta be a word for this. A mental condition. Group hysteria or something."

Dad whispered, "I answered your prayers too, Bobby."

"More of your crap. I never prayed."

"You did. You know you did. After that night in Hershey Park, you prayed a lot. You wished I'd disappear. You wished me dead."

45

SHIT MY PSYCHOPATHIC DAD SAYS

I was guilty of my prayers as charged, yet hardly convinced he'd heard them. His God delusion confirmed what I'd suspected: he wanted to be caught. Peanut brittle as a weapon was out of character. Cute wasn't his style. Why after twenty-six killings (twenty-eight, counting Cori's folks) would he leave a calling card? Nor did he collect trophies, yet he'd kept the tire jack from Abel Willing's Dodge RAM. I'd naively believed he'd accepted responsibility for what befell him. Now, in his roundabout way, the sanctimonious bastard blamed me for derailing his spree. I could live with that. Happily.

"I'm sorry, son. I managed the disappearing part, it's the dead part that's been hard to come by."

"You ended up here," I said. "Banrum is the next best thing."

"Rob!" Cori admonished, like I cared.

"So, what are you saying, Dad, you're an avenging angel?"

"I don't know what I am. I just am."

"Great. I've got a wife who's a hundred different people and a father who isn't anybody. Please, just this once, be honest. No games. No lies. If there's more to you than cold-blooded murderer, tell me."

Cori objected. "Don't talk to him like that."

"I never murdered," he said. "I killed."

"Dead is dead. You don't measure it by degree."

"I do," he said. "The naturally dead. The tragically dead. The mercifully dead. The deservedly dead." And with eyes on me, an all-too-smug: "The spiritually dead."

"You think I care what you think? Cut the crap. Just tell me who you are. This is your last fucking chance. You owe me that."

"You'll think I'm insane."

"That's the problem. Had I thought for one second you were in any way crazy, I might have forgiven you. But you weren't crazy. You knew exactly what you were up to. The scariest thing about you has always been your sanity."

"He was saving people." Cori clung to their mutual fantasy. The righteousness.

"I have kept who I am to myself for good reason," Dad said. "It would make no difference."

"I warned you, Cor. Told you this would be a waste of time."

The touchy-feely serial killer was hurt. "Seeing you two, the three of us together, shouldn't this be good enough?"

"Christ! No."

"Please, Rob ..."

"He owes me, goddamn it. He fucked up my life. You owe me, old man."

"Your life is good, son. Look at her. You've got Shannon. Your Cori."

"Not for long. Not after this. And I have you to thank for that, along with all the other fucked up shit you've dumped on me. You think because you've been out of my life you haven't been part of my life? You're my whole fucking life, for God's sake. Every goddamn day, every goddamn night. I don't know when you're going to die and, frankly, I don't give a shit. But you fucking owe me an explanation."

Dad pushed back from the table as far as the leg irons would permit. "You won't like it."

"As if that'd be something new. What you going to tell me, you have a character flaw?"

"You won't believe it."

"If it's the truth ..."

"You won't think it is."

"Just fucking tell me. I need to know who the hell you are. Because it's the only way I'm going to know what the hell I am."

"It's tricky." The debate with himself was in full swing, the con weighing the pros and cons. "I can't tell you who I am."

"Perfect."

"Only where I began."

"Whatever you got ..."

All at once, the old degenerate was holding court atop the Tower of Babel. "I was born on my feet at the age of thirty-seven in the Classics section of Mara's Book Nook at 43 Main Street in Hillsdale at 10:28 on a Thursday morning in 1988."

46
HOW GOD MAKES A SERIAL KILLER

"This ought to be good." I settled into my seat for the entertainment to come.

"You were born where, Henry?" Cori questioned her Savior's sanity, at last.

I revised my previous opinion. He was some kind of crazy, after all, at the finish line of a decades-long decline. I needed to ease off the acting-out, let this mistake of a day run its slapstick course.

"I tried to tell you," Dad said. "Hey, if some jailbird hit me with a whopper like this, I'd think he was nuts too."

"I don't think you're nuts." Cori rested her hand on his.

"The deluded leading the gullible," I muttered.

Cori talked over me. "I've never thought that Henry. Please, I want to hear."

"It gets crazier," he said. Had it been thirty minutes earlier, I'd have accused him of stringing us along. Now, I sensed he believed every word that spewed from his sorry trap. Serial killers are by nature conniving and manipulative, but my father never was. Unless he'd connived and manipulated me into thinking he was neither. "In the end, all you'll know is what I know."

"Or what you pretend to know," I said.

He sighed, crumpled forward as if his batteries had died, then set his eyes on the floor and the wackadoodle tale unspooling on the widescreen between his feet. And suddenly his delivery was that of a TV preacher stirring up his flock. "I don't know where I've been or where I'm going. I've stepped out of one dream and entered the next, except I don't remember what the other dream was. And I'm in a bookstore, of all places, perusing the stacks, three books at my nose: Henry James's *The Turn of the Screw*, Samuel Taylor Coleridge's *The Rime of the Ancient Mariner*, and Charles Dickens's *Pickwick Papers*. It's my name. Right there. Plain as day. Henry Taylor Dickens. It's who I am, who I've always been. And hey, the sun is shining, and out I go. The air is fresh. Feels good. So I feel good too. Alive. Excited. Like this dream is going to be a great dream. Like good is coming my way.

"And right off the bat, there's this hearse moving up the street, and close behind a second. Two hearses, one funeral. If this isn't an omen, what would be? What's a soul to do? I follow, right alongside the others, and up into the church.

"Two coffins rest by the altar. Big, shiny boxes. Cherry wood. Brass fittings. Quality, if I've ever seen. And taking her seat at the front is this woman dressed in black. Her lips the reddest of red. Hair like ginger. Eyes so green, her inner light reaches all the way to where I stand. She's my calling. My raison d'être. I push through the pews, take the seat beside her.

"She wants to know why I'm in the family section. Am I a friend of her parents? A relative she's never met? I look to either side. It's only the two of us. I tell her nothing. Nothing. And then, *then*, she thanks me for coming. She thanks me, because she did not want to be alone.

"The eulogies begin. She doesn't cry. She coughs. She has a cold, maybe. I offer her a candy. A cinnamon candy from my pocket. An Atomic Fireball. She laughs and takes it. She laughs at her parents' funeral and takes a candy from me. This is when I tell her, 'I'm a sinner too, like you.' She snorts, tries not to laugh, but can't help herself. Except she makes it look like she's crying.

"People pray. They sing hymns. And just as the whole shebang wraps up, she asks if I'm coming to the cemetery. Or the reception. 'No,' I tell her, but promise we'll be seeing plenty of each other. 'You're going to be my wife,' I say, and she looks at me same way you two are looking at me now—like I'm out of my mind. And I look at her, same way I'm looking at you now, as if I'm saner than sane. She bursts out laughing. She doesn't care who sees it now. She opens her purse. She gives me her card. Heather Blythe-Blessing. A hyphenated surname, no less. And she says—get this!—she says, 'If only you had let me know in advance, we could have killed two birds with one church visit: I'd have worn a wedding gown.' It's my turn to laugh, and laugh I do.

"The mourners file out. And all that's left is this big, beautiful church, God, the devil, and me. And it's only then I see I'm dressed for the occasion. Black suit. White shirt. Black tie. Shiny black shoes. And my earthly purpose becomes abundantly clear: I have been put here for funerals."

I couldn't let the line stand unchallenged. "To attend them or to make more of them?"

"And there you are and here I am," he said, as if reemerged from baptismal waters. "Whatever dream I dreamed, I'm dreaming it still."

What could I say? I couldn't despise him more than I already did. The old fart was impenetrable. A wall within a wall, baloney, bunk, and Cheese Whiz bricks.

When did the lines between reality and fantasy blur? Was he a psychopath playing a sociopath playing a narcissist? Would an early diagnosis have prevented the pain and misery he inflicted?

I did not debate the illogic of his logic. "And the prayers, the killings?"

"Your mother facilitated all, of course."

"Huh? She was in on it with you?"

"Were you not listening? Was I not clear? She had a hyphenated last name. A good Christian name. Blythe-Blessing. Your mother made me respectable, beyond reproach. A good family with standing in a small town. Any avenger wishing to evade detection cannot ask for more."

"Avenger? That's how you see yourself? Holy cow!"

"What then?" He patted Cori's hand. "Ask those I saved."

Cori looked a little sickly, Henry's lunacy at odds with the imaginary friend she'd nurtured since childhood.

I capitalized on the lull, asked the question I'd once posed to my mother. "Did you know what Mom was up to? Her other life?"

"God, how I miss her." He inhaled, savored the memories. "I wasn't blind. I was aware she had hastened the deaths of her mother and father. Not by premeditation, but with a malevolent benevolence. You witness your daughter performing the unspeakable, and should your health be precarious to begin with, well ... their misfortune was my good fortune."

"How romantic," I said. The twofer funeral had brought my parents together, their secrets had kept them together. It was in line with what Dr. Cutcheon had said: The foundation of every successful marriage rests upon not what a husband and wife share with one another, but what they choose to keep from one another.

"Did you always hear the prayers, Henry?" Cori continued to take him seriously.

"From the moment I opened my eyes."

"You heard voices."

"More like notions. Like the dusty bits that go floating through your eyes. I could ignore them some of the time, but not all of the time. And once I started, I could not ignore any of them, any of the time."

I expressed my next thought in the nicest way possible. "You ever been checked for schizophrenia?"

"Give it a rest, Rob."

"It's okay, Shannon. Years ago, I checked myself in for a battery of tests. You need to understand, I did not answer a single prayer until I was confident they were real. Schizophrenia. Brain tumor. Epilepsy. Ménière's disease. Tinnitus. I saw doctors for anything and everything that could have put the notions in my head."

"Mom knew about this too?"

"The prayers? Never."

"What about amnesia?"

"I am not a soap opera."

"But goddamn close to one."

"With amnesia, there's this sense a part of your life has gone missing. Not me. My life was all there. It was waiting for me to find inside Mara's Book Nook. Don't forget too, after my arrest, my mug was everywhere, on TV, newspapers. If it was amnesia, wouldn't someone have recognized me?"

There were so many holes in his story I didn't know which to fill first. The town never had any bookstore, none I remembered. "Why didn't you just use a gun? It would have been way simpler, don't you think? Your killings were messy. Vicious. You enjoyed what you did way too much."

"I did not enjoy any of it."

"C'mon! Taking a drill to some guy's head and sticking candy in the hole?"

"I took pleasure only in the knowledge I had helped a soul in need."

"And he says it with a straight face! C'mon, Cor, you can't be buying this crap?"

Dad rattled his chains. "You think you have all the answers."

"A damn sight more than you."

Cori pitched another softball. "Do the prayers still come to you, Henry?"

"The range is limited in here, so it's mostly prayers I don't want to hear. There are people in Banrum who deserve to be and a good many who don't. But every man here is wished dead by someone, if not himself. On visitors' day, you would not believe the prayers I hear: 'Please let this be the last time I see Jerome alive.' 'Dear God, may someone run a shiv through Chazzy's ribs.' 'Sweet Jesus, I pray you take my Donald now.' 'Please kill Enrico and I promise never to ask more of You.' They fill my head and fade away and fill my head again. If I could help, I would."

I played along with Cori's reasoning. "Before. Back then. Did you answer every prayer?"

"Lots of people pray other people dead. Lots pray themselves dead. I heard them all. But you must believe me, I answered only the prayers of those who deserved to have their prayers answered."

"Judge, jury, and executioner, eh?"

"The calling is higher. When good people pray to you, you know. There's a clarity of purpose." He pressed his trigger finger to his temple. "The prayers that mattered stayed here."

"Like Cori's—like Shannon's prayers," I said.

"Like yours," he said.

Cori bit her lip, hesitated. "It took you forever to answer mine, though, Henry."

"I didn't get up to Michigan much. I had a candy business to keep up. I worked you in first chance. I worked everyone in. Until I couldn't."

"How many prayers did you answer, Dad?"

"Life is the dream. Death is the awakening."

"More than twenty-seven, for sure," I said. "There's Cori's parents, plus .... Give me a ballpark, at least."

"I killed before I was born. I will kill after I am dead."

Hoo, boy! No stopping him and his whack-job narrative.

Cori tried to bring him back to Earth. "Do you know about the murders in Hillsdale, Henry?"

He wasn't clear on what she was asking. "I never killed anyone in Hillsdale. It was the only place I ever was where nobody prayed anybody dead. Until you, Bobby—until you prayed me dead."

47

THE JUICY PARTS

Cori gave him the rundown on Willow and family. "The police think Rob did it, Henry." She capped her recap with a jarringly upbeat, "Rob's prime suspect," and looked to me as if I'd made the honor roll.

My father kept to the loony lane. "You hear prayers too?" he said to me, enthused by the prospect.

"I what? Jesus, Dad!"

"It's possible you black out when you kill, Bobby. Your mind shuts down until the deed is done. Happens all the time. I know a fellow in here who—"

"Don't go there. Don't lay your psychobabble on me. I'm not you."

"Unless you are, son, and don't know it."

"Right. And, during these blackouts, I suppose I wash the blood from my hands and burn my clothes and carry on enjoying the best that life has to offer. Of course."

"Yes. Exactly. You would do all the right things."

"Fuck off." I kicked the chair aside and stomped to the door. "Time to go, Agent Ambrose."

Cori stayed the course. "Rob didn't do it, Henry."

"How did they die?" he asked.

"Bludgeoned with a lamp. Stabbed with a ski pole."

"Sounds like me, except I never killed kids. I didn't answer those prayers." And then to me: "I don't see why the killer can't be you, Bobby."

"What the fuck is the matter with you? You're the murderer in this family."

"Killer," he corrected. "I am a killer."

"If not Rob, who then, Henry?"

"Someone like him."

"Fuck you." For a would-be writer, my arsenal of scathing rejoinders was severely limited.

"Life and death balance out, son. Maybe your job is to answer the wrong prayers. I'm yang, you're yin."

If there was any person I had ever wanted to kill, it was my father then and there. I'd covered off a hundred possibilities as to how this reunion might go. Uncomfortable. Bitter. Sloppy. Sentimental. Remorseful. None touched the ape-shit reality.

"Could it be a copycat killer, Henry?"

"Every killing is a copycat. There's no imagination nowadays. Bang bang. Stab stab. But the way you describe this one, it bears all the earmarks of revenge. What did they do to you, Bobby?"

"Who?"

"The dead family."

"I didn't know them."

"Except for the girl," Cori corrected.

"Willow, yeah. But I didn't really know her."

"Did she hurt you? Something to disturb you? Rebuffed your advances?"

"Please," I pleaded to Agent Ambrose, "end this."

"Have there been other killings?" he asked.

"A man is missing," Cori said. "Joe Di Iorio."

"This man, he wronged you, Bobby?"

"Who says he's dead?" I kept quiet about the delivery kid and ballcap.

"But he knew you, didn't he?"

"It was me he really knew," Cori said.

"Were there killings before you returned to Hillsdale, Bobby?"

"How should I know?"

"If you didn't commit the murders, Bobby—and I'm not prepared to say you didn't—you could be the guiding light. It's you who's decided who should die. The catalyst."

"Wow, that's some leap."

"Are there are others whom you've crossed?"

"This is idiocy."

"Do the prayers come to you too? I'm your father. I will understand. You can tell me."

"Fuck off."

"Or did you pray them dead? The girl and her family. Shannon's gentlemen friend, Mr. Oreo."

"I told you, I don't pray."

"The Messners, Rob," Cori said, fear dawning. "They wronged us, didn't they?"

"These Messners, they're dead too?" my father asked.

"They're fine," I said dismissively. "They did nothing. They're absolutely fine."

"A wish from you could be all it takes, Bobby."

"Yeah, that's it. You got it. One wish from me and *poof!* you're dead. Funny though, you're still breathing, aren't you?"

"Are you saying someone is answering Rob's prayers, Henry? Like you answered mine?"

"Someone is answering prayers. But not the prayers I would have answered."

"It's over," I said. "If you don't end this, Cor, I will."

"He's right, Henry. I'm sorry, but it's probably best if we finish up."

The ordeal was over, except for the cringeworthy melodrama of their goodbyes.

"I'll never forget," Cori promised.

"I should never have left you to them for as long as I did."

"I had faith you'd come, Henry."

Dad placed a hand over his heart. "Of all the souls I saved, yours has meant the most to me."

"I wouldn't be here without you."

"You take care of yourself, Shannon. You have a good life. You take care of Bobby too, you hear?"

"If he'll let me, Henry."

Their embrace was at risk of triple overtime when the attention returned to me.

"Well, son, this is how it ends for us."

"They're not going to kill you," I said. "They never will."

"We'll see how your argument holds come March."

He parted his arms, chains jangling, and invited me in for a hug. *Fuck that.* The eight feet between us was fine with me.

He said, "I am sorry for what I did to you. I am sorry for who I am and who you think I am."

I studied my shoelaces, recalled reading how the plastic tips were called aglets.

"For God's sake, at least shake his hand," Cori cried.

Pleasing my fraud of a wife was the least of my priorities, yet I found myself giving in. Not for her, for me. I hadn't expected much, though I had hoped for more. I'd come looking for revelation, not for whatever this was. Exasperation. Bloviation. Capitulation.

Dad and me, we locked eyes for the only time that morning and shook hands with no shared understanding of what we were shaking on. My only goal was to break the grip before he did. I felt no satisfaction when I succeeded. "You don't deserve even this," I said. "I've forgotten nothing."

"Why do you speak in the negative? Why didn't you say, 'I remember everything?'"

"Because negative is all you are to me."

He couldn't raise his shoulders high enough to pull off a credible shrug, only enough to rap the chain into my knee. (Looking back, I'm pretty sure he was aiming for my nuts.)

"Sorry," he said, with no hint that he was. "I didn't mean to hurt you."

"You didn't. You can't. You never will again."

Cori watched impassively. She gave the red button by the door three quick beeps. We waited for the guards.

"Shannon tells me you're writing a book," he said.

"She tells you too much."

"Is it about me?"

"As little as possible."

"Your mom and me, we gave you some juicy material, huh?"

"One way of putting it."

"Your book, I'd like to think it'll be my last words."

"No, Dad. No. The words will be mine. And they won't be my last."

"Okay, if that's what you think. Son."

48
FATHER VERSUS FATHER-IN-LAW

Assistant Warden Curtis Mangold had left a note for Agent Ambrose at the main gate. It could have been worse. He could have come to say goodbye in person.

I watched as Cori read. It was typewritten on yellow Banrum stationery. By typewritten, I'm talking Smith Corona. Had I been ready to talk to her, I would have asked if it was a marriage proposal. Instead, I feigned disinterest.

She sighed, snorted, laughed, and sighed again before reading the note aloud, behaving as if nothing had changed between us. For Christ's sake, I'd yet to shake off the sewage that was my father.

From the desk of
Curtis C. Mangold, BSCJ
Assistant Warden

January 1, 2020

Dear Shannon,

Regrettably, unforeseen events prevent me from seeing you off in person. I enjoyed chatting with you. I hope we can renew our acquaintanceship soon.

I trust your interrogation proved fruitful. Your assignment seemed daunting. However, I have every faith in your professional ability to achieve the desired outcome. In the short time I have come to know you, it is evident you are a credit to the Bureau.

Henry Taylor Dickens will be executed on March 16 at 2200 hours. Should you wish to attend, I will be pleased to reserve a seat in your name. Perhaps we could go to PF Chang's afterward. Please let me know at your convenience.

Fondly,
Curtis Mangold, BSCJ
Curtis

Banrum Correctional Institution
Office of Administration
Gator Jump, Florida 34144

I maintained my silence and she made no effort to draw me out. At first.

We returned the Suburban to Alamo, reclaimed the Pilot.

I hit the gas hard, anxious to make good our getaway. Anywhere was better than Gator Jump and Banrum, even the hometown of the Brittle Butcher and his head case of a son. The sooner we got home, the sooner Cori and I could sort out our future. Not that I saw one.

In her own way, I suppose, she'd already begun the sorting, babbling before we reached the Interstate, looking to fill the void my sulking left. Far as I could tell, guilt had never been much of a factor in her life, and she wasn't about to make it one now, whatever her wrongdoing.

"I get it," she said. "You're worried about Mangold or the warden discovering what I've done—who I am."

She was too cool. Too flippant. Worse, she was reading my mind, as closed as it was.

"Do you think for one second either of them will risk the embarrassment of going public, that their security can be so easily breached? By a woman, yet? And if anyone does get suspicious, actually investigate, all they'll find is that Agent Shannon Ambrose has gone deep undercover. You think I haven't thought it through? Believe me, Shannon Ambrose is as real as any agent, right down to the personnel records at 935 Pennsylvania Avenue Northwest, Washington, DC. You should see Shannon's commendations. They'd blow you away."

She had all the angles covered. She was so damn sure of herself.

"Deception is rarely about facts, it's about style. FBI Agent Ambrose is as real as she'll ever need to be."

I yawned cynicism.

"Don't think I'm not aware of the consequences. Title eighteen, U.S.C., section 912, I know it by heart: 'Whoever falsely assumes or pretends to be an officer or employee acting under the authority of the United States or any department, agency or officer thereof, and acts as such, or in such pretended character demands or obtains any money, paper, document, or thing of value, shall be fined under this title or imprisoned not more than three years, or both.' Even if it came to pass, three years isn't the end of the world. A fine most likely. Minimum security at worst. Time off for good behavior. Six months at most."

Nothing she could say or do would surprise me anymore.

"Curtis wrote a nice letter of reference, don't you think?" Her irreverence grated. "Please, Rob, are you never going to talk to me?"

"Who would I be talking to—Cori or Shannon? My dentist or my lawyer?" So much for my vow of silence.

"Whichever makes you hornier."

"Funny."

"Or would you prefer a Mandy or a Bambi? Or how about Amber? Lots of guys like Amber."

"You would know."

"You can't accept the truth even when it's staring you in the face."

"You're joking, right? You. My father." I pinched the air. "This much truth would be refreshing." Was there anyone in my life who didn't have some other life?

Her mood darkened. She folded her hands into her lap. When she spoke again, her voice was so low key, so uncharacteristically without emotion, she could have been rattling off the mileage markers that lined the ramp to 75. "Shannon Ambrose was the name my dead parents gave me. I changed it to Corinne Meredith Widdoes as soon as I was old enough. It was the first ordinary name I found that didn't have any exact Google matches. I don't know what my birth mother named me. I've never found any records. And I've tried, believe me. My past is as murky as your father's. For all I know, I was kidnapped as a baby."

"Or born in a bookstore." I didn't want to be talking, yet here I was.

"Seeing your father meant a great deal to me."

"The two of you, it was nauseating."

"He saved my life."

"If you'd only been open with me, it wouldn't have mattered."

"But it matters now?"

"You made a fool of me."

"You are a fool. You had the chance for closure and you threw it away."

"Closure doesn't exist."

"You finally get to see your dad and you behave like an immature asshole."

"Were you there? Did you hear a word he said?"

"Did you hear the things you said to him?"

"He called me a murderer, for fuck's sake. Where does he get off—?"

"One mistake doesn't dismiss all the good he's done."

"Twenty-nine mistakes and counting, from what I gather."

"They weren't mistakes. The Ambroses were not mistakes."

"Name me one serial killer who hasn't claimed to be God in one form or another. They all answer prayers. Their own."

"I prayed for my parents to die every morning and every night from the time I was four. The one who answered my prayers was your father. I knew he was coming. He told me he was."

"He told you? What, like in an email, a text, divine revelation?"

"I can't explain it, all right? All I know is he was with me from my first prayer. He comforted me. He kept me alive. And you want to know something else? I saw him kill them. I saw exactly how he did it. I saw how he put them to sleep, how he dragged them to the car. It was the most beautiful thing I ever saw. And when he was done, you know what he did? He hugged me and told me everything was going to be all right. I was going to grow up to be smart and pretty and happy. And that the good in my life would outweigh the bad. And he carried me into the kitchen and sat me at the table and made me toast with butter and apple jelly. And he warmed up some milk and poured it into a cup. And he tucked me into bed and kissed me on the head and promised me I'd have only good dreams from that night on. The last thing he said to me was the same thing he said to me this morning: 'I should never have left you to them for as long as I did.' He stayed until I fell asleep. And then he called the police and left."

"A serial killer with a heart of gold. Really, Cor? And your aunt, Maureen or whatever?"

"She wasn't my aunt. She was my last foster mother. I must have lived in a dozen different homes before her. Those families, they taught me a lot. They taught me how to be whoever I needed to be. But that stopped with Maureen. She was the first real mother I knew. I lived with her from the time I was twelve till she died. I was seventeen."

"But not in Eden Prairie. Not in Minnesota."

"Ann Arbor. Eden Prairie just sounded like a nice place to live."

Her eyes were wet. I should have pulled off the highway and consoled her. I wanted to. "My father manipulated you."

"You're impossible."

"You know how psychics and mediums work? Ever see those phonies on TV who talk with the dead? It's all crap. They read people. Demographics. Body language. You were a child. You were easy prey, Cor. My father conned you. Murderers are good at that. The fact your parents might have deserved it was a fluke."

"He cut the crusts off my toast. I didn't ask him to. He knew how I liked it. No one ever did that for me."

"Yeah, well, I didn't like crusts either, but you think he ever cut mine?"

"It's a competition now?"

"You've seen what he's capable of. There's nothing mystical about murder. If there's anything supernatural about him, it's that he's less than human."

"He's still your father."

"Think so? I saw him in action too, Cor. You told me yours, let me tell you mine."

49
THE STORY I TOLD HER

It was summer. Mom was in Europe on what she called *a buying trip*, and Dad had candy business in Pennsylvania to tend to. I was excited. I'd never gone on a business trip with him.

There was shoofly pie, the pretzel factory in Lititz (I laughed my ass off at the name), Wilbur Chocolates in Lancaster, and the Hershey factory tour. But none of it had been much fun. Not really. I was with my dad, but he was never quite with me.

His attention had strayed from the outset. Although his business was mostly in and around Lancaster, he'd taken us miles off the beaten track on each of the seven days we'd spent in the state. The last night began as more of the same.

Dusk dissolved into darkness as we flanked the outskirts of a deadbeat town. The headlights of our Impala flicked from high to low, each click an empty chamber in a game of Russian roulette. Through straightaways and S-curves we drove, along a stretch of rutted asphalt, before slowing along a lengthy dip between a graveyard and a drive-in movie.

An A-frame cottage stood back from the road. Like you see in ski country. Overhanging eaves. Steeply inclined roof. More windows than walls.

Every lamp in the place was lit, a giant Christmas tree illuminated from the inside out.

In the driveway, a car and U-Haul trailer.

"Is the roof slopey on the inside too?" I asked.

"Gotcha!" Dad said. "Game, set, match."

"What, Daddy?"

We coasted further up the road and onto the gravel shoulder.

The screen of the drive-in loomed ahead. Slivers of Marvel's *X-Men* flickered through the trees. I watched the fragmented action, as Dad ruminated beside me, his breathing the soundtrack. I asked if he knew the people who lived there. "Are they like friends?" Something was off. Like his brain was on a break from his body.

He steered the car into a shallow gully. Branches scratched at the doors and windows. *Witches' fingers, werewolf claws.* "You stay here, Bobby. Don't move until I get back."

He rummaged about the trunk for a bit, and lowered the lid without the customary thud. He handed me a grape Tootsie Pop and warned me again to stay put. He wore gloves. He carried a flashlight. The beam bobbed like a Wiffle ball as he hiked up through the bushes and into the night.

Crickets chirped.

Less of the screen was visible from the gully. Mostly foreheads and hair.

The Tootsie Pop was down to its chewy chocolate center when impatience got the better of me.

I scrambled up to the road. I walked as taught, facing the traffic, though any traffic thereabouts was confined to the drive-in.

Jhit! Jhit! I heard the house before I saw it. Squadrons of suicidal bugs divebombed a blue zapper. *Jhit! Jhit! Jhit! Jhit!*

Set back from the road up a grassy knoll, the chalet shone distinct and still. *Jhit!*

The front of the house was largely glass, though my view of the upper level was limited from where I stood. Bookcase. Headboard. Paintings.

I inched through the dirt, walked my fingers across the panels of the U-Haul, and froze at the sound of a clunk from within. I listened for more, heard nothing, moved on.

Two porches fronted the cottage, a broad lower and a narrow upper, small, perfect hearts routed into the railings. I thought to knock on the door and ask for my dad, but the windows were bare and, considering his warnings, I decided a peek inside a wiser option.

I crossed to the base of the A and center stage. My private drive-in.

At the fireplace, some beer-bellied guy steadied himself against the mantel. A brass poker hung at his side. A coffee mug lay broken at his feet, a brownish puddle at his heels. His hair was thick and wet at the crown. The wet was red. Had he bumped his head? I once cracked my head on a kitchen cupboard and bled all over the place.

In the foreground, a woman slouched on a loveseat. Her back to me. Black hair to her shoulders.

Across from her, at the TV, my father. His flashlight dangled from his belt. He was holding a knife. The blade was long, flat, and gleaming.

Andy Griffith was on the TV. Not the show with Opie. The other one. The lawyer one.

Why I thought my father would be glad to see me, I do not know. I rapped on the glass of the patio door. "Daddy!" I waved, forgetting I had disobeyed.

The paunchy guy goggled, bewildered by my appearance, and my father made the most of the distraction. He was on the guy in a flash, and with a move both quick and deft, he drove his knife through the man's mid-section and impaled him to the paneling.

My heart dropped to my gut and caromed off the lining. Pee streamed down my leg.

The man hung suspended from his gut. Scarlet tears welled in his eyes. Fluids burbled from his mouth. Slowly, gravity dragged him to the floor, his descent a graven signature of tissue, blood, and scarred paneling. *Jhit! Jhit!*

The woman leapt from the sofa, dashed for the door, but my father cut her off at the pass. She was tall. Taller than she'd appeared sitting down. Taller even than my dad. And I'd never seen anyone so scared in all my life. Her whole face was mouth.

She swung around the couch, snatched up the brass poker, flung it at my father, and disappeared up the stairs.

Purposeful. Methodical. *All the time in the world.* Dad returned to the dead man. He planted his foot on his chest and pulled out the knife. He motioned for me to stay put. He wasn't fooling this time. He was not happy to see me. And not only because I'd peed myself.

He took to the staircase, three steps at a bound. I waited as bugs fried. *Jhit! Jhit!*

Watched TV.

Watched the dead man and his blood. And not just blood. *God, no.* This was blood at high tide. I swear. And it was wending away from the body and coursing to where I stood at the patio doors.

From inside and overhead, a crash of glass and metal, the fight carrying to the balcony above. Grunts. Scratching and tearing. Screams and shouts. Words packed in terror. The woman. Begging my father to spare her. Cursing him. Pleading for mercy. Hollering for help. The most horrific sound I've heard in all my life. A voice I've tried to forget. A voice I never will. Nails creaked resistance.

Wood ripped from wood.

Gargling. Gagging. A soprano's fart.

A dust jacket fluttered down from above. *Lonesome Dove* by Larry McMurtry. (Years later, I read it just to see.)

Then nothing. Not a peep for one whole commercial break. If I'd been home, I would have flipped channels. The show was lame. Andy Griffith mostly, with actors sticking their noses into his bushy ears.

And the dead man's blood kept coming.

Up the window it streamed. *Up.* I'm not kidding. A gallon of red paint in a topsy-turvy world.

The dark-haired lady reappeared, tumbling down the stairs, crashing into the TV, sending Andy Griffith to the floor face-first.

She staggered to her feet. Spotted me at the window. *The boy who'd peed his pants her only hope.*

She lurched toward me. Frankenstein on weed. Her face a cartoony muddle, lips and teeth petitioning secession from her mouth. *"Save me, little boy. Save me."*

Blood chugged from her nostrils.

Blood soaked her hair and eyebrows.

My father's knife protruded from her belly, lodged to its hilt, her fingers curled around it. Three fingers, anyhow. Two were MIA.

She reached out, rammed herself flush against the glass dividing us.

The barrier baffled her. *An invisible shield?* She stretched her arms above her head, jumping jacks the evident solution. And again she drove herself into the glass, humping the patio doors, howling as she pounded my father's knife beyond the hilt, deeper into her mangled middle, till the knife was only a nub.

The window popped.

A hole the size and shape of an egg, the nub resting within the curve, propping her upright, until the hole sprung leaks.

Spider legs. North. South. East. West.

The glass collapsed.

And the woman splashed down in a grisly backwash. Enough to benefit your local blood bank for a year.

From inside came a fatherly: "How ya doin', Bobby?"

I could not see him.

"Go wait by the trailer."

I could not move.

"Do what I say. Now."

My feet refused to budge.

He strode onto the porch, chuckled. "Looks like you got yourself some red vengeance."

It brought to mind the fake waterfall at Wok In The Park. Except this waterfall ran red, and it was rushing up and over the sill and rail and onto the porch toward dumbstruck me.

Eddying.

Down and about.

Bridging the cracks.

Carrying shards and slivers.

Consuming the dust jacket that had fluttered from above.

Seeking me out. Closing in. Surrounding me. Lapping at my Nikes. I spun to escape and slammed my foot into a post.

"Red vengeance," my father repeated. He unwrapped a package of rubber gloves and handed them to me. They were oversized and yellow. I slipped a hand into each and he carried me through the busted doors into the house.

He plunked me onto the toilet seat, and went about extinguishing the lights.

"Strange to say, son, but blood draining from a body has a mind of its own at times. Gets attracted to the last person the freshly dead saw. That's red vengeance for you. In the case of those two, it happened to be you. Just the way it works."

"Will it come after me again?"

"Not likely." He winked. "Unless you get to be the last person some other freshly dead sees."

"I don't want to be."

"It's not always our choice to make."

"They were bad people, right?"

"Bad doesn't begin to describe it, son."

"But you're good, right?"

"What do you think!"

I should have been on his side, based on family ties and whatnot. Problem was, there was damn little I could salvage from what I'd seen. "I peed myself," I said.

"So I see."

"I hurt my toe too."

"It'll heal." He had this huge honking smile, all teeth and gums, as he fussed about the place. A blind guy could have seen how crazy happy he was. Like he'd just been invited to come on down, *"Because you, Henry Dickens, are the next contestant on The Price is Right."*

"Did you smell it?" he asked.

"Smell what?"

"Death."

"I don't know."

"There's a sweetness to it. Smells like glee."

"What does, Daddy?"

"Death, Bobby. Death smells like glee."

I loved my father. But from this moment on I would love him less. He was not a good man. I knew this. He was a scary man. I saw this. The guilt filled me up. It would have been so easy, had I the frailty of character to reverse my sense of right and wrong.

I could snitch on him, of course. But what would become of him? *What would THEY do to him?* Think the worst of me, sure. Accuse me of backtracking on history to save my own skin. But I swear to you and any God to whom you pray, it never crossed my mind that others had died by his hand, or that others would. The adventure was a one-off. *A very special episode of Daddy & Bobby.*

"I got blood on me," I said.

"Me too."

We stripped to our socks. Dad sprayed our clothes and sneakers with Wisk and ran them through the washer and dryer, while I kept watch for red vengeance.

We took showers.

While we waited for our clothes to dry, Dad returned the knife to a leather sheath that hung from a hook on the back door. I'd thought the knife had been his.

When the clothes were dry, Dad examined each item for blood. We dressed and got the hell out.

The bodies lay where they fell.

You'd think we might have run or at least moved at a getaway clip, keeping to the shadows. Nope. Not Dad.

He hauled a crowbar from the trunk of the dead people's car and smashed the padlock on the rear of the U-Haul. He did not open the U-Haul doors. *Jhit! Jhit!*

"What's in there?" I asked.

"Will knowing change your life, Bobby?"

He took my rubber gloves and threw them under the U-Haul.

We got to our car as the drive-in was letting out. Headlights and taillights in either direction. "We'll wait," Dad said. "No point fighting traffic." His jubilation was on the downswing, raising my hope he might yet show concern for what had happened. But something was off with me too. I should have been crying. I should have been in shock. Where was the trauma? What eleven-year-old witnesses shit like this and doesn't react, short of pissing his pants? A kid has to be pretty damaged. He either blocks it out or stores it for future trauma.

We slumped low in our seats, bided our time among the bushes, loath to breathe should the vapors betray our presence.

Cars kept coming. Shafts of light carved up the dark, lacerated the trees. Halogen mortars flared in our faces.

Tires screeched. Horns honked. Boys shouted. Girls laughed.

I pulled off my shoe and sock, massaged the toe I'd stubbed. I reached for the dome light, but my father swatted my hand. "No lights." Only time he ever hit me.

"Will my nail turn black?" I asked. "The toe I stubbed?"

He craned his neck, squinted through the herky-jerky bursts of dark and light. Somebody was out there. Closing in on our car.

"Have you ever had a black nail, Daddy?"

He retrieved a paper bag from under his seat. He put his hand inside the bag and left it there. I thought the bag might be peanuts or jujubes. Hoped he'd share.

A girl emerged from the bushes, raced up to our car. A boy followed. He was happy and drooly, and slowed as he saw her. He shed his tee and she faced him square, raised herself up onto the hood.

The boy kicked off his jeans. The girl leaned back, spread her legs. The boy stepped toward her and the girl threw off her tank top.

The boy hopped onto the bumper, and up went her legs, scissoring him at his waist, easing him down on top of her. They kissed, slobbered, gobbled each other up, hands all over, in and out of everywhere, the girl's bare butt suctioned to the windshield, inches from my face, and in all of thirty seconds she became my first true love.

Dad rested the paper bag and his hand atop the steering wheel.

The kids rocked, and the car rocked too, their bodies slapping and whacking in sweaty acclamation. The boy thrust down. The girl thrust up. She squeegeed to the right, her fingers in his hair, pushing down on his head, forcing him to her waist, until the boy began to slide, floundered for purchase, failed. She lunged to catch him. His chin hit the hood and the hood clunked open. The boy dropped from view and the girl did too.

They rushed to retrieve their clothing, pouncing, bouncing, laughing, jostling. Dad followed their retreat, his paper bag trained on them as they skedaddled the way they'd come.

"She was cute," I said, as yet unaware my predilection for sex on low carbon steel had been imprinted on my nascent libido.

Dad returned the paper bag to where he'd found it.

"Who were they, Daddy?"

"Stupid kids," he said.

"Not them. The man and lady, back at the house. What did they do that was bad?"

My father's face was blue-gray, like Andy Griffith's on the dead people's TV. His lips moved, though words failed to follow.

"I'm sorry, Daddy," I said, without knowing why.

"Do you have any idea what this world would be like if bad people had their way?" His voice was steady, a murmured narrative set to a cricket serenade. "They go about their business, confident in their anonymity. But I know."

"What do you know?"

He pumped locked fists onto the horn. Whatever he was thinking had him smiling again. I had liked his smile. I didn't like it anymore. Never would again. "I'm going to need your help," he said. Did he want me to be his sidekick, the Robin to his Batman?

"To kill people?"

"You cannot tell anyone about tonight. Not Mommy. Not your friends. Not Wade Griffiths. Not anyone. Not ever. Do you understand?"

I wished I didn't.

"I've got your back, son. You need to have mine. Bad people are everywhere. If I don't stop them, there's no telling who they'll hurt next. People we love, even."

"Are you a crimefighter?"

"You've got to promise me, Bobby, no matter what." He squeezed my hand and I squeezed back. I'd like to say this was a special moment, the bond between my father and me up there with the all-time great father-son duos. His hand was cold. My flagging faith had turned his blood to ice.

"I promise," I said.

He went outside and popped the hood shut.

The Impala groaned out of the embankment.

"What were their names?"

"The bad people?"

I switched on the dome light, checked out my toenail.

"I'll know tomorrow," he said, "when I read the newspaper."

"It's blue. I bet it turns black. Wade had a black thumbnail once."

"Listen to me, son. I'm not playing at this here. You can't tell anyone. Because if you did, well, I'd be sad if the bad people came looking for you."

Child psychology was not my dad's forte.

50

THROUGH GEORGIA AND INTO THE CAROLINAS

"THE CORI MONOLOGUES"

"My God, Rob, why wouldn't you have told me any of this before? If I'd known ... It's all so contradictory to how he was with me. Even the way he went about it with the Ambroses. I don't think they suffered much. A little, sure, but no worse than what they gave. Except for the dying part, I guess. But what Henry did to you, that's unforgiveable. You have every right. I'm so sorry. I'm saying it all wrong. I just don't want you to think ... I don't know. I just want to make it right with you. With us."

I was talked out.

"I cried when the police came. I put on this big show. I was convincing even then. Little Orphan Shannon was a heartbreaker. Crying on the outside, laughing on the inside. Okay, maybe not laughing, but I wasn't sad. Not one bit."

I focused on the road.

"I've thought of doing the DNA thing, find out who I am. But what if the person I am isn't anyone I want to be? What if my birth parents, my brothers or sisters ... what if they're bigger monsters than the monsters I've known? It'd be like opening the door."

I said nothing.

"You laugh at my prayers, my belief in your father, yet I'm supposed to believe you were chased by blood? Perhaps we should accept who we are —two stark raving crazies in love."

I clicked on the radio. She clicked it off.

"There was this old movie—*The Great Impostor*. TCM was all Aunt Maureen watched. That, and Lifetime. Anyway, it was supposedly this true story about this guy, Ferdinand Demara. Ever heard of him? He spent his whole life pretending to be other people. A navy doctor. A deputy sheriff. A prison warden. Even a dentist, if you can believe it. It's where it started. I read everything I could find on him—and people like him. Grey Owl. Stanley Clifford Weyman. Laurel Wilson. And then, later, there was that Leonardo DiCaprio movie, *Catch Me If You Can* ... If you've got the confidence, the stomach for it, papers that look legit, there's not much you can't get away with. When people believe you are that person, you become that person. It's easier than you might think."

She'd scammed me same as anybody else. What'd she want, an Academy Award?

"Are you even listening to me? Are you ever going to talk to me? C'mon, Rob, please. I'm sorry. You know I'm sorry. You know I love you. I know you do. And you love me too. I know you do."

Love, my ass! The night my father was arrested—him down on the ground, my mother kneeling there—this was the only time I saw my parents show affection for one another. It wasn't love they had. So what was it? The psycho connection? A business arrangement? An agreement to shut up and cover up? And why didn't my mother abort me? She must have thought about it. Now there was a conversation starter.

"Serial killers are cowards. They prey on the defenseless. They rely on surprise. It's not like TV. You confront them with any kind of force, they run. They're not fighters. They can dish it out, but they can't take it. But your father could. He wasn't afraid of confrontation. He'd stand and fight. Whatever else he might have been ..."

She was wrong. My father wasn't different, only a more proficient sociopath.

"The more I think about it, it's like your dad gave me my freedom and took away yours."

I was a banzai skydiver. That's what I was. The plane takes me up to three thousand feet or so. I throw my parachute out and then I wait. And wait. I wait for as long as I dare and then I dive out after it. The trick is to catch up to the chute and open it before I hit the ground. Yeah, my life in brief and in total—trying to catch up before I hit the ground.

"I've never taken a vacation without looking to benefit in some way. The more skills a person has, you know ... Survival training. Italian cooking. Archery. Same, I guess, with some of the men I've dated along the way. I spent eight months with an Israeli who taught me Krav Maga. I shouldn't tell you this, but I would have happily married him too, had his mother not hated me so much."

My mother wouldn't hate Cori. She'd teach her the ropes. The knots too.

"Look, you can have all the doubts in the world about me. My intentions. My identity. I'm a world-class fraud, no argument. But don't you dare doubt my feelings for you. I've never lied to you about that and never will. Have I omitted stuff I shouldn't have? Yes. But haven't you done the same? I know more about your childhood shrink than I do about your mom. And that night with your dad in that house, the killings, if that wasn't omitting details, God! I'm a liar. You're a liar. C'mon, we were made for each other. Aren't we worth saving? Goddammit, Rob, pigheadedness is your least endearing trait. Let's move on, please."

Her least endearing trait was pointing out my least endearing traits.

"I love you. What more can I do to prove it? Die for you?"

I took the first exit past Charlotte. Looked for a place to spend the night.

51
THE CAROLINA BELLE

The Carolina Belle was a strip motel with motor court pretensions, twelve units, twelve vacancies, a non sequitur Hawaiian theme, and a prize location on a secondary route amid bankrupt towns and abandoned shopping malls. The flashing neon skirt was the clincher.

"I want the room at the end," Cori pointed, and shifted over to the driver's seat before the door had shut behind me.

The weather was cool for Charlotte. On the drive down, the air had been so damn thick with humidity, lifejackets should have been a requisite. But not now.

I sauntered up to the office. A teenage boy ushered me inside like he'd been expecting me all along. "We don't get early birds," he said, "only late birds. But, heck, New Year's round these parts, a graveyard."

I chuckled along with him, though nothing he'd said was all that funny. When in doubt in the company of strangers, best bet is to laugh.

I asked for the unit at the end.

"Number twelve, sure. But it's an extra twenty, 'cause of the rollaway. How many y'all, anyhow?" He peered out into the lot.

"Me and my wife."

"No kids or nothin'? You sure? Pets?"

"None I'm aware of."

"Yeah, you bet. Well, let me give you number ten then. Save yourself twenty."

"My wife likes ends," I said. The kid cracked up. I fanned four twenties onto the countertop.

"You're funny, man. You should get over to the open mike night thing at Crown Station, ya know, on Elizabeth? I get my jokes up to snuff, I'm there, whoosh, whoosh! Five solid minutes and I'm set. The loonies I see come in here, I swear, crazier than a runover cat ..." He tossed a hitchhiker's thumb at the small TV in the corner. "Crazier than Jimmy Fallon even."

"You're like a young Jeff Dunham," I said. "Minus the dolls."

"You mean it?"

"I do."

"Shit, man." He slapped the key into my hand along with one of the twenties I'd just forked over. "You take twelve and don't think twice about the extra. You have a real nice night now. Jeff Dunham? Shit, man, shit."

I was almost out the door when I spied Tusk's book face down on a wicker armchair. *The Stainless Steel Ride* by Raymond T. Culley. "Any good?" I said.

He had to think for a moment. "My mom is making me read it. She says it'll keep me on the straight and narrow. It's okay, I suppose, if you got to read. Slow, kinda, until Walrus gets sent up. Some of the shit those fellas get into, I tell ya."

"Good to know," I said.

"You bet, Mr. Blessing, sir."

I envied the kid, wished I'd had the guts to try stand-up when I was his age. Might've changed my prospects, milking comedy from tragedy. Domme mom. Death row dad. No denying, I had killer material.

I stepped outside and my career in comedy was promptly forgotten. Cori and the Pilot were gone.

52
MY CAROLINA BELLE

I didn't panic. Cori throwing curves was routine. Still, it was the middle of the night in the middle of nowhere, and I wasn't without concern. Just didn't want to show too much too soon. Didn't want to be embarrassed when it turned out to be nothing. My guess, it was a ploy to get me talking.

We hadn't had a real bite to eat since lunch. Maybe she'd gone to pick something up. Chicken. Ribs. I could go for either. Better yet, a combo. And if she'd taken off on me, made the break, I guess I'd asked for it. Not that I accepted all the blame. Say fifteen percent. She was the liar, not me. Well, the bigger liar, anyhow.

I unlocked Room 12. Sat on the bed. Decided I'd give it ten minutes, lasted two. Where could she have gone? A rendezvous with Curtis Assistant Fucking Warden Mangold?

I ambled up to the road, mind wandering in sync with my feet. Car lights flared in the distance, only to blink to black, detouring to pastures greener than the Carolina Belle.

What would I do if Cori didn't turn up? What if something bad had happened? Stories of women abducted from motels were a dime a dozen. And yet again, I couldn't call the cops. You don't mess with a mess. Agent Ambrose. Banrum. The dead kid and his chainsaw. The Hillsdale murders. Vanishing Joe Di Iorio. Then lover-boy Mangold would be called in for his take, and every lie would expose the next, any truths buried six feet down with the rest of me.

I'd give her till morning before I'd move to Plan B, not that I had a Plan B. Best I could do was return to the room and wait.

I tramped down the knoll, back to the motel, and a glint of chrome caught my eye, followed in short order by an eyeful of Cori. She was doing it her own way, once more.

The Pilot had been backed onto the grass, to the side and rear of unit 12. It'd be tough to spot from anywhere, except from where I now stood. Darkness added to the privacy. *All the angles covered. So damn sure of herself. Time after time after time.*

She teased, "I thought I'd freeze to death before you found me." She was a sight, all right, posing in centerfold profusion, perched upon the hood of the Pilot in bra, panties, and goosebumps, her hands on her knees, her toes at the bumper, her hair just so. An auto show goddess as a luxury option.

She unsnapped her bra and pitched it to me. "Nice catch," she said, and with a sultry grace laced with languor, she parted her long, lovely legs. "Well, what are you waiting for?"

I scoped out the driver's side, sought assurance no one crouched behind the wheel, neither paper bag in hand, nor hand in paper bag.

I stepped closer, stopped, fought off the urge. "You think this is why I told you the story?"

The catch in her voice cut to the quick. "I just thought ... I just wanted ..."

"It's not that simple, Cor. This isn't how we make it right." I tossed back the bra and walked away.

A worrisome hour passed before she followed me inside and crawled silently into the second bed.

She tossed, I turned, and vice versa through the night.

Maybe I was wrong. Maybe it would have made everything right.

PART FIVE

WHAT WE MEAN WHEN WE TALK ABOUT DYING

53

HOW TO WALK INTO IT

Hillsdale could do to me whatever it wanted. I didn't care. Our relationship was in the crapper. Didn't see how it could be repaired. Not after what she'd done. Or what I had and hadn't done.

The weather had pulled an about-face in the days we'd been gone. The further north we drove, the warmer it got. The morning we arrived home, the sun was shining and the front yard was a mushy pastiche of yellow grass and dog-dirty snow. This was unlike any January I'd seen. Global warming had its plusses.

The stakeout at the corner of Robards and Appleton was no surprise. The lone cop was on the phone the instant we pulled into view.

A moving van was parked at the door of April Bright's salon. Tusk was supervising, deep-throating a hoagie from the tailgate of his 450.

I interrupted our current cycle of silence. "April's moving out early."

"No point now. Tell her she can stay, if you want." Cori opened her door, dropped a foot onto the driveway. "You need to know, there is one thing I've been keeping from you. I hadn't meant to. Honest. Had it gone better with Henry ... but then, after ... well, how it's been, you and me."

I gripped the wheel, studied the dashboard. *How much worse could it get?*

She stepped out, leaned in through the window. "I'm pregnant. We're pregnant." Laughing through tears, she added, "And if I don't get inside this second, I am going to pee all over myself." She grabbed her purse from the seat and off she jogged, up to the house, onto the porch, and out of sight.

I dipped into the slipstream of my addled brain, and all the reasons I loved her came flooding back. I should have chased after her, begun to mend what was broken. But the news was too damn much to process and, while I hated to think it, more than I could believe. Her timing was suspect. Yeah, I was an ass for going there, but how could I not?

April observed from the cottage as I pulled the bags from the trunk. She had a hand on the railing and another at her mouth, her expression a queasy potluck of revulsion and resentment. I looked to disarm her. "Cori's pregnant," I said, though too quietly for anyone to hear. There was an unfamiliar spring to my step and I coupled it to a too cheerful wave. My intent was bygones. Tusk and April had a different take. *The cocky little prick was gloating.*

Hillsdale's celebrated handyman and author, Raymond "Tusk" Culley, reared onto his hinds, and through the slough he slogged, upturned muck and sod erupting in his wake, slurping at his heels, sucking on his toes. Mid-field, he transitioned to goose-step, coming on like a hammered Oktoberfester in lederhosen three sizes too small. I missed the red flags. I trod out to greet him. And the troll launched himself at my head.

Smack onto my back I fell and smack on my chest Tusk landed, raging garlic, mustard, onions, and lunacy, as he pounded me into the mud. "I'll kill ya. I'll kill ya. I'll kill ya. Stay away from her or I'll kill ya. I'll kill ya. Ya think I won't kill ya? I'll kill ya."

He weighed a shitload, his belly quaking at my chin.

"What you done to her," he cried, and slapped my ears till my skull rang hollow.

Fuck him. Fuck this.

I bucked, rammed a knee into his spine and clobbered him on the recoil. His head snapped left, my arm flew right, and I hauled a fistful of knuckles up through his chin and into his face, slicing up my hand on his goddamn tusks. And there, at his belt, I saw it, my freaking coup de grâce—his trusty staple gun. *Fucking touché!* I squeezed off the whole damn clip, and *The New York Times* best-selling dunderhead wriggled and writhed like bacon on iron.

"That's enough." April Bright towered over us, to the extent she was capable of towering. "Enough."

Tusk sniveled to his knees, clawed at his belly, and wherever else the staples had stuck. But April wasn't much concerned with her brother. She sidled up till her hip met my head and slowly raised her pant leg. "You did this to me," she said. Her flesh-toned prosthesis extended down from her knee.

"I what?"

"Everyone knows now. Now everyone knows."

"Knows what? What?"

"Children commit the vilest of mischief. Your youth I can forgive. But who you are now, who you've become, to profess your innocence—have you no shred of decency?"

Tusk yelped. He'd used a pocket screwdriver to pry a staple from his rib cage and was working on another.

"If only Officer Griffiths had spoken up sooner ... so many lives so needlessly lost. Why, Robert, why?"

"What about him? What about Griffiths?"

"They're coming for you, same as they came for your father." She turned her back, limped off in a mawkish display of heavy heart and stoic dignity. For three triumphant paces, anyhow. And SPLAT! went the old bat as her prosthesis broke out of its socket, and rooted fast in the quickening muck.

The leg held upright, a practical white shoe buckled to foot, mute testament to a fallen beautician.

April regarded her leg from afar. "Damn strap." She appealed to Tusk. "Need your help, bro."

"Can't, sis." He was working on the staples in his nuts.

I dislodged the prosthesis, the *squoosh-woot* not unlike a CO_2 cartridge powering up a canister of whipped cream, and with my sick mind exploring the potential components of a *Prosthetic Parfait*, I passed the leg to April.

I called to the two movers who'd been watching by the rear of their van. "Hey, guys! Any chance you can help her into the cottage?" They were the same two creeps I'd caught prowling on the day Cori blew out our window. Rat-face George and Heavy Lennie. "Guys?" For movers, they didn't exhibit much movement, their hands twiddling in the bibs of their coveralls.

My magnanimity went unrewarded. April was unappeased. "And then what you did to my fruitcake."

"We're going to have a baby," I said, trusting in the possibility.

"I baked it with love, a Christmas treat for you and your wife, and you trashed it as if it meant nothing. That hurt. More than anything, that hurt so much."

"Wait! You been going through our trash?"

"You are an unkind man, Bobby Dickens."

I couldn't disagree, whether or not I'd returned her leg or been leery of her fruitcake.

Again, I appealed to George and Lennie to help her out. True to form, the dicks had taken off to parts unknown.

Tusk wallowed. Too many staples remained beyond his reach.

I volunteered my services and he relinquished the screwdriver. "So I'm the town's go-to scapegoat now," I said. He sucked up the pain as I wrested a staple from his brow. "But April's leg, c'mon, man, I had nothing to do—"

"My ass! You sent that truck crashing onto Main. You busted up April good. Them others too. You're out in the open now, sicko. The cop saw you."

"What cop? What are you talking about?"

"You was a kid. Griffiths says he saw you pitch 'em bowling balls out the truck and then you pulled the brakes and the rest is misery. The Calamity on Main. That was you."

"Wade's full of shit."

"Says he kept it to himself 'cause him and you was best pals, but now, folk dying and disappearing, he puts two and you together. You got revengers all over your ass now, Bobby-boy."

April chimed in. "Dalmatians don't change their spots." She'd made some headway in reattaching her leg. Or legway, I suppose.

"You know me, Tusk. C'mon, you know I wouldn't."

"Save it for your book, Bobby-boy."

"A perfectly good fruitcake. A full cup of Captain Morgan's."

"I was at the bowling alley that morning, but I never ... Hell, man, I'm not guilty of anything except stupidity. You think I'd come back if I was? I was in the clear."

"'Bayard's attorney hid his conceit beneath a cloak of arrogance tailored in Hong Kong.'"

"What?"

Tusk clicked his tongue. "Good, huh? Straight outta *Ride*. Chapter Eighteen. You know, where Bayard's snitch pulls the fast one on Walrus."

"You need to listen to me, man."

"Not me you gotta convince." Tusk gestured toward the street. "Them's the problem."

The cop who'd been staking us out pounded the sidewalk with a jittery nonchalance. Like I wouldn't suspect anything was up. Like I'd be too dense to guess he'd be carrying, locked and loaded.

"Let 'em come. I haven't done anything."

"Chapter Four: 'He acknowledged his tiresome declarations of innocence were championed solely by libtards.'"

"Quoting lines from your book. That your idea of help?"

"In your size-twelves, Bobby-boy, I'd hightail my fucking ass outta here."

"We're pregnant. Cori's pregnant."

"The Hillsdale Hacker, that's what they're calling you now. No way round it."

54

THE HILLSDALE HACKER

I left Tusk to his staples and April to her leg. I did not hightail it anywhere. I carried our luggage into the house.

Cori's purse lay open on the hallway floor. "Hey, where are you? We need to talk."

She did not answer. Couldn't blame her.

The light burned in the downstairs bathroom. The faucet was running.

"Cor?" She wouldn't be on the hood of the Pilot this time, but I held out hope for the bedroom. No luck.

I checked out the backyard from an upstairs window. Not that she'd have cause to be out there.

I heard sirens, distant, as sirens initially are. But I couldn't be sure. Anxiety hoodwinks hearing, turns bumps in the night into sleepovers with the Manson Gang. The Hillsdale Hacker was cornered. A noisy heads-up wasn't likely, even by Hillsdale law enforcement standards.

"C'mon, Cor. Joke's over. Come out, come out, wherever you are. I'm sorry, okay? Does that help?"

It doesn't take much for a woman to disappear in America. It's like drowning. Twenty seconds and gone.

I fell back to the kitchen, keeled into a chair, spotted blood on the floor, and hoped it wasn't. "Cori?"

A droplet. A perfect circle of iron-enriched red, glistening as might a pupil excised from an eye. One tile over, a second drop. A third. And then a smear, thin, streaky, and pointing the way. *Jeez! Was this what a miscarriage looked like?*

I wadded up some paper towels, followed the trail to the cellar door.

I paused, gave her cell a try. From below came the custom ring she'd assigned to me. *Ode to Joy.* The call skipped to voice mail.

I took the stairs one at a time, erasing the spots as I went. I wanted to see where the blood led, before it led the cops to me.

The trail went cold on the cellar floor.

"Where are you, Cor?" I said, as though she were next to me. "Where are you, dammit?" I shouted out, hoping to hear in reply, *"Why the panic, Bobby? I'm here. Right here."* My outburst would rank alongside Chicken Little's, but at least Cori would be alive and at my side. And then the condom caught my eye.

It was plastered knee-high to the post that supported the railing. Black and gloppy and full. A vibrant helix of red swirled within the ejaculate. And there, beneath the stairs, more color. The flamingo pink case of her iPhone.

If the fucker touched one hair on her head. One hair.

Should they make a movie of my story, this is where the scriptwriter will send Tom Holland or Channing Tatum or a grossly miscast Tom Cruise to his knees, mouth contorted in a Dolby-enriched *no-o-o-o-o-o.* Do not believe it. I kept my wits.

I welcomed my old self again, Son of the Brittle Butcher, Little Bobby Dickens, all grown up, with malice aforethought. Cori's lies meant nothing now. Her life was all that mattered.

I stacked up alongside any whack-job who had ever sliced and slashed.

I was who they needed me to be.

I had it all: The deranged posture, every pore hell-bent and hairy. Glassy eyes, the fevered twitch. The spastic fists. The mindless stutter clotted with drool.

I was who I needed to be.

The Hillsdale Hacker.

55
TUNNEL VISION

"One hair on her head," I said. A vow, not a statement.

From the wall of stored odds and ends, four hard-shell suitcases protruded. Two green. Two gray. I knew what I had to do. And while it shames me to say, I suppose I'd known all along.

I dragged the suitcases aside, peered into the vacuum created, and crept in.

The tunnel was anything but half-assed. Wooden joists and rafters ran its length, supporting the assorted junk that served as camouflage above and to the sides.

Remnants of orange shag overlaid the concrete, the path worn, dusty, and dim. A flashlight would have helped.

A funky odor resurrected memories of my bus ride to Albany after I'd dropped out of school. Six hours seated beside a middle-aged free spirit in woolen overcoat and knit cap. Six hours of dope, urine, and armpit.

The design was odd, constructed to discourage. Straightaway. Zigzag. Hairpin. Zagzig. And back to straightaway. Here, the rafters ascended, and I ascended with them, replicating the evolution of man poster I remembered from a classroom wall—Dryopithecus to modern Homo sapiens.

There was cold concrete to my left and a kaleidoscope of keepsakes to my right. Games. *Mouse Trap. Hungry Hippo. Life. Sorry.* A Ouija board. Ice skates. Lampshades. Dishes in open cartons. Bowls. Lots of bowls.

Deeper I went into the thickening gloom, feeling my way until there was no way to go. A door. Metal. And just enough light to discern a black and yellow Civil Defense decal.

Holy cow! A fallout shelter. If my parents were aware of its existence, they'd kept it to themselves. It would have made a great hideout for a kid. Or perhaps they hadn't known. There had always been a load of junk down here. Not as much as now, for sure, but enough to conceal the wall where I stood.

I steadied myself, turned my brain to what would be, rather than what might.

I put my shoulder to the door. Prayed for it to give, covered all my bases: God, Jesus, apple pie, the flag, Cori, my indeterminate unborn, and Henry Taylor Dickens.

Fear at its most pure. Fearlessness at its most reckless.

56
LAST CHANCE TO TURN AROUND

"It's him," came an anxious whisper and disembodied shadows skittered giddy through the murk. The utterance and images were so fleeting, I felt deceived by the blink of my own eyes, the pitch of my own breath.

Slender spirals of smoke moped white and aimless in the dark, the taste queerly metallic, like blood. Or, in the parlance of Anna Carmen Hope, *red vengeance on gossamer wings*.

I churned saliva. Same stench as the tunnel, albeit with artificial florals.

The shelter was half as large as the adjoining cellar, but more spacious than I expected, based on snippets of Cold War documentaries I'd seen on PBS. Light emanated from an open door and a brighter second room beyond. The builder had anticipated a lengthy nuclear winter.

I was no expert on the spiritual. I could count on two hands the times I'd set foot in church. Weddings. Funerals. Catering ice cream on bingo night. Yet, there was no dismissing the notion I'd trespassed upon a sacred precinct.

I called her name. My voice fell flat.

My eyes adjusted. Ahead, two seashell sconces cast a sickly pallor. Below, on a small Parsons table, a fat candle perspired within an aluminum bowl. A cigarette smoldered in an ashtray. I edged closer. In fact, it wasn't a table, rather a pile of books squared and stacked, as if laid by a mason. And then: "Oh, shit."

On the wall above the table, a collage of photographs extended the breadth of the room.

Once more, I called her name. Sound did not travel here.

I ran my fingers across the photos, connected invisible dots, divining answers from counterfeit Braille. Grim. Smiling. Clowning. Solemn. Relaxed. Pensive. Burdened. Every photo was of my father, some I'd forgotten, many I'd never seen, several swiped from family albums, others torn from papers, books, and magazines.

Dad in his swim trunks. The Brittle Butcher in shackles. The cropped shot the wire services had picked up after his arrest, my mother's hand on his shoulder. Dad and his Impala, his sample case in hand. Not just a few photos, but dozens. Hundreds. Originals and blow-ups. Duplicates. Quadruplicates. The handiwork of a fan gone amuck. And still amucking.

The door of the shelter whumped shut behind me, the seal dull, like a widower's refrigerator.

"Are you pleased?" A snappily dressed gent materialized from the shadows, his skull split between dark and light, doom and deliverance. "It is a fitting tribute to your father, yes?"

I should've known. I'd crossed paths with him plenty. The chubby guy in the suit. The mustache. Basil Bloomfield of Basil's Blooms, the flower shop on Main. "So, you're—"

"Indeed, the white rabbit, whom you have chased into the warren." Basil Bloomfield's delivery was spot on, the line reserved for the proper occasion.

It had been a long day; I wasn't much in the mood for apt. "Where's my wife?"

"You can do better, son. Her lying, her fabrications, you can't trust a woman of her ilk. 'The more beautiful the bride, the more troubled the marriage.' The proverb Ethiopian, if memory serves."

I grabbed him by the Windsor knot. "Where the fuck is she?"

His eyebrows bracketed his frown. "Go slowly now, lad. Rush not to judgment. This must be overwhelming, stepping into it as you have."

The door to the second room swung wide, and a guy and girl surfed in on a plenitude of beatific radiance.

The guy was dressed casually, jeans and shirt, while the girl sported a lopsided red wig and a getup worthy of *Astride-OM*: black satin corset, G-string, garters, silk stockings, delivering a visceral jolt I repelled on sight. The gear was easily two sizes too large for her, open parachute on skin and bone. I recognized the pair, though I couldn't recall from where. My priority was Cori.

Basil hailed the couple with handshakes and hats.

The hats were novelty items, premiums once sent by suppliers to my dad. A red Airheads hat with balloon tassel. A red and blue Dubble Bubble cap. A silver Hershey Kiss beanie. A fluorescent Jelly Belly hat.

I declined Basil's offer of the Dubble Bubble.

"The fundamentals of every great religion." He mimed an arc from the photos of my father to the Planters Peanuts top hat upon his head. "A messiah plus a funny hat, and you're preaching to capacity, voilà!"

I weighed my odds. Run for the second room in hopes of finding Cori or take it slow, get a handle on the what and wherefore. So far, it had been musical comedy, with damn little of either. This trio was more kooky than threatening.

"Just tell me where she is and I'll be out of your hair."

Basil knelt before the table of books. Titles came into focus. *The Serial Killer Files. Talking with Serial Killers. The Murderer Next Door.* "Your arrival is fortuitous," he said. "Another ten minutes and you would have missed everything. Well, not everything, but certainly this."

He extended a fist over the candle. "Lest we forget the fundamental of ritual. In the formative stages, we employed your father's socks and such exclusively, but have since intuited your mother's garments, most appreciably her undergarments, also possess a spiritual provenance of homologous atavistic profundity."

"Amen," the boy and girl chorused, their holy rolling diluted by effervescent tee-hees.

"Cut the crap," I said.

Basil blathered undeterred. "We have you to thank, Bobby. Until your homecoming, our knowledge of your mother's role in his life had been woefully ambiguous. Such is the deficiency of contemporary crime reportage. The grisly prevails to the detriment of substance. But your writing, your little notes and comments have proved enlightening. The reappearance of Anna Carmen Hope's instructional tome is proving helpful, I trust, elevating your cogitation to a coherent whole? I ask only because we have observed exiguous evidence of your progress of late."

"Willow? You? You," I said, my indictment gut-wrenchingly implicit. I didn't know all that I was up against, but my florist pal would be sure to fill me in. The posturing. The mouthiness. The bullshit. Unlike my father, Basil Bloomfield was a pop-culture psycho. Ego would rule. Answers would fly.

The trio wasn't anywhere near kooky. Not anymore.

"Have you had the opportunity to view that terribly insipid docudrama devoted to your father on Netflix? We anticipate your worthy composition, when complete, will cast the man in a more equitable light." He relaxed his fist and a pair of lacy panties flared within the candle flame before evaporating in a wisp of silken smoke. Face over the bowl, residue wafting into his eyes, he threw the flats of his hands onto the wall and collage. He meditated on the incline, his mantra swelling to chant, his sidekicks supplying backup vocals. "Hentaylickens. Hentaylickens. Hentaylickens ..."

Oh, yeah, it was nutzoid creepy. "You gotta be kidding," I rasped in disbelief at the truncated version of my father's apparently holy name. "Cut the fucking theatrics. I get it. I get it. You're crazy, scary, loony fucks. I've seen the movie. Now where the hell is my wife?"

Basil clapped his hands, the others chortling their approval. "Wonderful!" the florist cried. "Such a joy to have an audience— someone who can appreciate our little show. You grasp, of course, it is infinitely more rewarding for victims to believe they are dying at the hands of the criminally insane, as opposed to dying at the hands of everyday folk—folk like themselves."

"Josh Groban," the girl said. "Nobody wants to be murdered by Josh Groban or a Jonas Brother. They want Gary Ridgway, Jeffrey Dahmer, Anthony Hopkins, Henry Dickens."

"I'm no victim," I said, knowing it was all I ever planned to be.

"Marvelous to hear." Basil snuffed the candle. "Exactly what we prayed you would say."

The guy and girl motioned me toward the second room. Goatee and Caitlin, that's who they were. They'd come to see my Christmas display. They had argued over my dad's execution date. Goatee had asked for my autograph, and I had declined.

57

A GREATEST HITS COLLECTION

The stadium lighting stung my eyes. My nostrils powered down at the worsening stench. Lemon-scented Glade was no match for death and dung.

Floodlights burned from a false ceiling. Fantails of red and brown spattered the surface. Work lamps on tripods squared off from opposing corners in a ten-thousand lumen duel. No wonder our utility bills had been sky high.

My feet were firm upon the ground, but the rest of me was weightless, grappling for purchase. Life in 8K resolution. No detail escaped illumination, every facet defined and distinct. Reds were redder. Blacks blacker. Twitches twitchier.

Furnishings were sparse. Plywood bunks dominated three walls, lending a funhouse imbalance to the rest of the space. The beds were broad and crude and numbered twelve.

Four of the bunks were occupied, two covered in bed sheets, two in plastic tarps. But only an upper toward the rear showed signs of life. The sheet billowed at intervals, its occupant struggling in vain beneath.

Ten quick strides, that's all it would take. Ten quick strides to save her. But a hulky kid stood guard at the bunk, watching me watching him.

And that face, I tell you, it was nothing I'd ever seen outside of Manga. Bedhead spikes and kewpie-doll bangs, XL eyes, a brushstroke nose, and a fungal grin that crept under my skin, nestled in, and laid eggs.

Manga-Face winked, punched the sheet into submission. He winked again, made sure I saw his captive's shoes were men's. *No wifey here.* Nice kid. Bloodlust with compassion.

Nearer, to my left, Goatee and Caitlin had settled in at a card table. An associate misfit dealt hands by twos.

He was another old pal—Scuzzball—my hallway apparition from the morning Cori set off for "New York." Rubber-bands circled his arms from wrists to elbows. As reunions go, this was shaping up to be the doozy from Hell.

Between the bunks, resident number six rocked self-absorbed upon an upended crate. Fortyish. Good hair. Square jaw. The most normal of the bunch, discounting the khakis at his ankles and the ice pack on his dick.

The emerging profile was a greatest hits collection.

The wouldn't-harm-a-fly types. *Check!*
The quiet-as-a-church-mouse types. *Check!*
The never-bothered-anyone types. *Check!*
The deranged-from-birth types. *Check!*
The best-ever-neighbor types. *Check!*

How many were there, anyhow? What the hell were they doing hanging out? Wasn't this category of whack-job supposed to be the always-kept-to-themselves type?

I liked my chances less, and Cori's less and less. No way this wouldn't get messy. It was already messy. And getting messier.

Mailsacks were scattered left and right. Most flat and empty, *Property of USPS* stenciled on each. On one, a police badge had been pinned.

Here and there, the now familiar plastic cups. Butts, ash, and condoms.

Two of the bunks served as a pantry: Beer, canned soda, bottled water, cigarette packs, Rice Krispies, M&M Peanuts, jerky.

Off to the sides, a galley kitchen, a portable toilet, and a crawlspace with a dirt floor.

To my right, a wall of graffiti. A guestbook, perhaps. Too many scrawls to count.

Keep on *fuckin'* God bless Henry Taylor Dickens
The Deacon!!!

I did willow with a pillow
Then I smote her with a poker
MILF MAN WAS HERE
When I saw what I had done

TJ & Duster
3/3/18   THANKS ALL.
          GOOD TIMES.
I took it out and did her mom.

Fanboy55

Your main man,   **See yous in hell**
They died   *Mason forever*   **DVN**
for our sins.
                                    Parting tis such sweet storrow
John Cougar Mellonball   *-Shakespeare in the heart*

It's been a slice! AC   *8 down, 19 to go!*   **Black is the**
                                                 new black

FREE HENRY TAYLOR DICKENS!   Fuck 'n *snuff*

Godspeed BB   Goose on the Loose
from TTD   Pass the *catsup*, please
                                    remember
                                    hammerhead
"Someday we'll be 2gether *again*"   **Murder**
-D. Ross and the *supreems*   **is**   *Best of luck!*
                                     Mercy   *-Missy*

Praise be, HTD
Kill or be killed.   **XXOO LK**
Thrill or be thrilled.   *The Marsh Pond Killer was here June '08*

BOO! 1/30/11   Knock! Knock!   **ARTIE CULLY HE THE MAN**
                    Chop! Chop!
                    -Cyrus Mulligan, Jr.   *Betty & me, sitting in a tree K-I-L-L-I-N-G*

Wish you were here, Mr. Dikkens sir.   kil4thril   WHO LOVES PEANUT
                                                      BRITTLE? ME! ME! ME!

Behind me, near the door, a laptop and a printer. The freaks had hacked me. My book was on the monitor. My opening paragraph, anyhow. My only paragraph. I did not ask if they liked what they had read, though I was tempted.

Trigger warning: I've saved the worst for last. I do not like to relive it. I do not like to write about it. To gloss over the violence, however, would be to understate the horror and suffering of the victims, and cast the perpetrators in a kinder, less odious light than facts attest.

Put simply, the action gets hairy from here on out. In summary, really bad shit happens. If you prefer to wimp out and skip ahead, Chapter 63 offers a relatively safe space to resume your reading.

A butcher block dominated the floor in front of me, a machete embedded in the wood, a severed head occupying pride of place.

Male.

Unknown.

A pink Post-it affixed to an ear, CAITLIN in block letters.

Beneath the butcher block, limbs protruded from a bulging mailbag. Bony. Skin taut and sinewy. Air-dried sausage in an all-beef casing.

Adjacent to the butcher block, a frail old woman languished, gagged, bound, and breathless in a busted office chair, casters missing. With a flamboyant sweep of his hand, Basil Bloomfield conjured a blade from a sleeve and affixed the edge to the woman's cheek.

"It's high time she updated her photo, don't you think? Her current one must be, what, forty years out of date?"

I stared dumbly, which suited me to a T. I mean, who in their right mind would have barged into this unarmed? And who, but me, would stand by dumbly, his wife and unborn child in peril, if not dead?

For all my bluster, I had no moves. There were too many of them.

A lineup card would've come in handy.

Cellar Roster

1. Basil Bloomfield, local florist
2. Goatee, Xmas visitor, autograph collector
3. Caitlin (a.k.a. Astride-OM-in-training), Goatee's girlfriend
4. Scuzzball, card dealer, one-time hallway apparition
5. Manga-Face, young, sensitive psycho
6. Ice-Dick, 40-something guy with ice pack on his junk

"Sure you don't recognize her?" Basil pressed me for an answer. "No guesses?"

"Lenora-Jo Coffey?"

"Good gracious, Bobby."

Here, a yellow Post-it was affixed to the woman's upper-arm, *Basil* in a fussy cursive.

The florist chuckled, amused by my confusion. "The stickies denote ownership. The noggin on the chopping block, for instance, he's Cait's doing." Caitlin saluted from the card table. "And this little lady, well, Edith is mine."

"Edith?"

"Dengler? From the *Bargain Bugler*?"

"Jesus, man!" She'd connected me to the Storrows in her *All Eyes! All Ears!* column, but no way did I wish the gossipy granny dead. She was watching me now. Following me. Seeking forgiveness, maybe.

"Don't you worry, Dengler is getting her due. My goodness, casting aspersions, subjecting you to unwarranted attention. Unkind!"

"Fuck that!" Caitlin slammed down her cards and stamped to center stage. "The bitch gives Bobby credit for our doings. Fuck that!" She whipped off her Heather-red wig and tied a BBQ apron over her corset, *Well Done!* embroidered on the bib.

"Now, now, Caitlin. Let's not lose perspective." Basil transferred his Mr. Peanut top hat to Edith Dengler's head. "Let us be adult about this."

"Fuck adult!" From Caitlin's skinny wrists to the anorexic rounds of her shoulders, crude tattoos offered up a catalog of barbed wire and all its permutations.

By contrast, her voice and the soft contours of her face bordered the prepubescent. Were it not for the augmented reality of her spectacular breasts, she could have been mistaken for a boy.

Peter Pan, unhinged.

"Is everything around here up to me?" Caitlin shoved Basil aside, batted Dengler's hat to the floor, and ground the woman's head into the crook of her arm. "Gimme the razor, Bloomie."

Basil replied, trim and prim. "I'll cut her in my own good time, thank you very much."

"Me too," Caitlin said. She jerked the machete from the butcher block and, without a moment's hesitation, hacked off Dengler's brow, nose, and lips.

With any luck, this was a truck stop on my road to Hell. With any luck, I was still outside, mired in the muck, lungs busted from Tusk's tackle, oxygen deprivation marking my colorful passage to Eternal Damnation. Yup, I'd be there with horns and pitchfork to welcome Dad in one month's time.

Basil seethed, speechless for once, while Caitlin got intimate with her machete: "Bitch won't be sticking her nose where it don't belong no more, will she now, Betty?"

I updated the lineup:

Cellar Roster (Version 2.0)

1. Basil Bloomfield, local florist
2. Goatee, Xmas visitor, autograph collector
3. Caitlin (a.k.a. Astride-OM-in-training), Goatee's girlfriend
4. Scuzzball, card dealer, one-time hallway apparition
5. Manga-Face, young, sensitive psycho
6. Ice-Dick, 40-something guy with ice pack on his junk
7. Betty the Machete, Caitlin the psycho-chick's freaking big knife

Meanwhile, back at the card table, Goatee and Scuzzball slapped their sides silly. Manga-Face, the kid at the back of the room, yucked along with them. Only Ice-Dick, the dick on the crate with the ice pack on his dick, failed to see the humor.

With no little annoyance, Basil repositioned his blade at Dengler's throat. Despite the loss of face, the old lady hung on, conscious, eyes yet speaking to me. "You don't want to do that," I said.

"Oh, but I must. Now more than ever. The execrable little minx has challenged my authority. Watch and learn, dear boy. See, starting here, at the wattle, an incision to about say here, and then, if she's not a bleeder, as her facial wounds would predicate, I shall slice as far as—"

"Let her go. Please, man."

"Good gracious, if it so distresses you, Bobby, cast your eyes elsewhere. Surely, you witnessed your father's work. By all accounts, a first-rate cutter."

"Just stop, okay? You've proved your point."

"It's not about proving anything, it's about righting wrong. All of this, it's for you, don't you see?"

"All of it," Caitlin affirmed.

"You are the son of Henry Dickens. This beastly woman did you harm. We are defending you. What do you think we have been doing all these weeks, but exacting retribution from all who have mistreated you? It has given us purpose. We honor the father by safeguarding the son."

The logic was too damn warped not to appreciate. Dad had suggested the possibility.

Provoke? Placate? I needed a strategy. An out. I needed to do fucking something.

"You've got a funny definition of honor," I said.

Caitlin detonated. "Sweet Jesus Joseph Mary! I knew he'd be a pill. Ready, Betty?" She nicked the ceiling as she entered her wind-up, and down came Betty with force and fury, a two-handed swipe that split the severed head on the butcher block into symmetrical halves. Hell, rotten coconuts had given me a harder time than the skull had given that girl.

"You can't have it both ways, Bobby." Caitlin appealed to Basil. "He can't, he can't."

"It pains me deeply, Bobby. However, I must agree with our friend." Hand on Dengler's chin, Basil guided her head to his and kissed her ardently upon the mutilated cross section of her lips. He looked up with a smile, worked her jaw, speaking for her. "Thank you for teaching me the terror of my ways, Mr. Bloomfield."

I was being punked, right? I'd be watching myself on YouTube before the night was done. Hysterical.

"Don't look at me so high and mighty, Bobby. You know you want this."

"No, man. No." I was on my toes, desperate, yet still without a script.

"Oh, but you do, dear boy. 'For revenge is always the delight of a mean spirit, of a weak and petty mind. You may immediately draw proof of this—that no one rejoices more in revenge than a woman.' See, Bobby. She likes it. She wants it. She is woman. She rejoices."

Oh, fuck, a villain who spouted poetry, no less.

"Juvenal," Basil said, like I knew what the hell he was gabbing about. "Centuries ahead of his time."

He turned the edge of his blade to the old lady's throat and cut into her with the gusto of a cowboy on prime rib. He drove that godforsaken blade so goddamn deep within her gullet, his fist went missing, only to reemerge with an empty-handed twist at the sternum, the blade suspended, the handle a pearl brooch at Dengler's neck.

The incision wasn't as surgical as he had promised, yet Basil threw his bloody hands to the heavens and took his bows, Copperfield in Vegas.

I have no excuses. Chalk it up to DNA. I was removed from the gore yet immersed in the gore. No different than that soulless little geek, the 11-year-old who had borne witness at the window of the A-frame chalet.

I flicked bony splatter from an eyebrow. Where was she, dammit?

Bunk one, bunk two, bunk three, bunk none? "Anyone I know?" I said, a nod to the butcher block and halved head. I was invested, eager.

Caitlin's hand shot up. "Me and Betty did him. Our sixth."

Goatee snarled from the card table. "You and Betty, my ass! Me too. Me too."

Basil dabbed at his hands with a pre-moistened wipe. "A member of our merry band, alas. Lawrence of Lawrence, Kansas. A postal employee with a penchant for certified mail and the signatures of lonesome MILFs."

They killed their own. An encouraging sign.

"He left our family shortly after his ill-advised assault on the young vandal with the chainsaw. 'Patience, patience,' we beseeched. 'Follow the boy home, catch him unawares. But not in broad moonlight on Bobby's lawn.' We duly exiled the misguided lad. Alas, Lawrence revisited our fold last evening under the fallacious assumption all was forgiven. We could not abide his imprudence. Believe me, Bobby, we seek to protect you, not incriminate you. Restraint and subtlety above all."

"Yeah. Like slaughtering a family of four for no good reason. Restrained. Subtle."

"The girl belittled you."

"I deserved it."

"Yes, well ..." Basil sagged to sheepish. His knees knocked. "I do admit to a certain self-interest. The pre-holiday season is typically slow and, well ... nothing lifts the florist trade like a community in grief. As we like to say, one family's tragedy is another family's memorial wreath, gift basket, or floral arrangement with plush toy. A mass shooting is florist nirvana."

I poked the sack of arms with a toe. "And this guy's crime? He look at me wrong?"

"You think us frivolous?" Basil was indignant. "This man was disrespectful to you. Thoroughly."

"Call out the National Guard."

"He had eyes for your dear wife."

"Who doesn't?"

"You'd just arrived in town, Bobby. We felt it important for you to get off on the right foot. His rudeness was inexcusable. We—all of us here—were guests in your home. Coming to your aid was only natural. Your father would have wanted it. We knew immediately."

"Joe Di Iorio," I said.

"An older gent, as I recall. A driving instructor. From Albany."

"Saratoga."

Scuzzball claimed credit from the card table. "Tracked him to the Chinaman's place. I don't do nothing. He comes up to me. Lost like a pig in a poke, he is. Hasn't the foggiest. Wants the bus depot. I says I'll drive him. And what's he do? Bitches how I hold the wheel. 'Ten and two,' he tells me. 'Nine and three,' I tells him. Old bugger knew shit."

I laughed. Resigned. Ironic. Ha-ha the extent. (Were I the academic sort, I'd launch a study on the link between criminal behavior and grammar, with an emphasis on syntax.)

"What's so funny?" Basil cocked his head in a jackass pose, his upper body more boob than chest. Edith Dengler's sundry residue soiled his suit, the lunatic equivalent to black tie and tails.

"You think we're a joke? Bobby thinks we're a joke." Caitlin seized a half-head by the ear and plopped it onto Dead Edith's lap. "Lawrence terrorized Kansas for six years and we ripped him quicker than spit. Think we won't do the same to you?"

Goatee and Scuzzball upended the card table.

Manga-Face made like Bruce Lee mashing potatoes. He straddled his bunk-buddy and let loose with a frenzy.

"Just like his wife." Ice-Dick shifted his ice pack from his penis to his nuts. "Bobby needs a lesson in humility."

58
EVERY CLICHÉ IN THE BOOK

I summoned a page from Dr. Cutcheon's playbook: *When you have everything to lose, act as if you have nothing to lose.* "You ever listen to yourselves? You're every cliché in the book. The quirks. The twitches. The nutso crap. Where'd you learn your shit? *Mindhunter? Silence of the Lambs?* Machetes. Straight razors. What year you living in, 1896? Use some fucking imagination for God's sake."

Basil reddened. "It's not any razor. An astute observer would note it has been modified for extreme usage, and is significantly longer and broader than conventional models. The blade is Japanese stainless steel and coated with chrome for maximum durability. It stays sharp forever."

"A knife is a knife, asshole."

"Are you suggesting Lazy Green lacked creativity?"

"Ski poles? Lamps? You ripped off my Dad. You guys don't have an original thought in all your brains put together."

"Copycat killing is a wholly honorable methodology. It is highly regarded by the authorities."

"No, not so much these days. Where you been? You think anybody cares about your kind? You're yesterday's news. You're nothing but dabblers. Rampage killers, they're the ones people notice. Numbers make the headlines."

"To the contrary." Basil gasped his contempt. "Rampage killers are sorely lacking in finesse."

"And you, you pompous dick. The drivel. The platitudes. Your dumbass poetry. It's tired, man, so tired. Same for the rest of you and your screwball shtick. 'Ooo, we're so scary, look at us. Ooo, we're bad to

299

the bone.' Christ, I'll bet half of you live at home with your mommies and daddies."

"Critique as you see fit, but you cannot fault us for refuting the banality of evil. Hannah Arendt, Herman Kahn, Edward Herman. These so-called experts tell you one thing, Bobby, but let me tell you another: role-playing ups the ante. We succeed not by normalizing the unthinkable, but by destabilizing it. We are anything but banal."

"Case in point, dweebo. Hannah, Herman, and Herman—you think your genius colleagues know who the hell you're blabbing about?"

"Who cares?" Caitlin answered for Basil. "Who you ever killed, fucktard?"

Scuzzball and Goatee moved to Caitlin's side, a united front with the florist. Goatee piped up. "We are a disruptive technology. We are the Uber of murder, the Airbnb of death."

"He's an ingrate, that's what he is," Scuzzball said. "A shitty ingrate."

"Damn right, I am. I never asked for your protection. I don't want your protection."

Scuzzball hocked a loogie onto his palm, slicked back his hair. "Keep mouthing off, and you're going to need it plenty."

"Indeed. Why this contrarian turn, Bobby? Why such unpleasantry? Your churlishness is grossly uncalled for."

"Are you dumb or stupid? You have my wife, you idiots. Hand her over and I'm out of here. Promise. Not a word to anyone. But if you've hurt—"

"She's dead," Caitlin said. "Just like you."

"Is that what you want?" They couldn't see my heart or the beats it skipped. "Are you asking me to kill you?"

"Oh, I'm so scared. We're all so scared." Caitlin patted the handle of her machete. Betty was on break, lodged tip to spine in the butcher block. "Aren't you so scared too, Betty?"

"Deedy-weedy," Betty replied from her station. Unlike Basil's hammy act, Caitlin was a talented ventriloquist. Her lips barely moved. "Terribly, terribly scared."

"Don't underestimate me," I said. "Don't."

"Please, Bobby." Basil was almost motherly. "In the name of your father ..."

"You know fuck-all about my father. None of you do."

"I am saddened to hear you say this. The man is an inspiration. To achieve as he did, all the years that he did. This house! The magic! How can you not feel it? And your charming mother, a murderess in her own right. My goodness, a parricide!"

"The jury's still out on her."

"Come now, take pride. Your lineage is impeccable."

"My father didn't kill kids. He didn't kill indiscriminately." I stopped short of sharing the hooey about Dad answering prayers. One whiff and these freaks would have sprouted wings.

"We are not indiscriminate. We kill for you, when not for ourselves."

"Don't. Don't kill for me. And sure as hell not for my father. You think you would have been his buddies? Hell, you would have been his prime targets."

"Such an end would have been my privilege." Basil teared up, bloody hand over bloody heart.

Ice-Dick reentered the fray from his perch on the crate. "I've got more of his father in my little pinky than he does in his whole body. All of us do. We're wasting our time here. The kid's a zero."

Caitlin liberated Betty the Machete from the wood. "I say we off his wife while he watches. We take her slow, till baby boy here gets to bawling. Then we do him. Frame him up easy. The pigs'll lap it up, no question. He's already their pussy. We get away clean."

Ice-Dick labored to his feet. The crate teetered behind him. "The girl is mine. I took her, I finish her." He snapped the waistband of his boxers, lowered them to his thighs. He lifted his package to optimize our view. Show and tell never did sit well with me, and less so now. His testicles were blue and trending black. Bruising radiated from pee-hole to mid-way down his dinky dong, like a thermometer parked at 50°F.

Exhibition complete, Ice-Dick pulled up his boxers. "The cunt owes me. What's it her business where I choke my chicken? Barging in when she did, going ballistic on me, sadistic bitch. She found out right quick how a real man handles a woman. And now ... just you watch and weep." Legs bare and bowed, he waddled with delicacy to the bunk in front of him.

59
CLUBHOUSE FOLLIES

A skittering and a scuffling erupted from the crawlspace and Heavy Lennie crashed the snuff show. "The cops. The cops. People going bananas out there. Mr. Culley, Tusk, he wants us to evacuate. We got to —" He stuttered to silence at the sight of me. "Holy shit! What's he doing here?"

"Following his dream," Ice-Dick deadpanned. He leaned an elbow on the bunk, licked his lips, stroked the surface of the sheet.

"Jesus Christ Almighty, Mr. Blessing, if you'd stayed away, we'd be sitting pretty." Lennie spanked the dirt from his coveralls and green hoodie. A Skidmore College hoodie. A streak of blood between the E and C of the logo. Like Dobsie's hoodie. *Jeez!* How long had these Dexters been onto me? How wide was their net? "All due respect, we had a good thing going here. Until you and your lady showed up, squeezing us out like you owned the joint, coming on like your shit don't stink."

I looked down to a yipping and a yapping, and Françoise, the Messners' stupid Bichon, popped onto the scene, also via the crawlspace.

She scampered up to me, tail clocking 90. She sniffed my shoes, then pounced on Joe Di Iorio's remains, pried a drumstick from the sack.

Caitlin boogied over to the pup, jazz hands and happy feet. "OMG, is he not the cutest! I am going to explode in my undies."

"You bet you are," Goatee said, and flung the tarp off the nearest bunk. Al Messner, Jesus.

Just when I figured I'd hit rock bottom, the bottom dropped out.

If not for the sweater, I'd never have known it was Al. His green and white Argyle. "My signature." Goatee elaborated for my benefit. "I melon-ball the eyes and then I melon-ball the rest, you know, like make orifices where they aren't. And then I like to, well, you know?"

Basil rose for the defense. "Don't tell me he didn't deserve it, Bobby. Ruining your Christmas dinner was unconscionable. Whatever your opinion, necrophilia is a victimless crime."

"Uh-huh." I breathed deep, a lifetime of vomit in check. A human emotion. A rare slip for me since blundering into the chaos. "No denying, the punishment fits the crime," I said, far too subtle for Basil.

"Now, you're getting it, Bobby. Wait till you hear the other surprise we have for you." He called over to Heavy Lennie. "You going to tell him or should I?"

Lennie was dashing about, gathering belongings into a moth-eaten rucksack. "Did you hear me, Bloomie? The cops are swarming out there. Culley wants us out. Pack and run, man. Pack and run."

"I shall be your proxy then," Basil grinned, and then to me: "Guess who took care of the lady cop who badgered you? He's got her all trussed up as we speak. Sedated to the gills, she is. Hawkins, is it?"

"Hochstein," I corrected.

"Her husband too. Or wife. Or whatever they call carpet-munchers nowadays. We would have taken the Justin kid too, but he's a slippery little lad, that one."

"My gratitude knows no bounds," I said.

"See, gentlemen, ladies, I told you: he is his father's son."

"Never mind who he is," Heavy Lennie barked. "Finish him off with the others. Mr. Culley won't like it, but so what? We're done here. The sucker needs to take the fall." He scooped up Françoise, a bag of M&Ms, and clambered back into the crawlspace that was, in fact, a tunnel.

I was eager to know how Tusk figured in this, and I'm sure Basil would have been thrilled to pontificate had I asked. But my attention was riveted to Ice-Dick's bunk of choice as I calculated the path of least resistance.

Caitlin pressed Betty to her breasts. "Chop-chop time, Bobby-boy." *Bobby-boy* sounded strange coming from her, rather than Tusk.

"Not so hasty," Basil chided. "It's not right. We cannot permit his father to go to his grave grieving his only son. Henry deserves better. We owe the man."

Ice-Dick disagreed. "Stop dreaming, Basil; he's not his father, never will be."

"But if we explain to him, let him see—you'll see, Bobby, we're on your side. You see that, don't you, son? Tell them, Bobby. Tell them."

"Up yours, tubby-fuck," Caitlin said, and with a two-handed backhand Serena and Venus would have envied, she rode her machete into Basil Bloomfield's belly. If not for his high-fructose gut, the guy would have been watching himself die in halves. As it was, he flopped forward from the waist, his head a ten-pound kettlebell between his knees, and down he crumpled. No parting poetry, thank the Lord.

Caitlin and Betty had me all to themselves. "Snuffing the son of the Brittle Butcher, gonna be sick-awesome."

They stalked me Samurai-style, Caitlin with an affectionate two-fisted grip, Betty the Machete reciprocating in kind. Neck or knees. Swift or slow. High or low.

"Don't be an idiot," Ice-Dick cautioned. "It's got to look like he offed himself."

"He's right, Cait," Goatee said. "C'mon, sugar. What's it matter, dead is dead?"

"But I really, really want to," she said.

"Like who doesn't, sweets?" Scuzzball surveyed the room. "Anyone got a gun?"

Manga-Face's hand shot up. "I do." He tore the sheet from his captive. A cop. Wade Fucking Griffiths, yet, mummified to the core of a hundred yards of braided rope. He called my name. As spoken through duct tape, anyhow. And, I tell you, my heart went out to the prick. Till this moment, the most pitiful thing I'd ever heard had been elderly twins sing *Happy Birthday* to themselves one Saturday afternoon in Loony Scoops. Wade's muffled mewling had them beat.

Manga-Face fumbled with the ropes, redder and sweatier with every tug. The knots wouldn't give. He couldn't get to Wade's holster.

"Brilliant." Ice-Dick flung his icepack at the wall. "You didn't take his gun before tying him up?"

"I never thought ..."

Caitlin grasped her machete with two hands, raised it to the stars like Princess Leia gone mad, lightsaber dialed to annihilate. "It's up to Betty now, Bobby-boy. And she's gonna fuck you up but good."

"Wait. I have a gun." The voice was faint and weak and unexpected. "I do. I have a gun."

We turned to Ice-Dick's bunk. He pounced on the sheets like a man possessed of two good balls and a healthy penis.

60
DEATH PORN

There was no gun, only Cori. Like I'd never seen her. Like I never wanted to see her. Like the photos they terrorized us with in Drivers Ed, how our faces would end up if we didn't buckle up.

Her left eye was a patch of blue, lid the color of plums and swollen to a slit. A gash at the hairline. Bruising at the jaw. Bloodied lip. Bloodied nose. Bloodied ear. Blood matted in her hair. *I'd been playing for time and she'd been lying there like this? What the hell was wrong with me?*

She didn't move. Zip ties secured her wrists and ankles.

The six surviving dirtbags, Betty included, breathed a collective sigh of relief, roared with laughter and mutual goodwill, shamed by their skittishness.

Caitlin squirmed in her G-string. She hauled Goatee to her side and pushed him onto the butcher block, set to blow him then and there.

Ice-Dick had ideas of his own. "Round two comin', bitch."

"Hey, fuckers! Over here," I called. I'd made the most of the commotion. The blade from Edith Dengler's throat now rested tight in my hand. Wasn't much, but it would do. And as the fuckers' attention swung to me, Cori unwoozed and unwound. She wasn't far gone, after all.

Up went her arms, elbows to ears. Up went her hips. And down came her wrists fast and hard upon her pelvis. The zip tie went flying, flicked off Ice-Dick's ear. He swatted at the nip, lurched to retaliate, but she caught him high, two thumbs to opposing carotids, and he withered into the tender trap of Cori's thighs.

She had him where she wanted him, her scissor hold made all the more efficient by the plastic ties around her ankles. His resistance was clumsy, comical. She lifted him to his tippy-toes. Elongated his spine. Crushed his esophagus. And as the "real man" powered down, arms limp, face the shape and color of a clearance bin eggplant, she discarded him like the same.

I'd hoped she'd break his neck. But she had other ideas in store.

She drew her knees to her breast and double-downed on the zip ties at her ankles. A thumbnail to the locking tab was all it took, and the plastic cuff snapped loose. A master class in the basics of escape. She made it look easy, like she'd done it a thousand times. My wife, Houdini.

She reached behind her back and hit the floor feet first, Dobsie's Bersa Thunder now in her grip.

"See this?" she said, addressing Ice-Dick. He shook his head in a panicked *no* and Cori blew away the disbelieving scumbag's crotch, along with the two hands shielding it.

Up jerked his legs in spasm, air-pedal, and denial, a quaint folk dance to commemorate his Slavic roots, before splurting through the breakdance basics. Coffee grinder. Windmill. Baby freeze. Penectomy. Orchiectomy. End of *me*. I'm telling you, that bastard scorched the floor.

The surviving freaks looked on, a judging panel in a quandary, whether to award Cori's performance a 9 or perfect 10. *Why hadn't they killed her outright? Why had they allowed this take-no-prisoners bitch into their lair?*

"Oh, wait, I almost forgot, you gave me these for safekeeping." Cori slid a hand down the front of her pants and out she came with a bouquet of black condoms. She wished Ice-*Dickless* an adoring "best of luck" and mashed the wad into the newly minted boy soprano's mug.

The dead acoustics came to life, his polyphonic agony on reverb and repeat.

On our drive up 95 from Banrum, Cori had claimed serial killers were cowards by nature. Big on domination, not so hot on confrontation. Scuzzball lent credence to her theory. The freak decamped into the crawlspace, a rosette of brown blossoming from his butt, as if a can of cola had exploded up his ass.

Goatee was of a similar mind, but Caitlin dug in her heels. He held her from behind, tried to drag her off. I moved to sidestep the lovebirds too late, and Caitlin ran him bleating up and onto my razor. Down he went, from something to nothing, from hipster to corpse, his spinal cord sliced clean through.

Caitlin took to the high ground, a competition level gymnast, Basil's body her springboard to the butcher block. She was Queen of the Castle up there, swaying and swiveling, her naked machete mirroring her move for move.

She was a smart one, that freak. She had the territory covered. Taking her down was not an option, dissection by Betty the certain outcome. But then she wobbled suddenly and Betty thudded point down onto the butcher block. Princess Cait sunk to her knees, regarded me as though I were Saint Peter, and made like a Slinky onto the pulped remains of Basil the Florist.

A tin can rolled to my feet. Maple Cured Beans. Bush's brand.

At the far end of the room, Manga-Face gaped in shock, his empty hand cocked at his ear, Tom Brady's pose for Topps. "Damn," he said. "I was gunning for you. A hundred times out of a hundred I make that pass."

I kept an eye on the mutant and crossed to Cori. Manga-Face wasn't quite sure where to look or what to do. He was plum out of canned food. But there was Wade's baton. *Shit!* The kid was on it, wrenched it out from under the ropes, and popped it to full extension. "I need to get home. My folks will be wondering where I am."

"You live nearby?" I said.

"Passing through."

"Exit's right there."

"You'll let me go?"

"My pleasure ..." And it would have been too.

"Hell, yeah!" he cried, gave Wade a parting punch, and came screeching down on us. No telling whether he was aiming to maim or aiming to clear the track. And Cori, for one, was hardly keen to wait and see. She fired off a round, shot high. Gave it another try and the clip chaffed empty. If the kid had been intent on running, he wasn't now. He was looking to kill. And smart about it too, closing in on her blind side. Flying, he was. Feet off the ground. Hollering some kung fu hyena banshee crap. Baton whipping lethal as it hummed for Cori's head. She'd never see it coming. *She didn't see it coming.*

I lunged to intercept, thrust myself up, blade going for broke, while Manga-Face and his mother of a nightstick hurtled down.

Boom.

My ears rang silent. My head bled dead.

Night fell.

The Milky Way.

The Big Dipper.

Sandra Bullock in that stranded-in-space movie.

A warm and fuzzy feeling coursed through and over me. Bedtime on a cold winter's night. Spooning with Cori. Red vengeance lapping at my nose. Manga's guts sloshing onto my face and down my gullet. *Fuck!*

I sputtered back to the unrelenting unreality, flogging the shit from my face and clothes, gagging, spitting, sputtering whatever Manga had last scarfed down, as Cori lugged me out from under the lug. I waved her off, got to my feet, and staggered over to Wade.

My head pounded, Charlie Watts and Travis Barker dueling drums in my frontal lobe.

I yanked off Wade's gag. His voice was weak, hoarse. "Oh, God," he sobbed. "What I did to you. What I did to you. God forgive me, what I did to you."

The ropes cocooned about him from collarbone to heels. I worried Basil's blade might not be up to the challenge, considering its recent mileage through flesh and bone. Still, I cut him loose with ease. No slighting Basil and his pride in the tool.

"C'mon, man, we need to get you out of here."

"Can't. Can't. They cut me." The psychos had done a number on his tendons and hamstrings. His hands were pocked with cigarette burns. His thumbs were beef jerky, chewed, swallowed, regurgitated.

"Wait here," I said, as if the guy had a choice. "I'll get help."

Wade coughed weakly. His eyes fluttered red to white to red. He needed to tell me something. He wanted me to know something, to see something. He patted his holster, his hand a beached trout.

"What is it, man?" Caitlin's cackle and Betty's swish replied.

The slasher chick had Cori up against the wall. Betty tickled the tip of Cori's nose. I loved that nose, goddammit. And the confounding woman who went with it.

61
SMORGASBORD OF DEATH

I ripped the gun from Wade's holster. There was no clear shot. "C'mon, Cait, it's over. Go. You still got time."

"You wish." Her face was the warning label on a bottle of strychnine. Her apron clung to her corset, the blood that soaked it now darker, wetter, heavier.

"Take him with you," I said.

"What?"

"Your boyfriend. Look. He's alive. He's coming round. You two can make it out before the cops—"

Caitlin blew me a raspberry, snuck a peek at Goatee, and Cori made her move, ducking Betty and clobbering the psycho-chick with a slamdunk of Bersa steel. And there she was, my Kung Fu Dentist-Lawyer-Fed-Wife, revived to her former glory, stomping Caitlin's hands same way she'd put down Dobsie on that stormy night in Loony Scoops. Same way a woman might protect her unborn child.

I used the rope I'd cut from Wade to tie up Caitlin, while Cori fetched water for my dear old pal. He spoke between sips. "There's something I need to tell you, Bobby."

"Later. When we're out of here."

"No, I need to tell you now. It was me. I told them it was you. But it was me." The guy was losing it, three burbles shy of coma.

"Sure, man. Whatever."

"I saw you in that truck."

"Let it rest."

"Wanted to make it up to you ... my mother keeping me away ... after your dad ...not right ... we were best pals. Me. I sent the truck onto Main."

"Okay. Okay. Later. We'll talk later."

"I told them it was you ... thought you'd killed the Storrows. I'm sorry. Gonna make it up. What I did to you."

"Rest, pal. Rest." And finally he did.

Cori wanted to know what he was rambling on about. "Old timey times," I said.

"Sweet," she replied.

I took a closer look at her eye. "You need ice on that." I offered to fetch Ice-Dick's ice pack. She politely declined, retched a little. For a sec, I worried she might introduce Betty to my spleen.

"You look like shit," she said. I didn't tell her she looked the same. Husband-sense, you know. Maybe I was cut out for this relationship schtick, after all.

We fell into each other's bloodied selves and hung on. There was nothing more to say. Not then.

Must have been a decade earlier I'd read this piece in *Rolling Stone*. The writer made mention of the Brittle Butcher and the tools he'd employed along the way. The line that stuck was "smorgasbord of death." I'd thought the reference snarky, trivializing the victims, disrespectful of the bereaved. Now, as I looked out upon the carnage, the portrayal was more than apt.

Manga-Face. Disemboweled.

Ice-Dick. Alive. Barely. In shock. A good chance he'd luck out by bleeding out.

Basil Bloomfield. Folded at the waist. A human calzone. Leaking marinara.

Goatee, the autograph seeker. Animal. Vegetable. Mineral. Anybody's guess.

Caitlin. Battered. Bound. But not out.

Lawrence of Lawrence, Kansas. The misanthrope who'd bowled down the Chainsaw Kid with the Virgin Mary's head. Talk about karma. Half a head here, half a head there, no body anywhere.

Edith Dengler. Al Messner. Joe Di Iorio. And probably Dobsie too.

Lastly, my poor buddy Wade. Battered, crippled, remorseful, and hanging by a thread.

My father had told me death smells like glee. Glee, it turns out, smells like sewage.

I pulled the tarp over Al's mutilated remains. I'd have said a prayer had I known any. "Sorry, Al, I never thought ..." Same applied to Joe's arms and Edith's bits and pieces.

One bunk remained covered. I could have left it, I suppose. Two boys lay side by side in weird white underwear, bottoms, tops. Best guess, late teens or early twenties. Hard to tell. Betty the Machete and Goatee's melon-baller had been there, done that.

"Mormons," Caitlin volunteered with good cheer. "They came by while you and your ho were on vacation. Bitches wouldn't leave the fucking doorbell."

"We should gag her," I said.

Cori disagreed. "She opens her mouth again, I'll do to her face what I did to that bastard's nuts."

Cori insisted on staying with Wade while I went for help. He was lapsing in and out of consciousness by then. She kept his gun at the ready, with Betty on standby. Even with one good eye, Cori wasn't likely to be taken. Not three times in one day, anyhow.

"You keep watch on the crawlspace. If any of them come through, don't hesitate," I said.

"I doubt they will," she said. "But don't think I'm not hoping."

62
GLEE

I retraced my steps, past the Shrine of Henry Taylor Dickens, the photo collage, the hallowed hats, the candle. I pulled on the heavy metal door and dropped into the tunnel.

I felt pretty good, considering. I'd overcome. I'd conquered. I'd saved my wife.

This was the closest I'd ever come to hero. I'd be hoisted onto shoulders, paraded up Main. I would be respected, never to be shunned or feared again. So much was clear to me now. My father was a lunatic, but not the raving kind, which made him the most dangerous kind. And though I had some of my father in me, I knew for certain I was not my father.

Elated as I was, the game was yet in play. Lives to be saved—Wade's and Detective Hochstein's. Slayers to be slayed—Scuzzball, Heavy Lennie, Rat-face George, and God-knew-how-many others. And no forgetting Tusk. But man, I was so frigging happy. Nothing like disembowelment, split skulls, slit throats, and severed limbs to lift a man's self-esteem.

I bolted up the cellar steps. (I didn't exit cellars, I fled them. That much, at least, had not changed.)

The crystal chandelier in the hallway tinkled rainbows across the walls and ceiling. The grandfather clock tolled through the hallway. And by the living room arch, Marie Messner stood waiting. "Don't come any closer," she said. She had a gun. A shiny gun. A new gun.

"Marie, it's me. Bobby. Bobby." I must have looked a sight. Bloodbath fresh. Slaughterhouse spiffy. "I need your help. Below, the cellar—"

"What did you do to him?"

"Look, I know what it looks like, but you got it wrong. No matter what you—"

"Where's my husband?"

"Please—"

"Don't you move."

"You need to listen to me, Marie. There are people down there who—"

"What did you do to Al? Tell me, you bastard."

She said more, but her voice was drowned out by the hiss and pop of the loudspeaker outside. "Bobby, Bobby Dickens ... er ... Blessing. Bobby Blessing. It's me, Scur, Chief Goldwater. I need you to come out, son. Drop your weapons. Put your hands on top of your head and step out slow and easy. No one needs to get hurt here, Bobby. Let's not make this any harder than it already is."

"Please, Marie. Look in the goddamn cellar, for Christ's sake. Wade, he's in bad shape and—"

"Drop it," she said.

"Drop what?"

"Is that what you did to Al?"

I raised my hand, stunned I still held it. I'd been hanging onto it for so long, it had become a part of me, bonded to my palm by blood, guts, and sweat. But Marie, she didn't appreciate Basil's razor with the same affection I did. Perhaps if I'd mentioned the Japanese steel ...

I heard her first shot.

Turned my head to the windows, saw faces creased with hate. Men. Women. Canes and crutches brandished aloft. April Bright. Tusk. Cops in protective vests.

So much for my reign as town hero.

"You killed him. Say it, you bastard. Say it, damn you. You killed my Al."

I did not hear her second shot. Felt it.

The commotion on the porch carried to the four sides of the house. People scurried in panic, dove for cover, convinced the shots were coming from me. *The Hillsdale Hacker is out to kill us! Kill us all! He'll kill us all!*

And was that my blood? My blood running from me? Heading straight for Marie Messner? *Well, wasn't that something!*

I did not hear her third, fourth, and fifth shots. I was either dead or getting there.

He'll kill us all!
He'll kill us all
He'll kill us
He'll kill
He'll
He
H

63

BANZAI SKYDIVING IN A HOSPITAL BED ON THE FOURTH FLOOR OF ST. JOSEPH'S HOSPITAL IN KENNER

Mom

"I never thought angels wore black."

"Some of us do."

"Are you Rita Hayworth?"

"I get that all the time."

"My funeral, is that what you're here for?"

"Depends on you."

"Why didn't you abort me?"

"All that red tape at the time, I didn't have the patience."

Dad

"Do you remember how it went down, Bobby?"

"I don't want to."

"How the police made me lie in the snow?"

"Yeah."

"The shotgun at my head?"

"Stop it."

"And your mother, what she was wearing? Beautiful, wasn't she? You liked her, didn't you? Really, really liked her."

"Do I really, really have to?"

"Have to what?"

"Remember."

Willow

"I didn't mean to laugh at you."

"It was my fault."

"It wasn't fair. My mother and father. My brother. I didn't want to die. I wanted to be a singer. Or a writer like you."

"I'm sorry."

"I don't know why they couldn't have killed Justin, instead. He was the mean one."

Caitlin

"You're not a doctor."

"As long as the uniform at your door thinks I am...."

"You here to kill me?"

"You're all Betty and me got left."

"Where's Cori?"

"Bitch fucked my teeth up plenty. Punched me in the kisser. Imagine, her a dentist and all."

"She's got a solid right hook."

"It was nice of you to leave her alone with us."

"I did, didn't I? I left her alone with you."

"You did. You left her alone. Well, with that cop. But he was nothing. Tell him, Betty. Tell him."

Curtis Mangold

"Since you're no longer with us, Mr. Blessing, do you suppose Shannon might marry me?"

"Ask her yourself, asshole."

"I have a Bachelor of Science in Criminal Justice. I make a very nice living."

Basil Bloomfield

"You take issue with calzones?"

"You're dead, man."

"Good gracious, yet another trait we have in common."

Heavy Lennie

"Rat-face George and me, we was wondering. You mind if we take some of your old man's junk from the cellar? It'll fetch a pretty penny on eBay."

"It's mine."

"A shame to leave it lying there unappreciated. You wouldn't keep the Moaning Lisa in your attic, now, would you? We're open to cutting you—"

"I know. I've seen."

"No, not that. Cutting you in. Ten percent, say?"

Ice-Dickless

"You seen my cock? The cunt blew off my cock."

"You can grow it back."

"I can?"

"Absolutely. You can do anything you want in a subconscious state."

April

"Please. A little tongue. In, out. Two seconds, all I'm asking."

"Get off of me."

"Where's your compassion?"

"Go away."

"Pucker up."

"Get the fuck off."

"My leg, let go my leg."

Raymond T. Culley

"Let me tell ya, Bobby-boy, the line between us writers and them killers is a blurry slurry. Some choose to fantasize, but us pros, we choose to contextualize."

Anna Carmen Hope

"Ah, Mr. Blessing, my second most favorite student."

"Miss Skunk-head."

"Pardon me?"

"That's what Tusk said to call you. Because of your hair."

"I prefer Anna."

"Anna."

"You were asking about *Bestselleritis!*"

"Yes. Now that I've caught it ..."

"Regrettably, there is no known cure."

Mom

"How many times must I tell you? I am not Rita Hayworth."

"Then why are you here?"

"I am not here, nor do I intend to be. I have no tolerance for teenage angst."

"I'm not a teenager."

"Since when?"

"You're wearing black. You must be here."

"I look good in black."

"I know."

"Here. Touch."

"No."

"Do as you're told."

"Ouch! That hurt."

"It was meant to."

Dr. Cutcheon

"You are not unique, Robert. All young people of your generation are, according to the vernacular, fucked up to one degree or another, in bondage to the vagaries of adolescence itself. Having a father who is a convicted felon may warp the psyche to an appreciable extent, yet it need not be the quintessential kink of one's existence. Each of us is, after all, the master of our own destiny. Or, as your dear mother might say, mistress."

Cori

"Rob? You're awake. He's awake. Can you hear me? It's me, Cori. Rob? Rob? He's awake!"

Tusk

"I never figgered it'd go haywire, Bobby-boy. Don't touch nobody in Hillsdale, I told them. No killin' local. Keep a distance. Make like the Brittle Butcher. But then they took you under their wing.

"Since the beginnin', thirty, forty, more or less. They come and went. Not all at once, by Jesus. Had to keep it *un*conspicuous. It wasn't like ol' Henry's devotees hadn't been showin' up for years, but us, we was true beliefers.

"Some stayed a day. Some longer. Most had jobs back home, mouths to feed. Let's face it, military and the fuzz aside, killing's an avocation, not a vocation. That flower shop fellow, Bloomingfields, he moved his whole kit and caboodle here. Nice family. Distressed a mite, now, naturally.

"It was all word of mouth. A place to go, you know, breathe the same air Henry Dickens breathed. What the fancy folk call a retreat.

"They're loners by nature. Like you, Bobby-boy. It was about givin' them the opportunity, you know, to network. It was special, no denyin'. Where else you gonna find the likes of them under one roof, outside a penile institution?

"Only two rules, outside of killin' local. No guns. And they got to let me chat with 'em to my heart's content. A gabbier lot you never met. Yappety-yap-yap. They give me enough material for twenty books. I was moving along too, mowin' down pages, then you come along. My next book is gonna be lots different now.

"They had the run of the ol' place, for Chrissake, till you and your missus. If staples in your face didn't send you running, threats and ghostly doings didn't, feeling was you'd been sent for a purpose. You was too.

"Got all I need now. For my next book, I mean. You're it, Bobby-boy. You are it. Of course, 'any resemblance to actual events or locales or persons, living or dead, is entirely coincidental.' Hah! Now, don't go telling anybody I told you. Don't sic no lawyer fucks on me, hell nope.

"The cops are going to nail me good. And all a guy was doin' was a little research, huh? Amazing any books get written anymore, how tetchy folk get about the teensiest disruptings."

Cori

"What day is it?"

"January 25."

"I'm not dead?"

"You would be if Marie was a better shot."

"And you? Caitlin didn't—"

"She's under a suicide watch. Separation anxiety, apparently. She keeps asking for Betty."

"So she didn't ..."

"Didn't what?"

"Nothing."

"Look. My eye's almost healed. I might have a scar on my forehead, but compared to Wade and Al, Willow and her family, I'm not complaining."

"Wade?"

"He was down the hall until yesterday. They transferred him to rehab. He told them everything. Including when you were kids. That crazy truck thing. The bowling balls. He wants to be your best friend again. Detective Hochstein didn't make it though. They got her wife too. It's the worst. They had kids. Two girls."

"How many in all? How many in my name?"

"Does it matter?"

"Does to me."

"They're still counting. Attributing."

"Jesus."

"They're looking for the ones who got away. Trouble is, Scur says, they don't have leads on most."

"He was here?"

"Every day. Never said much. He regrets he didn't do more to help you."

"My mother? Was she—"

"April let her know. She said she'd try to come. She did call April a couple of times after, to see how you were doing, but ... I'm sorry, Rob."

"The cops pick her up, April, I mean?"

"Insufficient evidence."

"And my father?"

"It was all over the news. I expect he knows. I wrote to him, but it takes forever for letters to get through. The censors and so forth. By the time it's cleared, it may be too late."

"But Tusk was here, right? He was, wasn't he?"

"Twice. In fact, they arrested him right outside your door. No evidence he participated directly in the murders, but they've got him up on other charges. Aiding and abetting. Accessory to murder. Parole violations. Like that."

"I thought you were a lawyer or a federal agent or a Supreme Court Justice or whatever. Aren't you supposed to know this stuff?"

"I've decided to focus on my dental career."

"Stop. Laughing hurts."

"What about fucking?"

"I hope not."

"Does this hurt?"

"No."

"This?"

"Ooo ..."

"Should I stop?"

"God, no."

Me

"I always expected to be murdered, Cor."

"Life doesn't always turn out how we expect."

"Five bullets, jeez, can you believe?"

"Perhaps it's time you revised your expectations."

64
LAST WORDS

I was transferred from Saint Joseph's to the Pillsbury-Lange Convalescent Center on March 2, 2020, where Wade and I met for the first time since the cellar. Our near-death experiences had worked wonders: we were both less dickish. We cleared the air. We reminisced. He asked if Cori had a sister and contained his disappointment when I told him she did not.

On March 9, 2020, Assistant Warden Curtis Mangold sent an email to FBI Agent Shannon Ambrose. The subject header: URGENT!

Dear Shannon,

It is with deep regret I must withdraw my invitation to attend the execution of Henry Taylor Dickens as scheduled on March 16, 2020 at 2200 hours. Despite my counsel, Warden Bucara has chosen to heed the nervous nellies and liberal elitists. All non-essential visitations to Banrum Correctional Institution are now prohibited for the duration of the Chinese virus hoax.

I had been looking forward with great anticipation to reuniting with you. I apologize for any inconvenience this unwarranted turn of events may have caused. Till common sense returns, I remain…

Affectionately,
Curtis

I was discharged from rehab on the afternoon of March 16. My father was put to death later that night, as scheduled.

Cori cried. I wanted to. I tried. I swear. The only loss I felt was for what should have been, rather than what was.

I consoled her as best I could, which was pretty good, considering how far I'd come in the years we'd been together. I won't deny, her assuming the needy role was a welcome change of pace. I was happy to be on the giving end.

We settled into bed for the night, each of us aching for the closeness of the other. I moved my head onto her pillow and she moved my hand to her belly. We stayed like this for a long while, drifting in and out of thoughts and sleep, before Cori broke the silence, an errant glint of moonlight in her eye: "Did you feel it? Just now? The baby. There. There. Do you feel it, Rob?" I didn't, but said I did.

It was around 3:00 in the morning when Cori awoke to find me sitting up in bed beside her. "Should I get you a painkiller?"

"It's not that."

"Your father?"

"In a way."

"What way?"

"I'm not sure how to say it."

"What? How to say what?"

"Probably just a bad dream."

"How bad?"

"She's there and then she's not."

"Who? Where?"

"I don't know, Cor. A girl. Young, older, whatever. She's praying. She's praying I'll come save her."

"Oh," she said, and took my hand in hers, grazed the folds of my palm with the blood red nail of her thumb. "Oh, Bobby."

ACKNOWLEDGMENTS

There's a sense of exhilaration when the final line is written. The joy lasts for about eighteen seconds before the doubt kicks in. *Is this thing any good? Will anybody read it?* I do not share details, let alone pages, during the writing process. I keep all inside my head—concept, characters, story, genre. Not even my wife, Pat, knows what I'm working on until I hand her the so-called finished manuscript. She then takes the pages in hand and begs me to leave her alone. Yes, *begs*. For some inexplicable reason, she prefers to read in peace, without my staring from around a corner, pacing the floor in front of her, or breathing down her neck to see what chapter she's on. What's more, she won't tell me anything, good or bad, until she's turned the final page. She does, however, sprinkle audible clues along the way. It is for these periodic gasps, sighs, groans, and giggles that I remain eternally grateful to her. Pat has been my first reader since the day I met her and, without getting too mushy, first in countless other ways as well.

My second reader for over twenty-five years was my friend Matthew Cope. This book is for him as much as anyone. Media personality, critic, journalist, screenwriter, photographer, and my personal sounding board, Matthew relocated from the UK to Canada in the early '70s. He quickly established himself among those irreplaceable Montrealers who make this city the unique and lively center it is. He loved this novel from the first draft and, at one point, had even started writing a screenplay based on it. Matthew died unexpectedly in January 2021, and not a day has gone by since that I haven't thought of him. The void he leaves is vast. To see this novel in print and not have him here to share the moment has been more emotional than I could have ever imagined. I also know what he'd say were he to read this brief tribute. "Dear God, Mike, would you stop being so damn maudlin! Shut up and get on with it." Okay, Matthew, okay. *Jeez! Stop shouting.*

This book is also for the extraordinary father-son dentist team of

Stan and Mark Reich. They not only offered valuable feedback on an early draft, but also served as dental consultants for Dr. Corinne Meredith Widdoes. Indeed, Cori would surely credit Stan and Mark for their roles in guiding her career.

And then there's Shelley Paris, who generously gave of her time and expertise on the public relations and marketing fronts to help promote my earlier work. Thank you! As for this novel, Shelley, I expect you'll come up with a ... uh ... killer plan.

Several people reviewed different versions of this novel. Their input was vital to the edition in hand. Many thanks to Sean Campanie and Joel David Ramsey (both early boosters of the book), Grace Hodgson, Ramon Kubicek, Lewis Olishansky, Robert Paris, Shelley Reich, James Ladd Thomas, and the late Ian Turner, Tim Ramsey, and Dave Fisher.

I am also grateful to Barry Malzberg, Bruce McAllister, and William Shunn. Their unequivocal embrace of this novel provided the impetus to all that followed. Similarly, for their assorted encouragement and support, I thank Clark Blaise, Al and Marie Campanie, Lawrence C. Connolly, Marilyn Jackson, Timothy S. Johnston, Robert Linney, Ralph Lucas, Charlotte "Charlie" Lunn, Ian Rogers, Gordon Van Gelder, Sheila Williams, and the late Bruce Scott. Within this group, as well, is the remarkable Kurt Olsson. On top of everything else, he consented to my using an excerpt from his poem, *Some Stories*, as part of the epigraph, the full version of which is found in his award-winning *Burning Down Disneyland*.

Notably, this book would not have been possible were it not for WordFire Press publisher, Kevin J. Anderson and my ever-patient editor, Marie Whittaker. Thank you for making this such a rewarding experience. Same goes for the entire WordFire editing team. Talk about a sharp-eyed crew! Whatever their ultimate fates, the Serial Killer's Son and his wife are on the loose because of you.

Likewise, I thank my friend and agent, Christine Cohen, of the Virginia Kidd Literary Agency, for her insightful notes on what *I thought* was my final draft, and for her tireless work that followed on my behalf. She made this book happen.

In addition to my wife and daughters, Carrie, Lindsay, and Margie, there are other family members whose support ensures them a spot in every list of acknowledgments I might write: My parents, Bert and Mollie. My sisters, the constant and true Shandyl Wiseberg and the much-missed Mara Libling, the legendary Jerry Wiseberg, tech advisor

Jean-Philippe Lebel, my stalwart nephews Sean Loucks and Michael G. Loucks, and my good-luck charms Andrew Davis and Maude Barlow.

Lastly, to Bobby and Cori, it was interesting getting to know you. Now, please, get the heck out of my head.

ABOUT THE AUTHOR

Michael Libling is a World Fantasy Award finalist whose short fiction has appeared in *The Magazine of Fantasy & Science Fiction*, *Asimov's Science Fiction*, *Realms of Fantasy*, *The Year's Best Fantasy & Horror*, *The Year's Best Science Fiction & Fantasy*, and many others. *The Serial Killer's Son Takes a Wife* is his second novel. His first, *Hollywood North: A Novel in Six Reels*, was published in 2019.

Creator and former host of the long-running CJAD Trivia Show in Montreal, Michael is the father of three daughters and lives on Montreal's West Island with his wife, Pat, and a big black dog named Piper. Among other things, he claims to be one of only a handful of North American authors who has never owned a cat. You can find out more about him at www.michaellibling.com, where he has been known to blog on occasion, or feel free to track him down on social media.

facebook.com/michael.libling

twitter.com/MichaelLibling

instagram.com/michaelliblingwriter

amazon.com/stores/author/B091RJ1Z1K

IF YOU LIKED ...

If you liked *The Serial Killer's Son Takes a Wife*, you might also enjoy:

Hollywood North: A Novel in Six Reels by Michael Libling
Empty Rooms by Jeffrey Mariotte
Drumbeats by Kevin J. Anderson and Neal Peart
Banshees by Mike Baron
Jewel of the Seven Stars by Bram Stoker

OTHER WORDFIRE PRESS
TITLES BY MICHAEL LIBLING

Our list of other WordFire Press authors and titles is always growing. To find out more and shop our selection of titles, visit us at:
wordfirepress.com

www.ingramcontent.com/pod-product-compliance
Lightning Source LLC
Chambersburg PA
CBHW030238120726
47903CB00005B/1540